The Dragonslayer
of Edgewhen

The Dragonslayer
of Edgewhen

JASON A. HOLT

Edgewhen® is a registered trademark of Jason A. Holt.

Published by the author.
JasonAHolt.com

print ISBN: 978-0-9860717-1-3
epub ISBN: 978-0-9860717-0-6

For Sierra, who makes Edgewhen possible

Prologue

THE ELEMENTALS were breaking into the world, and the deities would not stop them. Nine deities, nine excuses. Yolim, god of wealth, said fighting the elementals would violate the bargain with Nature. Zharnov, god of justice, said divine intervention was against the law. And so on.

Even Lashrefi, goddess of luck, had an excuse: She didn't like the odds. Oh, she could descend into the world and stop the elementals—all by herself, if she had to—but a massive influx of divine power would open the world to an attack from foes far more dangerous. The demons were always watching for an opening.

Nature had created the world as a wall between Heaven and Hell to keep the demons and deities from fighting. The demons, of course, wished to destroy this wall. The deities sought to defend it. Stability depended upon balance, so the Laws of Nature required the deities to remain in Heaven. Lashrefi could break the laws, but that would break the world.

And that was the problem with letting the elementals roam free. As beings of pure chaos, the elementals cared nothing for Nature's laws. They would twist a rule here, break a rule there, poke a hole in this, and smash that flat. Nature could withstand nine or ten, but the elementals numbered fifty-seven. Lashrefi thought Nature needed a little help.

And she already had the means to help: A thousand years ago, each deity had made eighty-one people, and Nature had allowed these people to enter the world. Their purpose was to defend against the demons, reproduce, and pass the mission on. Their generations had multiplied and spread themselves across the land. Perhaps it was time to put them to the test.

Lashrefi liked the people—all nine species. They were resourceful, courageous, and (best of all) unpredictable. How would they react when they discovered the elementals? How could they defeat beings with powers greater than their own? Lashrefi was intrigued.

Very well, then. Let the elementals enter. She wanted to see what would happen.

But she did not want to lose. She was betting on the people, and she had no qualms about improving the odds. A massive influx of power was against the rules, but the deities were allowed to help people in small ways.

Just one little push. Lashrefi knew exactly where to push. She found a sleeping man and whispered to him a single word:

"Dragon."

CHAPTER 1
Danwel

THE SEEDS FLEW from Danwel's fingertips, catching rays of springtime sunlight as they fell. They landed on the black earth, where they gleamed like golden nuggets until his sister's rake passed over and hid them beneath a blanket of dirt.

Danwel's sister Bethinesi was solidly built, but raking was work, and Danwel could push the pace enough to keep the girl puffing. This was good because it kept her from talking, which meant that she would not be raising any topics that, as far as Danwel was concerned, had already been discussed to Yolim's Heaven and back.

From the top of a nearby maple tree, a bright red cardinal proclaimed his love, whistling, "Sweet, sweet, sweet, sweet, sweet!"

Poor fool, thought Danwel. *He doesn't know what he's gotten himself into.*

The cardinal's mate answered from the brush with a call that sounded like, "Eat wheat! Eat wheat!"

A flock of crows, who had gathered in an oak tree to discuss clan politics, announced that they planned to get the wheat first. They were bigger than the other birds who were watching Danwel's family work, but Danwel reckoned it was the tiny sparrows who would get the most, because they had the advantage of numbers.

This bag of seeds was almost empty. Soon it would be Bethinesi's turn to scatter seeds and his job to hide them from the spectators. At which point, his sister would probably start talking again. If he could find something else to talk about, maybe she wouldn't bring up Kethwin.

Thinking of something else was difficult, though. Kethwin stayed on his mind.

Danwel was rescued by the sight of Benwel, their brother, hurrying toward them.

"He's supposed to be watching the cattle," Bethinesi said.

Danwel nodded. Apparently, Benwel had abandoned his task and gone to their house in the village: He was carrying three spades over one shoulder and a rope on the other.

"Have you decided to become a miner?" Bethinesi called.

If Benwel had been in a good mood, he would have had an answer for that. If he had been in a bad mood, he would have scowled. But Benwel just kept coming. The hem of his tunic bounced against his knees as he hurried toward them. His shoes kicked up loose dirt which clung to his leather-bound leggings.

He came to Danwel and looked up at him with worry in his eyes.

"What happened?" Danwel asked.

"Grobo fell in a hole," Benwel said.

Grobo was one of the younger oxen. Because Danwel's family was sowing, the plow teams had the day off. Benwel was supposed to be helping their cousin watch the two families' combined herd. The cattle should not have been anywhere near a hole.

"Dumb ox," said Bethinesi.

"It wasn't his fault," said Benwel.

"I mean you," said Bethinesi. "Why did you let him wander off and fall into a hole?"

"He didn't wander off," said Benwel. "He was grazing right in the middle of Kestrel Meadow, and the ground collapsed under him."

Bethinesi frowned. "In the middle of the meadow?"

Benwel turned to Danwel and asked, "Can you help me get him out?"

"I reckon I can try," Danwel said, taking one of the spades.

"I'll go, too," said Bethinesi.

"Go where?" their dad asked. Their parents, trailed by the two littlest girls, had come over to see what the trouble was.

"Grobo fell into a hole in Kestrel Meadow," Benwel explained.

"There's no hole in Kestrel Meadow," their dad said.

"Well, there is now," said Benwel. "And Grobo's in it."

"Is he hurt?" their dad asked. He had put a lot of work into training the ox that spring. He wouldn't be happy if Grobo had to go to the stew pot.

"His legs are buried in the dirt, so he can't get out," Benwel said. "But he didn't act like he was in pain."

"Well, I reckon I'd better take a look." Their dad reached for the third spade.

"Dad, we can get him out," said Bethinesi. "Don't worry."

Danwel doubted that Benwel had fetched that third spade for Bethinesi, but neither brother said anything.

Their dad considered it. "All right," he decided. "I'll let you handle it."

Bethinesi didn't wait for their dad to change his mind. She took the third spade and set off across the field with strides that made the red hem of her gray work dress writhe like a snake. The brothers trotted to catch up.

Danwel looked for Benwel's grin, but his brother's face was still flat with worry. Could be that Benwel was getting old enough to realize that responsibility wasn't an adventure.

As the oldest child, Danwel was used to responsibility. He had first driven the plow team by himself seven springs ago. Now he was twenty-two, and everyone in the village treated him like a man, even though he wasn't married yet. Danwel tried to be worthy of their respect, but it was hard to meet their expectations. He was huge—a head taller than anyone else in the village of Kwoshim—and everyone expected a big man to do big things.

People sometimes called Danwel a giant, but real giants—like the Stripedfolk or the Riverfolk or the Redfolk—were said to be tall enough to see over a horse's back. They were twice as tall as Clanfolk. The stories said that Yolim, the god of wealth, had made the Clanfolk small so they would not eat so much, and he had given them strong oxen so they could plow a lot of land. Their dad joked that when Yolim was making Danwel, he'd gotten confused and told the baby to grow into an ox instead.

Bethinesi slowed her pace once she was sure their parents would not call her back. Benwel caught up to her and strode on past.

"You're really worried, aren't you?" Bethinesi said.

"It's a deep hole," Benwel said over his shoulder.

"How deep?" Bethinesi asked.

"So deep that Grobo can't see out," said Benwel.

That was deep. Not even Danwel was as tall as an ox.

They headed away from the village. At the base of Kestrel Bluff, they met their cousin Pafweth. She and Benwel were about the same age, and they were supposed to be watching the cattle together. Pafweth was wearing a brown dress with a brown hem— as always. She said keeping a colored hem bright and clean was too much trouble for a cowherd.

"I got the shovels," Benwel said. "Did you find the beastshaper?"

"Aye," said Pafweth. "She's looking at a sick calf right now, but as soon as she's done, she'll come up and look at Grobo." Pafweth glanced at Danwel. "Kethwin might come, too."

"Well, isn't that nice?" said Bethinesi, also looking pointedly at Danwel.

Danwel just grunted.

Kethwin was the beastshaper's younger sister and also her apprentice. Of course she would come, too. But Danwel didn't see why he should let that bother him. There was nothing Kethwin could say to him that she hadn't said already. On the other hand, she'd already said some things that he didn't want to hear again.

"I don't think he wants to talk about it," Benwel said. He took the lead, and they set off on the path that followed the crease in the face of the bluff, through a wildwood of oak and hickory.

"I think that's the problem," said Bethinesi. "Danwel, it won't get better unless you talk to her."

Danwel thought that was the dumbest thing he'd ever heard. The more he and Kethwin talked, the worse it got.

"There's nothing to talk about," Danwel said. "The Clan is out of marriage marks."

"Well, could you marry into her clan?" Pafweth asked.

Bethinesi shook her head. "Pafweth, would you want to marry into Clan Walker?"

"Oh," said Pafweth. "I see."

Of the four clans that farmed the land around the village of Kwoshim, Clan Walker was the poorest. Kethwin had good reasons for wanting to join Clan Broadfield.

"So what are you going to do, Danwel?" his cousin asked.

"I reckon we have to wait," Danwel said.

"Waiting is what got you into trouble in the first place," Bethinesi said. "You've been engaged forever."

Actually, they had only been engaged a few months. Last fall, on the day the first snowflakes fell, Danwel and Kethwin had gone for a walk. They weren't used to the cold, and the new snow made their cloaks feel thin. When they passed the hollow oak that marked the edge of Shom Springwater's flax field, Kethwin had suggested they duck inside to warm up a bit.

They had warmed up a bit.

After that, they had an understanding. It wasn't a contract, and it wasn't really a bargain. They hadn't even said enough words for an agreement. But it was an understanding.

The troubles had begun a few days later. Kethwin thought they should make the trip to the city of Tarthil right away, before winter set in. Clan Broadfield only had twelve marriage marks left, she reminded him.

Well, she had thought she was reminding him, but actually she was informing him. Until that moment, Danwel had not given a thought to whether his clan had the means to mark the debt they would incur when they took Kethwin from Clan Walker.

Of course, if Clan Broadfield had held any Walker marks, they could have just returned one of those in exchange for Kethwin, but this was not the case. To make Kethwin a Broadfield, Danwel would have to convince his clan to give up another Broadfield mark.

Still, Danwel had not been worried. Each clan had one hundred marriage marks. Danwel reasoned that if Clan Broadfield was down to twelve, then that meant eighty-eight Broadfield marks were held by other clans. It seemed likely that some of those marks would be traded back.

But it was a good winter to marry a Broadfield. The Clan was not only dominant in Danwel's village; it was among the wealthiest clans in the state of Dwen-Tarthil, only behind Goodharvest, Fairweather, and Blackfield—and a late flood along the river Tartholin had washed away some of Blackfield's ancestral holdings last year. By the time Danwel started plowing that spring, the twelve marks were down to nine.

Kethwin decided that they needed to make the journey to Tarthil at once, but Danwel liked driving the oxen. Besides, it wasn't right to leave his father to do the plow work alone, nor to make extra work for Benwel and Bethinesi.

By the time plowing was done, the marks were down to five. Apparently four other young Broadfields had found the time to make the trip to the capital city. They were not Broadfields from Danwel's village. They were not even from nearby. But somehow, news of how many marks were left made its way up the valley of the Tartholin and then up the Grigolin to Kwoshim, as though carried by fish instead of by the wagging tongues of womenfolk.

With only five marks left, the situation was getting serious. Danwel could see that. He had even been considering skipping planting to get an early start. But five days ago, Tholom and Zhoswin Highmeadow had come back from Tarthil.

Tholom had left the village as a Broadfield, and Zhoswin been planning to become a Broadfield, too, until the Marriage Clerk had informed them that the number of marks was down to three and that none of these were available.

Under Broadfield clan law, the Marriage Clerk had the authority to conserve marks when the supply ran low, to save them for exceptional circumstances. What qualified as exceptional was at the discretion of the Marriage Clerk. One rumor said that the wharfmaster's daughter wanted to marry into Broadfield and one of the marks was reserved to pay for her. Another rumor said that the Clanhead had instructed the Marriage Clerk to hold back a mark or two in case one of his daughters caught a husband that summer.

Whatever the criteria were, Tholom and Zhoswin, a boy and a girl from some backwoods hutville, did not meet them. They were Highmeadows now.

"What I don't understand," said Bethinesi as they hiked up the trail, "is how many marks are left now."

"Three," replied Pafweth, who had just been to Tholom and Zhoswin's to find the beastshaper. "Tholom said there were three left."

"But was that before Tholom got married, or after?" Bethinesi asked. "Because if there were three left before Tholom joined Clan Highmeadow, there should be four now. They should have given us one of our marks back."

"I'm no marriage clerk," said Benwel, "but I reckon that when he considers how many Broadfields might want to get married this spring, four marks is not a lot more than three."

"Aye," said Pafweth. "It sounds like only important people can get married this year—unless a lot more of our cousins decide to marry out."

"But Kethwin Walker won't wait forever," Bethinesi said. "You know how she is."

They did. Kethwin was as lively as a sparrow and as ambitious as an ant hill. She could also scold like a squirrel.

"Your problem, Danwel," she had said during one of her scoldings, "is that you have no ambition. Sometimes I think you want to spend the rest of your life plowing."

What is wrong with plowing? Danwel wondered. *It's honest work. If Kethwin doesn't want a husband who spends his life plowing, why is she courting Danwel Broadfield? And what would she have said if I had asked her that then, instead of thinking of it now?*

Could be she would have told him that she was done courting Danwel Broadfield. And then what would he do? The truth was, he did have no ambition. But everyone expected him to do big things to match his big feet. Well, maybe he could do big things if he married Kethwin: She seemed to have ambition to spare.

They emerged from the woods onto the rolling green of the upland meadow. The spring grass had already gotten a good start, and the wildflowers that hadn't been picked for Tholom and Zhoswin's wedding celebration were still in full bloom. Cows, oxen, and the herd bull snuffled about, grazing happily, oblivious to any danger.

"The hole is over there," Benwel said, waving his arm at the middle of the meadow.

It appeared gradually as they walked closer. At first, it was just a dark spot in the green. Then they could see an edge of black earth. The closer they approached, the deeper it looked, and they still couldn't see Grobo until they were nearly at the edge, standing with the tips of their shoes on the cracks in the sod that warned them not to get any closer.

"That's a deep hole," Danwel said. He reckoned a man in the hole would need to stand on Grobo's back if he wanted to see out.

The ox, buried up to its belly in chunks of turf, looked up at them with mournful eyes. The earth had sheared away from the sides of the hole, leaving vertical walls that would have made it impossible for the beast to climb out even if its legs had not been trapped. A dark crevice in the earth near the ox's right shoulder hinted that the hole might be even deeper than it looked.

"Do you think we can get him out?" asked Benwel.

"You can get him out," Pafweth assured them. "Can't you, Danwel?"

Danwel studied the hole. "I reckon so," he decided. "We'll dig there, and turn that wall in front of Grobo into a slope. Then if we can get his legs unstuck, he'll be able to walk out."

"If he can still walk," said Bethinesi.

"The Walker sisters can fix him up," Pafweth said.

"Aye," said Danwel.

He put his spade in the ground. Loose turf flaked off the edge of the hole and landed near Grobo's nose. Grobo gave a resigned sigh.

"Be careful," Pafweth said.

Bethinesi started digging a couple paces away. "I don't like this," she said.

"I don't like that smell," Danwel said.

Benwel sniffed. "That's just Grobo," he said.

Danwel had spent quite a few days plowing with Grobo this spring. He knew Grobo's smell.

"I mean that other smell," Danwel said.

Benwel asked, "Are you sure that's not just Grobo making a special smell for a special occasion?"

Danwel was sure it wasn't. He recognized that smell from seven springs ago, the first time his father had let him drive the plow team by himself. Halfway through the second furrow, the right ox had started shaking his head. Coming to the front of the team to investigate, Danwel had spied a writhing mass of scales flowing across the field.

"No, that's not Grobo's smell," Danwel said. "That's the smell of snakes."

CHAPTER 2
Kethwin

BY THE TIME Kethwin Walker and her sister Feshwin arrived at the hole, afternoon shadows were spreading across Kestrel Meadow. Danwel and his siblings were digging. Rays of sunlight illuminated the copper tints in the beautiful brown fuzz that covered Danwel's scalp. With long, strong arms and a powerful back, he surely could work that spade. Everyone in Kwoshim admired Danwel Broadfield. Too bad he didn't know how to use his popularity to his best advantage.

Kethwin knew. Danwel was respected enough to become the Broadfields' councilman someday, and Kethwin would be the councilman's wife. The "wife" part could have been accomplished already if Danwel hadn't spent so much of this spring dragging his huge feet.

"Oho! That *is* a deep hole."

This exclamation came from Councilman Highmeadow. He and Tholom had decided to come along.

The cheerful, gray-bearded councilman had arrived at Tholom's while Feshwin and Kethwin were working on the calf. Tholom had told him about the hole, and the councilman had decided to investigate. If it had been a Broadfield meadow, any livestock hazards would have been Broadfield business, but Kestrel Meadow was held in common. The mysterious pit was a problem for the village council.

The diggers stopped working long enough to exchange greetings with those who had just arrived. Kethwin's sister conferred with Pafweth Broadfield a moment before descending into the hole. Kethwin would have followed, but Danwel's sister, Bethinesi, was giving her a look.

Bethinesi whispered something up into Danwel's ear. Danwel

frowned. Bethinesi smirked and nudged him in the back.

Danwel shuffled over. Kethwin stood her ground, even though she didn't want to talk to Danwel with all these people watching. She'd been mighty angry with him lately.

"Good day, Kethwin," he said to the green hem of her dress.

"Good day, Danwel."

Well, that was a start.

Danwel raised his eyes to meet hers and asked, "How is Tholom's calf?"

"A bit sick," she said. "Feshwin thinks he ate one of Zhoswin's wedding garlands."

"Why would that make him sick?"

"Could be he ate the string, too."

"Oh."

With their beastshaper sight, Kethwin and Feshwin had looked inside the calf. They could see his cramped gut, but they had to guess about the cause. They wouldn't be able to see a string because the fibers would be long dead. Kethwin considered explaining this to Danwel, but decided against it. Her ability to resonate with elemental Life made no sense to him. There were a lot of things about her that made no sense to him.

"Are you still mad at me?" Danwel asked.

"Yes," she said.

"Bethinesi said I should tell you that I really do want to marry you."

"Danwel, you've already said that dozens of times."

"Aye. That's what I told her, but she thinks you don't believe me."

"It's none of her business," Kethwin said.

"Aye, I told her that, too. But Kethwin: do you believe me?"

"I believe you, but—" She looked up into his brown bull-eyes. "Danwel, when you want something—when you really want something—what do you do?"

"Something like what?"

"Well, say you wanted a pair of oxen. What would you do?"

"Well, I reckon I'd ask my dad if I could have the pick of the calves next spring."

"But what if you wanted them right now?"

Danwel shrugged. "My dad would let me borrow a pair of his."

"But what if you'd borrowed and borrowed for months and months, and what you really wanted, deep in the deepest part of your heart, was to *own*—what would you do then?"

Danwel frowned. "Are we still talking about oxen?"

"We were never talking about oxen!"

"Oh."

Pafweth, Bethinesi, and Councilman Highmeadow were staring at them. Tholom and Benwel were very interested in the dirt they were digging.

Kethwin sighed. What was the use of talking to him?

"I should go help my sister," she said.

The slope into the hole was steep, but thanks to the digging, it was now climbable, even for a slender girl in a dress. Kethwin descended into the black earth until she reached her sister's side. Feshwin was kneeling by Grobo. The mournful ox was buried so deeply in the lumps of sod that, even while kneeling, Feshwin could rest her head on his shoulder.

Feshwin's arms were buried in the sod so that she could keep her hands on the ox's right front leg. That leg must be injured. Feshwin used the physical contact to enhance her resonance with the ox's Life.

"What's that smell?" Kethwin asked.

"I don't know. Maybe there was a snake den here this winter."

Kethwin looked around. She didn't see any egg shells or snake skins.

"Don't worry about it," Feshwin said. "If any snakes were still here, I would have been able to sense them."

That was true.

"Here," said Feshwin, "look at this leg."

Kethwin knelt down on the cool, loose earth and closed her eyes. She didn't need physical contact to use her beastshaper's sight, but she did need to shut out visual distractions. Feshwin needed contact, but could work with her eyes open. Feshwin said this meant that Kethwin was more perceptive, but less focused.

Kethwin opened her extra senses and allowed herself to

become aware of the ox. He was in pain, but his spirit was in a helpless, sorrowful sort of calm, as though he knew his only option was to wait and see if things got better.

A bit like Danwel, Kethwin thought. *I hate waiting.*

As her senses opened more, she became aware of the blood flowing through her veins. Then, through resonance, she felt the blood in Grobo's veins. She and the ox were separate, but they shared the vibrant element of Life. This allowed Kethwin to see inside him, to see how Life flowed through him.

"The joint doesn't look too bad," she observed.

"No," Feshwin agreed. "The flow is sluggish there, but we can heal it quickly."

To be precise, Feshwin could heal it quickly. Kethwin could resonate with the flow of the ox's Life, but manipulating that flow was tricky. Kethwin did not yet have her sister's fine control.

Kethwin moved her focus from the joint and inspected the bone. There it was: "He has a fracture."

"Yes," said Feshwin. "How did he get it?"

By falling into a hole, Kethwin thought. But that wasn't the right answer.

"Look at his muscles," Feshwin prompted.

Kethwin looked, but she couldn't see anything wrong. "He looks strong to me."

"He is," Feshwin agreed. "His muscles held the joint together, and that is what cracked the bone."

"He cracked his bone with his own strength?"

"Something had to give," said Feshwin.

Kethwin's concentration was about to give. She opened her eyes, allowing her focus to fade. Sitting at the bottom of the strange-smelling hole right beside the massive ox, Kethwin remained aware of Grobo's Life. That was not difficult for her. She just found it fatiguing to focus on his leg.

"So what is your plan?" she asked. She knew that even with Feshwin's help, the fracture would take days to heal.

"Well, right now, I'm making the fracture's edges sticky so that they can fuse together again."

"I saw that," said Kethwin.

"But if he tries to walk out under his own power, he could widen the crack. I'll have to show his muscles how to hold the bone together."

"How do you do that?"

Feshwin smiled. "Watch."

Kethwin closed her eyes and focused her senses. She was willing to watch. At least the muscle training technique was one she could see. Kethwin only had half of the beastshaper's sight; some beastshaper skills would always be mysteries.

Beastshapers cared for sick or injured animals, but they got their name because their primary job was to shape animals in the womb. Kethwin had helped shape Grobo three springs ago. She had altered the flow of Life in his genitals so that he would be born a trainable plow ox instead of a bull. Feshwin had checked her work, made a few corrections, and told her she'd done a good job.

But then Feshwin had asked her to help with Grobo's markings. He needed a white blaze on his face and a white stocking on his right hind leg so that everyone would know he belonged to Clan Broadfield. Feshwin did the blaze to show her how. Kethwin had tried to shape the hind stocking the same way, but Feshwin said she was making the fur darker, not lighter. Kethwin's second attempt took the hair off completely. Feshwin had spent the rest of the afternoon convincing it to grow back in.

Feshwin had promised the talent would come to Kethwin in time, but it had not. Kethwin could geld, but she couldn't see colors in the womb. Eventually she had realized what that meant: She would never be a beastshaper.

Even so, she still wanted to learn what she could. It was interesting work, and it gave her an excuse to get out of that small, crowded house.

Danwel would get her out of that house for good.

"Are you watching?" Feshwin asked.

"What? Oh, sorry."

"You've been scatter-minded ever since Tholom and Zhoswin's wedding celebration," Feshwin said. "You and Danwel need to make up."

"We've already made up," Kethwin said. "Mostly."

Danwel had apologized. She'd accepted. They had both agreed there was nothing they could do. But that didn't make things right; that made things awful.

She hated not having something she wanted, but even worse was having no way to get it. She was powerless, and it was Danwel's sluggishness that had put her in this position. That was the offense she could not forgive.

"If you've made up, then why were you shouting at him?" Feshwin asked.

"Because he needed to be shouted at."

Feshwin should understand that. There were plenty of times when she had shouted at her husband, Zhamel.

"Shouting won't make marriage marks appear," Feshwin said. "You'll just have to wait until the Broadfields get some marks back."

"I know."

"Or you could invite him to marry into Clan Walker."

"Don't be daft."

"What's daft about it?"

"Feshwin, his family has land."

"We have land."

"We have enough land to support Mom and Dad," Kethwin said. "And maybe a few kids."

"Do you think we're daft for staying in our clan and helping our parents?"

Their brother Hameth had been the first to get married. He had chosen to stay in the Clan so he could eventually take over their dad's carpentry trade. At least he and his family lived in a different house.

Feshwin and Zhamel still lived in Kethwin's parents' house. Their little girl was a handful now that she had learned to walk, but she was cute enough to make up for it.

Kethwin's brother Vanim had been the third to get married. He and his wife Zhosethi slept in the stable. At least they didn't have any kids yet.

Kethwin also had a younger sister, Beswin. At sixteen, Beswin was finally mature enough to be bearable. In fact, Kethwin could tolerate any one of the people who lived in her house, but there were nine of them—more, if Hameth brought his family over for dinner—and nine was just too many. Kethwin sorely needed to marry out. And soon.

"Feshwin, don't you think Mom and Dad have enough 'help'?"

"What do you mean?"

"I mean that we have more help than we have food. Remember when we were little, and we all just grabbed our own chunks of bread? Now Mom cuts the bread and we each get one slice. And when was the last time anyone got a second bowl of soup?"

"It's spring," said Feshwin. "Food is always scarce in spring."

"Food is scarce because we keep adding more mouths to feed with the same amount of land," Kethwin said.

"But we have trades," Feshwin said. "You and I didn't plant anything today, but we still brought in food. Between this ox and Tholom's calf, we should get enough milk and eggs to stretch the pantry out for a few days. Dad is getting old, but he can still get a lot of carpentry work done with Hameth's help. And Vanim— Well, Vanim sometimes gets those timber cutting jobs."

"Aye. 'Sometimes.' But we have to eat every day. And Feshwin, I don't have a trade. Even if I could learn the skills, this village doesn't need two beastshapers."

"You can learn the skills, and you will," said Feshwin. "And there is plenty of work for two in the early spring, when everyone needs their calves and foals colored."

"Feshwin, I can't color. You know that."

"Well, you need to learn. Next spring, you'll be doing it by yourself."

This brought Kethwin up short. "What do you mean?" she asked.

"I'm pregnant," said Feshwin.

"Since when?" Kethwin asked in dismay.

"Since the third of Bluemonth."

"Feshwin, you're a beastshaper! You can control things like that!"

"I can control them a bit," Feshwin admitted. "Bluemonth is a good time for babies."

Kethwin stared at her. "So you *planned* this?"

Feshwin gave her a funny look. "The opportunity arose and I decided to take advantage of it."

Kethwin didn't want to believe it. Another mouth to feed by next spring.

"Does Mom know?" Kethwin asked.

"I haven't even told Zhamel," her sister said. "But I'm surprised you didn't notice. A beastshaper needs to be able to see things like that."

"Well I surely do not spy on your womb, Feshwin."

"It's not spying. It's just looking at what you can see. Go ahead."

"The very idea!"

She thought about it.

"Go ahead," Feshwin repeated.

"Surely?"

"Surely."

It seemed a bit too personal. But she *was* curious.

Feshwin wiggled one of her arms free from the earth and withdrew her knife from her belt. She set it aside so that the iron blade would not interfere with Kethwin's magical resonance. Kethwin no longer noticed her own blade's interference—no more than people notice their noses when they look at their feet—but Feshwin's blade would have been in the way.

Kethwin closed her eyes and allowed her Life to resonate with her sister's. It was much easier than examining an animal, because she and her sister were so similar—elementally, at least. The new life was difficult to sense. It was small. But there it was: a tiny glowing spot that was inside and yet not a part of Feshwin.

"It will be a few months before it starts to look cute," Feshwin told her.

Kethwin opened her eyes. "Do you have a name picked out yet?"

Feshwin smiled. "I think I'll wait until I can tell if it's a boy or a girl."

Kethwin nodded.

Names were troublesome. Every baby had to be named after

one of the first people Yolim had put into the world, but there were a lot more than eighty-one people now. The informal endings helped a bit. A girl named Kethi could be called "Kethwin", "Kethinesi", "Kethesi", or "Kethefi". Kethwin considered herself fortunate to be the only Kethi Walker who was called "Kethwin".

Clan Broadfield already had a Kethwin, but she was so old that the nickname no longer sounded right. Everyone called her "Granny Kethi". Kethwin's name would still be unique when she joined Clan Broadfield.

If she joined Clan Broadfield.

Feshwin re-sheathed her knife and said, "Now look at this leg again."

It was a mark of Feshwin's skill that she had been able to work on Grobo while carrying on a conversation. Kethwin doubted she would ever be able to split her concentration like that.

With eyes closed, Kethwin reached out to resonate with the ox again. She studied the leg and the work that Feshwin had done on the muscle. It was holding the fracture closed now. Kethwin thought the leg could probably support Grobo's weight, but she worried about him walking on it.

"Will it hold?" she asked.

"He needs time to heal," Feshwin admitted. "But he can't heal here."

Kethwin opened her eyes to see if the diggers were making any progress. It looked like a healthy ox could climb out of the hole now, if its legs were free.

No one had talked about that part of the plan, yet. She supposed they would just dig around Grobo's legs until he started climbing out on his own. The soil was surely loose enough.

Could be it was dangerously loose. The gaps between the chunks of sod hinted at hidden depths. And was that a trick of the wind or was there really a breeze coming from underground? That strange smell was getting stronger.

"Are you still seeing the leg?" Feshwin asked.

Kethwin tried to re-establish her resonance with the ox, but something else was vying for her attention. It was like trying to listen to a conversation while a bull bellowed nearby. She was about to push the thing out of her mind when she realized that something that big should not be ignored.

"Feshwin? What's that?"

"What? … Oh."

It was big. It was distant, yet it was closing rapidly. Resonating with the thing did not require Kethwin's concentration; she felt as though the thing were resonating her. It seemed to move with an animal passion, impossibly deep underground, impossibly huge.

The ground shifted. Feshwin gasped.

Kethwin clambered to her feet. The diggers were all staring wide-eyed, as though they could sense the thing as well. That was when Kethwin became aware of the deep rumble coming from below.

She reached down to help her sister up.

"Feshwin, we have to get out of here!"

"Go," was the reply. "My arm is stuck."

CHAPTER 3

A Dragon

DANWEL WENT STILL, stopping with his spade in mid-swing. The ground was vibrating. It shook with a rumble so deep that Danwel heard it not with his ears, but with his bones.

The other diggers—Tholom, Benwel, and Bethinesi—were also frozen in place, trying to understand what was happening.

The rumble was getting louder.

"Danwel!"

Kethwin's cry swooped through the air like a hawk. Danwel jumped like a rabbit.

"Come here!" Kethwin yelled. "She's stuck!"

Danwel was already moving, lumbering down the slope that they had dug into the sinkhole. The ground beneath his feet was uneven, but he kept his balance with momentum and determination.

Kethwin's sister was pleading, "Kethwin, get out of here."

Danwel did not have any breath for pleas. He grabbed white-faced Kethwin by her slender elbow and pushed her toward the slope. Then he began to dig.

Feshwin had made a hole by Grobo's shoulder so she could work on the ox's leg. Grobo's weight must have shifted, for her arm was now trapped in this hole. With a bit of time, it would have been no trouble to set the woman free, but the ground was shaking, a breeze was blowing up between the chunks of loose sod, and the air was filling with the smell of snakes. Danwel reckoned his time was short.

He plunged his spade into the earth. He had to dig fast, he had to strike deep, and he had to avoid stabbing the spade into Feshwin's arm—which was what made the task so difficult: Spadework did not normally require precision.

The ground shifted. Whether because of this or because of Danwel's efforts, Feshwin suddenly pulled her arm free. Placing a hand on Grobo's shoulder, she pushed herself to her feet.

"Kethwin, don't just sit there!" she yelled. "Get out!"

Kethwin was indeed sitting, only halfway up the exit slope, staring at her sister and Danwel with terror in her eyes.

Danwel took a step toward his girl. The ground shook, and Danwel crouched to keep his balance.

With a bellow, Grobo began sliding backward. A new hole had opened up behind the ox. Under Feshwin, chunks of turf danced like dirt clods in the harrow.

Danwel wrapped an arm around the woman's waist and dove for the slope. Earth disappeared under his feet, but his belly landed on solid ground. He reached out and planted his spade in the dirt.

Feshwin's body slipped in his grasp. Her ribs slid against his arm. He squeezed tighter. Feshwin caught herself with a hand on the crook of his neck. She dangled there, above the empty darkness of a newly opened pit.

Danwel wasn't sure the pit had a bottom. *Yolim save us,* he prayed.

He had one hand on the spade and his other hand tucked under Feshwin's arm, preventing her from plummeting into oblivion. He clung to a ledge of earth with only his body and his prayers.

A chunk of dirt crumbled away under his knee. Danwel tightened his grip on the spade and discovered that the spade was actually quite loose.

His brother Benwel came rushing down the slope then. Benwel brushed past the petrified Kethwin and sat down straddling the spade. He wrapped both hands around the handle.

"Hang on," Benwel said.

Kethwin stood up. "Don't just watch!" she screamed at the others. "Come help!"

"The rope!" That was Pafweth's voice, from up above.

Legs scrambled down the slope and a rope fell across Danwel's back. Feshwin grabbed for it, pulling Danwel a thumbwidth closer to the edge.

"Hold on tight," said Tholom.

"I've got it," Feshwin said. "Let me go, Danwel."

Danwel loosened his grip on Feshwin. Her ribs slid past his fingertips as Tholom, Pafweth, Bethinesi, and Councilman Highmeadow pulled her out of the hole. With Feshwin's weight gone, Danwel now felt like a man simply lying in the dirt instead of a man a handsbreadth from doom. The deep rumbling sound had died away.

"Do you need the rope, too?" asked Tholom, once they had Feshwin safely out of the pit.

"Just a hand," said Danwel.

Tholom sat down beside Benwel and took Danwel's free hand. Pulling against them, Danwel hauled himself out.

For a moment he contemplated the blackness that had swallowed up a good ox. There was no way to see how deep the hole was, not in the shadows of sunset.

"Let's get out of here before more of it caves in," he suggested.

The others readily agreed with this idea.

As soon as Danwel was off the excavated slope and back on seemingly solid ground, white-faced Kethwin left her sister's side and wrapped her arms around him, burying her face in his chest. Danwel patted his girl on the back. She was shaking.

"Good thing you saved Dad's spade," Bethinesi said in a soft voice. She put a hand on his shoulder.

In the distance, an ox bellowed. For a moment, Danwel thought it was Grobo's voice coming up from the pit, but then he realized it was one of the yearlings. The milk cows had started the herd on the path to the village a while ago, but there had been a few stragglers still at the edge of the meadow when the rumbling started. They were doubtless running to catch up now.

Pafweth gave Benwel a worried look. Panicking cattle didn't always remember the way home.

"I reckon we'd better go," she said. "We don't want those yearlings to get into trouble."

"Aye," agreed Benwel. "I've lost enough of Dad's cattle today."

The two of them wished Councilman Highmeadow a good day and set off down the path at a trot.

Danwel doubted his father would be very mad. There wasn't

much Benwel could have done. But Benwel was used to having things be his fault.

The rest of them walked down the path through the trees at a slower pace, respectful of Councilman Highmeadow's years. Kethwin walked right beside Danwel with her arm around his waist. She even leaned her head against his arm when they emerged from the woods. The blue evening sky was streaked with flame-bright clouds lit by the setting sun. The purple moon was sinking toward Katydid Ridge.

They followed the path to the village, walking between newly plowed fields. "I shall have to call a meeting for tonight," Councilman Highmeadow said. "Although, I do not know what I shall say."

"What *was* that thing?" Bethinesi asked.

Danwel was wondering, too. People told stories about tornadoes. Villages downstream occasionally had floods. Thunderstorms were commonplace and lightning often struck Kestrel Bluff. But Danwel had never heard of anything that shook the ground and opened gaping holes in the earth.

"It was an animal," Kethwin said.

"Are you sure?" asked Councilman Highmeadow.

"We could sense it," agreed Feshwin.

The Councilman cocked his head like a robin. "Do you know what it was, Feshi?"

"No," Feshwin said. "I could just tell there was something there—something that was so full of Life that I could feel it from a distance."

She looked at Kethwin.

Kethwin frowned. "It's difficult to describe," she decided. "It had enough Life for a tree, but it was an animal kind of Life."

"Was it bigger than an ox?" Danwel asked.

"Much bigger," said Kethwin.

Feshwin nodded in agreement.

This thought disturbed Danwel. He didn't know any animals bigger than an ox. A horse was taller, but it wasn't bigger. A moose might be bigger, but moose lived far up the river Yarl in the land of Dwen-Maisil. He had never heard of a moose in the land of Dwen-

Tarthil.

"Bigger than an ox, and smells like a snake," he murmured.

"It was a dragon," Tholom said.

They all looked at him.

"What is a dragon?" Bethinesi asked.

"It is a giant beast that lives on the plains," Tholom said. "I heard about it when Zhoswin and I went to Tarthil to get married."

"I have never heard of such a creature," said Councilman Highmeadow. "Tell us what you know about it, Thol."

"Well, some merchants say there is a dragonslayer in Brin," said Tholom. "He's not Clanfolk; he's one of the Stripedfolk. And he sang a song about killing a dragon with his spear."

"Did you hear anyone sing this song?"

"No, Councilman," Tholom replied. "But those who had heard it told me what it was about. A great beast was attacking the Stripedfolk and eating their horses. And then this dragonslayer stabbed it and saved them all."

"Do you know anything more about this beast, besides the fact that it is big enough to prey on horses?"

"No, Councilman."

"That's quite all right," said Councilman Highmeadow, giving his newest cousin a pat on the arm. "I am sure that what you have just said will be of interest to the rest of the council."

"Zhoswin might remember a bit more," Tholom said. "I'll ask her."

Danwel wasn't sure what to think about Tholom's idea. Not many animals were big enough to eat a horse. Wolves could prey on horses, but Stripedfolk probably wouldn't need a hero to save them from a wolf. They were giants, twice as tall as Clanfolk, and they made their living by hunting.

This was all Danwel knew about Stripedfolk, except for the legend of how they had gotten their skin. The story was a strange one, which meant that it was probably true:

When the nine deities were creating their people, each gave their creations a special gift. Yolim, the creator of the Clanfolk, gave his people mutable skin color, so that they would always be the same color as the people they wanted to trade with. By that time, most of the other deities had already given their people colors: Zharnov's people were blue, Kashram's people were red, and so on. But Lashrefi, goddess of luck, was still trying to decide whether her people should be as white as the snow or as black as the night. When she heard about Yolim's gift, she laughed at him and made her people striped.

Clanfolk would turn red when talking to Kashram's Redfolk and blue when talking to Zharnov's Riverfolk, but when they wanted to bargain with the Stripedfolk, they had to concentrate on holding one color; otherwise their complexion would waver between light and dark and they would be laughed at.

The story always made Danwel think of Kethwin. Kethwin's skin changed color, but she couldn't control it the way most people could. In Kwoshim, the custom was for people to keep their skin the color of lightly tanned leather. Kethwin was usually pale, but she might turn dark if she were working on a bay horse. This was embarrassing for her—and when she was embarrassed, she turned pink.

Everyone blushed pink sometimes, if they didn't pay attention. Bethinesi said Danwel turned pink every time he kissed Kethwin. Danwel said she should mind her own business.

Sometimes Danwel could make Kethwin turn pink just by holding her hand or by whispering the right thing in her ear. Bethinesi acted as though Kethwin's inability to control her skin were some sort of defect, but Danwel was glad his girl's moods were so easy to read. Kethwin didn't hide much.

So now, with her arm around his waist, Danwel felt pretty sure that Kethwin was done being angry with him for a while.

The meeting was set for moonset, right after supper—that is, right after supper for everyone but Benwel. He and Pafweth spent suppertime convincing a yearling cow that she really did want to go into the courtyard with the rest of the herd instead of into the adjacent courtyard, which held Pafweth's family's herd. Danwel and Bethinesi went looking for Benwel too late to be of any help, but just in time to get his detailed account of the escapade.

"You're just lucky Pafweth was there to help you," Bethinesi told him when he had finished his comic tale of woe.

"Aye," agreed Benwel. "Because you two were too busy eating to help."

"Sorry," Danwel muttered, and he handed Benwel half a loaf of bread.

"We were busy telling Mom and Dad about what happened," said Bethinesi.

"Well, I hope you got practice," Benwel said, "because now you'll have to tell the whole village at the meeting."

"Oh," said Bethinesi. Danwel could see she hadn't thought of that.

They set out for the center of the village with their dad. Sheets of clouds had spread themselves over the Grigolin Valley, diffusing the purple glow of the setting moon. The village was dark except for the torches burning outside the Meeting House.

Kwoshim was laid out like a wheel, with four roads for spokes and the Meeting House for a hub. The roads divided the village into quarters: Broadfields, Highmeadows, Walkers, and Spring-waters. They were quarters in the sense that there were four of them, but the parts were not equal. Clan Broadfield and Clan Highmeadow owned seven-tenths of the land around the village of Kwoshim, and the number of buildings in these quarters was correspondingly larger.

Still, on the council, each clan had one councilman and one vote. On the other hand, they didn't really vote; they mostly just talked about things and then worked out some sort of agreement. No clan would elect a councilman who couldn't see both sides of a bargain.

Pafweth and her folks met them in the street, so they all walked toward the Meeting House together. The torches at the entrances illuminated the faces of those who stood in line outside.

"When did you find time to brush your hair?" Benwel asked Pafweth.

It was a fair question, considering that they had just been chasing a yearling together. Benwel still looked like a cowherd and she, despite her brown dress and worn shoes, looked like a miller's daughter. It was amazing what women could do just by brushing and re-braiding their hair.

Pafweth ran her hand over Benwel's fuzzy head. "I have time to brush yours, too, if you like."

She was teasing, of course. Men couldn't grow hair long enough to brush.

Bethinesi told Benwel, "If you hadn't spent so much time complaining about your extra work, you would have had time to clean up a bit, too."

"I have time now," said Benwel, pulling out his knife to clean his fingernails. "This line isn't moving."

"We're moving," their father said. "It just always takes time."

Benwel did get all ten nails cleaned before they finally got inside. The Meeting House was round on the outside, in accordance with tradition. Inside, however, the tiers of seating were built on the four sides of a square, one side for each clan. The entrances were at the corners of the square, so to get to the Broadfield tier, they had to squeeze through a narrow passage on the diagonal between two tiers of seating. Well, it always felt like a squeeze to Danwel, but even normal-sized people could only walk through in single file.

The high walls of the passage gradually stepped down as they proceeded toward the center, so that by the time they had reached the front tier, the wall was nothing more than a support for the bottom step. Danwel's father had one foot on that step when Councilman Bil Broadfield caught his eye.

"Dom, bring your children over here," he said, indicating the bench in front.

Benwel's smile glowed in the rushlights. Bethinesi looked startled.

Councilman Broadfield consulted with Councilman Highmeadow a moment and then called, "Pafi, you too."

"Thought you could sneak away?" Bethinesi asked as they sat down on the front bench.

"I was hoping so," Pafweth murmured.

"Don't be so scared," Benwel said. "This will be fun."

Kethwin, who had been sitting on the front Walker bench, came over to the Broadfield section and took Danwel's hand.

"Sit on the end," she murmured up into his ear. "So I can talk to you if I need to."

Danwel did as he was told, while Kethwin slipped back to the Walker section. She had held his hand. That was nice.

She was smiling, too. But it wasn't like that sweet smile she got when she wanted him to kiss her. It was more like the smile women got when they knew something men didn't. Why did she think she would need to talk to him during the meeting?

The councilmen took their seats in the center of the Meeting House. They sat on four sides of a square desk, the sides chosen so that each councilman could see his own kin behind the councilman on the opposite side. Once everyone was quiet, Councilman Highmeadow—who sat in front of the Broadfield bench—stood up and addressed the village:

"Thank you all for coming. I am sure we all have many questions about what transpired in Kestrel Meadow this afternoon. The best way to answer those questions is to begin with the people who were there at the beginning."

He nodded to Councilman Broadfield and sat down.

Councilman Broadfield rose and addressed the village in his deliberate voice:

"Thank you, Councilman Highmeadow. Pafi and Ben Broadfield, it is my understanding that you were both present at the occurrence of an unusual event this afternoon. Please rise and tell us what you saw."

They stood up. As it happened, Benwel was quite a bit more nervous than he had pretended he would be. He talked fast enough to cover the entire afternoon in half the time it had taken him to tell Danwel and Bethinesi about the troublesome yearling. Even so, he did a fair job of representing the Clan. Poor Pafweth just looked at Benwel or her shoes.

Benwel did have some funny ideas about what had happened. He made a great deal out of how much danger Feshwin had been in, saying, "If Danwel hadn't run in to save her, she'd still be stuck there," which was absurd, because the turf that she had been stuck in had fallen away with Grobo. He also made it sound as though Danwel had leapt across empty space and planted his spade into the side of a cliff as the ground gave way beneath him. But Danwel couldn't blame his brother for wanting to make a big impression with his first chance to speak at a meeting.

"Do you have anything to add, Pafi?" the councilman asked.

Pafweth shook her head.

Danwel was called on next. He could only think of one detail his brother had left out.

"Benwel saw everything I saw," he said. "Although, I reckon I was a bit closer to it there at the end."

He looked over at the Walker sisters. "According to Kethwin and Feshwin, there was some big animal down there, but I'm not sure it was trying to eat us. Could be it was just making holes. Grobo wasn't grabbed by anything; he just sort of slid backward into this hole that opened up behind him. Feshwin and I stumbled a bit then, but we managed to hang on until the others pulled us out."

Councilman Broadfield asked, "Bethi, do you have anything to add?"

Bethinesi looked at the councilman, then at Danwel. Her hands were gripping her skirt.

"Yes," she decided, standing up.

"Danwel didn't stumble," she said. "He grabbed Feshwin and leapt. And he didn't just hang on. He saved her life."

Bethinesi sat down and squeezed Pafweth's hand. Murmurs of approval rose from all four tiers. Danwel was surprised. It was strange to think that his sister might be proud of him—and standing up to say so was a lot braver than anything he had done.

"Very well," said Councilman Broadfield. And he nodded to Councilman Highmeadow.

Councilman Highmeadow passed the meeting to Clan Walker so that the two sisters could tell their story. Feshwin took the lead, describing how she had sensed something alive in a place where life was not usually found, but Kethwin was not shy about interrupting her to emphasize, "It was *deep* underground. And it was not just alive like a tree: It was like an animal *seeking* something."

Feshwin gave her sister a funny look, but she let that statement stand.

Danwel was impressed at how strong and steady Kethwin's

voice was. She was not at all afraid of speaking before the entire village.

When Kethwin sat down again, she gave Danwel a smile. But it was still the I-have-a-secret smile. What was she up to?

Danwel's speculations were interrupted by Councilman Highmeadow announcing, "Zhosi and Thol Highmeadow will now tell us about dragons."

These words produced a low murmur because, of course, everyone had already heard a bit of Tholom's tale. The villagers were eager to hear it first hand.

Tholom and Zhoswin stood up.

"As you know," Zhoswin began, "we recently went on a little trip to Tarthil." She beamed as the village's applause interrupted her.

"Thank you. Thank you. While we were in Tarthil, we heard many a tale about the goings-on in neighboring lands, as well as news from all corners of Dwen-Tarthil. But could be the most intriguing story of all was from the distant prairies of the Stripedfolk."

Danwel had not known that Zhoswin Highmeadow could spread her butter so thick.

"It seems that, not long ago, a dangerous beast stalked the plains—a beast larger than anything known on our side of the Yarl. This beast was so large that it frightened even the wild Stripedfolk, who lived in fear of it until a brave hunter took up his spear and vowed to slay it. They called this beast a dragon!"

She must have practiced this story before the meeting, Danwel thought. *I should do that next time.*

"Word of his brave deed spread all along the Yarl, until it reached the very tavern in Tarthil where Tholom and I ate supper!"

The audience, especially the female portion of it, made sounds of approval. Danwel realized that by leaving out the fact that the Stripedman was actually in Brin, she had avoided giving them the impression that Tarthil might be second-rate.

"My husband—" And here a rush of applause answered the gush in her voice. "Thank you. My husband would now like to tell you about what he saw this very day." She turned and smiled at Tholom.

"Well," said Tholom, "when I saw that hole up there in Kestrel Meadow, I got to thinking that it would take a mighty large beast to make a hole like that. So I got to thinking, and I thought, 'Could be we have a dragon of our own, right here in Kwoshim.'"

Although not as polished, Tholom's words drew every bit as much a response as his bride's had. Zhoswin beamed at him.

The four councilmen leaned across the desk then, taking advantage of the noise to confer without being overheard. All conversations in the tiers rapidly died away as each villager strained to overhear.

"Aye, that much is clear," said Councilman Broadfield.

He clunked his stool back from the desk and stood up. Turning as he spoke, so that he could see and address everyone, he said, "It seems to me—and the council agrees—that this dragon could be rather a destructive creature. When it has finished its meal of ox— and it will surely do so by the end of the month—it seems to me that it will come back for more. And unless we want Kestrel Meadow renamed to Kestrel Pit—" he paused for the quiet chuckles, "—we need to exterminate this vermin."

This sentiment met universal approval.

"So I ask you," finished Councilman Broadfield, "does anyone have any ideas on how to do that. Yes? Kethi Walker?"

Danwel was startled to see that Kethwin had left her bench to stand beside him. "Say you will slay the dragon!" she hissed in his ear.

All eyes were on them, and Kethwin was blushing. "Kethwin, I can't slay the dragon," he replied. It was difficult to keep his voice to a whisper.

"Yes you can. Show some ambition," she hissed.

Now even Councilman Highmeadow had turned around on his stool to look at them.

"I think Danwel can slay the dragon," Kethwin said to the council.

Sensible people would have laughed at this ridiculous idea. Danwel was appalled to see heads nodding.

"If the Stripedfolk have dragonslayers," Kethwin went on, "then so can we. And no one is bigger or stronger than Danwel."

People murmured in agreement.

In a voice pitched so that only Kethwin would hear, Danwel asked, "Are you trying to get me killed?"

"Danwel, this is our chance!" she said. "You'll be a hero. Once you've saved an entire village, they'll *have* to let us use one of those marks."

So that was her scheme!

He raised his voice and spoke to the council. "I can't slay the dragon. I'm not even a hunter."

"You slew that wolf last summer," said his cousin Shimeth, from the third tier behind him.

Heads nodded.

"I didn't 'slay' it," said Danwel. "I just killed it. Its back was broken by your deadfall trap."

"But you helped me build the trap," said Shimeth.

"And he saved Feshwin's life," Kethwin added.

"You surely did that, Danwel," his brother agreed.

Why is everyone going daft? Danwel wondered. He looked at his dad, who shrugged.

People were murmuring to each other: "Danwel can do it." "Danwel can fight this thing, whatever it is." "We've got our own giant right here."

Danwel had to make them see reason. He stood up and the room quieted to hear his words.

"Look, the dragon is big," Danwel told them. "It might even be as big as a moose. And it lives deep underground."

He looked at their faces.

"I can't be your dragonslayer," he said. "I don't even know what a dragon is, much less how to kill one."

All eyes were on him, begging him to help. If the biggest man in the village could not kill it, who could? There must be something Danwel could do.

"Now ... could be there's a trick to it," he admitted.

The councilmen nodded.

"Could be there's a way to make some sort of trap for it," he went on.

Everyone was looking at him hopefully.

"Well, I'm just big," he told them. "I'm not smart. But we know there's a way to kill the dragon, because somebody else already did it. So it seems to me, the thing to do is to go find this dragonslayer and ask him to help."

"Would you do that, Dan?" Councilman Broadfield asked. "Would you bargain with the dragonslayer on behalf of the village of Kwoshim?"

Danwel shrugged. "I suppose so," he said. "I reckon I'm a better bargainer than I am a dragonslayer. If Dad thinks that's what I should do."

His father nodded.

Councilman Broadfield sat down and addressed his colleagues: "I propose that Dan, son of Dom and Marshi Broadfield, be given authority to represent the village of Kwoshim in negotiations with the dragonslayer, and that he be supplied with a stipend so that he may journey there and back."

"I support."

"I support."

"I support," said Councilman Highmeadow. "Proposal passed."

As the village's applause poured over them, Kethwin gave Danwel a hug and said, "Oh, Danwel, I knew I could count on you!"

CHAPTER 4

Summerwind

THE KALAIBO LED THE SONG as the band rode their horses across the rolling plain. Summerwind Dawnracer sang the girls' part on some choruses and the women's part on others, depending on whether she felt more like Summerwind or more like Dawnracer.

In the Olden Time, she would have been given a name like "Half-Mask", because the entire left side of her face was black. Or perhaps she would have been named "Fork Cheek", because of the stripe that curved under her right eye and split into three just below her cheekbone. It was said that the tribes who lived near the mountains still named their children according to their stripes, but the Flamebringer Tribe used modern names because it was the Modern Time.

Summerwind was the spring name she had been given by her mother. Dawnracer was the name she had chosen for herself three autumns ago. It suited her, for she often raced the dawn.

When the blue of night gave way to gray, when the stars began to fade, Summerwind would creep out of camp and find the silhouette of her horse against the sky. Their ride would start at a careful walk. When the clouds in the sunward sky grew red, she would allow the horse a gentle trot, to add distance between herself and the camp. When she saw a hint of yellow, she would guide the horse around until they faced the pointed peaks of the waking lodges. An instant of tension, while the horse gathered itself and then: Speed! Wind through her hair, thunder through her spine. Racing, racing to reach the lodges before the first ray of the sun. She was Dawnracer, the fastest horsewoman of the prairie!

Not that she had played games this morning, of course. She only did so when she and her horse did not have a long ride ahead of them. Summerwind was adventurous, not stupid.

Scouts appeared at the top of the rise. They were returning to report on the campsite at the Acorn Ravine. Summerwind envied the scouts because they had more opportunities to gallop than she did.

They were galloping now as they rode down to meet Gethrav Lowsinger—only two of them. If the scouts had seen a buck in the ravine, a few would have stalked it and the rest would have come back. If the scouts had seen a distant bison herd, they would all have come back and waited for the gethrav to organize the hunt. Why had these two come back alone?

Summerwind had to find out. Still singing the traveling song, she encouraged Whitefoot to move up toward the front where the broad-shouldered gethrav and the white-haired taishrefi rode. She was only two horselengths behind them when a gray mare veered to block her path. Whitefoot balked.

It would be a poor lesson to let Whitefoot be intimidated. The filly needed to learn that horse-herd hierarchy didn't apply when the saddle was on. As long as she had a rider, she was safe from bullies.

Summerwind looked into the scornful eyes of Primrose Breezekenner, the rider of the gray mare. The traveling song caught in Summerwind's throat. If she tried to pass, Whitefoot would learn that presumptuous fillies got bitten very hard.

Breezekenner's eyes narrowed to slits, as though she were staring into the sun. Summerwind affected a serene smile, implying that her horse had stopped precisely where she had intended. In response, Breezekenner's scowl grew darker, which made Summerwind's smile more genuine.

The scouts had arrived at the front of the band by that time, and the kalaibo gave the signal for the traveling song to end. Summerwind joined in the last chorus, making sure to keep her smile on Breezekenner until the woman turned away in disgust.

Pompous goose, Summerwind thought.

Breezekenner was Summerwind's age—old enough to make a lodge and take a husband, yet not so old as to have actually done so—but she acted as though she thought she were a wizened taishrefi instead of a taishrefi's fledgling apprentice. She was from

Slowtalker's Band, and everyone in Lowsinger's Band disliked her.

Once the end notes of the traveling song had been sung, the scouts addressed Gethrav Lowsinger and Taishrefi Smokewatcher. The four of them spoke in low voices, and Summerwind was just far enough away that she could not hear clearly.

Thanks to that foul-tempered vixen and her gray mare.

At least she was close enough to watch their faces. Gethrav Lowsinger showed surprise, but Taishrefi Smokewatcher's expression did not change. The white-haired woman was the oldest person in Lowsinger's Band, and nothing ever surprised her. However, there was much that interested her, and her keen eyes were always watching.

The gethrav and the taishrefi conferred a moment. It was the gethrav's duty to lead the band; it was the taishrefi's duty to guide the band. From the very moment that Taishrefi Smokewatcher had named Lowsinger the band's gethrav, she had always accepted his decisions and yielded to his leadership. And in the ten years that Lowsinger had been leading the band, he had never once made a decision without first consulting the taishrefi to be certain it was one she would accept.

The gethrav turned his horse and announced, "There is a sight ahead that I shall not describe, for we must see it with our own eyes. Forward, Kalaibo Stormdrummer!"

The kalaibo nodded and began a new song. Instead of a traveling song, he chose a sweet melody that sounded best when sung by few voices. He knew that the band was now too curious to sing.

Summerwind's brother Greenpool would usually sing along with the kalaibo even when the song was intended as a solo—he said this was allowed because he was the kalaibo's apprentice—but this time, as the band resumed riding up the gentle slope, he used his breath to chastise his sister:

"You should not have provoked Breezekenner."

"I provoked her?" Summerwind was amazed. "She was the one who encamped her fat mare in my path."

"Sister, the burden of the taishrefi's apprentice is not light. A taishrefi must think always of what is best for the band, even if this may result in some hard feelings."

Hard feelings? Summerwind didn't have hard feelings. She just thought that Breezekenner was a foul-tempered vixen.

"My brother, I thank you," she said sweetly. "I had forgotten that becoming an apprentice makes one boring, serious, and unpleasant."

He gave her a look that he probably thought was disappointed and dignified, and then fell back to sing with the kalaibo.

Perhaps she had been unfair. Greenpool was not, in truth, unpleasant. (And no one could be as unpleasant as Breezekenner!) But he was serious and boring. Summerwind had three brothers, and the most boring one was the only one who had stayed with the band.

Frogfoot—who traveled with his wife's band—was even more serious than Greenpool, but he was now Summerwind's favorite brother. Summerwind saw him only a few times a year, but whenever they met, he gave her a new fleet-footed filly to train. The arrangement suited her father, who would have been responsible for supplying her with a horse himself if her brother had not done so. Her father said he was grateful that he had one less horse to look after. Her mother, however, worried that Frogfoot's fine horses were keeping Summerwind from finding a husband to supply her with mounts. Summerwind had to admit that there was truth in this. As long as she had a fast horse to ride, she saw no need to marry.

Zephyr would have been her favorite brother if he hadn't left three summers ago. As children, they had been so close that they could share thoughts. Far from being serious, Zephyr was so whimsical that he had run away to sing for the farmers along the river Dothedarl. A brother who traveled with a different band was called a "left-brother", but Summerwind knew no name for a brother who went to join a tribe of plow people—"stupid-brother" seemed to express her feelings best.

As the band trotted over the rise, the sight that met their eyes seemed, at first, to be exactly what they saw every year. They continued to travel through a green plain of new spring grass—last year's dead grass having been cleared by a fire their tribe had set the previous month. A short lope ahead was the edge of the Acorn

Ravine, where topography stopped the spring fires and allowed the trees to flourish. Lone oaks ventured out from the ravine onto the prairie, like scouts watching for trouble around the perimeter of a camp. The trees were beginning to leaf out, and their solid gray trunks wore gray-green halos, except for that gap in the wood where a trick of the light made the budding leaves appear purple.

That gap was new. And perhaps that light wasn't a trick.

"What knocked down the trees there?" Summerwind asked at the same time that Breezekenner asked, "Why are the oak leaves glowing purple?"

Breezekenner gave her a frown. Summerwind, willing to be generous, gave her one back.

"If those questions can be answered," the taishrefi said, "they cannot be answered from here."

More of the scouts appeared then, riding on the bison trail that led up out of the ravine. The gethrav's eyes watched them sharply, and his back relaxed when he had accounted for all the men he had sent out.

The scout in the lead beckoned to indicate that it was safe for the band to approach. That explained why only two had been sent back: The rest had been investigating the ravine, looking for danger.

The gethrav led the band to meet the scouts at the gap in the trees. Arriving at the edge of the ravine, they could see that the trees had been smashed. Trunks lay flat, amid a litter of leafing twigs and branches. The splintered stumps proved that they had been snapped from their bases, not chopped with an axe. It was a scene that Summerwind might have expected to see in the wake of a tornado, except for the swath of purple-tinged grass leading to the gap and the glowing purple leaves on the trees.

To get a closer look, they had to dismount. They followed the gethrav into the chaos of brush and branches. The only way to move about was by walking on the fallen trunks.

Summerwind plucked off a nearby twig and studied the infant oak leaves. They were soft, fragile, and slightly sticky, just as one would expect of leaves that were seeing their first day of sun. But their color was a bright bluish-purple, and as Breezekenner had said, they glowed, illuminating the white skin of Summerwind's palm.

"That truly does not look natural," murmured the gethrav.

"Perhaps it is not," said the taishrefi.

The kalaibo climbed on top of a tree stump to get a better view.

The gethrav asked, "Kalaibo Stormdrummer, is a scene such as this described in any song that you know?"

The kalaibo surveyed the swath, which extended through the bottom of the ravine and up the other side. Summerwind noted that on the far side, the trees had fallen up—that is, they had been knocked flat against the hillside with their splintered stumps left below them.

After contemplating the scene, the kalaibo addressed the gethrav: "I know eight tornado songs. Two of them describe purple flashes of lightning. And one of those mentions a purple sky."

That was what was strange about the color, Summerwind realized. It was a natural color, but it was found in the sky: the moon early in Purplemonth, just as it began to take on its new hue; or the glow in the sunaway sky, just as the sunward sky was turning golden.

"Lightning did not eat this tree," Summerwind's father observed.

Summerwind craned her neck to see what he was looking at. The gethrav scrambled over to investigate.

"The bark is shredded," the gethrav agreed. "And those are teeth marks."

"Porcupine?" suggested Greenpool.

"Something bigger," said her father.

"Beaver?"

"I think not," said the gethrav. They waited for him to say what he thought it was, but he remained silent.

"Aha!"

All heads turned to look at Peltswapper, one of the band's traders. He held up a curious object, which he brought to the gethrav.

"Have you ever seen a feather such as this?" Peltswapper asked.

"It looks almost like a fish scale," said the gethrav, taking the object into his hand. Summerwind moved to get a better view. The thing was shaped like an eagle feather, but it had no quill. Like the baby oak leaves, it glowed, giving the gethrav's skin a purple tinge.

"I believe it to be a feather from a dragon," said Peltswapper.

"From what?" asked the gethrav. "I did not hear you truly."

"A dragon," repeated Peltswapper.

"You will have to tell us what you think a dragon is," the taishrefi said. "We do not know."

Peltswapper answered her, "I think a dragon is a flying beaver with glowing purple feathers that it uses as brushes to paint the landscape."

"And to crush the trees flat?" inquired the gethrav.

"Yes," said Peltswapper.

"And is this a tale you heard from the Yolimites?" asked the gethrav.

"It is," replied Peltswapper.

After the spring gathering, the trader had not traveled with the band, but instead had ridden to the great Yolimite village of Minroshi. That is, the village was great in area and in population. Peltswapper said the lodges and the Yolimites themselves were small.

Peltswapper visited them to exchange his pelts for iron. This time he had brought back seven iron bars, two broken knives, and one long, curved blade. Summerwind knew this because her father, Buckslayer, now had all these things in his possession. He would turn the iron into spear points, knife blades, and axe heads, giving some of these tools to Peltswapper as payment for the material.

Peltswapper explained, "In Minroshi, the Yolimites told of a Lashrefite hunter who had sung for them in the great village of Brin. This hunter had not only seen a dragon, but had slain one with his own spear."

The gethrav surveyed the width of the swath the dragon had left in its wake. "He must have had a very large spear," he observed. "Unless, perhaps, a dragon is some other animal?"

"What animal is there that is not in our songs?" asked Peltswapper. "This destruction was caused by a giant animal we have never heard of before. A dragon matches this description precisely. Can there be two such beasts? And if there were, is it likely the dragon would come to our knowledge at the same time that another beast made its appearance?"

The gethrav considered this. "Peltswapper, do you know the way to Brin?"

"Truly I do," the trader replied. "One simply travels to Minroshi and then rides along the river Kailanarl until one comes to Brin."

"Then would you find this dragonslayer, ascertain if his story is true, and invite him to come and give our band a dragonslaying demonstration?"

"I could," the trader admitted, "although I have not had a chance to obtain more pelts since my return."

Breezekenner spoke up: "Gethrav Lowsinger, this dragon threatens the entire Flamebringer tribe, and perhaps all Lashrefites. You should choose someone who represents more than just your band."

Who is she to give orders to our gethrav? Summerwind wondered.

The gethrav, however, was merely amused. "I thought I should choose someone who knows about Yolimite villages, someone who has proven himself to be persuasive. Did the Goddess reveal to you that you could do this better than Peltswapper?"

The taishrefi murmured something into her apprentice's ear. Breezekenner scowled and hunched her shoulders.

Addressing the gethrav, the taishrefi said, "Peltswapper may indeed be the best choice, but there is much about this that we do not know. Anyone who is sent to ask an unknown person to slay an unheard-of beast will need to go with the blessing of Lashrefi. Perhaps this makes Breezekenner a better choice, or perhaps there is some other."

"Ah. I hear your words," said the gethrav. "You are proposing that we leave the decision up to the Goddess."

"Precisely."

"And will you begin the dice game immediately?"

"Let us hold the game this evening, once we have built our lodges," the taishrefi suggested. "The winner can depart tomorrow morning."

"Very good," said Gethrav Lowsinger.

A dice game with adventure as the prize! How exciting!

"And who will be allowed to compete?" asked Breezekenner.

"Anyone who wishes to be chosen," the taishrefi said evenly.

Breezekenner seemed about to object, but instead she said, "Very well. Lashrefi makes her own odds."

What an arrogant toad! Summerwind wished she could win the dice game and remove that superior smirk from Breezekenner's face. A vixen like Breezekenner did not deserve the right to quest for the mysterious and romantic dragonslayer of Brin.

CHAPTER 5

Rolling the Dice

SUMMERWIND unloaded the yellow-painted lodge hides and the smooth, straight poles from the back of the lodge horse. She removed its saddle. The horse was not eager to trot off, so Summerwind began brushing its back with her wooden horse brush. She would gladly have done the same for Whitefoot, but the frisky filly had refused to hold still. Summerwind had let her go to graze with the rest of the herd.

The lodge horse, by contrast, stood as still as a stone while Summerwind scratched its back. Soon its head was nodding in the cool springtime sun. Despite the load it had dragged across the prairie and the four fat ticks that Summerwind picked off its back, it seemed to be of the opinion that it was a good day to be a horse.

Summerwind had to stop brushing well before the lodge horse would have liked. Her mother had lashed the three main poles together and needed help setting them up. Sometimes Summerwind wondered what the woman had done before she had had a daughter.

"I should make you do this yourself," her mother said, as they pulled the lodge poles into place.

"Ah, Mother, you say that every time."

"Until you get daughters of your own, you *will* have to build your lodge by yourself. I feel I should be giving you a chance to practice."

"Perhaps I should give you the chance to practice for when your only daughter has her own lodge."

"Ah, but still she will help me, for I shall be old by then. My loving daughter would not leave an old woman to build her lodge alone."

Summerwind laughed.

Her mother tugged the sunward pole into place and continued, "In all seriousness, daughter, when do you plan to sew your own lodge? Your father's smith work has already earned you enough hides."

"Perhaps I prefer to follow the old ways, Mother. Taishrefi Smokewatcher said that when she was young, no woman would start sewing the skins for her lodge until she had received a promise from her suitor at the spring gathering."

"Speaking of the spring gathering, what did you think of your suitors?"

Summerwind laughed. "None of them suited me."

It was true. The bands of the Flamebringer Tribe met twice a year, and Summerwind was familiar with all the marriageable men. There were three or four who had fast horses, but none of them were truly intriguing. Only an exceptional man could convince Summerwind to exchange the life of adventure she pursued for a life of nursing babies while plodding along beside the lodge horse.

"Perhaps you expect too much," her mother said. "Men are like horses: They need to be trained."

Summerwind expected to marry a man who could make her feel as excited as she did when she was riding in the bison hunt. It was not possible to train men like that. A man was either exciting, like Dragonslayer, or he was not.

How could she get her mother to let her join the dice game tonight?

"Check the poles," her mother suggested.

The bases of the three lodge poles were at the points of an imaginary triangle. Summerwind stepped into the center, directly below the apex where the three poles met. She turned in place to sight lithward, moonward, and sunward. The lith was nearly at its height, so its metallic facets marked lithward exactly. The purple moon was on its way down, but still close to due moonward. Sunward had to be guessed at—somewhere to the left of the setting sun. Each pole was supposed to line up with a cardinal direction.

"The poles look proper to me, Mother." At least, they were close enough.

Her mother nodded—not to indicate that she trusted Summerwind's judgment but rather to indicate that Summerwind had given the correct answer.

Next they put up the auxiliary poles. As they arranged the slender poles around the supports to form a cone, Summerwind tried to think of a way to convince her mother to let her compete in the dice game. Getting her father's permission was simple—she could usually persuade him with a smile and a hand laid on his arm—but her mother could be stubborn.

So Summerwind was caught off guard when her mother asked, "Are you planning to play in the dice game tonight?"

"I was thinking about it," Summerwind admitted.

"I think you should leave it up to the scouts," her mother said. "Young men need a chance to prove—"

"But the taishrefi said anyone may join!" Breezekenner certainly did not plan to leave it up to the scouts.

"Yes," said her mother.

"So why do you forbid me to play?"

"Summerwind, I cannot stop you. You are old enough to have your own lodge and old enough to make these decisions."

"But you said—"

"You interrupted me. I was saying that young men need to show off their bravery for young women, and young women make themselves less attractive if they do well in young men's games."

"I do not see why that matters." People in the same band could not marry, so Summerwind didn't really care whether her band's scouts found her attractive.

"It matters because you are getting a reputation. I do not want this to turn out like those horse races at the spring gathering."

Those had turned out wonderfully well. Summerwind and Whitefoot had won four of them.

"If you are not forbidding it, then I will play."

"As you will, daughter," her mother said. "I will ask the Goddess to guide your path. She knows that I can no longer do so."

Lodge poles went up all over camp. Mothers and daughters dressed them in hides of red, green, brown, and yellow. Summerwind's mother's lodge was the prettiest because Mother had painted a black horse on the yellow hide.

Once they had the lodge built, Summerwind went into the ravine to forage. She managed to find a few mushrooms that others had overlooked. Her parents still had some jerked deer meat left over from the previous camp. Their meal that evening was sparse, but Summerwind barely noticed. She was anticipating the call to join the competition. The purple moon hanging over the pointed peaks of the band's lodges reminded her of the glow of the dragon's feather. Stars were appearing by the time Kalaibo Stormdrummer began drumming.

Normally, people took their time to gather in the music circle, but tonight the circle filled quickly. Those who wished to play their instruments after the game carried their lutes, flutes, and drums to the inner ring, where they could see the kalaibo in the light of the flickering flames. The fire was not large enough to provide much warmth, but they had buffalo robes they could put on over their buckskin dresses and tunics if they got cold.

When it looked as though everyone who wanted to watch had gathered, the kalaibo blurred his hands into a drum roll. The sound diminished to silence before it burst into a shout. The event had begun.

The gethrav stepped into the circle. "My band," he said, "I bid you good evening. As you know, our territory has been invaded by a dragon, a strange beast with the power of a tornado, the appetite of a bear, and the trail of moonlight."

His words carried. Before the taishrefi had decided Lowsinger would be the gethrav, he had trained under Kalaibo Storm-drummer. Kalaibos knew how to make sounds do what they wanted them to, and this skill had served Lowsinger in good stead as gethrav.

"It may be possible for us to live with this beast, as we live with the wolves who follow our bison herds. It may be possible to drive this beast out of our territory as our ancestors did with the Kashramites. Or our survival may depend on our ability to kill it."

The people shifted uneasily, wishing for a clearer direction, but the gethrav told them, "We do not know. This dragon is not in our songs."

Kalaibo Stormdrummer nodded in agreement.

"But:" announced the gethrav, his voice smothering the murmurs, "a dragon song exists. And the one who sings it dwells just beyond the Flamebringer territory. Peltswapper tells us that in the Yolimite village called Brin, there is one who has seen such a beast—not only seen it, but slain it! This very night, he sings the song."

Having filled his people with hope, the gethrav then asked for their help: "One of us must go to Brin. One of us must speak with Dragonslayer. Then we will know what we face, and how we must deal with it."

This call brought Summerwind to her feet, and she was not alone. All the scouts came forward to play for the right to seek Dragonslayer, as did all the traders, including Peltswapper. Greenpool came forward to play, despite having three young children to provide meat for.

Breezekenner came forward, too, and a few other maidens came after her. Summerwind wondered if they had decided to join just to make it more difficult for Breezekenner to win.

"There are too many of you," the taishrefi said. She could have declared it in strident tones as the gethrav did when he spoke to the entire band, but that was not Taishrefi Smokewatcher's way. She simply said it, and yet her voice carried.

The taishrefi sat down with her back to the kalaibo's fire and spread out a buffalo hide. She rolled a bone-white die onto it and studied the result within the secrecy of her wrinkled hands. Looking up, she announced, "The Goddess smiles upon those who can roll a four." She placed the die on the hide.

One by one, those who wished to become contenders in the game sat down opposite the taishrefi and rolled the die. Greenpool's wife looked relieved when his roll came up with six spots.

Breezekenner passed this first test, which was not surprising. No girl could become a taishrefi's apprentice without having demonstrated a strong connection with the Goddess. Peltswapper also passed, which amused the gethrav and the taishrefi both.

Summerwind had played dice before, but never with the entire band watching. As she sat down opposite Taishrefi Smokewatcher, she realized that Lashrefi, too, was watching her. The Goddess knew that Summerwind was ignoring her mother's advice.

The die was damp in Summerwind's palm and slightly sticky. It felt like it was the wrong weight. Summerwind closed her eyes and prayed, *Lashrefi, please allow me into your game.*

Summerwind took a deep breath.

"That is not for you to keep, Dawnracer," the taishrefi told her. "Toss the die and let us get on with things."

Breezekenner snickered.

Summerwind tossed the die and stood up.

"Sit back down, Dawnracer," said the taishrefi. "The Goddess has not dismissed you yet."

Summerwind looked at her roll. On the buffalo hide, the die showed a four.

Summerwind sat down, as did the others who had been allowed into the game. They were all smiling. Those who had not rolled a four were forgotten.

The taishrefi scooped the die off the hide and added two more.

"Two against three," she said. "No second rolls."

The taishrefi turned and looked up at the gethrav, who was standing behind her.

"They will use your dice," she told him.

The gethrav chuckled and handed two dice to the contestant sitting on the taishrefi's left. In turn, each player would roll the two dice, trying to match or beat the highest number rolled by the taishrefi.

Summerwind was glad the taishrefi had chosen a pure game. Some of the games were more a test of how well one could bluff than a test of how much Lashrefi favored one's rolls. Of course, Summerwind was playing against her mother's wishes and attempting to steal victory from the taishrefi's apprentice, so perhaps the Goddess would not favor her at all, but at least she would not have to think. She was too excited to do well at a thinking game.

"Six!" the taishrefi announced triumphantly, indicating the highest number she had rolled on the three dice before her. A few people groaned.

"You may begin," the taishrefi said.

The first contestant failed to roll a six, and no comment was made. He simply stood up and joined the spectators. The second likewise failed and left the buffalo-hide mat in silence. But when the third contestant failed, the crowd began to murmur. What if no one could match the taishrefi's dice? What would that mean?

It was Summerwind's turn then. Not wanting to be the object of the taishrefi's amusement again, she gave the dice only the briefest squeeze before tossing them onto the leather.

One of the dice came up six, causing sighs of relief and words of congratulations from the crowd.

Peltswapper was the next to throw. His dice came up five and four, which seemed to disappoint him. Perhaps he regretted having balked at the gethrav's request.

There were only two people left to play. If neither of them rolled a six, Summerwind would be going to Brin!

Rabbitpaw, the youngest scout, who only last autumn had named himself Wolfstalker, was next. It made Summerwind glad to see someone more nervous than she was. The boy looked almost sick as he picked up the dice in his shaking hand.

"Two sixes," proclaimed the jolly kalaibo in response to Rabbitpaw's throw. The scouts cheered, for he was the last of them left in the contest. The boy beamed.

Breezekenner, sitting at the taishrefi's right, was the last to play. She confidently scooped up the dice, gave Summerwind an intimidating smile, and held Summerwind's eyes as she tossed the dice out onto the hide. She did not have to look. She knew she had thrown a six.

Murmurs of approval came from those who had been impressed by her attitude. But the taishrefi, whom Breezekenner could not see because she was still gloating at Summerwind, narrowed her eyes. The taishrefi smiled, but her eyes held neither congratulations nor approval.

Taishrefi Smokewatcher scooped up all the dice, including the three she had thrown to start the game. She handed two of them back to the gethrav. It did not matter which two. All fair dice belonged to Lashrefi. The taishrefi put the rest of the dice into her pouch and withdrew from it the Die-of-the-Heavens.

The quiet conversations that had begun in this interlude gradually ceased as people caught sight of the object in her hand. It had been forged from iron and copper, long ago. No one knew how long it had been with the band.

In a way, the Die-of-the-Heavens *was* the band. When Low-singer died, the band would have a new gethrav and a new name. When the taishrefi died, the band would have a new taishrefi. But the taishrefi of the band—whoever she was, and whatever the band's name—would always carry that Die-of-the-Heavens.

Like the bone dice, it had six sides, but instead of having dots carved to indicate numbers, the die had six engraved symbols.

The taishrefi moved to sit between Summerwind and Rabbit-paw. "This is the sun," she explained. "And this side is called anti-sun." She showed the symbol on the opposite side. "This is the lith. And this side is anti-lith. This is the moon. And this side is anti-moon. The game is called 'Around the Heavens'. Do you know it?"

Summerwind nodded, although she had only seen it played once. Rabbitpaw looked worried.

"You play it just like One Above Six," the taishrefi explained. "You roll the die as you would when choosing a direction." The taishrefi ignored the fact that she was the only one in the band who ever rolled the Die-of-the-Heavens to choose a direction.

"Two directions can beat your roll. If the next player rolls either of these, you are out. Two directions lose to your roll. If the next player rolls either of these, she is out."

Breezekenner frowned at this.

"You can learn as you go along," the taishrefi said to Rabbitpaw. To the band, she said, "Since he has not seen the game before, Wolfstalker will begin."

This earned the taishrefi a glare from Breezekenner that Summerwind would not have given even to her mother. It was the sort of look one should reserve for people who overstepped the bounds of politeness, such as brothers. It was truly not a wise scowl to give to the woman who owned the lodge where one slept.

Serenely ignoring Breezekenner, the taishrefi handed the Die-of-the-Heavens to Rabbitpaw.

He rolled lith.

Summerwind was not certain if this was a good roll or a bad roll. If the game was like One Above Six, then any roll could be beaten.

"Lith," the taishrefi said. She pointed to the lithward horizon, where indeed, that heavenly body was rising, its shiny, irregular facets reflecting the purple glow of the moon.

"Two rolls beat lith," she said. "Anti-sun." She pointed sunaway. "And moon." She pointed moonward.

"Your roll, Breezekenner," the taishrefi concluded.

The taishrefi's apprentice picked up the Die-of-the-Heavens and rolled it deliberately, staring at Rabbitpaw.

"Lith again," said the taishrefi.

Breezekenner checked the die for herself and frowned.

"No one is eliminated by a matching roll," the taishrefi said. "Your turn now, Dawnracer."

Reluctantly, Summerwind leaned over and picked up the metal cube. It was cold in her hands. It felt heavy with the weight of decision.

Summerwind tossed the die.

"Anti-lith," said the taishrefi. "That is like a match," she explained to Rabbitpaw. "No one is eliminated. But now the winning and losing rolls are reversed: Summerwind is eliminated if you roll sun or anti-moon; you are eliminated if you roll anti-sun or moon."

The boy picked up the die and gingerly rolled it back into the center of the hide.

The taishrefi chuckled. "Anti-lith again."

Breezekenner picked up the die and rolled it with a contemptuous flick of her wrist.

"Sun," she said, almost before the die had stopped bouncing.

"Sun beats anti-lith, Wolfstalker," the taishrefi told him. "But be proud that Lashrefi wanted you to play this game."

Shakily, Rabbitpaw arose and left the buffalo hide to find consolation among his brother scouts. Obviously, he was disappointed, but Summerwind thought that he also looked relieved.

It was not much fun to have the entire band watching one play a game of chance against an apprentice taishrefi.

Unless one were to win of course.

"What beats sun?" Summerwind asked as she picked up the Die-of-the-Heavens.

"Anti-moon or lith," the taishrefi replied.

"And moon and anti-lith lose," added Breezekenner.

Summerwind rolled the die.

"Anti-sun," chuckled the taishrefi. "The game goes on."

Breezekenner snatched up the die.

"It is time for it to come to an end," she said. The die spun from her fingers and landed in the middle of the hide with a solid thud.

There was a moment of silence as all regarded the symbol on top.

"Anti-moon," the taishrefi said. "Moon loses to sun; anti-moon loses to anti-sun."

Breezekenner looked from the taishrefi to Summerwind in confusion.

"Dawnracer wins," the taishrefi affirmed.

The band cheered.

"You set it up so that she would win!" Breezekenner's hiss did not carry beyond the buffalo hide. "The third player has an advantage!"

"Only in games where Lashrefi chooses not to intervene," said the taishrefi.

"Did she intervene?" demanded Breezekenner. "Did you ask her to intervene?"

The taishrefi's reply was quiet, yet easy for Summerwind to overhear: "What we ask for and what we receive are two different things, Breezekenner. Perhaps Lashrefi keeps you here with me so that you may learn this."

As Summerwind accepted Rabbitpaw's congratulations, she wondered whether the Goddess had chosen her or whether the Goddess had simply rebuked Breezekenner. Ah, but it did not matter. Either way, Summerwind Dawnracer was the one who would seek Dragonslayer!

CHAPTER 6
Journey to Brin

DANWEL rode astride the high saddle with his feet firmly on the mare's back. He held the reins loosely, for the mare was sensitive to every movement of his hands. The reins were attached to loops around her ears.

The road through the valley of the Grigolin was lined with familiar sights—newly plowed fields, paddle wheel flour mills, whitewashed houses—but no place was exactly like Kwoshim. Each new village seemed exotic.

Tevishi, the bay mare, kept a steady pace and held her head high, as though she, too, enjoyed seeing new country. She had served Danwel's father as a cart horse for nine years, but she had been retired because keeping her old knees healthy had required too much beastshaping. Her legs were still good enough for a riding horse—as Kethwin confirmed whenever she and Danwel went riding—but Tevishi had never been ridden very far. Until now.

Could this horse carry him all the way to Brin? The question was Danwel's chief concern as he approached Grizhil, on the river Tartholin. He was nearing the end of his second day of riding, and his legs and back were getting sore. How much worse was it for Tevishi?

Maybe he should check her legs again. He reined the mare to a halt and loosened her nape catch so she could lower her head and nibble the spring grass on the edge of the road—an opportunity Tevishi took at once. Next, Danwel untied the slipknot that bound the saddle ladder. The wooden rungs clicked against each other as the rope ladder unrolled. Danwel climbed down.

Walking around the horse, Danwel was unable to see any sign that Tevishi might be favoring one leg. She seemed to be standing well enough, considering the softness of the ground. Did that mean she was all right, or did it just mean that he didn't know what to look for?

Kethwin would know. Danwel wished she were with him.

* * *

Kethwin raised the well bucket to her lips only to discover that it was dry again. Water. Where could she find water to slake her thirst? She should seek the Grigolin. The stream was over an oxlength wide and powerful enough to turn a mill wheel. That was where she needed to go. She slithered through the earth, driving her body upward until she found that for which she thirsted.

Kethwin awoke in the darkness to find herself sitting on the edge of her bed, with one bare foot already set upon the packed-earth floor.

Had she been awakened by a noise? She listened. All she could hear was the breathing of the others in the sleeping room—her parents and her younger sister Beswin.

No, she remembered, she had been dreaming about the well bucket. It was thirst that had awakened her, but she wasn't thirsty. Someone else's thirst, then.

This sort of thing had happened before. Kethwin sometimes dreamed of water when Beswin needed a drink. Or last summer, before her brother Vanim had patched the water trough in their courtyard, Kethwin had been awakened by the thirst of the milk cow. Kethwin felt this was an aspect of her beastshaping talent, but her older sister Feshwin never had dreams like that.

Well, Kethwin was nearly out of bed anyway. She might as well go check on the milk cow.

She could see nothing, but her feet knew the way. Six steps took her through the curtained doorway, across the main room where Feshwin's family slept, and out the front door. Her feet found the soft mud of the street. Stars peeked through the gaps in the fluffy black clouds, giving just enough light to show her the whitewashed walls of the house and the gray rails of the courtyard fence.

Shivering in her sleeping frock, wishing she'd taken time to put on her shoes and cloak, Kethwin squished along the fence to the courtyard gate and let herself in. She latched the gate behind her.

At first, all she could see was the house's back wall, which formed the rectangular courtyard's nearest corner. She decided that the indistinct shape against the wall must be the milk cow.

Kethwin walked over to check on the water trough. She verified that the trough was three-quarters full by splashing her hand into the chill water. There was no reason for the milk cow to be thirsty.

Could it be the calf? Probably not. The calf got enough milk. Besides, Kethwin's brother Vanim and his wife slept in the stable where the calf was kept. Kethwin didn't want to wake them.

One of Uncle Tharnwel's oxen grunted in the adjacent courtyard. Had its thirst been the thing that had awakened her? Not likely. Surely the beast was too far away to affect her dreams.

Kethwin opened her senses to see if they could show her which animal was thirsty. Feshwin had explained in detail how the flow of Life changed when an animal was becoming dehydrated, but Kethwin had never found it to be as complicated as Feshwin made it seem: She simply imagined the need to drink and waited to see if there was any resonance.

The milk cow was not thirsty. Stretching her senses, Kethwin could feel the calf sleeping in the stable room. It was dreaming of galloping, but it was not thirsty either.

How good was her range? Could she learn anything about Uncle Tharnwel's cattle?

Yes. She could find them at the limit of her senses. They were growing nervous. Their shifting feet rumbled in the darkness.

Kethwin also sensed a strong drive to move, guided by a tiny candle of curiosity. That was strange. It didn't seem to be coming from the herd but rather from … underground.

That rumbling was not Uncle Tharnwel's cattle shifting their feet. It was the dragon. That was what had woken her up. She had dreamed she was the dragon, looking for water. Now the monster's thirst was fully quenched, and curiosity was driving it through the earth. It was coming toward the village.

"Wake up!" Kethwin screamed. "Wake up!"

Her thin voice drifted out of the courtyard to be absorbed by the night air. What could she do?

Let the calf out. Everyone knew that if there was a fire, you had to go into the stable and let the animals out.

But this isn't a fire, a part of her mind said as she jerked open the stable door. *This is a monster.*

The calf was bawling, answering the bellow of the milk cow in the courtyard. Kethwin ran a hand along the gate of the calf pen, trying to find the latch. The calf banged into the gate. Startled, Kethwin jumped back.

She collided with her brother Vanim, who grunted. She hadn't heard him climb down from the hayloft. His arm wrapped around her shoulders—whether to steady her or himself, Kethwin did not know.

Twice more the calf banged into the gate before—with a scraping of hooves on wood—it cleared the top pole. Crying for its mother, it passed as a black blur through the open stable door.

"Vanim!" called his wife from up in the loft. "What is it?"

And then they heard the crash. Vanim's arm squeezed Kethwin tightly as Uncle Tharnwel's herd thundered through the courtyard, snapping and splintering the wooden fences that stood in their path.

Kethwin, too, felt the urge to escape—to move toward safety and trample anything that got in her way. This was not her own will, but rather an emotion that seemed to fill all the space around her, driving everything into panic.

Kethwin's own will was to hide, to disappear. Her legs collapsed and her brother eased her down onto the coarse straw that littered the stable floor. There she lay until the dragon's rumbling died away, taking the panic with it, leaving behind only the echoes of cattle bellowing in the distance.

* * *

In the morning, things were looking better. The cousins who had put Danwel up for the night had found a beastshaper to look at Tevishi.

"Your mare's knees look sound to me," the man said. "What sort of exercise has she been getting?"

"My girl and I have been riding her four or five times a month," Danwel said. "But we don't go very far."

"Well, I don't recommend you push your mare too much now, either. Be sure she gets plenty of rest and give her a chance to build up her strength some. But it looks like exercise has been good for her. As long as you take it easy and stop before she starts getting sore, this horse can carry you all the way to Brin."

* * *

Kethwin and her cousins found Uncle Tharnwel's cattle in Ashturn. Kethwin's family's milk cow and calf were still with the herd, grazing on the Ashturn common meadow. At least they were uninjured.

No one in Ashturn complained about the trespass. They were just excited to learn the news. They had already heard the story of the Broadfield ox, and they seemed pleased that their upstream neighbors had come to visit that morning with more tales to tell. Having Uncle Tharnwel's cattle on their commons just made the stories better.

I wonder if they'll be so pleased when the dragon comes after them, Kethwin thought.

A hole had opened in the bed of the Grigolin so that the creek now disappeared underground. The dragon had somehow caused a swath of wheat seedlings to grow a half-month high in a field that was planted yesterday. And Uncle Tharnwel's cattle weren't the only ones that had stampeded through the streets last night.

Kethwin shivered, remembering the panic. Part of her wanted her cousins to stop gabbing so they could take the herd back home. Part of her knew that home was no longer safe.

Eventually, they got the herd rounded up and on the road back to Kwoshim. Her cousins started discussing whether the Ashturn fashion of embroidered cuffs was elegant or frivolous. Kethwin reckoned that depended on whether the embroidery would prevent a girl from rolling up her sleeves.

She kept her opinion to herself, however. They weren't really talking to her anyway. And that was why she was the one who noticed that the mill wheel was still.

The Walker mill was on the opposite bank of the Grigolin, just upstream from the village. It ground the grain for all the Walkers in

Kwoshim and Ashturn. Any transaction that required giving Walker flour to someone from another clan had to go through that mill. Why wasn't its wheel turning?

After promising her cousins she would catch up, Kethwin took the side road and crossed the creek. She saw the problem from the mill bridge: Only a thin stream of water trickled in the creek bed.

The miller sat in the dry stream with his head in his hands.

"Good day, Cousin Miller."

He looked up at her. "Good day, Cousin ..."

"Kethwin. Of Kwoshim."

The miller blinked at her. "Kwoshim?" He stood up. "Say, did someone dam the creek?"

Kethwin shook her head. "It's worse than that. The dragon dug a tunnel into the bed."

"What?"

"The water is disappearing into a hole."

"You mean the hole the big Broadfield boy's ox fell into?"

"No," Kethwin said. "This is a new hole. The dragon attacked Kwoshim again last night."

The miller frowned. "You know, they dug exploratory mines in this valley before it was settled. I don't see why people have to invent monsters to explain holes in the ground."

"Cousin Miller, the dragon is real," Kethwin said, wishing it weren't.

"Oh, and you've seen one, have you?"

"No, but I have felt it, moving under the earth."

He gave her a skeptical look.

"I have the beastshaper's sight," Kethwin explained.

The disbelief faded from his face. "Oh. You're that Kethwin."

"Yes," Kethwin said, although she assumed the miller was actually thinking of her sister.

"So this ... tunnel: How deep do you think it is? How long before it fills up and the creek starts running again?"

"I have no idea," Kethwin said. "The dragon seems to travel underground, like a giant earthworm. The creek might never fill all its tunnels."

"That's bad," said the miller.

"Yes," said Kethwin.

"Your council needs to do something."

"Well, we did send a man to find the dragonslayer of Brin."

"Not about the dragon. About the water. You've got to dig a channel around the hole. Otherwise, our clan is out of flour."

This had occurred to Kethwin. It had also occurred to her that if Ashturn had no water, the Walker mill would have to be moved to Kwoshim. As the saying was: "No catastrophe is without opportunity."

But it would be up to the clan elders to decide that. Could Kethwin find an opportunity here for herself?

"I will be happy to take your idea to our village councilman," she said. "Everyone is so busy cleaning up this morning that I doubt they realize the dragon has harmed your village as well."

"What are they cleaning up?" asked the miller.

"Well, you saw that our cattle were loose. They broke through two courtyard fences and trampled a flax field. And that was not the only herd to escape last night."

"Is that so?"

"Aye," said Kethwin. "And the dragon made plants grow, too. That might not sound so bad, but it means some people suddenly have a half-month's worth of hoeing to catch up on. And what will they do if one swath of wheat comes ripe earlier than the rest of the field?"

"Cousin, that is surely a strange tale. You make it sound as though this animal could be magical."

"I reckon it must be," Kethwin said. When she considered the power she had sensed, calling the dragon "magical" was like looking at an iron rod glowing orange in a blacksmith's forge and declaring that it could be warm.

Thinking about the dragon made her sick. A calf had once butted her in the stomach hard enough to make her sit down. That was the way she felt when she thought of the dragon and what it could do. And there was no telling how long it would stay away. Would it be two days again, or would it come back that very night?

"I hope it doesn't come after Ashturn," she said.

"Do you think that's likely?" asked the miller.

Kethwin shrugged. "I reckon no one can tell where it will strike next—except maybe the dragonslayer."

"Well, good thing your village sent that Broadfield boy to fetch him, then."

"Aye," agreed Kethwin. "Only …"

"Only what?"

"Well, Danwel is the best man in the village, but he doesn't always get things done fast."

How long would it take him? She wished he would come riding back right now—with or without the dragonslayer. She wished she'd gone, too.

"Well, with all the trouble your village has been having, I'm sure he'll hurry," her cousin said.

Kethwin shook her head. Danwel never hurried. And: "He doesn't know."

"Doesn't know what?"

"When Danwel left, the dragon had just made one hole that accounted for one ox. He doesn't know about what happened last night. He doesn't know we may have lost the entire Walker mill. I'm not sure the dragonslayer will realize how bad things are."

The miller rubbed his chin. "Well, rumors travel mighty fast. The dragonslayer might hear about this even before the Broadfield boy gets to Brin."

"Or he might not," said Kethwin. "Or he might hear and not believe the rumors. Can we take the chance?"

"Cousin, are you saying we need to send someone after the Broadfield boy?"

"Yes. Do you have a fast horse?"

The miller shook his head. "You don't want a horse. You can overtake a man on a horse if you walk fast to Grizhil and take a boat down the Tartholin."

He grinned. "But, yes, cousin. I will help you chase after your boy."

* * *

The Clan elders had given Danwel a bag of brinnacs, but he did not have to spend many in the state of Dwen-Tarthil. Broadfields were widespread enough that Danwel had no trouble finding a cousin who would put him and his mare up for the night, feed them a hearty breakfast in the morning, and send him out with a loaf of bread to eat along the way.

No one questioned his claim of kinship. Tevishi's white rear stocking and white blaze marked her as a Broadfield horse. Danwel was marked by the plow-and-furrow brooch that fastened his cloak. Any Broadfield was entitled to wear the clan badge, although most, like Danwel's family, did not travel far enough to justify having one made. Danwel had asked to borrow this brooch from Councilman Broadfield, and the councilman had presented it to Danwel as a gift symbolizing the trust that the village was placing in him.

Danwel saw many villages no bigger than Kwoshim as he and Tevishi followed the road along the river Tartholin. The towns, however, seemed to grow larger the farther they went downstream. Gafi's Ford was so large that the local clans could afford to maintain majestic clan houses overlooking the town from the tops of high, grassy mounds.

It was at the Broadfield clan house that Danwel learned of the road from Gafi's Ford directly to Brin. The overland road was little used because boats could haul so much more than carts, but it was just the route for a mounted man.

Danwel rode away from the river at daybreak.

* * *

The planks of the boat made a hard bed, and the food was rationed almost as strictly as at home, but at least Kethwin's cousins traveled quickly. By Kethwin's reckoning, they would overtake her boy before he reached the city of Tarthil. For the first time, she was glad that Danwel was so slow.

Kethwin kept a sharp eye on the road when it was within sight of the river—which was frequently, but not often enough to suit her. The Tartholin had too many bends, and the road took too many short cuts. Also, Cousin Sam had the annoying habit of moving the boat all over the river instead of staying close to the bank she was watching.

Cousin Sam and his son did not move the boat themselves, of course. They gave orders to a crew of six bald, blue-skinned Rivermen who sat two-by-two at the front, middle, and end of the boat, each wearing a garment that was merely a loosely wrapped sheet. These exotic giants could alter water currents with elemental magic. Although helpful for steering, the Rivermen were not actually needed while the boat was traveling downstream, but Cousin Sam kept them on because after stopping in Tarthil, he planned to travel up the Yarl to Brin.

Cousin Sam said elemental propulsion was expensive, but still the best way to go upstream. The only cheaper way was to use a winch to pull the boat from tree to tree, and that was only cheaper if one placed no value on speed. Other methods required large crews of Clanfolk. Kethwin had seen one boat—decorated with the buck's head symbol of Clan Deerfield—rowed by twelve oarsmen on each side. A boat bearing the knife-and-hide of Clan Skinner had been pushed upstream by eighteen men with poles. Cousin Sam said that Clan Walker's profit-sharing laws made it too expensive for him to hire so many cousins, so he used Rivermen.

"Gafi's Ford is just ahead, Dad," Cousin Lon announced. A gap in the woods revealed a huge earthen mound with a house on top.

"Thank you, Lon," said Cousin Sam. He moved to the front of the boat to stand between the two Rivermen. With him standing and them sitting, their heads were at the same level.

Cousin Sam looked downriver. "Aim more for the right side of the channel," he said. "The ford is deepest there."

The Riverman sitting on Sam's right held out his naked blue arm, palm down above the water. When he bent his elbow and made a fist, the boat glided gently to the right.

"Harder," said Cousin Sam.

The Riverman's fist went higher and his crewmates followed the command.

"That's it," said Cousin Sam. "Keep the boat headed for that tree until we cross the ford."

The Riverman nodded and stopped signaling.

Kethwin spared a moment to watch Gafi's Ford drift past—it was her first glimpse of a town big enough to build mounds and clan houses—but she did not let her eyes linger. As soon as they had crossed the ford, she returned her attention to the River Road, hoping to catch sight of Danwel.

* * *

After spending so many days traveling through the state of Dwen-Tarthil, Danwel had expected that crossing Dwen-Brin would take several days more, so he was surprised when his cousins on the border told him the journey could be made in one day. This was fortunate, because once he crossed the border, he would have to start patronizing inns: Only nine clans owned land in Dwen-Brin, and Clan Broadfield was not among them.

Danwel crossed the border at sunrise. By noon, he had already passed through a dozen villages, and Danwel realized why the one-day crossing was possible. *Dwen-Brin is just as big as Dwen-Tarthil,* he thought, *but they cram it into a smaller space.*

Lacking woods, hills, and meadows, Dwen-Brin seemed to be nothing but flat fields and dense villages, with the villages crowding closer and closer together as Danwel neared Brin. It was late in the day when Danwel finally saw the waters of the mighty Yarl. At first, he thought he was looking at a lake, until he realized that it was much farther away (and hence much bigger) than he had thought. The greatest river in the world, and Danwel was seeing it with his own eyes!

The Yarl marked the edge of civilization: square fields of the Clanfolk on one side, overgrown forests of the wild Stripedfolk on the other, tiny riverboats traveling the broad water in between. Danwel's gaze followed the graceful curve of the river as it slid behind the city of Brin.

And now Danwel understood that a city was not simply a large village. High-peaked thatched roofs grew in thick patches on the plain before him. Rising above the roof tops, grassy mounds punctuated the landscape. Each mound was capped with a large clan house and attended by clusters of houses at its base. In the center of these was the highest mound of all, rising above the city like Kestrel Bluff rose above his village. It was the Great Mound of Brin, topped with the Brinnen council chambers known as the Round House.

Danwel patted Tevishi's neck as he rode toward the Great Mound. "You did it, old girl. It's been a long road, but you did it. Now we just need to find that dragonslayer."

CHAPTER 7
Zhen and Shamon

THE MARKET surrounding the Great Mound of Brin was always busiest in the morning. Waist-high Children of Wealth scurried from stall to stall, purchasing the food they would need for the day. Chamfo, too, had been looking for food—the Dry Mill Inn did not serve saltfish—but instead he had found Pugoku, the girl from the boat he had once called home.

Pugoku stood out in the crowd. Like Chamfo, she was a Child of Justice: bald, blue, and taller than the multicolored awnings of the market stalls. But she was not like Chamfo, because she still had a home.

Pugoku had much to share about the people who lived aboard *The Mud Mother.* Chamfo followed every word—watching her beautiful green lips, listening to the sound of his own language—until Pugoku's final story reached its conclusion.

"Well," she said.

"So," he replied.

Pugoku gestured with her basket of bread. "I should be leaving," she said.

Chamfo nodded.

"I am glad I saw you," she said.

"And I am glad I saw you," he replied.

"You could have seen all of us if you had come down to the docks," she said.

"That is true," Chamfo agreed.

Yet he had no reason to go to the docks. The little people of Brin called him a Riverman, but he was no longer of the river. He had left his own kind because he was useless to them. Seeing his people's boats only reminded him that no boat would ever be his.

No, he had no reason to go to the docks—except to see Pugoku's smile.

"I think someone wants to talk to you," Pugoku said. She nodded her head to indicate a brown-haired Child of Wealth. The little man stared up at them politely.

He was blue, but all Children of Wealth turned blue in the presence of Children of Justice, so this was not a distinguishing characteristic. His gray tunic with the brown collar indicated that he was not from Brin, where the fashion was for more colorful clothing. He wore shoes instead of clogs beneath his mud-spattered, leather-strapped leggings, which meant that either he was accustomed to standing all day in the mud or that leather was so cheap in his town that people could afford to let their shoes get muddy.

The iron brooch binding his cloak was marked with the plow-and-furrow. So he was a Broadfield. That made him a foreigner, like Chamfo. Clan Broadfield had no land holdings in the state of Dwen-Brin.

When the smiling little man saw that he had Chamfo's attention, he said, "Good day. I am Dan Broadfield Dwen-Tarthilen."

Chamfo did not feel obliged to translate this for Pugoku. His people made their living trading with the Children of Wealth, so they all spoke enough of the second language to be able to exchange pleasantries.

"Good day, Dan Broadfield Dwen-Tarthilen," Chamfo replied. "I am called Shamon."

Pugoku giggled, and echoed, "Sha-mo-na."

"They can't pronounce 'Chamfo'," he explained to her.

"Good day, Dan Broadfield Dwen-Tarthilen," Pugoku said in the second language. "I am called Pugoku."

Her beautiful, thick accent was like a melody to Chamfo's ears.

"Glad to meet you, Shamon and ... Pugoku," Dan said. "Shamon, I was told that you are partners with the dragonslayer."

Pugoku gave Chamfo an enquiring look, but he did not even know how to begin a translation of the word "dragonslayer". Instead, he replied to Dan, "I accompany the man known as 'the dragonslayer'."

"Will you take me to him?" Dan asked. "My village—in Dwen-Tarthil—has a dragon that needs to be slain."

Chamfo winced. Judgment had come at last.

"Is he asking to meet the Child of Luck who makes music with you?" Pugoku asked, in their language.

"Yes," Chamfo said.

Pugoku nodded. "We have heard stories about you," she said. "So it is true? You are earning coins by playing your lute while this Child of Luck sings?"

"Yes," Chamfo said. "That is true."

Pugoku laughed and shook her head in disbelief. "Shugo, Priest of Justice, is preaching that our people should not work for the Children of Wealth. But I don't see how you could earn coins playing your lute on one of our boats."

"I could not," Chamfo said.

She kissed his cheek.

"I am happy for you," she said. "I am glad you have found a way to use your talents to earn your boat money."

Chamfo felt like his heart was caught in an eddy. Dan had come to punish him for his sins, and yet Pugoku had kissed him. While his emotions spun him dizzy, the beautiful girl spoke to the Child of Wealth.

"I am sorry," she told Dan. "My boat leaves now. I am nice to meet you."

Then she gave Chamfo's hand a squeeze, and said, "Do come visit the docks the next time *The Mud Mother* is in Brin. We will all be glad to see you."

Chamfo watched her skirt sway as she departed.

"If I came at a bad time, Shamon, I am surely sorry," said Dan.

Chamfo looked down at him. "No," he said. "She is— How to say? She would leave anyway. Her home is a boat. Come with me. The man you want to see is at the Dry Mill Inn."

Pugoku was right, Chamfo decided as he led Dan out of the market and onto the muddy cart street: It was good to earn coins from music. He and Zhen had been doing nothing wrong—not until Zhen had dreamed that song and invented the word "dragon".

Chamfo had known it would lead to trouble. They had been popular enough. The Children of Wealth paid well to hear the songs of the "wild Stripedman" and the "serene Riverman" who accompanied him. Zhen and Shamon had made a name for themselves, and they did not need to pretend that they were more than musicians.

But once Zhen had dreamed that song, he was not content to be Zhen Stormsinger anymore. He became Zhen Dragonslayer.

The song told of how Zhen had slain a hideous, scaly beast as big as a horse. He called it a dragon because that was the name it had been given in his dream. Chamfo's parents had always told him to listen to his dreams because they could guide him to do what was right, but Zhen's dream had led them astray. Zhen never admitted to anyone that the monster was only a song.

At first, Chamfo did not realize that people were taking the song literally. The Children of Wealth were accustomed to songs which were not true narratives of events. Yet the way Zhen held his spear, the way his buckskin tunic showed off his muscular, striped arms and legs, and the way his melodious voice carried throughout the room somehow lent his words an aura of authenticity that convinced listeners who should have been more skeptical.

The song had made them popular even beyond Zhen's immodest expectations. They had been able to afford cloaks, custom made by a tailor whose usual clients were half their size. And the coins in Chamfo's personal trunk were accumulating. He *had* earned his boat money, but he still felt he had no place among his people.

Zhen did not care much about the money, which he spent or gave away. Zhen wanted the fame. He wanted the name of Dragonslayer to be known not just in Brin, but all along the Rivers. Well, he had his wish. And now that he was famous for something he had not done, he would have to deal with the consequences.

Chamfo led Dan to the Dry Mill Inn, which was easy to distinguish from others in the city because it had a mill wheel attached to it. The story was that the original owner had been a miller whose mill had been destroyed by a flood. He had salvaged

the wheel and re-built his mill on high ground so that the next time
the Yarl got that much water, his mill would be the only one in
business. So many people came to laugh and point at his dry mill
that he made a fortune selling them food and drink.

The story was absurd. Any visitor inside the Dry Mill Inn could
see that there was no mechanism attached to the wheel. Even so,
Chamfo liked the story because it had a moral: Prosperity comes to
those who seek it. Most of the customers did not see the moral,
however. They just laughed at the story and bought another drink.

The door was open to let in light. Chamfo led Dan inside.

Chamfo did not have to duck because the door was big enough
for Children of Justice and Children of Luck. Likewise, the
whitewashed walls were high, and he did not have to worry about
hitting his head on the cross beams that supported the roof. Most
buildings in Brin were designed for Children of Wealth, but an inn
that was tall enough for Children of Justice and Children of Luck
could expect customers of all sizes.

The Dry Mill Inn even had a special bench for normal-sized
people, but Chamfo did not use it. A Child of Justice from Delta
City might use a bench to eat, but among Chamfo's riverboat
people, the custom was to sit on the deck.

Zhen's people did not use benches, either. The Child of Luck
sat on the deck of the inn, striped legs crossed, with the belly of his
lute resting in his lap. Although Zhen claimed he was not as skilled
as Chamfo, he could play the lute well. He often practiced in the
mornings, but he had not performed on the lute since Chamfo had
started accompanying him. He had, however, composed a few
melodies for Chamfo to play, and he was working on one of these
now.

Chamfo led Dan over to where Zhen was playing and indicated
that he should sit on a bench to wait until the song was done.
Chamfo sat down as well—on the deck—and listened.

As Zhen played, he drew the sound out of his lute and wrapped
it around the three of them like a cloak covering their backs against
the cold. The melody was powerful and Zhen played it well—
except for the trills, which he played with precision instead of with
feeling. Trills were an effort for Zhen, and this melody needed trills

that sounded effortless.

"I don't have to play the trills," Zhen told Chamfo as he moved into the coda. "This is your part."

Chamfo nodded.

Zhen said, "This is my part:" and he sang a series of notes that brought out a melody hidden within the one his fingers played.

"It will be a lute duet," said Zhen, when the song was over. "The simple part is mine, and you will not hear it again until I teach you yours."

Chamfo felt that he could already hear it as he listened to the under-melody in his mind, but he did not contradict his friend. Instead he said, "This is Dan Broadfield Dwen-Tarthilen."

The little man nodded. "Call me Dan," he said.

Chamfo said, "This is Zhen, who is sometimes called 'Dragonslayer'."

"But you may call me Zhen," said Zhen with a smile.

"Pleased to meet you," said the little man.

Many Children of Wealth became flustered at meeting a person with striped skin, but Dan retained his composure. His complexion remained blue, like Chamfo's. Either Dan Broadfield Dwen-Tarthilen had met Children of Luck before, or he was not easily perturbed.

"Did you come all the way from Dwen-Tarthil just to meet the dragonslayer?" Zhen asked.

"Aye," agreed Dan. "And to ask for your help."

This seemed to please Zhen. "And what would you like my help with?" he asked.

"Well, we have a dragon that needs to be slain," Dan explained.

Zhen was amused. He looked at Chamfo to see if this were news to him. Chamfo regarded his friend sadly.

Zhen ran his fingers through his long black-and-white hair and said, "Tell me about this dragon, Dan."

The little man leaned forward, resting his elbows on his knees. "Well, Zhen, it all started when my family's ox fell into a hole that smelled like snakes. We tried to dig the ox out, and while we were digging, the ground started rumbling. Then the ox slid backward, and a bigger hole opened up, and he was gone."

Zhen looked at Chamfo to see if he was laughing. Chamfo wasn't. He was feeling a little sick.

Zhen still found the situation amusing. "Well, now, Dan, that is quite the tale."

"And it's true," said Dan, "may Yolim witness."

Did Zhen really think the little man would come all the way from Dwen-Tarthil just to lie to him? Why wouldn't he take Dan seriously?

"And you think this hole was dug by a dragon?" Zhen asked.

"Well, I don't know about that," Dan admitted. "We've never seen any dragons around Kwoshim. But my girl, Kethi, she's a beastshaper, and she was sure it was some sort of animal down there, and a big one, too. Only big animals we know about live above ground, so we reckon this one must be a dragon."

"A dragon," Zhen repeated. He looked at Chamfo again, but Chamfo still did not see anything funny.

"Dan," Zhen said, "I think I need to consult with my partner. I never slay any dragons without talking to him first."

He called to the innkeeper, who was swabbing the inn's deck: "Nesi? Could you get my friend here a bowl of something hot? And maybe a drink? Shamon and I will cover his expenses."

"Aye, we've got a porridge bubbling," Nesi replied, leaving her mop and walking into the kitchen.

"Just go sit on that bench by the kitchen," said Zhen. "She will bring it to you."

Dan Broadfield did as he was told.

Zhen leaned over and lowered his voice: "Tell me, Shamon, where did you find him?"

"He found me," Chamfo replied. "He was looking for the dragonslayer, and someone told him that I know you."

"What do you think of his story?" Zhen asked.

"He is not lying," Chamfo asserted.

"No," agreed Zhen, "but what do you think truly happened? Did his ox simply fall in a hole?"

"He said his friend is a beastshaper."

"Not his friend," Zhen corrected. "His 'girl'. That's more than just a friend."

"Thank you," said Chamfo. He sometimes had trouble with nuances when speaking the second language. "Yes, I missed that. Do you know what a beastshaper is?"

Children of Luck and Children of Wealth spoke the same language, but they did not always understand each other's culture. Chamfo thought this might be one of those words that was not known to Zhen, but he was mistaken:

"Yolimite beastshapers paint and geld livestock in the womb," said Zhen. "But I don't see why— Ah. Perhaps I do. A beastshaper can see the element of Life. Is that what you are leading up to?"

Chamfo nodded. "If she says there was a big animal underground, then perhaps she actually saw it."

Zhen considered this. "Very well," he said. "We can suppose Dan's ox was swallowed by a big underground animal, if that is what pleases you. But what does that have to do with us?"

"You are the dragonslayer," Chamfo explained.

"Yes," agreed Zhen. "But I made that up. If this underground animal is real, as you seem to think, then it cannot be a dragon."

"But he thinks it is a dragon," said Chamfo. "And he thinks you can slay it."

"And so what shall we tell him?"

"You are the one who must tell him."

"Very well, Shamon, what shall *I* tell him?"

"The truth, Zhen. Tell him that you made it all up."

"Well, then, word would get out," Zhen said, as though he thought Chamfo did not know this. "We would have a problem."

"We already have a problem," said Chamfo, indicating the little man who was receiving his bowl of porridge.

A figure appeared in the sunlit doorway. Zhen's eyes widened.

"And now we have a bigger problem," Zhen said. "That's my sister."

CHAPTER 8

A Happy Reunion

SUMMERWIND peered at the man sitting in the corner. The Yolimite lodge had no hearthfire lit, but the light that leaked in from the entrance and from the vent above was captured and held by the white walls, so that she could make out some distinguishing features on the man's face: a black forehead stripe that ran down to cover his nose before merging with the black patch on his right jaw; the left side of his face white, except for three black, flame-tongue stripes; his long hair mostly white, with few streaks of black. His eyes she could not see, but they were green like hers.

"Zephyr."

"Summerwind!" her brother called.

Her brother's blue-skinned companion—a Zharnovite!—turned to him and echoed, "Zephyr?"

"A steady wind, gentle, but stronger than a breeze," Zephyr explained.

"But not as strong as a Summerwind," she added as she came toward them.

The Zharnovite, who was dressed in a cloth garment wrapped around his hips and draped over his blue, well-muscled shoulders, looked from her to her brother. "Your people have many words for wind."

"Summerwind, I did not expect to see you in Brin," said Zephyr.

"I did not expect to see you, either, brother. We believed you to be living in the villages along the Dothedarl."

"I did live there a time," Zephyr acknowledged. "But I am in Brin, now."

"As I see."

"So, ah, have you run away?" he asked.

"No, Zephyr," she replied. "In truth, I have come to Brin to find the one who names himself Dragonslayer."

"Have you truly?"

"Truly," she asserted. She fixed him with a sister's stare: "Have you seen him?"

"Why, sister, truly you know that the dragonslayer is I."

His voice was loud—loud enough that the remaining person in the room, a waist-high Yolimite man, stopped eating and looked up at them. Clearly, the statement was intended to be overheard.

Summerwind maintained her stare.

Please, Zephyr thought, right on the top of his mind where she could hear it.

Coyote-pup, she thought, in case he wanted to listen. Ah, well. She would play his game.

"Truly I know it now, brother," she said. "But you forget that much has passed since you left Lowsinger's Band, and not all your accomplishments are known to us."

"Of course," he agreed readily.

"But if you are Dragonslayer, then I am glad to learn this thing, for your band is now in need of your services."

Zephyr smiled, as though they were sharing a secret.

"Ah, this puts me between the stampede and the cliff," he said, looking at the Yolimite. "That man there says he is also in need of my services."

At this, the fuzzy-headed Yolimite set down his bowl of food and came over to their corner of the lodge. He wore leather moccasins as she and Zephyr did, but his tunic was of linen. His leggings, too, were of cloth, and he had to remedy this flaw with leather bindings that wrapped around each leg. He seemed to be turning blue, and yet he remained calm, saying, "Zhen, I surely don't want to ask you to abandon your sister."

"Zhen?" asked Summerwind. Zhen had been one of the Eighty-One, the first ancestors who had been named by Lashrefi herself. It seemed a strange name for her brother to appropriate as his own.

"It is a common name among the Yolimites," Zephyr explained.

His Zharnovite companion chuckled.

"You must help your own people first," stated the Yolimite. "I understand."

"Truly, Dan, I thank you for your understanding," said Zephyr solemnly. "I can slay only one dragon at a time, after all. If you find your village still troubled by that dragon when you return, tell them I will be along after I have helped my sister."

Coyote-pup, Summerwind thought at him.

"You surely are generous, Zhen," said the one called Dan. "But please listen to my offer: I could come help you."

Aha! thought Summerwind. *That was well done, little man.*

This thought was too complex for her to communicate telepathically to her brother, so she let her smirk do the speaking.

Zephyr scowled at her.

"I fear that your proposal is too dangerous," said Zephyr.

"If the dragon is dangerous," persisted Dan, "then your sister will be in danger as well. I could protect her while you do your work."

Summerwind realized that he meant this seriously, even though his head was barely above her waist.

Zephyr looked at Summerwind. *Your idea?* he asked.

No, she thought, spreading her hands to indicate that she had never met the little man before.

"Truly, it is you who are generous, Dan," said Zephyr. "But as Summerwind can tell you—"

"I think that is a good idea," she said.

"What?" Zephyr squeaked.

"Truly, 'Zhen', I do not want to miss your exploit. Dan and I shall watch you fight the dragon and gather up the bits and pieces for you afterward."

She turned to the Zharnovite: "And would you like to come as well?"

"Excuse me, friends," said Zephyr. "I need a moment to speak with my younger sister."

He took her by the arm and led her through the entrance of an adjacent lodge—or perhaps it was actually a different part of the same lodge, for it was under the same roof.

"Have you been chewing lupine?" Zephyr asked.

"Have you?" asked Summerwind. "Giant porcupine-tornados start sweeping across the prairie, and you boast that you can slay them?"

"I— Giant—? What?"

"In the heart of the purple moon we went to the Acorn Ravine," Summerwind told him. "A great swath of trees had been flattened, as though by a tornado. But Father found signs that the trees had been eaten, as though by a giant porcupine. And Peltswapper found a magic feather that glows in the dark."

Zephyr blinked. "So you *have* been chewing lupine."

"No one has been chewing lupine!" Summerwind said. "That is what we saw. I was sent to find help. Peltswapper said there was a man in Brin who called himself Dragonslayer. I was chosen to fetch him. I sought him, and I found you."

Zephyr frowned. "But Summerwind, that was just a song. I made the dragon up."

"Good! Can you un-make it?" What a mouse-brain he was!

"Ah. … Hm. …" Zephyr fell silent.

"No wonder Lashrefi chose me to find Dragonslayer," Summerwind muttered. "I doubt that every heart will be filled with joy when I return with the news that it was only my brother making up songs about himself. What are you thinking about now?"

For he *was* thinking. That coyote-pup never seemed to run short of schemes.

"Summerwind, if I dream about a dragon, and then a few months later someone appears and says he has actually found one, that could just be chance, yes?"

She folded her arms and stared at him.

"But," he continued, "if my sister appears on the same day, in the same lithic, and says *she* has found a dragon, too, then that is no longer chance. That is luck."

"Speak plainly, brother."

"Come with me," he ordered, as though she were not old enough to have her own lodge and her own autumn name.

Zephyr marched back into the part of the lodge where the Yolimite and the Zharnovite were waiting.

"Dan Broadfield," Zephyr announced, "I accept your proposal.

You may travel with us."

The little man smiled broadly.

Zephyr addressed the Zharnovite: "Shamon, you are the greatest accompanist in all of Brin. Will you now accompany me to the prairie to aid me in my quest to rid my people of this dragon?"

The blue man's face grew sad. "I will, Zhen. I will help your sister pick up the pieces."

"Summerwind," said Zephyr, "please greet my friend Shamon, who has seen me through many a storm this past year."

"I am pleased to meet you, Shamon." She gave the well-built Zharnovite a smile.

"And please greet our newest acquaintance, Dan Broadfield, who has traveled from the distant land of Dwen-Tarthil to seek our aid," continued Zephyr.

"Well, it isn't that distant," said the little man. "Glad to meet you, Summerwind."

"And I am pleased to meet you, Dan Broadfield," said Summerwind. It was time to assert herself, however: "I am Summerwind Dawnracer of Lowsinger's Band, sister of Zephyr Stormsinger, but you may call me 'Dawnracer'."

"Dawnracer," repeated the Yolimite.

"Dawnracer?" asked Zephyr.

"There she is, guardsmen," said a Yolimite at the lodge entrance.

Three other Yolimites in green tunics stepped around him and entered the lodge warily, as though approaching an injured wolf. Each carried a club—firmly in the right hand and loosely in the left—ready to strike in a heartbeat.

"Step away from the Stripedwoman," ordered the one in front.

"She is my sister," said Zephyr. His forehead wrinkled in confusion. "What has she done?"

"Who are you?" asked the lead Yolimite, ignoring Zephyr's question.

"He is the dragonslayer," called a voice from another entrance. A female Yolimite stepped into view. "And this is my inn."

"Is this Stripedwoman your customer?" asked the lead club-wielder.

"No," conceded the female.

"Then this does not concern you," he concluded.

The other two green-tunics had edged up behind their leader, so that one was behind each of his shoulders. Despite the order to step away, neither Summerwind's brother nor his companions had moved.

This was exciting! It looked as though they were about to fight over her.

The lead Yolimite fixed a sharp eye on Zephyr. "Dragonslayer, does your sister own a horse?"

"No, of course not," said Zephyr.

"Then we are taking her to a magistrate," said the leader. "She was witnessed riding a horse earlier this morning." With a glance, he indicated that the witness was the Yolimite who had been left standing in the entrance. Summerwind now recognized him as one of those who had ferried her across the river.

"I left that horse on the Lashrefite side of the river," said Summerwind. "I did not ride it into your village."

"That horse was stolen!" said the ferryman.

"Oh no," said Zephyr. "Tell me Father did not loan you a marked horse."

"In truth, it is Frogfoot's horse," said Summerwind. "But I left it on our side of the river, just as Peltswapper told me to do."

"But if it has any stockings, they think it belongs to them," said Zephyr.

That was preposterous! The Yolimites could not claim every horse with stockings.

"Were you riding a horse with stockings?" asked the lead club-wielder.

"Only one," said Summerwind. "Ah, one stocking, I mean. Although, it was also only one horse. Zephyr, why is this troubling them?"

"One stocking and a blaze," corrected the ferryman.

"They think they own blazes, as well?" she asked.

"Whose mark is that?" asked Zephyr.

"Clan Skinner's," said the leader.

"Skinner's stock are bald-faced."

Everyone looked at Dan.

"Who are you?" asked the one who asked all the questions.

"I am Dan Broadfield Dwen-Tarthilen called Danwel of Kwoshim. Now tell me who you are."

"I am Guardsman Zol Joiner," stated the leader. "Do you know what a 'guardsman' is, Dwen-Tarthilen?"

"No," said Dan.

"A guardsman is a man empowered by the council to enforce the laws of Brin," said Zol.

"Oh," said Dan.

"Now if we are all done with our introductions, my comrades and I will be taking this woman to tell her tale to the magistrate." Zol paused. "You are welcome to come along, Mister Dragon-slayer, if you would like to plead for clemency."

"Front or hind?" asked Dan.

"Beg pardon?"

"Front stocking or hind stocking?" asked Dan.

"Hind stocking," said the ferryman in the doorway.

"That is my clan's horse," said Dan.

"It is not!" said Summerwind.

Zephyr grabbed her arm and thought, *Silence.*

"Mister Joiner," said Dan, "a blaze and one hind stocking are the Broadfield marks. I am a Broadfield. The woman is traveling with me. This theft, if there has been one, is clan business."

Zol squinted at the female Yolimite who owned the lodge. "Do you know Broadfield marks, innkeeper?"

"Blaze and one hind stocking, as the man says," she replied.

Zol frowned at Dan. "You could have said so earlier. Come with us to claim your clan's horse, Mister Broadfield."

CHAPTER 9

Out of Brin

THE DAY was only half over, but Zhen felt that he had already seen a month's worth of surprises. He was accustomed to people asking him for favors, but these were usually things he could do: play at a wedding dance, mention someone's shop between songs, buy a hungry man a meal. He had never expected anyone to ask Zhen Dragonslayer to actually slay a dragon. And then two supplicants had appeared in the same morning.

Dan's dragon sounded like a spring cave-in—some sort of sinkhole formed by ice melting underground. But Dan and Shamon were convinced that the beastshaper's interpretation was correct. Shamon, at least, should have known how easy it was for people's imaginations to bend their perceptions.

Summerwind's dragon was certainly a tornado, but unless the band had a new taishrefi, there had to be something more than that. Taishrefi Smokewatcher would not mistake a tornado for an imaginary beast.

The appearance of the Brinnen guardsmen had added a strange coda to the morning's intriguing song. All members of the same Yolimite clan marked their livestock the same way, so Zhen understood why they believed that all beasts so marked belonged to them. However, he did not understand why Dan, who seemed to be a foreigner from a remote farming village, would be given authority to speak for the entire clan of Broadfields.

"You did that well," Shamon said to Dan, once they had collected Frogfoot's horse.

Summerwind said, "Thank you, Dan, for helping me get Whitefoot back." She gave the black filly a pat.

"I do not understand why the guardsman was so easily persuaded," Zhen confessed. "One instant he was telling you it was none of your business, and the next instant you told him it was none of his."

"The Clanfolk have two laws," said Shamon.

Zhen gave Shamon a stare to let him know that this cryptic statement was no explanation.

"Brin and tributary villages are bound by state law," explained Shamon. "But each clan is bound by clan law. Dan argued that the guardsmen had no jurisdiction."

"Truly," said Zhen. "Let us leave aside, for the moment, the question of how you can know words such as 'tributary' and 'jurification' when you cannot even understand the lyrics to 'The Maiden's Third Lament'. Let us instead focus on the other question that is, I am certain, on everyone's mind, namely: What do those words mean?"

"I apologize," said Shamon—and the wonderful thing about Shamon was that his apology was sincere. "Under the laws of Brin, the guardsmen can take marked horses from people who—how to say?—who do not match the horse. Riding a different clan's horse is proof that you have stolen it. Because this is theft between clans, it is under the juri— It belongs to Brin law."

Zhen nodded to indicate that Shamon was finally speaking sensibly.

"When Dan said that Dawnracer was with him, it became a thing belonging to Broadfield law. Clan law cannot be judged by Brinnen magistrates. Do I have that right, Dan?"

The little man nodded. "Aye, that sounds right. Though I can't say I've ever thought about it like that."

"I thought it was truly clever," said Summerwind. She tilted her head coquettishly so that the braided half of her hair dangled before Dan's eyes. "Your quick thinking helped avert what would have been a brutal fight."

A brutal fight? Zhen could not believe that his sister thought they would risk broken knees just to keep her from explaining to the magistrate why she had been such a mouse-brain.

"It is unfortunate that the ferryman and the guardsmen do not know all the markings," said Shamon. "The Broadfield stocking is on the right. No clan marks with a blaze and a stocking on the rear *left* leg."

Zhen said, "There are forty clans along this river, Shamon. You cannot expect people to know every clan's markings."

"My people know all the marks the clans paint on their boats," said Shamon. "I do not see why people who live on land cannot learn all the ways they mark their horses."

"What do you do when you want to give or trade a horse to someone in another clan?" asked Summerwind.

"Geldings for trade are left unmarked," said Dan.

"What about mares and stallions?" asked Summerwind.

"Mares and stallions have to stay in the clan," said Dan.

"They do not trade beasts that can have babies," Shamon explained. "'Offspring', I mean."

"Why not?" asked Summerwind.

"Because that would be giving away the clan's wealth," said Dan.

"They say that wealth has three legs:" said Shamon, "health, land, and stock. These cannot be traded or bequeathed outside the clan."

It was the sort of fact that Shamon loved because it gave so much insight, he said, into why the Yolimites acted as they did. However, Zhen found it useless. There was nothing there to sing about.

Unless … what if there were a man who had lost his land and stock—to a flood, perhaps. All he would have left would be his health, which he could bequeath to no one. There should be some way to make a song about that.

Zhen worked on this idea as they fetched Dan's horse—the one that actually belonged to him—which was stabled at an inn near the market. Some Yolimites treated their horses as though they were no different from the carts they pulled, but Dan Broadfield seemed to understand that his mare was a living, thinking being. Before saddling her and leading her out of the stable, he took the time to talk to her. He walked all around her, inspecting the way she was standing to be certain that her legs were not sore. Next, he climbed a ladder and brushed her back until she seemed relaxed and ready for the leather platform that Yolimites called a saddle.

Yolimites' legs were too short to bestride a horse's broad back, so they built something like a toy horse on top and sat on that with their feet flat on the horse's withers. It was clear that Summerwind wanted to giggle as Dan bustled about his horse, climbing up and down ladders to reach all the buckles and straps that were part of Yolimite horsemanship. It had looked ridiculous to Zhen, too, the first time he had seen it, but he had learned not to laugh. A Yolimite on a horse believed himself to be as tall as a full-sized man. And Dan Broadfield seemed to believe this even when he had both feet on the ground.

Dan suggested they purchase food, so they went to the market next. Zhen held the horses, which gave him a chance to work on his song while the other two men taught his sister how to spend coins. Summerwind squealed in delight at the multitude of carts and stalls. She fawned over Dan and Shamon as they gave her advice on choosing bread. Zhen was certainly grateful for their help, but he found Summerwind's gratitude to be excessive.

Undersong, Zhen's mare, was stabled on the outskirts near the river. Once the bread was purchased, he led his companions to the stables, composing his new song all the while. By the time they arrived, Zhen had three verses to go with the melancholy chorus:

Once I did stand on three legs of wealth.
I've lost stock and land; all that's left is my health.
This last, I bequeath you. My son, do not cry.
Without stock and land, all that's left is to die.

Yet, oh, how they would cry, Zhen thought—the sons and the daughters, too, or he did not know Brin. It might not strike a chord with the foreign merchants, who had left their stock and land behind in favor of the high profits that tradable goods could bring, but it would be a good song for the Brinnen carters who trickled into the inns after the market day was over.

Zhen bought a tradable gelding—sorrel, with no markings—for Shamon. The former boatman did not argue, although from the expression on his face, one might have thought he were preparing to eat a meal of death's-head mushrooms.

With his remaining brinnacs, Zhen purchased cloth blankets. These would give Shamon something to sit on between his Zharnovite costume and the gelding's sweaty back. The blankets could also be traded for a normal saddle as soon as they were among normal-sized people. Zhen's own saddle was designed with convenient straps for his spear and his lute, and he wished to procure such a saddle for Shamon as well, as soon as they were among Flamebringers.

It was unfortunate that Shamon insisted on bringing his box with him. Shamon carried the loaf-sized wooden trunk wherever they traveled, although it was practical only on a boat. He could lift it easily enough, and Zhen admired the stamina he showed in carrying it, but there was no doubt that their journeys could have been swifter and more comfortable without Shamon's box.

Dan figured out a way to deal with the box, however. Using the stable's built-in ladders to reach the horse's back, he managed to secure the box to the gelding using a blanket and the rope.

Summerwind solved the problem of the reins. The stablemaster gave her a light cord which she fashioned into a child's bridle. Accustomed to Yolimite ear-reins, the gelding was astonished by the unorthodox head gear, but not as astonished as the stablemaster was when Summerwind succeeded in convincing the horse to wear it.

There was one final obstacle to getting Shamon on a horse: He had never learned to vault. In the end, Shamon had to use the Yolimite stable-ladders to mount. With his long legs flopping against the gelding's sides and his long fingers fumbling with the reins, he looked like a bullfrog. They all assured him that his bearing was the epitome of equestrianism.

"But try not to let your elbows flap about like wings," suggested Summerwind.

"And keep your back straight," advised Dan. "But not stiff."

Shamon looked ill.

Zhen wondered how the two of them would fare. The gelding was used to high Yolimite saddles and ear-reins; it would have no idea how to respond to a full-sized rider's commands. Shamon had no idea of the proper way to give commands that the horse would respond to. But the problem was solved as soon as they started moving. The gelding was a follower. Instead of waiting for commands from the helpless Shamon, the gelding just did what the other horses were doing. The arrangement seemed to suit both horse and rider.

The riverfront downstream from the city was unremarkable: a cascade of mills and millponds, another stable, and a village laid out as haphazardly as debris left by a spring flood. Nonetheless, Dan and Summerwind craned their necks about, looking at everything.

Everyone was looking at them, as well. Zhen liked the attention. And it was fortunate that he did, because the Yolimites stared at him wherever he went, whether he had mismatched companions or not.

They dismounted at the ferry landing, and Zhen banged on the iron drum which summoned the ferrymen. That was when he realized that he had forgotten to save brinnacs for the toll. Pelt-swapper must have given some to Summerwind, though; otherwise, she would not have been able to cross to Brin. "How many coins do you have left?" Zhen asked her.

"I will handle this," said Dan, striding forward to meet the first ferryman, a bearded man with dirt clinging to his leggings.

While Dan negotiated the price, other ferrymen arrived. Among them was the one who had accused Summerwind of stealing Whitefoot.

"Never thought I'd see a Broadfield cuddling up to stripeys," the man said.

The bearded one frowned.

Dan looked over his shoulder at Zhen and Summerwind and then back at the hostile ferryman.

"They haven't done anything wrong," he said.

"That tree-kisser will have her knife in your kidney as soon as you get in the forest," the hostile one said.

"Now, Gimin," admonished the bearded one.

"Truly, that is a strange thing to say!" protested Zhen.

Gimin pulled out his knife. "I'm not afraid of you, or your spear either," he told Zhen. "I killed plenty of stripeys in the war."

"It seems to me that your cousin doesn't want to ferry us across the Yarl," said Dan to the bearded one.

"Well I am surely glad I have made that plain," said Gimin.

"And yet, our bargain has already been struck," insisted Dan.

"Aye. That it has," agreed the bearded one. "Will you come, Gimin, or should we divide your share?"

"I've had enough of this Broadfield and his stripeys," said Gimin.

"Then I reckon we should leave at once," said Dan to the bearded man. "That seems to suit everyone."

Undersong and Dan's mare stoically allowed themselves to be led onto the broad, flat deck of the ferry, as though they traveled this way all the time. Shamon's gelding showed the whites of his eyes, but he was more afraid of being left behind. He boarded.

Whitefoot had already been on the ferry once this morning—when the boatmen had confiscated her. She danced nervously from side to side, making the boatmen nervous in turn. Summerwind started singing "Two Hearts Met in Moonlight" to calm the filly down, but that made Dan's mare nervous.

Summerwind finally coaxed Whitefoot aboard, and the five boatmen shoved off. Shamon offered to take the sixth pole, but the head ferryman refused. Perhaps he was afraid that Shamon would claim Gimin's share.

When the ferry finally made landing, they were all relieved, especially the horses.

"Thank you for taking time out from your gardening to ferry us across the river," Dan said to the bearded one. "May Yolim bless your planting."

"May Yolim smile upon your bargains," said the man, even as he pushed the ferry back out onto the river.

"I'm glad that's over," Dan said as they led their horses up the riverbank.

"What war was that man talking about?" Summerwind asked.

"It was something that happened when I was a boy," Dan said. "Some dispute over who owned the timber around Maisil—a city that is surely far away. I'm surprised anyone from Brin was involved in that."

"For people who live on the Rivers, all cities are close," said

Shamon. "During the Timber War, many people went to Maisil. Seeking opportunity."

Zhen had never heard the word "opportunity" uttered with such sadness.

"But what does that have to do with us?" asked Summerwind. "Our people fought over range once, with the Kashramites, but that was long, long ago. We have never gone to war over timber, have we?"

Shamon said, "It was a different tribe. They live in the forest, without horses."

Shamon had mentioned this strange tribe to Zhen before. It was difficult to imagine how a Lashrefite could survive without bison to hunt or horses to hunt them with, but he did not doubt Shamon's word. Lashrefi had given her people a love of travel, and now they were spread all over the world.

"So because of what this tribe did, the Yolimites now hate all Lashrefites?" Summerwind asked.

"No," Zhen told her. "Most of them like us and our music. The Goddess just decided you were going to cross paths with that one."

"Nobody in Kwoshim hates Stripedfolk," said Dan. "As far as I know."

"Oh, Dan," said Summerwind, in a voice as sweet as nectar. "That is truly comforting to hear."

She was playing with her single braid again, too. Zhen decided the two of them needed to have a talk.

CHAPTER 10

Riverside Conversations

"ZEPHYR, we need to have a talk."

"Yes, we do," her brother agreed. "Sit down."

Summerwind sat down next to the man whom she had last seen three springs ago. She had not thought of him as a man then, but she supposed he must be one now. He looked no different, except for the cloth cloak that he wore over his sleeveless buckskin tunic. The cloak was long enough for him to sit on, but he had laid its hem in his lap so that he would not get it muddy.

Trees rose above their heads, with young, green leaves that cast shadows over the murky waters of the river Kailanarl. She and Zephyr sat on the soft ground of the river's bank, a half day's ride from Brin. Ah, but her time in Brin had been short, thanks to that unpleasant ferryman that Dan had put in his place. Since she had discovered Zephyr, they had done nothing but hurry, hurry, hurry—as though he were eager to rejoin the band and tell them what a fraud he had become among the Yolimites. He had a coyote-plan, and now that the two of them finally had a moment alone, she was going to find out what it was.

So it was truly frustrating when he opened the conversation before she had a chance to compose her first question.

Zephyr said, "This is not the spring gathering, Summerwind."

What could he mean by that?

"No, brother," she agreed. "In truth, it is the Kailanarl, which is considerably wetter than most spring gatherings."

Zephyr replied, "Well said, sister. And yet I wish to be serious with you for a moment."

"Ah," she said. "And I was just saying to myself that you had not changed. Very well, dear brother, be serious with me. I shall enjoy the novelty."

Squirrel-tongue, he thought.

Puffed-up robin-chest, she thought back.

He continued aloud, as though the silent exchange of insults had not taken place: "With Mother and Father absent, I am responsible for your welfare. Don't laugh!"

For she *was* laughing. "Zephyr, I am grown. I am Dawnracer now. Perhaps I should make you call me by my autumn name so that you do not forget this."

"Grown or not, you have no husband, and you seem not to have the sense to realize that this is not the place to look for one."

Ah. That.

Swiftly sorting through her options, she rejected "Whatever do you mean?" in favor of: "Are we talking about the river again?"

"We are talking about your hair," he said. "You are wearing a single braid."

Instead of reaching up to touch it, Summerwind carefully kept her hands in her lap. Congratulating herself on her restraint, she replied, "Many young women wear a single braid to keep the hair from their eyes when traveling."

"They wear a single braid down the back," he countered. "Yours is on the side. The right side, even."

"Perhaps my other braid slipped loose while I was riding," she suggested calmly.

"Then you could have re-braided it," he said.

"Perhaps there has not been time," she suggested.

He cut his conversational tempo in half, emphasizing each word: "You have time now."

"Indeed I do," Summerwind acknowledged. She withdrew her comb from her pouch and started combing the un-braided half of her hair.

Zephyr thought he had won. "Truly, you say you are no child, and yet you carry on like this."

Like what? She was old enough to be courted—past old enough according to their mother. She had the right to wear a courtship braid. And why did he care that she chose to braid the right instead of the left? True, that indicated she was willing to leave her own band and join her husband's, but Zephyr had left that band himself three springs before.

The one-sided braid was usually only worn at the tribal gatherings, but she was an unusual girl. She had been chosen for an unusual task. It was only natural that any young man whom Lashrefi might happen to put in Summerwind's path would wonder whether she were willing to be courted. It was only polite to answer the question that her stately beauty and adventurous calling would provoke in this man's heart. Did Zephyr truly think that was childish?

Summerwind had not had the good luck to cross paths with a young man on her way to Brin. She had hoped this was because the Goddess wished her to focus her charms on the rendezvous with Dragonslayer. Ah, but that had been a disappointment!

She considered telling Zephyr that there was no point to wearing a courtship braid now that she knew Dragonslayer was a fraud, but that would counter her "perhaps it just slipped loose" gambit.

Her fingers split her hair into three strands. In truth, the left side made the prettier braid: She could get one strand mostly black, one all white, and one mixed.

She should have fought him, she realized. Despite the fact that the loose half of her hair blew into her face too often, she should have worn the courtship braid until they were back with the band. Now he would think he was in charge of her, unless she managed to put him in his place immediately.

"And now, if you will allow it, my dear older brother, I would like to ask you the question that required me to find you in privacy."

"And that is?" Zephyr was amused, but on guard.

"What do you plan to do when we rejoin Lowsinger's Band?"

"Slay the dragon, of course," he said, as though he believed that were within his capabilities.

Truly? she asked.

Truly, he thought.

That was no proof of his earnestness, however. The coyote-pup could bluff with his thoughts as easily as he could bluff with his voice.

At that moment, something erupted from the river with a great splash. Summerwind did not squeak, despite how Zephyr later described it. She may have given a shout, such as all adventurers must in preparation for meeting something unexpected which might prove to be a threat, but she certainly did not "squeak like a frightened mouse".

It was Shamon, the Zharnovite, his wet blue bald head gleaming in the sunlight. He contracted his exquisitely formed abdominal muscles and water gushed from his mouth and nose. He followed this with a deep breath that expanded his broad chest. A mighty cough expelled the last of the water from his lungs.

The spectacle was monstrous, yet fascinating, like the mating of bison. He climbed the river bank wearing nothing but a loin cloth. The wet thing clung to him in a way that revealed nothing, while suggesting everything. Summerwind had certainly been startled, but that was not the only cause of her racing heartbeat.

Unashamed—and the man certainly had nothing to be ashamed of!—Shamon smiled at her and waved. Then he bent over to collect the sandals she had not seen behind a log. This gave her another aspect of him to admire. Summerwind released the strands of the braid she had started. She could braid it later.

Zephyr called out, "My sister thinks I am a fraud, Shamon."

The blue man slipped into his sandals and retrieved his clothing from behind the log before turning to face them.

"Zhen, you *are* a fraud," he said, without a trace of humor or rancor.

"It is not so, Shamon," said Zephyr reasonably. "True, I was a fraud when I claimed to have slain a beast that did not exist. But if, in truth, the beast exists, all I have to do is slay it to become a hero."

"Zhen, I would be happy if it were that easy for you," said Shamon sadly.

"Ah, but it shall be, my dear friend. It is true that I created the song, but I believe that the song now plans to create me."

"Truly the lupine flowers early this spring," said Summerwind.

Zephyr pretended to ignore her. Addressing Shamon, he said, "I see you are skeptical. Consider, therefore, the following question: Before today, how likely would you have thought it that someone would come to me asking me to slay a dragon?"

"I thought it was possible," said Shamon.

"You did?" Zephyr was surprised.

"My people believe that dishonesty—how to say?—returns to a person."

"Very well," said Zephyr. "Let us suppose that, eventually, someone was bound to call my bluff. We can even suppose that my bluff would be called by asking me to slay a problematic beast, although that idea stretches the bounds of credibility. Even so, you must agree that, on any given day, such a thing was unlikely."

Shamon looked confused.

"Allow me to phrase it this way," Zephyr persisted. "Would you expect someone like Dan to appear once a day, or is once a year more reasonable?"

"Once a year," Shamon said slowly. By this time, he had finished wrapping himself up in his clothing, which appeared to be simply a long, rectangular piece of cloth. Somehow he had folded and twisted it to form a shoulder wrap and an ankle-length skirt, which mostly concealed the beautiful muscles that Summerwind could still see in her mind's eye.

"Precisely so," said Zephyr. "And now consider this question: Given that someone who needs the services of a dragonslayer should only appear, at most, once a year, is it not surpassing the bounds of chance that two such people should appear on the same day?"

This was what Zephyr had said to her at the inn that morning, and now Summerwind feared she finally understood her brother's reasoning. "You think the Goddess sent Dan and me as a sign."

"Not just you and Dan," insisted Zephyr. "But even the song! How could I have made a song about a beast that no one had ever heard of unless it was the direct inspiration of Lashrefi herself?"

With horror, Summerwind realized that there was the tiniest chance he was right. What if the Goddess had chosen her brother to be a hero? His arrogance would become unbearable.

"There is another possibility," said Shamon solemnly.

Summerwind looked to the Zharnovite for hope.

"Perhaps the Goddess of Luck gave you that song because she likes to hear you sing," suggested Shamon. "And then you decided to tell people the song was real. Perhaps the Goddess of Luck—or the God of Justice—sent Dan and Dawnracer as a punishment for your lie."

"But the dragons are real," said Zephyr.

"Then they can really kill you," said Shamon.

"Ah," said Zephyr, as though this were the first time he had considered that possibility.

"I have been thinking," said Shamon. "It is not right for us to bring Dan along. He is the only one who does not know that you cannot do this thing that you have been saying you can do. We should tell him now and send him back to Brin tomorrow."

"But what if I *can* slay dragons?" Zephyr protested.

"It seems unlikely," said Shamon.

"But if you do not believe I can, why did you agree to come with me?"

"I have accompanied you in your crime," said Shamon. "If the deities choose to slay you, I should be slain, too."

"That is truly—" Zephyr groped about for words. "Shamon, that is so loyal of you."

"No, it is not," said Shamon.

"Yes it is," insisted Zephyr. He had no tears in his eyes, but Summerwind could hear them in his voice. "When this is over, Shamon, I shall write a song about you—a song about Heartstringer, the loyal friend of Dragonslayer."

What a puffed-up robin-chest! Summerwind exchanged a look with Shamon. His blue face suggested he was thinking the same thing.

By the time they rejoined Dan, the busy little man had finished brushing his bay mare and had moved on to the sorrel gelding that Zephyr had obtained for Shamon. The blankets that had been on the gelding's back were spread out to dry on a hackberry bush.

While Zephyr tried to get a fire going, Summerwind worked on building a brush-lodge. A beaver-felled cottonwood provided the backbone. She laid dead branches against it for the ribs. Then all she needed was a skin.

She contemplated using the blankets her brother had obtained in Brin, but from what she knew of cloth, she suspected it would not keep out the rain. She could not find any trees with leaves growing thickly enough to suit her. Dead grass, however, was ample and waist-high. She began to cut grass bundles.

After watching her tie a few bundles with green willow twigs, Dan began tying them for her and attaching them to the framework she had set up. Sometimes when she handed him a bundle, their fingers would touch, so Summerwind did not mind that Dan's thick thatching technique required her to cut twice as many bundles as she had planned. The project did not take much extra time, and she would gladly have worked beside the thoughtful little man all night.

Zephyr came over to inspect their work. "Dear sister, I had thought we were continuing our journey tomorrow. Do you intend to build a village here instead?"

There was only one answer for that: "No, dear brother. I was intending to build something simple to shelter the four of us for the night. But as you remind me of the need to save time, I think I shall build it for three."

In truth, it was already done, for Dan was tying the last bundle to the brush-lodge, chuckling as he did so.

"You two remind me of me and my sister Bethinesi," he said.

"Is that good?" Zephyr asked.

Dan chuckled again. "I reckon so," he said.

"Do you have any brothers?" Summerwind asked.

"One younger brother and three younger sisters," Dan replied.

"I have only older brothers," she told him. "But the other two are nicer than this one."

Dan chuckled again, which pleased her.

They ate their bread sitting around the campfire under the trees. The stripes on Zephyr's face danced in the flickering firelight. Shamon's blue skin was dark in the red light, and the whites of his eyes glowed within the shadow of his face. Dan's skin was much the color of Shamon's, but being a cheerier companion, he smiled more often, revealing his bright teeth. Summerwind had always thought that her people's skin had been made for nights like this—

and in truth, her brother looked beautiful—but it was those two exotic faces that proclaimed she was on an adventure.

Zephyr and Shamon fetched their lutes, then, and began playing a duet that Zephyr was still composing. After a few choruses, Summerwind withdrew her flute from her pouch and threaded notes into the melody. Dan, who had no instrument, smiled and listened.

After a while, Dan leaned back and closed his eyes. Soon he was making little snuffly snores. Summerwind reached over and touched his small-but-manly shoulder.

Dan blinked and smiled up at her.

"It is good that you fall asleep first," she told him, "for you are the smallest and need to be the first one under the roof of the brush-lodge."

"Oh, I was enjoying the music," he said sleepily.

"They will keep playing," she assured him.

Dan yawned and stood up with a stretch. "I reckon you are right," he said. He ambled off toward the brush-lodge.

After playing through one last chorus, Summerwind arose and went to the brush-lodge as well. Dan had taken one of the blankets and wrapped himself up in it to augment his cloak. Summerwind had a warm buffalo robe to sleep in. The robe would be cozier with two.

"I bid you good night," she said, as she curled up against his back.

"Mmmmf," said Dan.

She wanted to offer to share the buffalo robe with him, but this was not exactly the conversational opening she required. Perhaps he would start shivering in the night, and then she could wrap it over him. Or perhaps Shamon would ask to share. Contemplating these possibilities, Summerwind fell asleep.

It was a very pleasant night. Sleeping between Dan and Shamon was as warm as sleeping in a lodge, and Dan's expert work on the roof kept the rain off them. The only disturbance came when Zephyr apologized for mocking her brush-lodge and asked if she would take his lute under the roof. Even this was not very disturbing, for she mistook it for a dream. Only when she awoke in the morning did she realize that she had graciously consented: Her hand was caressing the round belly of Zephyr's lute, and not—as she had been dreaming—Shamon's head.

"Did you really sleep out in the rain?" Dan asked when he saw Zephyr attempting to dry out his cloak at the morning fire.

"No," said Zephyr. "I slept under my horse."

"When she said you could not sleep under the lean-to, you thought she was serious?" Dan asked.

"She was serious," said Zephyr simply.

Dan looked at Summerwind.

She nodded.

"Among their people," Shamon explained to the bewildered Yolimite, "women own the houses. The owner of the house can keep out those who displease her."

"You do not have to worry," Summerwind assured Dan. "You are polite."

"Oho!" said Dan. "And I will surely continue to be polite now that I know where the bread is coming from."

"In truth, the bread is almost gone," said Zephyr. "We shall want to kill a rabbit or two today."

Dan frowned. "I did not pack a sling," he said.

"Ah, we will provide, dear Mister Broadfield," Zephyr assured him. "While you travel in Flamebringer territory, you shall be our guest."

A short time after this exchange, Summerwind saw Shamon talking with Dan alone, and she remembered that the Zharnovite had wanted to warn Dan not to travel with them. Perhaps he had changed his mind, though, and only spoken to Dan of the gelding that was standing nearby, for when they set off up the trail later that morning, Dan went with them.

The rain returned at mid-morning. This did not seem to bother Shamon, who actually took off his cloak so that his skin could catch the drops. Summerwind was too cold without her buffalo robe and too warm when she wore it, but she could not complain because Zephyr was not complaining—and Zephyr would not complain because he had just spent the night out in the rain. No doubt he had prepared words to mock her if she should mention her discomfort. Dan sat tall on his platform-saddle and watched the trees and the river with interest, so he was not complaining. The horses, however, slogged along with their heads down and their ears back. They were miserable, and horse-pride did not require that they act otherwise.

At midday, they stopped to rest on the river bank. Summerwind and Zephyr went looking for rabbits, but the animals had been intelligent enough to take shelter from the rain. By the time they returned to camp empty-handed, Dan had built a fire to cook the crayfish that Shamon had scooped up from the bottom of the river. Zephyr just laughed.

"Truly, this is the best band a dragonslayer could travel with," he said. "As long as we four remain together, we shall not want for food, shelter, or song."

Summerwind was preparing a similar remark about how any woman would consider herself lucky to be in the company of such fine men, but before she could voice it, Dan jumped up.

Staring at the river, he exclaimed, "That's Kethwin!"

CHAPTER 11

Onto the Prairie

KETHWIN couldn't help herself. As soon as she got off the boat, the first thing she did was run to Danwel's arms. For a moment, with her head nestled against his broad chest, it didn't matter that she was turning pink in full view of her cousins and those strange giants. Danwel had turned pink, too.

"Allow me to guess that this is the village beastshaper to whom you have promised your heart."

Kethwin released Danwel and contemplated the speaker. The striped giant had a male voice, but long black and white hair.

"Who's that?" Kethwin murmured.

"Oh. Kethwin, let me introduce Zhen Dragonslayer," Danwel said.

"I am pleased to meet you," said the long-haired man. "And please greet my friend Shamon, and my sister, ah, Dawnracer."

Shamon was tall, bald, and blue, just like the Rivermen aboard Cousin Sam's boat. If Shamon had slipped in among them, Kethwin would not have been able to pick him out.

The dragonslayer's sister wore her hair loose like her brother's on one side and braided like Kethwin's on the other. Although her leather skirt was short, her leather leggings revealed only a modest amount of her ankle. Her long sleeves were similarly modest. Even so, Kethwin found the woman unsettling. Perhaps it was the fringes decorating her dress just below her bosom. Or perhaps it was the way her bold eyes seemed to proclaim she was ready for a challenge.

"I am Kethi Walker Dwen-Tarthilen, called Kethwin of Kwoshim. But you should call me Kethi. And these are my cousins, Sam and Lon Walker."

Her cousins mumbled some sort of greeting. The two men had

been quick to offer an escort from the boat to the primitive campsite among the trees, but now they stood well behind Kethwin, as though reluctant to get too near the giants. Or possibly it was the grazing horses they were afraid of. Boatmen had strange prejudices.

"How did you find us?" Danwel asked.

"Well, it wasn't easy," she said. "We were lucky that one of the captains at the Brinnen docks had seen the four of you running away to Minroshi."

"We aren't going to Minroshi," said Danwel.

"And we are not running away," said Dawnracer. "We are off to slay the dragon."

"Then why are you traveling in the wrong direction?" Kethwin asked. "The dragon is in Dwen-Tarthil."

"Alas, I fear we have a dragon ahead of us as well as the one that attacked your village," the dragonslayer said.

"Two dragons?" Kethwin asked. "When until this month we had never heard of even one?"

He spread his striped hands. "It is strange, but it is so."

"Dawnracer's people have also seen a dragon," Danwel said. "Well, they haven't seen it, but they have seen what it can do."

"It flattened a forest of oak trees," the Stripedwoman said. She gestured with her arms. "Oaks this thick were snapped off at the base. This is much more serious than a few holes in the ground."

"'A few holes in the ground'?" replied Kethwin. "I'll have you know that one of those holes has swallowed up our creek. My entire clan will be without flour this spring because there is no water to turn the mill wheel. I doubt your people will go hungry without those trees."

"The dragon ate the Grigolin?" Danwel asked.

"Yes, it—" The memory of her dream overwhelmed her indignation. "It was thirsty," Kethwin murmured.

"Ah, pray tell us the whole story," said the dragonslayer. "I should very much like to know what would cause you to travel so far, when your village had already sent Dan."

So Kethwin told them. The dragonslayer was interested to learn that Kethwin had dreamed of the dragon's thirst. Danwel was impressed that the monster had spooked Tharnwel's docile herd through two fences. Dawnracer, however, seemed barely able to follow Kethwin's story. The Riverman even had to tell her what a mill was.

"And so Cousin Miller and I decided that I should bring you this news at once," Kethwin concluded.

"And you were right to do so," said the dragonslayer. "Well done. I appreciate the care you have taken to deliver this information."

"So you will come back with us?" Kethwin asked.

"Certainly," Zhen replied. "Just as soon as I have slain the dragon of the plains. Would you care to join us?"

"But our mill!" Kethwin protested. "Danwel, make him see sense."

Danwel shook his head. "Kethwin, we can't ask him to put our families ahead of his own."

"So you put his family ahead of yours?"

"Well, now ..."

"Excuse us a moment," Kethwin said. "Dan and I need to speak privately."

Kethwin tugged Danwel to the other side of an oak tree a short distance away. Speaking in a quiet voice despite her anger, she asked, "Just what do you think you're doing here, Danwel Broadfield? You were sent to fetch your village a dragonslayer."

"And I found him, Kethwin, but ..."

"But what?"

"Well, his sister has a dragon, too. I couldn't out-bid her."

This was a respected rule of fair bargaining. It was very rude to offer someone a better deal than what they were getting from their cousin. Competition between clans was expected, but forcing someone to choose between clan obligations and personal profit was like paying them to sin. Leave it to Danwel to apply Clanfolk ethics to hide-wearing, spear-wielding Stripedfolk.

"So you just go riding off through the wilderness with these savages and leave your village to suffer?"

"No. Well. But Kethwin, we made a bargain."

"What kind of bargain?"

"I offered to come help slay their dragon."

"And what do we get from this deal, Danwel?"

"Well, Zhen says that when he's done with that one, he'll come slay ours."

"So *you* won't come back with me, either."

"I can't," said Danwel. "Not right now. I was sent to bargain with the dragonslayer, and this is the bargain I made."

Kethwin put her head in her hands. Lives were at stake, and Danwel thought the problem could be solved with "I'll help with your threshing and you help with mine."

And now what would she do? The dragonslayer wouldn't come back with her. Danwel wouldn't come back. Would they make her go back alone?

Kethwin wouldn't stand for that. To lie in bed sleepless for fear of what might wake her up, to hear that terrible rumbling in the ground again, to sense the thing that could make those monstrous holes. No. Danwel couldn't make her face that.

"If you aren't coming back with me, then tell your dragonslayer I'm coming with you."

* * *

They sat two in the saddle with Kethwin holding Tevishi's reins. Danwel thought it was almost like going for a pleasure ride at home, except that the woods were so much wilder here. Cottonwoods and ash trees arched over their heads. In the open places, last summer's grass was standing high enough to tickle Tevishi's belly. Blackbirds called from among the rushes. Frogs boasted about how strong their lungs were. Crows laughed in the high branches of the trees.

Danwel could almost imagine they were laughing at him and the bargain he had made. He was riding farther and farther into the wilderness while the dragon did Yolim-knew-what at home. Yet what could Danwel have done for the village that the other men could not? He was bigger than they were and stronger than most, but he doubted this was a problem that could be solved with muscle. He suspected dragonslaying required technique. Danwel didn't know any techniques, but he reckoned a clever man like

Zhen would figure something out once he met up with Dawnracer's dragon. Danwel just hoped he would be learning from Zhen's success and not from a fatal mistake.

Danwel asked them to stop early that evening, ostensibly to give the old mare extra rest from the extra weight, but really to give Kethwin's legs a rest and help her ease into the physical demands of horse travel. Everyone—including the horses—was quite agreeable to the idea, each for his or her own reasons. Shamon slipped off toward the river. Dawnracer took her spear from its straps and rode toward the sinking sun. Zhen announced that he was off to set a snare for a rabbit, taking pains to explain to them that the cord he was using could also double as a lute string.

Dawnracer and Zhen both came back empty-handed—the difference being that Zhen smugly assured them that they would have rabbit meat for breakfast. It was up to Shamon, again, to find them something to eat, and he came back from the river with a turtle.

"Your people eat those?" Zhen asked, looking dubiously at the creature's hard shell.

"You ate one yourself last month," Shamon replied. "What did you think was in the 'turtle soup'?"

"I assumed it was a colorful Yolimite expression," said Zhen.

"What is a 'soup'?" asked Dawnracer.

Kethwin stared at her.

"It is a pot full of water with some food thrown in," Zhen explained.

"Like tea?" Dawnracer asked, wrinkling her striped forehead.

"Meat tea," Zhen agreed. "Or a very thin stew."

"Can we cook a turtle without a cook pot?" Dawnracer asked.

"Not likely," said Kethwin.

"Turtles can be baked in the shell," said Shamon. "I have never done it, but perhaps it is the same as crayfish."

Danwel nodded. That seemed plausible.

"But they do not have much meat," Shamon went on. "This one will be mostly shell."

Danwel knew his mother could make a turtle stretch to feed the entire family, but his family was merely big, not giant-sized.

"I found some biscuitroot when I was out looking for deer," Dawnracer said. "I'll go dig some up."

"I think I know where I can find some mushrooms," Zhen countered.

As brother and sister again went their separate ways, Kethwin asked, "Why didn't they do that in the first place?"

"I do not understand Zhen often," agreed the Riverman.

Danwel reckoned he had a good idea of what was going on. If a sister came back with venison and a brother came back with a few wrinkled mushrooms, the teasing would be merciless. It was much better to come back empty-handed.

"Do you have any brothers or sisters?" Danwel asked Shamon.

"No," said Shamon. "Not anymore."

"Oh," said Danwel. He could think of nothing to say after that.

It was Kethwin who broke the silence, saying, "Well, I won't spend the whole evening standing up. Danwel, bring that log over so we can use it as a bench."

Danwel was glad to have an excuse to leave the cookfire for a moment. He dutifully fetched the log.

"How long have you known the dragonslayer?" Kethwin asked.

"I met Zhen last spring," Shamon replied.

"So a year, then," Kethwin said. "Not like that, Danwel. Other side up."

Danwel rolled the log over. Kethwin shoved on the end until it was at the angle she wanted, and they both sat down.

"Is he an honest man?" Kethwin asked.

Shamon looked stricken.

Kethwin raised her eyebrows. Her green eyes looked especially pretty with blue skin, Danwel decided.

"Does he lie, cheat, or steal?" Kethwin asked.

"He— He does not steal," Shamon said.

"So he lies and cheats," said Kethwin. "Interesting."

"Not so," said Zhen cheerfully, emerging from the woods. "Flamebringers never cheat, for Lashrefi would curse our dice if we did."

Kethwin blushed.

"Of course," Zhen added, "I could be lying about that."

"What are Flamebringers?" Danwel asked, hoping to cover Kethwin's embarrassment.

"My tribe," said Zhen.

He was holding the corners of the front flap of his leather tunic to make a pouch for carrying his mushrooms. This revealed the entire length of his striped legs as well as his minimal undergarment. Danwel wondered if Kethwin was blushing only because she had been caught calling the dragonslayer a liar or if the sight of his bare legs was also a cause. Danwel decided that as long as she wasn't smiling while blushing, he had nothing to worry about.

Zhen dumped his mushrooms on the ground and said, "Keep the squirrels away from those and I'll find us some roasting sticks. No, on second thought, use the mushrooms to lure the squirrels in, and we can roast them, too."

He walked away, whistling.

"He is a remarkable man," observed Shamon.

"Remarkable," Kethwin echoed.

Dawnracer appeared then, carrying a dozen roots. She held their green tops in her fists instead of lifting up her clothing to make a basket, for which Danwel was grateful.

"I found a good tree back there for a brush-lodge," she told Danwel. "But I do not think we will need to make one tonight."

"What is a brush-lodge?" Kethwin asked.

"It's a lean-to made of brush," Danwel explained.

"Dan helped me build one last night," said Dawnracer. "It kept us quite dry and cozy."

Kethwin arched an eyebrow. "You built one for both of you?"

"And for Shamon, too," Danwel explained. Things were suddenly going very wrong. "For the four of us, really, except that, um, Zhen slept outside."

"In the rain?" asked Kethwin.

"Alas, I fear it is so," agreed Zhen, arriving with three willow sticks. "For my heartless sister did see fit to cast me outside when the weather grew most dire."

Zhen and Dawnracer exchanged a look.

Dawnracer grinned and started slicing the tops off the roots she had gathered. Shamon and Zhen began poking mushrooms onto the sticks. Kethwin scowled at the cookfire and said no more.

Danwel reckoned he'd be catching trouble for that lean-to.

* * *

On the morning after Chamfo roasted the turtle, Zhen decided to leave the river. Chamfo's friend said his empty snare was a sign from the Goddess of Luck, and they must now travel through the open prairie.

Chamfo had heard Zhen's tales of life "in the land of grass and sky". Aboard *The Mud Mother*, Chamfo had even traveled along prairie rivers. But he had never expected to be riding a horse through a shadeless grassland so far from water.

Chamfo was grateful when Zhen finally called a halt for the day at a cottonwood-lined creek. Chamfo slid off his horse's back and stood there panting, holding on to the horse's mane until the pain in his knees ebbed enough to allow him to walk.

Kethi soon had her hands on the leg of Chamfo's horse, examining it with her elemental talent.

"Perhaps you should look at Shamon next," Zhen joked.

"I can look at your legs if you would like," Kethi told Chamfo. "But I won't be able to do anything for you. All I can do is tell you that your legs hurt, but you know that already. Muscle aches are normal."

Chamfo didn't ask whether joint aches were also normal. For a Child of Justice, nothing about riding horses was normal. But normal or not, the pain was no worse than he deserved.

"I was always under the impression that beastshapers could heal leg pain," Zhen said.

"I can't," said Kethi.

"Kethwin is still learning," said Dan, who had come over to remove the ropes that held the blankets and Chamfo's personal chest on the back of the horse. "Someday she'll be able to heal anything."

Kethi's grunt did not indicate agreement.

Dawnracer came riding up to the creek with her half-braided hair dancing in the wind behind her. Chamfo had no idea how she stayed on her fast-moving horse while holding a spear in one hand.

"I was right," she announced. "There was a deer in those willows. A doe."

Zhen eyed her spear. "Did you miss, sister?"

"No. She bolted before we could get close enough for a throw. I think we could have caught her, but Whitefoot has had a long day. We can make do with biscuitroot tonight. I saw some over there." She nodded to indicate the direction, but Chamfo could see nothing special. The prairie seemed to be mostly grass.

Zhen said, "I believe you underestimate the value of stealth, dear sister. Yonder thicket is certain to hide a rabbit, and he shall be our dinner once stealth and cunning are properly applied, as I intend to demonstrate." Zhen gestured with his spear.

"Truly, brother, you have been stalking rabbits for two days now with no luck, but go have your fun. I shall take my digging stick and get us food."

Dawnracer dismounted. Kethi came over and put her hands on the animal's leg.

"Thank you, Kethi," said Dawnracer. "But in truth, I can tend to Whitefoot myself."

"I'm sure you can," said Kethi. "I'm just making sure she hasn't been ridden too hard."

"Kethi has a sensitivity to the element of Life that allows her to see inside an animal's leg," Zhen explained.

"Truly," said Dawnracer.

"Truly," affirmed Zhen.

"Whitefoot is young, fast, and strong," said Dawnracer. "There is nothing wrong with her leg."

"But her body is still growing," said Kethi. "And to grow correctly, she must be ridden correctly."

"Ah!" said Dawnracer with a brittle smile. "Please accept my apologies. I was not aware that I was maiming this filly by riding incorrectly."

"I didn't say that," said Kethi with a scowl. "Be quiet a moment so I can concentrate. There. Your filly looks fine. But it's a good thing you decided not to chase deer after a long day's ride."

"Do you hear that, sister?" asked Zhen. "The beastshaper brings you good news."

"She tells me what I already know," observed Dawnracer.

"As I said, good news. For you do love being right, do you not? Yes, Kethi, it is lucky for us that you chose to join our merry little band. We needed someone to monitor the horses for us."

"I'm glad you think so," said Kethi. "Because I want you to be more careful with Undersong."

The expression on Zhen's face made Chamfo chuckle.

"Undersong?" said Zhen. "She is a fine, strong lady."

"Aye," said Kethi. "But she has been locked up in a stable for too long. I can tell by her tendons."

"What? What's wrong with her tendons?"

"Nothing, yet," said Kethi. "But they aren't used to travel. You should give her legs time to warm up before you ask her to trot in the mornings. And be careful on slopes."

"Truly we are lucky to have someone to put you in your place, brother," said Dawnracer.

"What about Shamon's gelding?" Zhen asked.

"Well, the same advice would apply to the gelding," said Kethi. "But Shamon isn't likely to ride him too hard."

Zhen chuckled. "My apologies, friend," he said to Chamfo. "But it is true."

Chamfo shrugged. His people were never insulted by the truth.

"And now," Zhen announced. "I am off to find meat."

Kethi looked at Dan and said, "You should go with him."

Dan, who was standing on Chamfo's boat-money trunk so he could brush the back of Chamfo's horse, said, "I should?"

"Yes," said Kethi. "It's ridiculous that Shamon makes you take care of his horse every night. Shamon, you can do that yourself. We will show you how."

It had never occurred to Chamfo that he might be able to learn something about horses, but he saw that it was indeed wrong for him to watch Dan struggle to reach the back of an animal that he could brush easily.

"Thank you," he said. "I would be grateful."

"There, Danwel," said Kethi. "Now make a sling and go help the dragonslayer kill a rabbit."

"I think I'll go dig up some biscuitroot before she starts giving *me* orders," Dawnracer murmured in Chamfo's ear.

"Well, I reckon I can make a sling from the end of this," Dan said, indicating one of the leather straps that held up his leggings. "But I'm not likely to hit anything. I'm pretty good at scaring crows, but I've never killed a rabbit."

"Ah, there is nothing to it," Zhen said. "Hunting rabbits simply requires a keen eye to spot the signs, innate cunning to sneak into the proper position, and blindingly quick reflexes. Of course, I use a spear and not a sling, but the principles are the same, I assure you."

Zhen spotted Dawnracer edging away.

"Ah, dearest sister?"

She gave him a look.

"Since we are teaching the Yolimites how to survive on the open prairie, perhaps you would be so kind as to show Kethi how to identify biscuitroot?"

Dawnracer hid her scowl behind a bland smile. "Why I certainly would, dear brother, had Kethi not already committed herself to giving Shamon a lesson in horse grooming."

"Ah, yes," said Zhen. "I had forgotten. Kethi, I can show Shamon how to take care of his horse while I wait for Dan to make his sling. Feel free to go with Summ—ah, Dawnracer."

From Kethi's face, one would have thought that she was chewing on something bitter, but she said, "Aye, I reckon you're right."

To Dawnracer she said, "If you can teach me what plants out here are good to eat, I would be glad to learn."

Dawnracer was at a loss for words, as though unprepared for sincere humility.

"There," said Zhen, as the two women walked off together. "Did you see how I set them on the path to friendship?"

CHAPTER 12
Hunting

DAWNRACER BRUSHED AND BRAIDED her hair in the mornings. There was nothing wrong with that—Kethwin did, too. But Dawnracer had the audacity to make a show of it.

On the first morning, the savage had plopped herself beside Danwel and braided her black and white hair right in his face. The next morning, Kethwin had made sure to sit on Danwel's left side. Dawnracer had responded by sitting on Danwel's right and giving the loose side of her hair a thousand strokes right by Danwel's ear. Well, this morning Kethwin would not let the Stripedwoman win.

"Let's go sit beside Shamon," she suggested.

The Riverman sat in the grass near the ashes of the previous night's fire, hunched under his gray cloak.

Danwel, who had been moving to sit on the rock on the opposite side, said, "I thought you didn't like sitting on the ground."

"Oh, I won't mind just this once," Kethwin insisted. "Go sit down beside Shamon. He looks so lonely."

Danwel ambled over, exchanged good mornings with Shamon, and sat down beside him—but not quite close enough. It would be just like Dawnracer to try to squeeze herself into the gap between the two men.

Kethwin sat down hard, landing her hip on Danwel's leg.

"Beg pardon," Danwel murmured. To give Kethwin space, he shifted toward Shamon.

There! Let Dawnracer try to sit next to Danwel now!

While Danwel solicited the Riverman's opinion on whether the clouds on the treeless horizon were likely to be bringing rain, Kethwin undid her braids and began brushing her hair. She kept her face calm and serene, taking care not to smirk at the

Stripedwoman who was now pretending to wake up. The yawns and the stretches did not fool Kethwin. She knew Dawnracer had just been waiting to see where Danwel would sit.

The Stripedwoman sauntered over and planted herself in front of them, with her hands on her knees.

"Good morning," Dawnracer sang. "I hope you slept well."

The men mumbled something affirmative. Kethwin continued brushing her hair, masking her contempt.

The woman's designs were so flagrant that Kethwin was almost embarrassed for her. It was obvious that Dawnracer had assumed her unnatural pose solely for the purpose of exaggerating the size of her bosom—an effect achieved by gravity and by her dress's bodice fringes, which she was dangling in front of the men's eyes. Surely Danwel would recognize Dawnracer's pathetic show for what it was.

Well, actually, that wasn't very likely, was it? Danwel was just aware enough to notice the bosom and just oblivious enough to not notice that it was all fringes. Pathetic. Kethwin was a slender girl, but she had just as much for her normal size as Dawnracer had for her giant size. And Kethwin didn't need any fringes to get Danwel's attention. Her boy sat right beside her. If she leaned the right way, she reckoned she could give Danwel a view right down into her dress.

But she shouldn't have to. Danwel was hers. She had more to offer than just what was in her dress. Danwel knew that. So why was this savage making her fight for a man she had already won?

Dawnracer rose from her ridiculous pose and went to sit on the rock opposite them so that she could brush her hair right in the middle of Danwel's view. The woman was insufferable. Still, Kethwin had won. She was beside her boy. Her rival sat far away.

Kethwin braided her green ribbon into her hair, taking care to ensure the ribbon lay smooth, not twisted. Just because she was in the wilderness was no reason to look sloppy.

Opposite her, Dawnracer undid her crude leather braid tie and carefully set it beside her on the rock. Her striped face held a simpering smile as she brushed the black-and-white mane that served as her hair. Kethwin ignored the Stripedwoman and smoothed out her second ribbon. Dawnracer pretended to ignore everyone as she carefully knocked her braid tie off the rock with a casual motion of her hand.

The reason for this game became apparent as soon as Dawnracer had finished her braid. With a feigned look of alarm, she arose from the rock, turned around, and began wiggling her bottom in the air, pretending to look for the braid tie.

Please don't let Danwel be dumb enough to fall for that one, Kethwin thought. But she didn't know any man who could resist the chance to help a woman who didn't really need it.

Kethwin touched Danwel's arm. "Is Tevishi limping?" she asked.

Danwel's head swiveled to look at the bay mare, who was grazing with the other horses a short distance away. His forehead wrinkled with concern. Dawnracer's bottom wiggled some more, but Danwel kept his gaze fixed on Tevishi, waiting for her to take a step.

"Do you think she's favoring that back leg?" Danwel asked.

"Could be," said Kethwin. Actually, Tevishi did favor that leg a bit, preferring to put more weight on the other three. But it didn't affect her health. It was just a habit, like the way people always used the same hand to stir a pot of porridge.

Shamon got up and went to help Dawnracer look for her braid tie. Tevishi took a few steps and grabbed a bite of flowers to complement her meal of grass. Dawnracer's bottom wiggled.

"I wish she'd move a bit more," Danwel said. "I can't tell if she's limping or not."

"Well, she looks fine now," said Kethwin as Shamon's blue fingers handed Dawnracer the braid tie. "Could be she just had her hoof in a low spot."

"Aye," said Danwel. "Could be. I reckon if there's anything wrong, you'll find it when you check her."

"Aye," Kethwin agreed.

Dawnracer came over and sat down beside Danwel. Shamon, unaware of his treachery, sat down next to her.

"Isn't it a beautiful morning?" Dawnracer asked as she began re-braiding her hair in Danwel's face.

"Aye," said Danwel.

"It's so beautiful I can't wait to get moving," Kethwin said. "Come, Danwel. Help me check the horses now so we'll be ready to go when the dragonslayer wakes up."

* * *

Water seeped out of the ground to fill the small rock-lined pool where the Riverman washed his face. The spring brought life to the shrubs clustered around it; Danwel hoped it would help the unfortunate Riverman. Scabs dotted the backs of Shamon's hands, and whenever he pushed back his hood, he revealed his scaly scalp.

"He doesn't look so good," Danwel murmured into Zhen's ear.

Zhen, also speaking in low tones, replied, "It grieves me to admit it, but you are correct. I fear our journey across the prairie is not as pleasant for my friend as I had hoped it would be."

"Well, he's a Riverman," Danwel observed. "Don't they need to spend time in rivers?"

Along the Kailanarl, Shamon had jumped into the river every time they had stopped. Now that they were on the open plains, they got their water from springs, pools, and streams that Zhen led them to. These offered sufficient water for the horses and riders, but they were too small for bathing.

"Perhaps I should have followed the river longer," Zhen acknowledged. "But my band does not frequent the Kailanarl this time of year. We must seek them on the high plains."

"What if we gave Shamon more time to wash?" Danwel suggested.

"Ah! You think he hurries because we are all waiting for him. That is well thought of. Hmm. Yes, I have it."

Zhen walked over to Undersong and untied his spear from the saddle straps. "Please wait for me a moment," he announced. "I believe I saw a rabbit in yonder thicket."

As he strode past Danwel, he murmured, "Thank you. Keep an eye on our friend for me."

Well, that was not quite the way Danwel would have handled it, but perhaps it was best. Telling Shamon to take all the time he needed might have only made him wash faster.

"You could go look for rabbits, too, Danwel," Kethwin told him.

"Yes," agreed Dawnracer. "Come hunt with me, Dan. I am certain I shall bring you better luck than my brother does."

Well now this was a demon's bargain: If he did what his girl had told him to do, he'd get in trouble!

"None of you have any luck," Kethwin observed.

"Yes, Kethi," said Dawnracer. "We are fortunate you came along to forage for us."

Dawnracer did that a lot: She'd say words that sounded nice but meant something else. This time she was pointing out that she did as much foraging as Kethwin and that Kethwin hadn't known what was good to eat out here until Dawnracer had shown her.

"Maybe I should take up foraging," Danwel offered. "I can't hit anything with my sling."

"That's because you don't practice enough," Kethwin said. "You need to start bringing in meat. Yolim knows we can't depend on the dragonslayer. How is he going to hunt a dragon when he can't even kill a rabbit?"

"Well, smaller things are harder to hit," said Danwel. "And anyway, we don't see many rabbits."

"I think the wolves have scared them all into their burrows," said Dawnracer.

Kethwin bit her lip and went pale.

They heard the wolves howling some nights, while Zhen was singing and Shamon was picking his lute. Zhen said the wolves howled because they liked to join the songs. Kethwin said he shouldn't sing those songs, then.

Kethwin hated wolves. She hadn't seen the one that Danwel had killed last summer, but she had seen the milk cow that it had attacked. A bull had run the wolf off, so the cow had been left alive. Kethwin said that was the only beastshaper job that had made her sick up. Her sister could do nothing for the cow except slit its throat.

Most of the wolves around Kwoshim knew enough to stay hidden in the woods, but out here they roamed all over. Kethwin shuddered whenever they heard one. Danwel reckoned this was why Dawnracer liked to mention wolves.

Dawnracer vaulted onto Whitefoot.

"I trust my brother will return shortly," she said. "Tell him I've gone to scout ahead."

"'Gone to scout ahead,'" Kethwin mimicked as Dawnracer loped away. "She's always scouting ahead when there's nothing to see. This whole place is just one big meadow."

Danwel wasn't sure why the Stripedwoman scouted ahead either. He reckoned she just liked loping over the rolling hills.

Kethwin continued: "And then she'll come galloping back with her bouncing—her bouncing horse and tell us all about the meadow on the other side of the hill, and it will be just like this one. We ride and ride through this endless meadow, and we never get anywhere."

Danwel knew what she meant. Aside from the fact that they saw fewer trees every day, these lands had a certain sameness about them.

"Dawnracer said we're getting close to where her band was when she left them," Danwel said. "Could be that's why she's scouting."

Kethwin sniffed. "They have no idea where their band might be. I reckon we crossed the band's trail yesterday."

"Zhen said he was sure that was a different band."

"Oh, how would he know?"

Danwel shrugged. Trampled grass, fire circles, horse droppings—he had no idea what aspect of the recently occupied campsite had marked it as belonging to another band. But Zhen and Dawnracer had both been sure, and they rarely agreed on anything.

"And why are we even looking for their band?" Kethwin wanted to know. "I thought we were supposed to be hunting dragons."

"Well, I reckon Zhen wants to make sure his band is all right first. And could be they know where to find the dragon."

"I don't think those savages know how to find anything," said Kethwin. "They can't even pick a direction. Sometimes we travel moonaway. Sometimes lithward. That's no way to get anywhere.

And when they can't decide where to go, they look for some omen. Yesterday, they rolled dice!"

"Well, that's just their religion, Kethwin. They were asking Lashrefi for guidance."

Kethwin sniffed. "It's stupid."

"They have faith," Danwel said.

"I have faith in Yolim," said Kethwin. "But that doesn't mean I think he gives a cracked egg about me."

Danwel blinked. "But Yolim cares about all his people."

"You're just saying that because you're a Broadfield. In Clan Walker, we know that anything you want, you have to get for yourself. Go help Shamon onto his horse; it looks like he's ready to go."

The Riverman had not taken advantage of his extra time. He was leading his gelding away from the spring, looking for a rock or a mound of turf that might give him the height he needed to climb onto the gelding's back. Danwel reckoned it was Shamon's way of asking for help. The poor man's legs were so stiff and sore that he hadn't been able to mount unassisted since the second day of riding. Danwel went over to give him a boost, thinking, *I just wish he understood that he doesn't have to be in such a hurry.*

* * *

Kisses catch him; cooking keeps him. That was what the women said in Kwoshim. *Well,* thought Kethwin as she surveyed the biscuitroots, parsnips, and wild onions arrayed on the blanket, *this should be enough to keep him. At least for one more night.*

Kethwin bundled up the vegetables and set off toward the campsite and the setting sun. It had taken a lot of work to dig and clean enough food for Danwel and three giants, but Walkers knew how to work. And she would show Danwel that she knew how to cook, too.

She was more practiced boiling food in a cook pot, but she could roast vegetables. She would lay the roots on the rocks of the fire circle and add the onions between them to enhance the flavor. While they were roasting, she would chop the onion tops and use them as a garnish.

She would cook Danwel a meal, and it would be all her work. Dawnracer could take no credit tonight, for she had gone off hunting with her brother, leaving all the foraging to Kethwin. And when the Stripedfolk came back to camp empty-handed—as they always did—Kethwin would serve them the best roasted vegetables they had ever tasted.

In fact, they were already back. From the campsite on the other side of the willow thicket, Zhen began singing against the background of Shamon's lute. It was another of those weepy Clanfolk ballads about a simpering maiden who didn't have enough gumption to go get what she wanted. Zhen knew a lot of those. They were even worse than his Stripedfolk traveling songs, which were filled with nonsense like "haido, daido, dithm". Kethwin wished they would just play lute duets. Whenever Zhen started singing, it was impossible to hold a conversation.

As Kethwin made her way around the willow thicket, she caught a whiff of the campfire smoke … and the aroma of roasting meat. Kethwin's last bite of roasted meat had been at Tholom and Zhoswin's wedding celebration. Her mouth watered even as her heart sank.

Please let Zhen be the one who got the meat, she thought. *Or Danwel. Let it be Danwel with his sling.*

She pushed her way through the tall grass to see not one, but two rabbits roasting on a spit over the fire. Rising above them was Danwel's broad grin.

"Look, Kethwin! Dawnracer got meat!"

CHAPTER 13
Beef

"THAT WOMAN IS INSUFFERABLE."

Chamfo gave no reply, but Zhen's sister did not require one. When she was complaining about Kethi, she could handle the conversation all by herself. Perhaps that was why she liked complaining to Chamfo: The aches in his joints, the burning of his skin, and the dizziness in his head left him with no energy for talking back—especially not while they were riding.

"She complains all the time," said Dawnracer.

This was an exaggeration. Kethi complained more than the rest of them, but no one could complain all the time.

"And she treats Dan as though he were a lodge horse."

"What is a lodge horse?" Chamfo asked.

"I mean she always tells him what to do and never says anything nice to him."

Chamfo believed it was more complex than that. On the night Dawnracer became the first hunter to bring in meat, Kethi had found fault with everything Dan did. But the next day, when Dan had killed a rabbit during the midday water stop, Kethi had been quick to praise him. She gave Dan commands without including a "please" or a "thank you", but Dan never remarked on this. Apparently, that was how he expected to be treated.

Chamfo did not feel up to the task of expressing these thoughts in the second language. It was just as well. Dawnracer was not actually soliciting his opinion on the matter.

"Summerwind, come look at this," Zhen called.

Dawnracer gave Chamfo a sad smile. "Thank you for listening," she said.

She did something with her hands or her legs that made her horse run ahead to catch up to Zhen. In an attempt to keep up,

Chamfo's horse began bouncing its spine into Chamfo's sore rump. After three bounces, it gave up and resumed its usual plod. They always caught up eventually.

Zhen had discovered trail signs that even Chamfo could read: bovine droppings. *The Mud Mother* had once contracted to move some of Clan Fairweather's bovines along the river, and Chamfo had taken the job of removing the excrement. He knew it well.

"We have found the trail of a herd of bison," Zhen explained.

"You mean wildcows?" asked Dan.

"Is that what you call them in Kweshil?" asked Zhen.

"Kwoshim," said Kethi.

"It seems they travel in the same direction we do," observed Dawnracer.

"Their trail leads lithward," said Kethi. "I thought you had decided to travel moonaway."

Dawnracer gave Chamfo a heartfelt look: Kethi was complaining again.

Zhen said, "Lithward and moonaway are the same for our purposes, dear Kethwin." He had begun calling Dan and Kethi by their familiar names—to improve camaraderie, no doubt. That was his way. Zhen liked everyone, and he expected everyone to like each other. Chamfo could not be so optimistic.

"Let us follow their trail and see where it leads," Zhen suggested. "I feel this is a sign from Lashrefi."

The others pointed their horses in the new direction and Chamfo's horse plodded along behind. Chamfo had no idea what made them certain they were following the bison instead of backtracking to where the bison had been. They all seemed to be in agreement, however, so he assumed they were right. And they were. They caught up to the herd shortly after midday. Eighty wooly-headed bovines were grazing on the spring grass in a shallow valley between two ridges of rolling hills.

"We dine on beef tonight," Zhen said.

"How will you sneak up on them?" Dan asked, for the nearest trees were on the other side of the herd.

Zhen looked at Dawnracer. "I think they will come to us. Do you not agree, dear sister?"

Dawnracer studied Dan and Kethi appraisingly.

"It is truly worth a chance, dear brother."

Zhen explained that he and Dawnracer would ride back down behind the ridge until they were hidden from the bovines' view. Then they would follow the contour of the land to put themselves at the top of the shallow valley. "All you have to do is get them moving."

"You" referred to Chamfo, Dan, and Kethi—or rather, to their horses.

"We should be able to do that," agreed Dan.

"Shamon?" Zhen inquired.

Chamfo nodded to indicate that he understood the plan. He doubted that he had the ability to make the bovines move in the right direction, but he did not think that Dan expected much help from him.

"Do not delay," Zhen called over his shoulder as he and Dawnracer turned to ride off. "We will certainly be in position in time."

Dan looked at Chamfo. "Animals want to stay with the herd," he explained. "That is why your gelding always trots to catch up whenever you fall behind."

Chamfo gave a mental wince at the thought of the bouncing gait known as "the trot".

"Those wildcows should react the same way," Dan continued. "All we have to do is convince those in the rear that they are falling behind. Once they start moving, we can move the ones in front, until they are all walking. They should keep going until—well, until they realize that they don't have a yard to go home to. That should work, shouldn't it, Kethwin?"

"It could," said Kethi. "I've never herded cows on horseback before."

"Well, it can't be that hard," said Dan. "Otherwise Zhen wouldn't have left us to do it."

They advanced on the herd cautiously—perhaps a little too cautiously, for Chamfo's horse thought the pace was slow enough that it should be allowed to graze.

"Use your reins to keep his head up," Dan said.

Chamfo knew this was what he was supposed to do, but he also knew that if he fought the horse too much it would just stand there and refuse to move at all. He had to be satisfied with a horse that shuffled in the same general direction as the others while it grazed.

The bovines' shaggy winter coats were only half shed, giving them a scraggly appearance. The beasts hardly seemed to notice the riders, so intent were they on grazing the fresh grass.

Chamfo's horse kept moving, but only because it was following Dan's horse. They were getting quite close to the herd now—close enough that Chamfo could see the sharp horns on their shaggy heads.

Rushes and sedges grew in a low spot in the middle of the plain. Chamfo could hear frogs singing. Dan's horse squished through this marshy ground and sank in deep enough to cover its white hind stocking.

Apparently, Chamfo's horse had been too busy grazing to notice any of this, for when it began its trot to catch up again, the soft ground took it by surprise. It stumbled and snorted and tossed its head, stutter-stepping sideways to keep its balance on the soft ground. To stay on, Chamfo grabbed its mane with both hands.

By the time the horse was back under control (its own control—Chamfo certainly did not control it) they had the herd's attention. Shaggy heads were raised to stare at the horses. One bovine took a cautious step back. Another shook its head in a manner which did not seem at all friendly.

"We should let her be," Kethi warned. "She won't like it if we get too near her calf."

"Aye," said Dan. "Let's try to move this bunch over here. Shamon already has them started for us."

Indeed, a few of the beasts were grudgingly ambling away from the horses. Focusing on them seemed reasonable. It should not matter if some bovines were left behind. Zhen was not planning to eat the entire herd.

Riding along behind the strolling bovines, they put some distance between themselves and the bunch with the unfriendly mother. She continued to watch them with a suspicious eye. In a short time, their chosen bunch caught up with the main herd. The bovines dropped their heads to graze once more. So did Chamfo's horse.

"Now what, Danwel?" Kethi asked. "Should we move closer?" She did not seem to like the idea.

"I reckon we ought to try shouting at them," Dan replied. "Ho, cow! Ho, cow!"

Several of the beasts looked up. They did not seem inclined to move. Chamfo was not certain this was a bad thing: He preferred immobile bovines to charging bovines.

"Shout with us," Kethi encouraged him. She, too, began singing, "Ho, cow! Ho, cow! Hya! Hya!"

Chamfo's heart held no enthusiasm for shouting. He had an uneasy feeling, as though something awful were about to happen.

He looked back at the protective mother, who seemed alert to these calls. She was threatening, but she was distant. The danger that Chamfo sensed was getting nearer.

A storm was coming, and yet the sky held no storm clouds. He had felt such a thing only once before.

Icy dread gripped Chamfo's heart. He wanted to dive to safety, but there was no river to dive into.

"Dan," he said. "Dan, we need to—"

To hide or to flee?

"Oho!" shouted Dan. "Now they are moving! Ho, cow! Hya! Hya! Hyuh?"

A flash of purple lightning streaked over their heads and exploded in a ball of sound. The sky tilted at a crazy angle, and Chamfo opened his eyes to find himself lying in the grass looking up at the clouds. Two more explosions punctuated the thunder of hooves, and then a twisting form passed overhead and spiraled up into the air. It climbed until it appeared to be a tiny thing, like a winged garter snake or newt in the sky. Then it coiled around itself and plummeted toward its target with astonishing speed.

The dragon hunters had found their dragon.

CHAPTER 14

The Sky Dragon

"OHO!" shouted Danwel. "Now they are moving! Ho, cow! Hya! Hya! Hyuh?"

A flash of purple lightning streaked overhead and struck the ground with a boom. Tevishi jumped sideways, leaving Kethwin sitting in the air where the horse and saddle had been. Danwel pulled Kethwin back onto the saddle, holding himself in place with his other hand.

Tevishi bunched herself and galloped after the fleeing wildcows. Shamon's riderless horse had already decided to do the same. It galloped ahead of them with Shamon's open trunk banging against its rump and spraying brinnacs into the air.

Kethwin still held Tevishi's reins.

"Catch the gelding!" shouted Danwel. "I'll get Shamon."

As he spoke the last syllables, he was already leaping from the saddle. He landed well clear of Tevishi's hooves and rolled along the ground. Clambering to his feet, he saw Shamon's clothing billowing in the wind. Danwel ran toward the fallen Riverman.

The group of wildcows with the protective mother was also running toward Shamon's body, but from the opposite direction: Danwel and Shamon were between them and their fleeing herd. Danwel raced toward them, hoping to get to Shamon first. If tame cattle could smash a fence to splinters, what would wild cattle do to a man lying in their path?

A flash of lightning exploded beyond Shamon, causing the wildcows to scatter. Another flash shot overhead to explode somewhere behind Danwel. Not near Kethwin, he hoped.

Searching the sky for the source of these supernatural terrors, Danwel saw a giant snake soaring on two pairs of glowing purple wings. It flew over the approaching herd, splitting them into two bunches. Danwel was too slow to reach the Riverman. Whether the cattle went around Shamon or over top of him, Danwel could not tell.

The serpent writhed and twisted its way up into the sky. Danwel tore his gaze away. A dozen wildcows were stampeding toward him. He veered out of their path. Bawling beasts thundered past.

A straggling yearling bull galloped toward him with flashing hooves and tossing head. Danwel prepared to spring. Surely the beast would see him, but which way would it spook? Danwel wanted to jump away from it, not into its path.

He could have jumped either way, for when the yearling saw him, it decided to jump over. Danwel dove under its legs.

He sat up in the bright green grass and turned to watch the yearling gallop away. With a flash of blue scales, the plummeting dragon slammed the yearling's head into the ground. Bones crunched as momentum carried the yearling's body over its head. The body struck the earth and lay still.

The dragon's tail lashed around the lifeless young bull. The two were roughly the same size, although the comparison was difficult to make because of the dragon's serpentine shape. Danwel had been expecting something larger.

The monster grasped its prey in the talons of its two short legs. Striking with its spade-shaped head, it ripped a wound in the yearling's neck. Its sharp-toothed mouth gaped wide to drink the flowing blood.

A gray hand grasped Danwel's and pulled him to his feet.

"Come!" Shamon told him.

Danwel was still trying to catch his breath, but next to the feeding monster was no place to do so. He ran after Shamon, struggling to keep up with the long strides of the Riverman's sandaled feet.

Shamon stopped at the low, marshy spot in the middle of the meadow. When Danwel caught up, Shamon grabbed him by the shoulders and threw him down into the mud.

Danwel lay there gasping as water seeped into his clothing. Lying beside him, Shamon indicated that he should stay down. The Riverman's behavior was mystifying, but Danwel did not have enough breath to protest.

Then he heard it: a deep roar that grew louder than his haggard breaths. He tried to raise himself up to see what was making the sound, but Shamon pushed him back down, shouting something that Danwel could not hear.

A breeze blew across his fuzzy scalp, and then the noise diminished, as though traveling away.

Shamon sat up. "Can you run more?" he asked.

Danwel nodded.

"Then run more," said Shamon.

Danwel rose to his feet and began slogging through the soggy turf. A twisting cone of wind traveled away, visible only because of the muddy water that it scooped up and carried high into the air.

"There may be another," Shamon told him. "Keep moving."

Once they were out of the marshy spot, the going was easier. Danwel did not have enough breath for another sprint, but Shamon kept him jogging up the slope, back toward the place where Zhen and Dawnracer had left them.

Before they got even halfway, they heard the sound of galloping hooves.

* * *

"Catch the gelding," shouted Danwel. "I'll get Shamon."

And then he was gone, leaving Kethwin alone on a panicked horse.

A second blast struck somewhere behind her. Another flash exploded among the stampeding wildcows on her left. Why were thunder and lightning coming down from a blue sky? And why were the lightning flashes purple?

Dread grasped Kethwin's heart. Dawnracer had said a swath of mature oak trees had been knocked down by a supernatural storm that left them with glowing purple leaves. *Could be this is Dawnracer's dragon*, Kethwin realized.

Kethwin didn't want to face that terror again, but she had to know where the dragon was. She opened her senses, sick at the thought of what she might find.

Tevishi was in a panic that resonated with the alarm of the

stampeding wildcows. As Kethwin had suspected, the animals were propelled by a terror like that which had caused her uncle's herd to break out and run to Ashturn. But she sensed no dragon.

Yes, she was riding a runaway horse. Yes, the air was filled with the bellowing of terrified wildcows and the rumble of their hooves. But there was no overwhelming crush of animal purpose pouring into their fears. They were just running from bright lights and loud noises.

If there was no dragon, if it was just a freak lightning storm, then Kethwin needed to focus on calming the horse. The reins were useless. They were designed to communicate subtle movements of the rider's hands to the horse's ears, but Tevishi was in no mood to pay attention to Kethwin's commands.

The mare was gaining on Shamon's gelding. His mouth reins were actually a single cord that was now flopping about his mane. If she could grasp the cord where it sagged under his jaw ...

Tevishi overtook the gelding. Kethwin stretched out her arm. She got it!

Now she had the reins of two horses she couldn't control. But these weren't wild predators intent on gobbling her up. These were gentle Clanfolk horses that she worked on every day. She might not be a full beastshaper, but she knew how to calm frightened animals.

"Easy, Tevishi. Easy, gelding. Easy."

Tevishi's gait relaxed a bit. Kethwin could sense a part of the mare that wanted to be a good horse and overcome her fear.

"That's it, Tevishi. Easy does it, old girl."

With a gentle motion of the ear rein, Kethwin suggested that Tevishi turn away from the gelding. Because Kethwin still held the gelding's rein, he followed. Kethwin guided the horses around a wide circle and headed them back toward Danwel.

And that was when Kethwin saw the dragon.

Tevishi put on a burst of speed, racing toward Danwel and the cloaked Riverman. The glowing indigo serpent whipped its head around to stare at Kethwin and the horses. It was small, Kethwin realized—bigger than most animals, but much smaller than the dragon she knew. It did not resonate with her emotions. All she could sense was the horses' desire to keep away from it and her own desire to catch up to Danwel.

The horses were tiring, but compared to them, Danwel was hardly moving. Kethwin convinced Tevishi to come to a stop beside the men. Shamon's gelding rolled his eyes and tossed his head, but Kethwin did not let the gelding jerk the rein from her hand.

"Easy, gelding," she said. "You need your rider."

Danwel gave Shamon a boost onto the gelding. The horse was dancing so much that the Riverman nearly fell, but he managed to get himself astride.

With reins in each hand, Kethwin could not loosen the saddle ladder. Danwel chose not to waste time with it. Using the breastgirth for a handhold and then a foothold, he clambered up onto the saddle and sat down behind Kethwin.

She gave the gelding's reins to Danwel, then urged Tevishi into a trot. The gelding pranced nervously alongside.

Shamon held up his thumb and pointed back at the dragon.

Kethwin looked over her shoulder. Amid silent flashes of lightning, a whirlwind moved away from the dragon and stalked up the slope toward them.

Danwel whistled. This was the signal for Tevishi to break into a lope, which she willingly did. The gelding tossed its head in protest, but it did not want to be left behind, so it began loping as well.

Did the horses still have enough strength to outrun that whirlwind? The old mare needed a rest. Kethwin could tell she was willing to gallop herself to death.

The gelding was struggling to keep up. He wanted to stop. If Danwel lost the rein, it could mean death for the Riverman.

Shamon was riding with his eyes closed, and yet he seemed to be concentrating. He raised his fist.

Kethwin realized she knew what he meant. With a flick of the reins, she sent Tevishi sideways into the gelding. There was a floating sensation in Kethwin's stomach as the mare stumbled. Then Tevishi righted herself and brought the saddle back up under her riders.

Cut off by the mare, Shamon's gelding fell behind for a moment, but Danwel held on to the reins, encouraging the horse to keep up. Instead of fleeing over the hill, they were now running along the contour.

The whirlwind passed right through the spot where Shamon had told them to change direction.

Kethwin pulled Tevishi back to a trot, and then a walk. They watched the deadly wind disappear over the gentle curve of the hill.

"Good thing you turned the horse," Danwel said.

Kethwin nodded. "Good thing I learned Riverfolk boat signals."

* * *

Zhen and Summerwind had the bison's hide peeled off by the time their companions rejoined them. Zhen was proud of himself for working so quickly, but he was glad that help had arrived. He stood up from the butchering and waved a bloody hand at the approaching riders.

"Shamon, I wish you could have seen it," he said. "One spear precisely between the ribs. I've never seen a cleaner kill in all my years of hunting."

Puffed-up robin-chest, his sister observed.

"Of course," Zhen added, "it would not have been possible had my sister not slowed the beast with an expert thrust to its leg."

I can be generous, he told her.

Summerwind chuckled.

"You also performed your part well," Zhen continued. "Your use of thunder was quite effective."

In truth, the herd had been moving too rapidly, but it had been Shamon's first bison hunt, and Zhen did not want to criticize.

Kethwin was incredulous. "You think Shamon made the thunder?"

"Yes, Kethwin. Did you not know that I have been teaching our friend how to manipulate sound?"

"But Zhen," said Shamon, "I did not make that thunder."

"Then who did?" asked Zhen.

"That," said Kethwin, pointing to the sky.

Zhen could have mistaken it for one bird harrying another, but between the large wings and the smaller wings, it had a pair of legs.

Connecting these limbs was a snake-like body that ran from a triangular head to a thrashing tail. It was the dragon from his dream.

"It makes its own wind," Shamon commented as the dragon spiraled into the sky. "Its wings do not need the air of our world to fly."

"Shamon, may I suggest that you be cryptic at another time?" Summerwind requested.

"Oh he will," Zhen assured her. "Do not worry about him wasting cryptic comments. He has plenty."

"As you have plenty of mouse-brained comments, dear brother. Still, this is a poor time for either."

"Ah, but neither of us can match your repertoire of insulting comments, dear sister."

"Will you just stand there and argue?" asked Kethwin. "Or will you tell us what you plan to do about *that?*"

"Why, nothing for the moment," Zhen said. "It appears to be leaving us."

Indeed, the dragon had stopped spiraling upward and was now undulating through the sky toward the lith. All of them watched it fly away.

When it could be seen no more, Kethwin asked, "Well, where do we go from here?"

Zhen noted the gelding's bare back. "Did you lose my blankets and your chest, Shamon?"

"Yes."

"Then the first thing we should do is look for them," Zhen decided.

"You simply wish an excuse to avoid the work of butchering," said Summerwind.

"I know a bit about butchering," said Danwel. "I can help."

Kethwin's eyes flashed at him, but with her words she agreed: "Yes, Zhen can go. Danwel and I will stay here and help with the meat."

Summerwind smirked, but said nothing.

"We are looking for a chest of coins in the middle of a vast prairie," Zhen said. "Yolimites have an eye for such things. I think

Danwel should come with us. Kethwin can help you, dear sister."

Kethwin scowled. Summerwind showed her teeth in a feigned smile and thought, *I'll not forgive you this*.

Be kind, Zhen replied, wiping his hands on the soft spring grass.

Zhen mounted Undersong and led the men back to inspect the site of the dragon's appearance.

"Was that wise?" Shamon asked once they had some distance between them and the women.

"Was what wise?" asked Zhen.

"Dawnracer and Kethi do not like each other," said Shamon.

"Nonsense," said Zhen. "They just need a chance to get to know each other."

CHAPTER 15

Getting to Know Each Other

SUMMERWIND COULD NOT COMPLAIN about Kethi's competence at butchering. Yolimites knew how to use their knives.

Nor could she complain about Kethi's work ethic. The tiny thing could work like a beaver.

Regarding Kethi's other qualities, however, Summerwind had no shortage of complaints. The woman was rude, pushy, arrogant, ignorant, recalcitrant, and generally unpleasant. This list was just a beginning, but it amused Summerwind to make it. The rhythm of the words pleased her.

Whereas nothing pleased Kethi. Unpleasant and unpleaseable.

Many times along their journey, Summerwind had longed to tell Kethi what she thought of her. Always, she had restrained herself. Because she was good at getting along with others.

Whereas Kethi was not. Kethi was bossy—always telling them how to ride and when to stop—as though a person needed special senses to know how to take care of a horse.

Kethi was always looking for problems. She took great pains to point out other people's faults.

Summerwind did not do that. Except with Zephyr's faults, of course, but that did not count, for he was her brother. Kethi was related to none of them, not even to Dan—yet. Not even to Dan, whom she called "Danwel" in that squeaky sparrow-voice of hers.

Squeaky, shrieky, cheeky. Another pleasing list.

But Summerwind was too polite, too thoughtful, too sensitive to the feelings of others to say anything like this to Kethi.

At least, she would have been, had Kethi not said, "Don't cut it there; you'll ruin the roast."

What, pray tell, was "the roast"?

Summerwind reminded herself that she was a reasonable

person. And reasonable people do not stab someone in retribution for the crime of giving random, bossy orders. Reasonable people attempt to reason:

"If I do not cut here, the meat will stay attached to the bone."

"Aye," Kethi agreed, using that ignorant ejaculation that Yolimites took for an affirmative. Dan used it too, of course, but he said it slowly, almost with a drawl, turning it into a pleasing sound. Whereas Kethi's words were always as sharp as her knife.

Summerwind went back to her task of removing the bloody meat from the bone.

"Don't cut it there!" repeated Kethi. "Are you daft?"

It was said to be a custom among the red-skinned Kashramites to answer insults with a contest of knives. This idea had always struck Summerwind as chilling, barbaric, and strangely romantic. Now she saw that it had a practical side as well.

But she reminded herself that hers was a joyful, musical, thoughtful, enlightened people. Her people did not murder—not even when the victim might deserve it. Yet such brutality was something Kethi should be expecting, for when she spoke to Dan and thought no one else could hear, she often referred to Summerwind and Zephyr as "savages".

But no. Summerwind was a Lashrefite, descended from the goddess who had invented language. Her people had other ways to duel.

"Truly, Kethi, I am not 'daft'," she answered. "I am cutting the meat away so that we may cure it and take it with us. I truly was not aware that you would rather gnaw raw meat off the bone."

Kethi gave her a green-eyed squint, like a Yellowmonth rock lizard. "Don't be revolting," she said flatly. "And don't play with me. I'm not your brother. If you don't know how to cut a roast, then get out of the way and let me do it … and, uh, bring me a bonesaw."

So Kethi knew how to make a "roast" with a "bonesaw"? Well, for whom did she think she was showing off? The dead buffalo?

"Fetch your own bonesaw," said Summerwind. In addition to being appropriate, it was a clever way to avoid admitting that she did not know what a bonesaw was.

"Don't tell me that you survive by butchering meat but don't even carry a bonesaw," said Kethi. "How about a cleaver? Do you have a cleaver?"

A what? Coming from anyone else, Summerwind would have suspected it was a nonsense word invented to make her look foolish, but Kethi, although never shy about making someone look foolish, was as easy to read as a waddling baby. She was incapable of subterfuge—and probably incapable of the creativity required to invent words.

"No roasts, no bonesaws, and no clay-veers," snapped Summerwind. "Yet even so, we have managed to survive on this prairie for hundreds of years. If your people did not spend so much time worrying about how to cut your meat, perhaps you would have learned a few songs to sing after supper."

Even as she finished the sentence, Summerwind was impressed by her own brilliance. She had accomplished a complete reversal of positions by moving to the topic of music, about which Kethi was as ignorant as a toad.

"And if your brother would spend more time practicing with his spear and less time practicing with his lute, perhaps we would be rid of your puny dragon by now."

"There is nothing puny about that dragon!" exclaimed Summerwind. "Have you seen what it can do to trees?"

"Ours is bigger," said Kethi.

"You have never seen it."

"But I have seen yours, up close. It is no bigger than a yearling. Ours swallowed a whole ox."

Summerwind had no idea how big the dragon was. Distant objects in the sky could be any size. But a creature the size of a yearling could not have blown down all those trees.

"If it was so puny, why did you not kill it when you had the chance? You say you were close enough."

Kethi shivered and shook her head. "I do not claim to be the dragonslayer," she said. "Your brother does. Although if we had slain it, I am sure your brother would have been relieved."

"And what does that mean?"

"He's afraid," said Kethi.

"He is not!" said Summerwind. Zephyr was only slightly afraid. And besides, Kethi was the one quaking in fear.

"He's afraid to fight the dragon because he's afraid we'll find out he was lying," said Kethi.

The Yolimite had hit the mark there. "How did you— Why do you think he is lying?" demanded Summerwind.

"Because even though your brother is a bigger show-off than you are, he has never sung us his famous dragon-slaying song."

That was a keen observation. Zephyr had mentioned dragons and dragonslaying very little after that first day. He pretended to have complete faith in his ability to slay the monster, so he acted as though defeating the dragon were a foregone conclusion that did not need to be discussed.

Summerwind was not certain what Zephyr's plan was—or even if he had one. Her brother seemed to be focused on finding Lowsinger's Band. Possibly he wished to consult the taishrefi about his dream, or possibly he wished to give a great speech in which he claimed to have been sent by Lashrefi to deliver them from this terror. The former possibility was wiser, which meant that the latter was more likely.

It amused Summerwind to think of the entire band laughing at her brother. But that was something for her own people to share. She did not want these strangers laughing at him, for in laughing at him, they laughed at her as well.

"If the dragon is as puny as you say, then truly no one should be afraid of anything, for my brother and I could kill it as easily as we killed this bison."

"The dragon can kill, too," said Kethi. "When your brother sees what it did to the wildcow, he'll be even more scared."

"Wolves can also kill a bison," said Summerwind. "Yet we are their masters. Certainly we can master this dragon."

"This is the second time you say 'we'," observed Kethi, in her abrupt, clipped voice. "Do you really plan on helping?"

"Truly I have helped him hunt all along our journey," said Summerwind. "Dragon hunting shall be no different."

"Well, I am surely glad to hear that," said Kethi. "But do not expect the rest of us to do your job for you next time."

"Whether you help or not, Kethi, is truly up to you. My brother did not ask you to ride with us. I much doubt that the men would mind if you should choose to desert us now."

Kethi's eyes narrowed until they were slits. "Do not mistake Danwel for one of your men," she replied. "He may have the size of a giant and twice the courage, but he is surely mine."

"Ah, but how 'surely', dear Kethi? You must ask yourself that."

"You do not tempt him," Kethi sneered. "No matter how much you shake your bosom fringes in his face."

"My bosom fr—?" That attack took Summerwind by surprise, but she recovered quickly: "Truly I do have more to shake in his face than you. But I have something else to offer him as well."

"He does not want what you have to offer." Kethi's voice shook.

"He wants what all men want," said Summerwind. "Curving hips and pleasant lips. You just keep spitting out your poison on him as you do on the rest of us, and soon I won't have to shake anything to convince him to leave you."

"Don't you ever tell me how to talk to my boy," said Kethi, but her words were full of breath, and her bloody knife rested limply in her lap.

"Dan is not your possession!" yelled Summerwind. "Why does he submit to your bonds when you treat him so badly? You are the most unpleasant vixen I have ever met. That man deserves so much better."

Kethi looked as though she would cry. Summerwind did not want to see it. And she was about to cry herself.

Summerwind stood up.

"I must go find wood for smoking the meat," she said. "Do not let the wolves eat you."

She turned her back on Kethi and walked away.

CHAPTER 16
Coming Home

"I KNOW THAT you have trouble getting along with Kethwin, but it was beyond cruel to abandon her when wolves could be nearby." This was the rebuke that Zhen had prepared for his sister as a prelude to dictating the terms of her punishment. When he saw her face, however, he decided to leave the words unspoken.

Summerwind had a stripe that ran across both her lips. When the two halves of the stripe did not line up, it meant that she was holding her lips tight to keep them from quivering. Anything he said could cause her to burst into tears. Danwel had been unable to extract the story from the weeping Kethwin, and Zhen could see that he would get nowhere with his sister, either.

It was possible that the women would get over it. It was more probable that they would hate each other forever. It seemed like the type of quarrel that would cause a girl to marry into a different band.

As Summerwind built the smokefire, she did not look at Kethwin, who was sitting a short distance away, in Danwel's arms. From the way his sister was not looking at them, Zhen guessed that this was most of the trouble—not so much Kethwin, but rather the embrace that she could claim.

It was ridiculous. Had his sister not been in such pain, Zhen could have laughed. Danwel was a fine specimen of manhood, truly, but only in miniature. He was a Yolimite. No one ever married *that* far out.

Zhen had thought it was a game. He had thought that Summerwind had simply found a childish way to annoy him. But now he realized that when Danwel had confronted the Brinnen guardsmen, Summerwind had been smitten. It was truly lucky that Danwel already had "a girl", for had things been otherwise, who knew what sort of heartache Summerwind could have caused herself?

A consoling word right now would just make her cry. A consoling thought would be shut out. So Zhen did what any good kalaibo would have done: He picked up his lute.

"The Battle of Yucca Hill" seemed like a good choice. War ballads were usually sung only at the tribal gatherings. Summerwind did not know it well, so she would pay attention to the words and forget her troubles. Also, it had a part in the second chorus where Zhen drummed his fingers on the body of the lute to mimic the sound of galloping hooves. It was a dramatic effect. Shamon would be interested in the technique.

Like all war ballads, it included a list of the slain. Fourteen had fallen in the battle of Yucca Hill, which made it too long for a casual mid-afternoon song and too short for an evening epic. This meant that even at the gatherings it did not always get sung, which was unfortunate because Zhen liked the refrain: "His bones lie in the knives of the yucca!" Five of the fourteen refrains were "her bones", which made the song especially poignant.

The musical interlude had the soothing effect that Zhen desired. By the time he had finished, Danwel and Kethwin had brought Tevishi over so they could listen to the song while brushing the horse. Summerwind had the smokefire going and was slicing off strips of meat. Shamon had not only learned the melody, but had also invented an off-beat counterpoint which carried the idea of galloping hooves from the second chorus back into the verses.

Shamon was truly a marvel. Zhen resolved to learn that counterpoint at the first opportunity.

"What are 'the knives of the yucca'?" Danwel asked once the notes had died away.

"Leaves of a plant that grows in arid country," Zhen explained. "Yucca Hill is far lithward from here."

"Our tribe does not range there," elaborated Summerwind.

"Then who were those people leaving bones there?" Danwel asked.

"Ah, that was long ago," said Zhen. "All our tribes were in the war against the red-skinned Kashramites, because they kept crossing the Kailanarl to hunt our bison."

"Oh," said Danwel. "I thought it might be about the Timber War."

"Zhen's people did not fight in the Timber War," Shamon reminded him. "Those were other people."

"Aye, so you have said," acknowledged Danwel.

"We Flamebringers only have one war to remember," said Zhen.

"Sounds like you remember it well," said Danwel. "Beg pardon, Shamon?"

"I said, 'Some things are best left forgotten,'" Shamon admitted. "I apologize for speaking my own language, but I was only saying it for myself."

"Oh, no apologies," Zhen insisted. He had the women somewhat cheered up now. He did not need to have his partner slide into melancholy—further into melancholy. "Say, Shamon, why don't you sing us one of your songs? We will not even make you translate."

This brought a little light into Shamon's gray face. He began plinking out a melody in five-tone, to which he soon added his voice, warbling in the traditional Zharnovite style.

The melody was simple enough. Zhen picked it up at once. It was hard to play a wrong note in five-tone.

"What was that?" Danwel asked, when they had finished.

"The name means 'Let Justice Guide Me.' Or 'Let Zharnov Guide Me.' They are the same word in my language."

"I suppose all people seek guidance from their god," Danwel observed.

"My people do not see Zharnov as our only deity," Shamon replied. "We serve them all. When deciding what cargo to carry, we ask Yolim. When seeking knowledge, we ask Thafarsi. When the current is swift and the waters hold hidden snags, we pray to Lashrefi. But when we wish to know right from wrong, we let Zharnov be our guide."

"Play us another one," Zhen suggested.

They managed to sing through the evening without anyone

bursting into tears again. The girls were silent, however. Zhen feared that the next day would be a long one.

As he lay in the grass under the stars, wrapped in his Brinnen cloak, Zhen considered whether he would rather fight the dragon or spend the day with quarreling women. Neither seemed enjoyable, and he might have to do both. Having only the one deity, he prayed for Lashrefi to guide him.

Strangely enough, she did.

Danwel was the first one up the next morning, but his cry of "Hey!" wakened the rest of them while the sunward sky was still orange. The Yolimite had already fitted a stone into his sling by the time Zhen was awake enough to understand what the trouble was.

"No!" Zhen called. "That is a sacred bird!"

Danwel frowned at him. "Surely it is a common crow," he said. But he lowered his sling.

"In your wheat field it may be a common crow," Zhen told him. "Out here, it is a messenger from Lashrefi."

"Your messenger is eating our meat," Danwel observed.

"Ah, Dan, we have already smoked what we need," Summerwind pleaded. "Let the crows have their share."

"Well, I surely do not understand this," said Danwel, but he put his sling away.

"When we die, the crows carry our souls to Heaven," Zhen explained. "If Lashrefi has chosen to take in the soul of this bison, it is a great boon for us. She is blessing our meat."

Kethwin fixed him with her sleepy, skeptical eyes, but she said nothing. Perhaps the women's quarrel had some advantages.

The Yolimites killed crows, if they could. Shamon had once explained to Zhen that one seed eaten in spring was like ten eaten in autumn, but Zhen thought this was a poor justification. They had enough grain to share.

The crow gave a caw and flapped a short distance away to perch on the Yolimites' saddle. It cocked its head at them.

"It wishes to lead us somewhere!" Zhen exclaimed. "Let us mount at once!"

"And I thought I had heard everything," Kethwin murmured.

The bird took wing then, making a circle before heading

moonaway. Zhen knew he must follow, but the horses had wandered some distance in the night. Mounting at once was impossible. All the party could do was watch until the crow disappeared over the next hill.

"We will ride moonaway," Zhen told them. "Lashrefi has spoken."

Summerwind opened her mouth to remind him that they had already decided to ride moonaway.

"Be silent!" he commanded. "Lashrefi has spoken."

It took them some time to get moving. Zhen had to bring in both Undersong and Whitefoot himself because, instead of helping him, Summerwind was moping and braiding the loose side of her hair.

Danwel figured out a way to wrap the smoked meat in the blankets so that it could be carried by Shamon's gelding. Kethwin scowled as Danwel bundled the meat, observing, "Those blankets aren't very clean." People who lived on rivers had strange ideas about what made things clean.

"I just hope everything stays on," said Danwel. "I don't want to have to hunt through the grass for Shamon's brinnacs again."

The lid of Shamon's chest had popped open and spilled its contents all over the prairie when his panicked gelding had fled from the dragon. The three men had spent a considerable time collecting his treasure, with Danwel keeping a careful count. The Yolimite had been willing to keep looking until they found every last coin, but Shamon—to Danwel's surprise—had not known exactly how much money the chest had held. Now that Danwel had a precise count, it was important that the same accident not happen again. Yolimites would kill crows and they would leave to go urinate during the middle of a song, but money was sacred.

The ropes did hold, although their pace did not give Danwel's knots much of a test. They kept their horses to a walk. Even Summerwind did not lope ahead to scout, as she usually did.

Zhen, of course, was avoiding a trot out of consideration for his friend, Shamon, who truly was sore in the saddle these days. His choice of pace had nothing to do with the fact that the dragon could be somewhere ahead of them.

"We should go more lithward," Kethwin said, finally.

"The crow flew moonaway," Zhen explained.

"But the dragon flew lithward," Kethwin insisted. "Are we hunting dragons or crows?"

Zhen was hunting for his band. And now that he was back in their range, he was not so certain he wanted to find them. He admitted to himself that this might be the true reason he rode so slowly.

"We hunt dragons," he said. "But we follow the crow, for I have never slain a dragon without Lashrefi's guidance." Aha! That was even true!

"Brother, I believe I see a flock of crows."

"It is so!" cried Zhen. "Crows rise from the direction toward which we travel. The Goddess has shown us the way, Kethwin."

The girl said nothing, but her face looked worried, as though Lashrefi's revelations had finally broken the mask of her skepticism.

O, Lashrefi, great is your power! Zhen thought. Then, remembering how great also was Lashrefi's sense of humor, he added, *Please let something be there.*

The wanderers only needed to climb one more rise before they could look down on a plain and see that, indeed, they had found Lowsinger's Band. Colorful, conical lodges were set up by Spring Creek.

Zhen's eye was drawn to his mother's lodge—yellow, with a leaping black horse. Would she be glad to see him? What would she say? Now that he was about to find out, he was not certain he wanted to.

He wanted to pause on the ridgeline, to give himself a moment to prepare to meet his band, but the horses began exchanging whinnies with those on the plain below. Whitefoot knew those horses on the plain, and Undersong had grown up with many of them. It was Shamon's sorrel gelding, however, who whinnied the most. He truly liked company.

Summerwind preceded them down the hill, her two braids flying behind her in the wind. Zhen smiled at this. She was Dawnracer. She could return to her people no other way.

The gelding wanted to follow, but Zhen maneuvered Undersong so that the gelding was between the two mares. Shamon would not be able to hold the horse back, but two horses setting a good example might keep the gelding under control.

It worked out well. Summerwind's arrival drew an audience, so by the time Zhen arrived, all eyes were on him. Most fortunate was that the gethrav was among the crowd, which meant that Zhen could address him and not the hawk-eyed taishrefi.

"Gethrav Lowsinger," Zhen called, projecting his words so that they could be heard without him straining his voice, "we bid you and your band a good morning."

"As we do you and your companions, Zephyr Stormsinger."

Zephyr Stormsinger. That would be his name, now, until he could prove he was truly Dragonslayer.

Zephyr and his companions reined to a halt five paces before the gethrav. Summerwind had already dismounted and was embracing Mother. Their father was just arriving, with a spearhead-shaping hammer still in his hand. Their brother Greenpool, who had taken Zephyr's dream of becoming the kalaibo's apprentice, stood near the back of the crowd. On his shoulders was a little girl who had been just a baby learning to walk when Zephyr had left.

As they were a nomadic people, the Flamebringers seldom used the word "home". The Yolimites, by contrast, had at least twenty songs that were about nothing else, and all of these were popular with the travelers who passed through the inns of Brin. Now Zephyr knew why.

"Please greet my friends," Zephyr said. "This is Shamon Heartstringer, the greatest lutist in all of Brin."

Shamon gave him a pained look—whether because of the invented name or because of the boast, Zephyr did not know. In truth, mentioning Brin had been a mistake, for there were some who would equate the compliment with phrases like "fastest turtle" or "tallest mouse". Ah, but it could not be taken back now … and it gave Zephyr an idea.

"This is Dan Farmer," he continued, "the strongest man in Kweshil."

"Kwoshim," said Kethwin.

"And this is Kethi Beastshaper," he finished. "The—" *Inspiration, do not fail me now.* "The sharpest woman in Dwen-Tarthil." *Aha! At least she has the sharpest tongue.*

Gethrav Lowsinger gave no sign of noticing Zephyr's jests. He simply replied, "We greet you Heartstringer, Farmer, and Beastshaper."

"You can call us Dan and Kethi," Danwel said easily, as though the gethrav were an innkeeper interested in buying some of his clan's flour.

"And I am called just Shamon," said Shamon. "I have no second name."

This minor mutiny irked Zephyr. It was all right for him and Summerwind to call them by their spring names, but they were adults, and the band addressed outsiders by their adult names.

"We heard there was one in Brin calling himself Dragonslayer," the taishrefi said. "Do you know anything about this, Zephyr?"

Well, the taishrefi could call anyone by any name she wanted.

"In truth, Taishrefi Smokewatcher, the Dragonslayer you heard of is I." Zephyr could tell from the crowd's reaction that Summerwind had already revealed part of this story. Instead of registering surprise, they waited attentively for more information.

And now he had come to the technically challenging part of the happy reunion song. His travels had taught him much about how to address a crowd, but the taishrefi was a person to whom one could not "sell an egg for the price of a chicken", as the saying was in Brin.

Since crossing the river, he had known that this test would come. Thanks to the crows sent by Lashrefi, Zephyr now knew he would pass.

"Lashrefi sent to me a dream in which I slew a dragon. With her inspiration, I composed a song. The story that she chose for me was so powerful that word of this song traveled deep into the deepest forests—" here he indicated Danwel and Kethwin, "—even as it traveled across the wide prairies to you. For there is not one dragon, but two. And I have been chosen to slay them both."

Many of them nodded. He had spoken words they wanted to hear, infusing his voice with the confidence that the morning's signs had given him. Some were skeptical—remembering his reputation for "bragging about the size of the bison his spear had missed"—but no one openly scoffed. They would give him a chance to prove the truth of his words.

But the eyes of Taishrefi Smokewatcher looked into his and reminded him that the ultimate judge of his worth would be the Goddess herself.

CHAPTER 17

Bathing

SUMMERWIND had thought it most unjust when her grand adventure had ended with the revelation that Dragonslayer was merely her brother. But it was even more unjust that he should turn his humiliation into glory.

Zephyr sat in the music circle with Dan and Kethi, telling the band about the dragon as though he actually knew something. True, he *had* seen it—but not as well as the Yolimites had, and certainly no better than Summerwind.

The gethrav wanted to know more about the dragon. The taishrefi wanted to know about Zephyr's delusions. The kalaibo wanted to know if he had learned any new songs. Zephyr was already a hero, and all he had done was make up stories. Summerwind would not stay to listen to any more of his ravings. Dan and Kethi could hold him to the truth.

That was when Summerwind realized that she had lost track of the most truthful member of the party. This worried her. Shamon was a melancholy man. If he was absent, it was not because he was wandering about the camp making new friends.

She found the gray-skinned Zharnovite sitting in the splashing waters of the creek, pouring water on his bald head. Summerwind recalled how excited she had been the first time she had seen him wearing nothing but his loin cloth. Now, he looked different. His absurdly long arms were still beautifully muscled, but his slumped shoulders gave him the air of a defeated man. And hadn't his skin been blue before?

"Shamon, what has happened to you?" she asked.

"I came here to submerge," he said, missing the point of her question.

"You look unwell," she said.

"I am unwell," he agreed. "My people spend more time bathing than eating. My skin has become sore without water."

"Does it feel good to be in the water again?" she asked.

"Yes," he said. "Although this creek is still too shallow."

Summerwind grinned. "I can help with that." She slipped out of her moccasins and loosened the laces on her leggings so that she could roll them up above her knees.

"How are you thinking to help?" Shamon wondered.

"I can build you a dam," she said, standing up and wading into the water.

It was cold, but the chill dulled the pain of banged ankles and wedged toes, which were inevitable when one walked on slippery stones. She started by moving the rocks near the surface of the water, but she quickly realized she would either need to remove her sleeves or get them wet.

Well, the day was warm. It was more-or-less Redmonth. Even the taishrefi exposed her arms sometimes.

Summerwind waded back out and began unlacing her sleeves. As she did so, she could not help noticing Shamon's pile of clothing. A corner of his coin box peeked out from under his Zharnovite garment.

"Shamon, may I ask you a question?"

"Yes," he said.

"Why did you bring your box of coins with you? My people do not trade for them."

"Each person on a boat can have one chest, small enough to carry. Even the—how to say?—the poorest. Even the orphans may have a chest that belongs to them."

"Ah, I truly was not denying your right to carry it with you," Summerwind told him. "But I do not understand why you would want it."

Shamon looked at her with eyes full of sorrow. "It is all that I have," he said.

Summerwind thought of all she had. Except for the moccasins and sleeves she had just removed, she was wearing it. That reminded her: She removed her knife and pouch, as well, to keep them from getting wet should she be clumsy enough to fall.

"But what I do not grasp is why you should want to have those coins at all," she said as she waded back in. Surely he did not need to use the ferry that many times.

"Sometimes I wonder the same thing," he said, hanging his head. "We save coins so we can buy a boat someday."

"How many coins do you need for a boat?" she asked.

"Many many," he said. So it was probably more than ten. "We do not buy the whole boat," he added.

"Which part do you buy?" she asked. She began moving rocks to build up a dam.

"I mean that we share the boat with our wives and our wives' husbands."

"Do I hear you truly? Do you mean that your people have two wives?"

"A boat usually has three wives and three husbands," he replied.

"All married to each other? Not in pairs, but married to everyone?"

"All married to everyone," he agreed. "Or they can make pairs. It does not matter. What matters is that they all own the same boat."

That seemed like an odd thing to matter.

"My parents do not own anything in common," Summerwind said. "My father owns his horses and his smithing tools. My mother owns the lodge. She allows Father and me to sleep there, but we do not own it. It is difficult to explain."

"Oh, no. I understand. I have been allowed to sleep on other people's boats, but I have never owned one."

"I suppose a boat for you must be like a lodge for us," Summerwind said.

"Yes," Shamon agreed. "Except ... if your parents do not buy a lodge together, how do they know they are married?"

"Ah, that is simple enough. A man who is not married must sleep in his mother's lodge or sleep outside."

"Now I understand," said Shamon. "Do you have a lodge?"

"No," said Summerwind.

"So you cannot get married," he concluded.

"I cannot until I make my own lodge," she agreed.

"It is the same with our chests of coins," Shamon said. "Until we have enough coins to buy our own boat together, we cannot get married."

It was not exactly the same, but it was close enough.

"Now that I have explained the chest to you, will you explain something to me?" Shamon asked.

"Certainly I will," she said. "What will you have me explain?"

"Why did you braid two braids this morning?"

Oh. He had noticed that.

"I apologize," said Shamon. "I should not have asked."

"It was well asked," Summerwind told him. "I shall certainly give you an answer, since you were so generous in your answer to me: Girls my age often wear two braids."

"Yes," Shamon agreed. "I saw some in your village. And some with one braid down the back. And some with no braid. But I saw no girls who wear one braid on the side, as you did before this morning."

"I wear two braids when traveling with my band," said Summerwind.

"And when do you wear only one?" Shamon asked.

"At our gatherings," Summerwind admitted.

Shamon nodded. "Zhen told me about big gatherings where you do your courtships. I understand now."

"You do?"

"Yes. Before, you were wearing courtship hair. Now you are not."

"Yes," said Summerwind. "This is the hair I wear when traveling with my band."

"Yes," agreed Shamon. "But you did not know we would be meeting your band when you braided your hair."

She could think of no reply to this.

"I apologize," said Shamon.

"You have nothing to apologize for," she said.

"I thought, because you are asking me questions, that you want to talk. But you do not."

"I enjoy talking with you, Shamon. But I do not yet want to talk about—about him."

"I understand," he said.

"Is it my turn again? May I ask a question?"

"Which question?"

"Do you have 'a girl'?"

Shamon gave a rueful smile at the Yolimite phrase—or perhaps it was his own situation that made him rueful, for he said, "You cannot understand. You have a father and a mother and brothers who love you. But I— Among my people, I am nothing. Is there anyone in your band who travels with you, but is not one of you?"

Summerwind thought. "Well, there is Breezekenner. She is our taishrefi's apprentice, but she is from Slowtalker's Band."

"So she will one day be a priest," observed Shamon. "No, this is not what I mean at all. I mean a person who will never be anything."

"But everyone is something," Summerwind protested.

"I am not," said Shamon. "Or ... I was not until I met your brother."

"Truly?"

"He says I am the best lutist in Brin."

"He also claims he can slay dragons," Summerwind replied.

"Yes," agreed Shamon. "I cannot say if I am the best lutist in Brin, but before I met your brother, I did not even know that it was a good thing to be."

"Do your people not like lutes?"

"They enjoy music, but they do not—how to say?—they do not value it. No one ever thought my music had value."

"Not even your parents?"

"My parents are dead."

"Ah." Summerwind paused. "How did—?"

Shamon cut her off. "No. I do not yet want to talk about them."

"Then we shall not," agreed Summerwind. "Instead we shall go back to the question of girls. What I hear you saying is that you will not find a girl to buy a boat with because you are in love with my brother."

Shamon's mouth hung open. Summerwind congratulated herself on successfully taking his mind off an unpleasant topic.

"No," Shamon finally said. "It is not like that. We marry other men, yes, but we do not— It is just not like that."

"Shamon, I do not mean that you find my brother attractive like a woman. But look at what you have done to yourself because of him. You love him so much that you let your skin fall off."

Shamon was now, thanks to Summerwind's dam, submerged in a pool. And it was as she said: Floating in the pool were great flakes of gray skin that had peeled off his body.

But Shamon shook his head sadly. "In this thing you are wrong, Dawnracer. This is not suffering from love. This is punishment for sin."

"Sin?" It was a strong word, rarely uttered among her people. "For what sin?"

"For lying, Dawnracer. I love your brother so much that I lied with him."

Summerwind found herself in need of clarification. "You are talking about his dragonslayer song?"

"Yes," said Shamon. "I let others believe the story was truth. For this, Zharnov must punish me."

"I thought you said your people serve all the deities."

"We serve them all," agreed Shamon. "But everyone must face Justice."

"Zephyr is not facing justice," Summerwind observed.

"He will have to answer to Zharnov," Shamon said. "And perhaps to Lashrefi as well, if he pretends to have signs from her."

"Did he lie about the dream, too?"

"Perhaps I say that wrong," said Shamon. "I do not think he did lie about the dream. But I do not know if it was sent by Lashrefi. What do you think?"

What *did* she think? Zephyr was always so certain of himself that it was difficult to take him seriously. But why had he dreamed of a dragon before anyone had seen one? Why did the word he had invented fit so easily into Lashrefi's language? Why had the crow appeared that morning?

"I do not know, either," she said. "I cannot believe that my coyote-pup brother receives messages from the Goddess. But neither do I want to see him punished. Or at least, not punished too much."

"It is not for us to decide how much punishment is too much," Shamon told her. He shivered.

"You have been punished too much," she told him. "And it did not come from Zharnov. You chose to punish yourself."

"You do not understand the ways of my people," he said.

"Perhaps I do not, but I understand the ways of my brother. If calling himself Dragonslayer is the worst sin you have allowed him to commit, then I say you must have prevented a great many worse sins."

Shamon tried to stand up, but his knees buckled. He fell back into the pool with a splash.

"I— Would you—?"

Summerwind waded to his side. Water pushed against the hem of her leather skirt. She helped the Zharnovite to his feet.

"Thank you," he said. "My head. I—"

She waited until he was done vomiting, then led him to the bank, where he lay down, shivering. The strip of cloth that he wore as clothing lay nearby, but she had no idea of how to dress him in it. Instead she simply used it to cover him, as though it were a blanket.

"I will get help," she told him. "You wait here."

It was an absurd command: Clearly, he was incapable of going anywhere else.

Summerwind ran between the lodges. She did not understand what was wrong with Shamon, but she knew there was one person who could help.

She arrived at the music circle.

"Kethi, Shamon is very ill," she said. "Please come."

CHAPTER 18

Healing

"How is Shamon?" Danwel's great, fuzzy head was silhouetted in the entrance to the tent.

Kethwin scowled. "You stay out, Danwel Broadfield. Dawn-racer says no one may come into the tent without her mother's permission, and that applies to you, too."

"Aye, so Zhen said," agreed Danwel. "Then he sent me to ask in his stead. He thought I would get into less trouble than he would."

"Then he does not know Kethwin Walker," Kethwin said. She glanced at the sleeping form of the Riverman. "But tell him his friend will recover."

"Thank you, Kethwin," said Danwel, relieved.

He lingered at the entrance. "Zhen and the councilmen have made a plan for hunting the dragon," he said.

"Good," Kethwin replied. "I am glad to hear that."

"I reckoned you would be, so I— Well, I'll go tell Zhen the good news."

"Good night, Danwel."

"Good night, Kethwin."

The light grew dimmer as he closed the entrance flap.

"Oh! Good evening, Dawnracer!" said Danwel's muffled voice. "I was just leaving."

"I bid you good evening, Dan," the girl replied. Her voice was flat—not cold, but it held no smile for him.

Dawnracer slipped inside, carrying a pot of wet rags. They had been Zhen's blankets, but Zhen had been glad to supply rags for keeping Shamon's skin damp. Dawnracer knelt beside Kethwin, taking care to set the iron pot where Kethwin had asked her to put it—within reach, but not so close that it would interfere with beastshaper sight.

Kethwin closed her eyes and resumed the examination that Danwel had interrupted. It was difficult to tell what had happened to the Riverman's body. Dawnracer believed that Shamon needed to wet his skin daily and that his problems were caused by being too dry. This was quite unlike anything that had ever happened to the livestock Kethwin had healed.

Shamon's blood, muscles, and bones were just like any person's, but his skin was a mystery. Perhaps his skin was like a frog's. Kethwin knew nothing about frogs.

But she could heal him anyway. Most healing techniques were variants of the same basic method: Look at where the flow of Life is sluggish and try to help it flow better. The method applied to plants, to animals, and to people.

The flow of Life had been slow in Shamon's hands and feet. Kethwin had seen this before in the limbs of calves that had been born in a late snowstorm, so she knew he needed to be warmed up.

But he also needed to be cooled down. The flow of Life in his head reminded Kethwin of an ox that had collapsed after working too hard on a hot day.

Whenever an animal needed to be warm or cool, the place for it was in the stable, so Kethwin had asked them to bring Shamon indoors. Or at least "in". Dawnracer's people did not have doors.

Once Shamon was brought inside, Dawnracer's mother had sent everyone out. The female's total authority over the house was a good custom, Kethwin thought—certainly one that she would like to spread to Kwoshim. Only Kethwin and Dawnracer were left with the ailing Shamon.

The first problem had been to position the half-naked man the proper distance from the hearthfire. This had required a few adjustments, which were "problematic", as Dawnracer had said, because Shamon was a heavy giant. But they finally managed to get his feet close enough to the fire to get warmed up and his head close enough to the edge of the tent to allow it to cool down.

Life had returned to Shamon's hands and feet, and now the main task was to keep the warmth of the fire and the dryness of the air from harming his skin.

Whenever a wet cloth was placed against Shamon's bare skin, his Life would flow toward it. Kethwin believed this was his skin's way of healing. So Dawnracer brought her a steady supply of wet rags and Kethwin laid them on Shamon in various places, depending on where it looked like the Life needed to flow.

Now the Life flowed well.

Kethwin opened her eyes and looked up at Dawnracer sitting beside her. "His skin is healing," she said.

"How is his head?" asked Dawnracer. "Is it still weak?"

"No," said Kethwin. "Everything seems to have balanced."

"That gladdens me," sighed Dawnracer.

The girl had been right to be worried. Dry skin could heal. Cold feet could be warmed. It had been the overheated head that had been most likely to be fatal.

"I would send you to tell your brother," said Kethwin, "but he already sent Danwel here to ask me."

Dawnracer said nothing.

Kethwin swallowed and said, "You were very helpful." There. That was over with. It had not been so hard to say after all.

"The music has started," she went on. "If you want to join them, we will be fine here."

Dawnracer shook her black-and-white braids. "I can hear the melody, and I know the words. I would like to stay with Shamon until he wakes up. If you permit it."

So Kethwin was not the only one saying difficult things.

"He may not wake up this evening," Kethwin said. "But if he does, I am sure he will be glad to see you."

The coals, which had once been a pile of cow dung, were glowing red, lending the same hue to Dawnracer's striped skin. While tending to the Riverman, Kethwin had not worried about whether her skin were turning blue to match his or wavering between light and dark in an attempt to match Dawnracer's. Now she took time to be grateful for the darkness. It was like being naked under her clothing: No need to be embarrassed about what no one could see.

The sun had set, but looking at the vent above, Kethwin could see the crisscrossing poles against the pale sky, which was just beginning to light up with stars. Dawnracer must lie there and look up at the sky every night.

Of course, Dawnracer was the sort of girl who looked at skies. Kethwin always had to keep both feet firmly on the ground.

"I am sorry I left you," Dawnracer said.

When? Oh.

"I should not have left you when there were wolves about," Dawnracer said.

"I suppose it is easy to not fear wolves when you are a giant," Kethwin said. Her words had a bite to them, she knew, but she hoped Dawnracer understood that they were not intended to cut.

"I often forget that you are the size of a child," said Dawnracer. "You act like a taishrefi."

"I'm not pious enough to be a priestess," Kethwin said.

"Perhaps not," said Dawnracer. "But when you speak, you expect to be obeyed."

Kethwin was not always obeyed. But she had to admit, at least to herself, that people were more likely to do what she said when she acted as though she expected it.

"Is that a compliment?" she asked.

"Truly it was not intended as an insult," Dawnracer replied.

"Oho! It was an observation then?"

"I think it improbable that I would be the first person who has said this to you," said Dawnracer.

"My little sister Beswin says I am 'bossy'."

"Perhaps you are bossy," said Dawnracer with a smile in her voice. "But what I meant was that you speak with authority, which I would like you to take as a compliment."

"Oho! So now it is finally a compliment."

"No, it was an observation," said Dawnracer. "But I want you to take it as a compliment anyway."

Now Kethwin was confused. "Are you mocking me?" she asked.

"Kethi, do you never laugh?" asked Dawnracer.

"I laugh!" Kethwin protested.

"When, Kethi?" asked Dawnracer. "When was the last time you laughed?"

Kethwin thought about it.

Shamon chuckled. "She does not remember."

"Shamon!" exclaimed Dawnracer. "You are awake!"

The Riverman chuckled again. "Yes. You two argue above my head, and somehow: I am now awake."

"We weren't arguing," said Kethwin sternly.

"Were we not?" asked Dawnracer.

"No," said Kethwin. "Of course not. You were apologizing and ... making observations that were not intended as insults."

"And what were you doing, Kethi?" Shamon asked.

"I was—" What had she been doing? "I was trying to understand the observations."

"What observations?" asked Shamon.

"She said that I expect people to do what I say," said Kethwin, as Shamon pushed himself up with his elbows. "No, don't try to sit up yet."

He fell back down and laughed. Dawnracer laughed with him.

"But he's been ill!" Kethwin wailed. "He needs to rest. Why are you laughing at me?"

Dawnracer's huge striped hand enveloped hers. It was clearly intended as a warm gesture, although the hand was still a bit clammy from fetching the wet rags.

"Dear Kethi," she said, "your friends can laugh at you without mocking you."

"Dawnracer, that makes no sense."

"Then order it to make sense and perhaps it shall," Dawnracer suggested.

Shamon shook.

"I do not think this is good for him," said Kethwin weakly. "He needs to rest. His mind ..."

"My mind is good," gasped Shamon. "My belly hurts." And he kept laughing.

Kethwin closed her eyes and focused on Shamon. Dawnracer released her hand, but Kethwin did not need her hands to see what was happening inside the Riverman. He was full of vitality—in a way that he had not been when he was asleep. She had no words to describe it, not because she had never seen it before, but because her sister could not explain it to her. It was something Kethwin could see that Feshwin could not.

She looked up at Dawnracer's striped face. "The laughter seems to be good for him. It is lifting his spirit. But it sounds so strange, considering how dour he has been."

"I feel so light," said Shamon. "In here," he added, slapping his hand on his bare chest.

"Is he lupine-headed?" Dawnracer asked.

"I don't know," said Kethwin. "Does that mean 'daft'?"

"It might," said Dawnracer.

"No, I am not daft," said Shamon. "I am just—how to say?—relieved. I thought I will die. And then I talk to Dawnracer, and she—"

A strange look passed over his face.

"What is it, Shamon?" asked Dawnracer.

"Are we married?" he asked.

Daft, thought Kethwin.

"Ah ... no," said Dawnracer.

"You said only husbands may come into your house," Shamon said.

"Aha," said Dawnracer. "Men can enter the lodge; they just cannot sleep here."

"But—"

"And ill men may sleep wherever they need to," she finished. "Furthermore, this is my mother's lodge. Sleeping here would not make you my husband. It would make you my step-father."

Shamon's eyes widened.

"Do not worry, friend," said Dawnracer. "You have not married anyone."

Dawnracer turned to Kethwin and said, "Did you know that Shamon can marry three women?"

Kethwin kept her face blank, but the glowing coals must have made her look stern, for Dawnracer hastened to add, "That was an observation, not a suggestion. We all know you are marrying Dan. Just you. No one else."

So that claim was officially relinquished, then. It was a night for surprises.

"I would like to marry Danwel," Kethwin told them. "But I wonder sometimes if he wants to marry me."

"Kethi, he adores you," said Dawnracer.

"Yes, but—" These people had no currency. How could they understand marriage marks? "Is that the way it works with your people? Can you marry a boy just by convincing him to sleep in your tent?"

"No, it is not so simple," said Dawnracer. "The couple must choose which band they will travel with. And a taishrefi must pronounce them married before the eyes of Lashrefi. We usually do this at the autumn gathering."

"We can get married any time we want," said Kethwin. "But our clans have to agree."

"Is a clan like a band?" asked Dawnracer. "Or more like a village?"

"Not really," said Shamon, which Kethwin did not consider helpful.

"A clan is all the descendents of two of the first people," said Kethwin.

"The *very* first people?" asked Dawnracer.

"Aye," said Kethwin. "All Walkers are descended from Zol and Gafi Walker, who were placed into the world by Yolim a thousand years ago."

"All Walkers are descended from two people?" Dawnracer was shocked. "How is that possible? Do Walkers marry only each other?"

"No, of course not." Kethwin waved the ludicrous idea aside. "We cannot marry anyone in our clan. We have to marry people from other clans. So my sister's husband, for example, was a Springwater. But now he's a Walker. Well, I reckon that means he's not really descended from Zol and Gafi, but once he joins the clan it is *like* he's descended from them. And my sister's daughter is, too, because my sister is. Do you see?"

"Yes," said Shamon. "You all marry each other and then pretend that only certain people are ancestors."

"We don't 'pretend'!" Kethwin protested.

"I apologize," said Shamon quickly. "I did not mean 'pretend'. I meant— But if all clans are free to marry each other, then are you not descended from every clan?"

"No," said Kethwin. "'Descended' doesn't mean— Well, maybe, but— Look, the important thing is that we have clans, and we need their consent to get married."

"And will your clan give consent?" asked Dawnracer.

"Well, that is the trouble," said Kethwin. "I want to join Danwel's clan, and I can't."

"They will not buy you?" asked Shamon.

"Yolimites buy their wives?" asked Dawnracer.

Kethwin considered leaving it at that. It would certainly make Dawnracer look elsewhere for a husband if she thought that Danwel would buy his wife as though she were a loaf of bread. But no:

"We use marriage marks to record debts," said Kethwin. "They look like big coins, but they are not currency. Each clan in Dwen-Tarthil is only allowed to have one hundred. Each time two people marry, one person joins the other clan. The clan receiving the new person must give the other clan a mark. The only way to get that mark back is to have one of yours marry into their clan."

"Why must it be so complicated?" asked Dawnracer.

"Because otherwise everyone would marry into the rich clans, and they would get even bigger and richer," said Kethwin.

"When one of our bands gets too big," said Dawnracer, "we simply split it. The two bands go their separate ways."

"But how do you divide up the land they own?" asked Kethwin.

"Ah, I see," said Dawnracer. "Yes, each band will want to visit the same places at the same time of year. The new ranges must be agreed upon. Usually a taishrefi from another band will be asked to arbitrate."

Shamon nodded.

"Well, we do not split the clan," said Kethwin. "There were forty clans a thousand years ago, and there are still forty today."

"And Clan Broadfield has no more marks?" asked Shamon.

"They have three," said Kethwin, with disgust. "But they are saving them for important people. If Danwel can slay our dragon, then he will be important. That is why we are here: So that he can get some practice by slaying yours first. What?"

Dawnracer was giving her a funny look.

"That is not exactly what he told us in Brin," she said carefully.

"Well, could be things were different then, but this is the way they are now."

"Dan killed a rabbit," said Shamon. "But this dragon is no rabbit."

"It is no bigger than a wildcow," said Kethwin. She tried to say it dismissively, as though the thought of the monster did not make her tremble. "Even Dawnracer can kill a wildcow."

"Zhen helped her kill it," said Shamon. "And they are both bigger and stronger than Dan."

"They are bigger," acknowledged Kethwin. "That does not mean they are stronger."

Shamon thought a moment. "I withdraw that. I should have said, 'I believe they are stronger.'"

No one was stronger than Danwel, but Kethwin chose not to press her argument.

"This dragon is a weird beast," said Shamon. "It makes wind."

That tied a little knot in Kethwin's stomach. The wind, the thunder, the lightning—the dragon was much more dangerous than any beast she knew.

"Well, don't worry about it," Kethwin said to mask her anxiety. "You need to rest now. This is for Danwel and Zhen to figure out. And Danwel said they already have a plan."

CHAPTER 19

The Plan

DANWEL DID NOT THINK much of the plan. But he was no thinker. Zhen and the gethrav were experienced hunters, so their plan had to be better than anything Danwel could think up.

They were right about the wildcows, at least. The herd had come to the creek that morning, and they still grazed within sight of the camp. Danwel, Zhen, the gethrav, and three hunters rode toward the herd.

To keep Tevishi away from strange horses, Danwel rode on the outside, next to Zhen and Undersong. Tevishi knew Undersong. The gethrav's stallion, on Zhen's other side, also knew Undersong and kept trying to renew acquaintances.

The gethrav was an interesting fellow. His name was Lowsinger, but because he was important, everyone referred to him by title. Danwel had expected the leader of the band to be old, like a councilman. Zhen said young men made better leaders because they could ride and hunt.

This made sense. A clan wanted to be represented by their best bargainer, so the job of councilman fell to the wealthiest. And because good bargainers accumulated more wealth as they got older, the wealthiest man was always an old man. But a gethrav had to make decisions, not bargains, and most of those decisions involved where to ride and what to hunt—activities which concerned young men. For Stripedfolk, athleticism was more important than wealth.

But it would be wrong to think that Stripedfolk did not care about wealth. They owned no land, but they did have horses. The gethrav himself had over twenty, which made Danwel wonder why he had chosen to ride the annoying stallion this morning. The gethrav, fighting his mount, probably wondered the same thing.

"Spread out," said the gethrav, in a voice loud enough to be heard by the riders, but not sharp enough to draw the attention of the wildcows. The riders began to widen the gaps between their horses as they rode toward the herd.

The order was a bit premature. Danwel suspected it had more to do with the gethrav trying to control his horse than with their distance from the wildcows.

It was important to not disturb the herd. That was why the gethrav had decided to approach with only himself, Danwel, Zhen, and three scouts. "Scouts" was the name for men who slept outside, as Danwel had learned from sleeping among them the previous night. Zhen was technically a scout, too, because he was too old to sleep in his mother's tent.

As Danwel and Zhen eased away from the other hunters, they heard a gallop of hooves behind them. Turning, they saw Dawnracer riding toward them on her black and white filly.

Zhen made a face. After glancing at the herd to be sure they had not yet been spooked, he turned his horse to meet his sister at a trot.

Danwel followed. Tevishi exchanged whinnies with Whitefoot. Danwel hoped the wildcows were accustomed to whinnies.

"What are you doing here?" Zhen asked. "Gethrav Lowsinger and I agreed to take no more than three scouts."

"Ah, but no one told me the plan," replied Dawnracer, "so I could not have known. Regardless, dear brother, if you will recall, Dan promised to protect me when you went out to slay the dragon. How can he protect me unless I come along?"

"You would be best protected if you stayed in Mother's lodge," Zhen replied. "But I will not argue with you. Battling a dragon takes much strength; I will not exert myself by taking on a second beast."

"Truly!" said Dawnracer. "As though you knew how much strength it takes to slay a dragon."

Zhen glanced at Danwel, then gave Dawnracer a look.

"But he knows!" Dawnracer protested.

Another look.

"Yes he does!" she replied. "Tell him, Dan."

Zhen and Dawnracer could say quite a bit with looks, but Danwel sometimes had trouble reading them. "Tell him what?" he asked.

"Zephyr thinks you do not know that he has never slain a dragon."

"Oh, that," said Danwel. "Aye, Zhen. Shamon told me when we were still a half-day from Brin."

"He did?" asked Zhen.

"Aye. He said he felt bad about me coming along with you and not knowing you were a fraud."

"Truly?" Zhen said, in a voice that was almost a croak.

"Aye," said Danwel. "But I told him that I had already figured that out. I decided to come along anyway, because I reckoned you might find a way to slay this dragon. And if you did, I wanted to be there to see it."

"Ah, your faith is— Or, rather, your hope— You knew all along?"

Dawnracer was enjoying this.

"Well," said Danwel, "when I found out you were a singer, I thought, 'People who do things don't usually sing songs about it. Most people are good at only one thing.' So when I heard you sing, I reckoned that was the thing you were good at, not dragonslaying. And Shamon told me I was right."

"Does Kethwin know?" Zhen asked. "What are these words I speak? Of course she knows."

"Aye, but I explained to her that just being able to imagine a way to slay a dragon was more than I could do. And she agreed that we had to go with you."

Actually, he had explained why he had made a bargain with Zhen, and Kethwin had agreed that Clanfolk must honor their bargains. But Danwel saw no need to mention the fine distinctions.

"Now tell me the plan," said Dawnracer.

Danwel noted that she had brought her iron-tipped spear. Her father, a blacksmith, had offered a spear to Danwel, but Danwel preferred his sling. Actually, he would have felt better with a scythe or a hoe in his hands, but with his sling and his bundle of round stones, he thought he could do his part if needed.

"The plan is elegant," stated Zhen. "You will recall that the last time the dragon was looking for a meal, it attacked a herd of bison. Well, that is exactly what it shall do today. The six of us will be in place on all sides of the herd. As soon as the dragon descends upon its kill, we will all converge, and the first man there will deliver the fatal blow."

"Or I," said Dawnracer. "The first man or I will deliver the fatal blow."

"As you like it, dear sister."

"And if the dragon does not come?" asked Dawnracer.

"Then we shall kill it when it comes tomorrow," said Zhen.

"But let us suppose that the dragon finds its food elsewhere," Dawnracer persisted. "What shall we do then?"

"There is no sense in planning for failure, dear sister."

To Danwel's mind, this was the great flaw in the plan. They could see forever, and there was no dragon in sight. It was clearly elsewhere and likely to remain there as long as it had food. And if it ran out of food, how would it know to travel across unseeable distance to reach these wildcows?

"Very well," said Dawnracer. "Suppose instead that we do manage to bait the dragon. How do we know our spears can kill it?"

"If we can kill a bison with our spears, then certainly this dragon will present no problem," said Zhen. "As Kethwin constantly reminds us, our dragon is no larger than a yearling bull."

"And yet how can we get close enough to thrust our spears when the dragon makes thunder and lightning and whirlwinds?"

"Sister, we are a plains people. We deal with thunder, lightning, and wind all year long."

"So do our horses," said Dawnracer, "but they panic every time."

"You yourself have ridden a horse in a thunderstorm," Zhen replied. "As punishment for which, if I recall, Father made you ride the lodge horse for the rest of the month."

"Truly," said his sister. "But there are not many who have my skill."

"Truly?" said Zhen. "If I recall, even little Kethwin was able to stay mounted throughout the dragon's storm."

"But Dan got bucked off," Dawnracer said.

"He did not," said Zhen. "He jumped off. Tell her, Danwel."

"Well, aye," said Danwel, not really wanting to take sides. "I jumped off to get Shamon. But his gelding was going crazy. When they get scared, some horses run and some buck. Kethwin was just lucky that Tevishi is a runner."

"And now the scouts shall have the opportunity to learn whether their horses are runners or buckers," said Dawnracer. "Is that not lucky for them? Truly you have done them a service by allowing them to join you in your plan."

Zhen rolled his eyes. "If you think so little of my plan, then ride back."

"I will not," said Dawnracer. "I promised you in Brin that I would pick up the pieces, and a bargain is a bargain, is it not, Dan?"

"A bargain is a bargain," Danwel agreed. There was no sense in trying to dissuade the girl. Danwel had three younger sisters. Not one of them would allow herself to be told to go home once she had decided to tag along.

They rode in silence until Dawnracer murmured, "I do not think that even I could ride a horse in a tornado."

"The dragon just makes little whirlwinds," said Zhen.

"Big whirlwinds that flatten trees," said Dawnracer. "They are tornadoes."

"We shall avoid them, just as Shamon did when he led Danwel and Kethwin to safety. There are six directions. This means that your odds of choosing a safe direction are five against one."

"Those odds are good enough," Dawnracer agreed. "But there are six of you. That means one will be swept away."

"No, it simply means that one will have to flee while the rest of us race to the kill. Ah, and if you want a good view of the kill, stay close behind me, for to bet on me is to bet on Lashrefi."

"Truly!" exclaimed Dawnracer.

"Truly," said Zhen.

After a moment: "There," said Zhen. "There in yon patch of bluestem shall I make my stand. Sister, ride no closer, lest you alarm the herd."

Danwel and Dawnracer reined to a halt. Zhen kept Undersong walking until he was in the place he had said he would be. He looked over his shoulder once, to verify that his sister was staying with Danwel, and then returned his attention to the grazing herd.

The gethrav and the three scouts were already in their positions around the wildcows. There was still a big gap in the circle, however, and Danwel reckoned that he was expected to fill it.

"I need to get to my spot," he told Dawnracer.

"I shall come with you," she said.

Dawnracer studied the herd as their horses walked through the spring grass.

"Having reconsidered," she said, "I think you should come with me."

"Aye, then," agreed Danwel, for the girl seemed to have something in mind.

Dawnracer turned Whitefoot away from the herd and Tevishi followed, until they had wandered some distance from the wildcows and the other riders.

"Now let Tevishi graze," Dawnracer said, lowering Whitefoot's reins.

"Tevishi will not graze unless I dismount," Danwel reminded her.

"Do so," said Dawnracer. "We are in no hurry."

This was surely true. Danwel loosened Tevishi's nape catch, unrolled his saddle ladder, and climbed down.

The nape catch did not hold the horse's head up by force. It simply checked the horse by putting tension in the reins when she lowered her head. Tevishi had the strength to pull through the catch, but no one had allowed her to develop that bad habit, which was why she had lived so long. If a horse with Clanfolk reins lowered its head to the ground, it could pull the reins out of its rider's hands or pull its rider out of the saddle. Grazers, as such problematic horses were called, were useful only for carting, and Tevishi's carting days were over.

Dawnracer leaned forward until her head was resting on Whitefoot's mane. It was not the sort of thing Danwel would do on a horse, but she looked comfortable.

After a while, she said, in a lazy lilting voice, "So Shamon told you that Zephyr's song was just a song?"

"Aye."

"He said he would do as much," said Dawnracer. "But when you decided to come along anyway, Zephyr and I thought you still did not know."

"Well, I didn't see any profit in calling your brother a liar," said Danwel.

"Kethi did not keep her doubts to herself," said Dawnracer.

"No, that is not her way," Danwel agreed. "I tried to keep her from badgering Zhen, but …"

"But you could not tell her that you believed Zephyr's story, because that would have been a lie."

"Aye," Danwel agreed.

"That was how I knew you knew," Dawnracer said. "Because you did not tell her you believed Zephyr."

For a while there was no sound but the munching of grass. Dawnracer lay draped over Whitefoot's neck. Danwel walked beside his grazing mare.

"I understand now why you like her," said Dawnracer with a sigh. "She is very practical."

Danwel reckoned she was talking about Kethwin and not the mare.

"Aye," he said. "Of course, all the girls in Kwoshim are practical. They can't waste time on finery like the girls in Tarthil or Brin."

Danwel thought back on the women he had seen in Brin. None of them had actually seemed to be wasting time on finery, but it was common knowledge that Brinnen women did so.

"But Kethi is special, isn't she?" Dawnracer persisted. "She can heal sick people and animals. And use a bonesaw. And make soup."

"Well, they all can make soup," said Danwel. *A bonesaw?* "But, aye, she's a good healer. Beastshapers mostly work on livestock, though."

Dawnracer sighed again. "Kethi says you two would be married right now were it not for your family's lack of coins."

"Marks. Aye."

"Aye, marks," Dawnracer echoed.

The Stripedwoman rolled over onto her back. Apparently, White-foot was accustomed to being reclined upon, for the mare held still until Dawnracer had taken up her new position.

While grazing, the horses had moved at a leisurely pace across the meadow. The wildcows had been drifting as well. The result was that Danwel and Dawnracer were now in the front of the herd, right where Zhen had wanted them to be.

Dawnracer stared at the sky and murmured, "What a mouse-brain I have been."

"Actually, I was just thinking how clever you were to get us into position," said Danwel.

"Ah," said Dawnracer. "Yes."

"What were you talking about?" Danwel asked.

"Ah, I was—"

She jerked herself upright, causing Whitefoot to give a hop.

"We are all mouse-brains," Dawnracer said. She spun herself into her saddle. "The dragon is over there."

CHAPTER 20

Dawnracer

THERE WAS A TIME for sighing and moping, and there was a time for screaming and galloping. Summerwind decided it was now the latter time.

She had many things to say about her brother and his mouse-brained plan, but as she lacked the kalaibo's gift for projecting her voice, she left them unsaid. Instead she summoned all the breath in her lungs and put it into one word that sliced the day's stillness: "Dragon!"

She tugged on the reins to turn her dancing filly back toward the lodges.

In response to her cry, the men gazed skyward. Zephyr spotted the winged monster first and urged Undersong to a gallop. Gethrav Lowsinger and the scouts—Rabbitpaw, Fateater, and Whistler—began loping after him. Summerwind pointed Whitefoot's nose at the horizon and let the filly run.

The dragon was circling, but not above the bison. It was above the band's horse herd, which grazed on the plain between the bison and the lodges, unguarded.

Zephyr had been wrong about the target. However, he had been right about it being like a dice game: With the purple serpent striking outside their circle, one of the six riders would be closer than the others.

And Zephyr had won. As they all raced toward the dragon, he was in the lead.

Had he known? Had he told the other men one plan and then positioned himself so that he could get all the glory when the dragon went after the true target?

No, Summerwind decided. *Not even Zephyr would be so stupid as to think that was clever.*

It was luck then—blind luck or the will of Lashrefi—that Zephyr should be leading the charge. Would he be so lucky as to arrive in time to save the horses?

The dragon dove. Purple lightning streaked from its body and exploded among the horse herd. The pause between flash and boom told Summerwind that the distance was far. No matter. Whitefoot was young. The filly could sustain the gallop.

The other riders stretched behind her like a tail—the gethrav, the three scouts, and finally Dan on Tevishi.

Whitefoot was closing on Undersong. Summerwind leaned forward over her filly's neck and let loose a tongue-trill—to encourage the horse's speed and also to let her brother know that she was coming up behind him.

The dragon swooped like an eagle over the horse herd, then climbed into the sky, spiraling like a rising leaf in a whirlwind on the hottest day of autumn.

The loose horses were panicking. Like bison, they panicked in a bunch, but they were faster. Bison trusted the herd to keep them safe, but horses relied on speed.

Zephyr nudged Undersong to keep her nose pointed at the leading edge of the horse herd. Whitefoot followed.

As they closed with the herd, there was the danger that the dragon would see them as part of it. Summerwind knew stories of wolves nipping at horses that were being ridden in a bison hunt. The dragon would not nip. Dan said that it killed with one blow.

Zephyr craned his neck to look up at the sky. The dragon was somewhere above them.

Summerwind felt the thunder strike. The flash blinded her. She did not see the ground as it bounced up and hit her. She should have heard a thud, but it was lost in the thunder of the hooves and the gallop of the thunder.

She was lying on the ground. Pain filled her spear hand, but her other hand still held Whitefoot's reins, through which she could feel the horse bunching for another buck. She swung her feet in that direction and used the filly's leap to pull herself upright.

Had Whitefoot tried to run directly away, Summerwind would have been pulled off her feet and dragged until she let go, but because Summerwind was standing where she could pull the horse's neck sideways, Whitefoot was forced to panic in a circle, with Summerwind at the center.

As Summerwind blinked the lightning from her eyes, the plunging form of the horse came into view.

She heard her brother's voice: "Are you hurt?"

"I am whole!" she cried. "Go on!"

And then she heard a thud, accompanied by a crunch.

Whitefoot ceased bucking to stare at the scene. As Summerwind's vision cleared, she saw it, too.

The dragon perched on the body of Shamon's gelding. That accounted for the thud. The gelding's contorted neck accounted for the crunch and explained why there had been no scream to complete the trio.

Kethi had been right about the dragon: It probably weighed no more than a yearling bison. But she had been wrong, too, because the dragon was much more dangerous. Bison were prey. They fled or were eaten. The dragon lived by killing. It had to fight for every meal.

It had two short legs, like a bird's. Two claws pointed forward, and two back, like the toes of a woodpecker, but the sharp talons were clearly for grasping prey, not for clinging to trees. Its triangular head held a mouth filled with teeth—the kind that looked like knives for ripping, not stones for grinding. Although much bigger than a rattlesnake, the dragon had a viper's quickness as it struck at the neck of its kill to open a wound. Something was unnatural about the movement—about the way its head struck and flashed back. Big things could move fast, but they should not be able to change direction in an eye-blink.

Zephyr had stopped his charge to check on Summerwind, giving the gethrav and Rabbitpaw, the youngest scout, time to catch up. The other two scouts and Dan were approaching at a trot.

Zephyr lifted his spear and loosed a tongue-trill—to encourage the men if not the horses. Undersong resumed her gallop.

The dragon lifted its bloody mouth up from the carcass. Its purple wings glowed, and its eyes flashed red.

Instead of charging directly at the dragon, Zephyr passed to one side so that he could loose his spear while riding at full speed. His aim was true. The spear flew from his hand straight toward the life-point under the monster's jaw.

The dragon's head snapped back, leaving the spear motionless in the air. The slender wooden shaft with the gleaming iron tip hung without support, as still as if it were lying on the ground.

Gethrav Lowsinger had been following Zephyr's line of attack, but when he saw this eerie result, he veered off, keeping his spear in hand.

Rabbitpaw Wolfstalker was third in line. His horse veered away from the dragon to follow the gethrav's. Rabbitpaw leaned out and made a throw anyway, nearly losing his balance. His spear wobbled through the air, missed the dragon by a horse-length, and stuck in the ground.

As though suddenly remembering itself, Zephyr's spear also fell to earth.

Fateater and Whistler rode up then and drew rein beside Summerwind. She tried to vault onto her horse, but with her spear-hand sprained, she managed only to flop herself across White-foot's withers, from which undignified position she scrambled onto the saddle.

Fateater had probably been too far away to see what had happened with Zephyr's spear. Lifting his own weapon, he turned to Whistler and said, "Follow me."

They took a line that passed by the dragon, as Zephyr had. The scaly serpent must have grasped that these creatures intended to disturb its meal, for instead of watching them come, it lunged out to meet them. Its mouth caught Fateater's stallion at the knee, snapping the foreleg as the horse somersaulted forward. Fateater let go of his spear and rolled clear of the tumbling body of his screaming horse.

Despite colliding with a charging horse, the dragon was not knocked backward. Its head remained in place, immobile as a boulder.

Whistler's horse decided that enough had been asked of it for one day. It veered off and galloped after the retreating horse herd.

Whistler remained mounted, trying to rein his horse in.

The dragon now perched on Fateater's screaming stallion, watching Fateater, who crouched in the grass. The scout had drawn his knife, but while the monster watched him, he was as still as a hiding rabbit.

In Summerwind's experience, rabbits that tried to hide in plain sight did not live long.

There was a whirr through the air and the dragon's head whipped round to stare at Dan and his sling. The stone had been stopped in mid-air, but Dan was already swinging a second one.

With the dragon distracted, Fateater pounced. But his target was not the dragon. He raised his knife over the neck of his own screaming horse. One swift stroke and the screams died, never to come from that throat again.

Dan loosed a second stone as Fateater sprang away. This stone went wide of the dragon, but the beast's eyes followed it, allowing Fateater to make his escape. Instead of arcing toward the ground, the stone curved strangely and struck the gethrav on the elbow.

Dan's first stone, which was still in the air, started whirling then, making an eerie hum. The grass underneath it vibrated for a moment before being sucked upward. Grass and dust defined a twisting cone of air crowned by the orbit of the slingstone. The whirlwind drifted toward Dan and Summerwind.

Zephyr and Undersong had turned around. They were returning to the scene of carnage at a steady lope. Zephyr had no spear, but leaning out of his saddle, he could pluck up Rabbitpaw's spear from where it had stuck in the ground.

His luck had run out. He misjudged the speed of his horse and the depth of the spearhead. The spear remained stuck and Zephyr lost his balance. Undersong loped away, leaving Zephyr afoot.

Now certain of the whirlwind's direction, Summerwind rode around the gelding carcass, away from the whirlwind's path. Yet even as she did so, her eyes were on her brother.

Zephyr extracted the spear and charged with a yell. He used the kalaibo's trick to make his voice louder, but his eyes grew wide in surprise as the sound slid out of his control to become three yells, then nine, raging together in a dissonance that filled not only

Summerwind's ears but her chest as well, as though she could feel the echoes of her brother's shout in her own lungs.

Through this thunderous cacophony, Zephyr stumbled onward, until he was met by a contemptuous flick of the dragon's blue tail. It caught him under the chin and sent him flying through the air. He landed on his back in the grass.

Zephyr did not rise.

Summerwind turned Whitefoot toward him. She would not leave him lying there.

She leapt from Whitefoot's back, landing in a crouch beside her brother. Rabbitpaw appeared by her side then, and together they lifted Zephyr's body onto Whitefoot's saddle. There was no time to thank the boy. Summerwind scrambled back onto Whitefoot and galloped away.

She leaned over her brother's body and used her torso to hold it in place. With her injured arm, she cradled his head to keep it from bouncing against Whitefoot's shoulder. At any moment, she expected a flash of blue scales to drop from the sky and end their dash, but as long as she was riding, she was still alive.

Her other hand was wrapped around Whitefoot's neck to keep herself and Zephyr from falling off. There was no need to rein the horse. She could not see where they were going anyway, because she was gripping the filly's mane with her teeth. It was Whistler who finally grasped Whitefoot's reins and slowed them to a halt.

Summerwind spat out mane and raised her head to look at him.

"Where is the dragon?" she asked.

"It went to destroy the lodges," he said in a voice like a mourning dove's. "Does Zephyr Stormsinger live?"

With her body pressed against her brother's, Summerwind knew the answer: "He does not breathe."

CHAPTER 21
Zephyr

ZEPHYR hit the ground hard.

The tail. He should have been watching for the tail.

Warily, he sat up and reached for the spear. It should not be far from where he had fallen.

There it was—only an armslength from his outstretched body.

Hm. Now that was truly strange. Why was his body still lying on the ground?

Zephyr looked at his hands. They pulsed with shifting swirls of color. No flesh, no bone. So those were not truly colors. No, he was looking at his spirit—disembodied.

Probably no point in reaching for the spear, then.

Zephyr rose to his feet, but the dragon paid him no mind. It seemed focused on Gethrav Lowsinger and Fateater. Armed only with a knife, Fateater was standing beside the Gethrav's horse. The Gethrav, at least, had a spear, but his arm was injured, enveloped by the throbbing darkness of pain.

They held their weapons poised to strike, but the dragon realized they were too far away to do it any harm. It bit into the neck of Fateater's fallen horse.

A substance swirled inside the horse's body, but it was of a nature different from Zephyr's spirit. Its flow was sluggish. Instead of writhing away into the air, it seeped from the body and disappeared into the ground. The dragon was drinking what it could before the substance drained away.

It was Life—elemental Life that Zephyr could see with his own eyes!

Ah, but perhaps he no longer had eyes.

As his consciousness expanded, Zephyr realized he no longer needed to face a thing to see it. All spirits in the vicinity were perceptible, regardless of where he chose to "look". He could feel Summerwind's grief and determination as she and Rabbitpaw lifted his body onto Whitefoot's back. He could sense Danwel's alarm as he reined Tevishi away from the dragon's twisting whirlwind. He could feel the racing pulse of the gethrav's stallion, waiting for the command to fight or to flee.

Truly, this was an extraordinary experience! He wondered if he would be allowed to write a song about it.

Fascinating, too, were the things his new senses could detect only feebly. The Life inside Fateater's gelding was fading away. Shamon's gelding was barely perceptible. And the dragon itself, though its body glowed with a light of its own, seemed to have less of those shifting, swirling colors that illuminated the souls of the other living beings.

Suddenly he felt himself pulled from the scene. Summerwind was carrying his body away, and his spirit was compelled to go with it. The grass sped past under his spiritual feet as Whitefoot galloped off toward the horse herd. Zephyr allowed himself to be drawn up onto Whitefoot's rump, where he sat, facing backwards, waiting to see what the gethrav would do next.

The gethrav had shifted his spear to his reining hand. Little Rabbitpaw had picked up one of the spears on the ground and remounted. Their weapons looked small. Fateater's tiny knife flashed a sparkle of sunlight as he raised it.

They charged, the spearmen horseback, Fateater on foot. Fierce fires of aggression illuminated their souls.

Hope flared in Zephyr's heart. Three weapons attacking at once. Perhaps this time one would find its mark.

But the dragon chose not to deal with their weapons. Instead, it drew a wind from nowhere and blew it toward the trio. Zephyr heard it, but his hearing was as vivid as sight.

And Zephyr realized that the sound of the wind had always been there, but on the other side of some barrier, as though he had been standing on a Brinnen street outside a noisy inn and had noticed the noise only when the dragon had opened the door.

The horses spun away. The riders tumbled. The man afoot was blown down.

The noise grew louder and the grass flattened before it, shining silver in the sunlight, bowing to Wind, the master of the plains. And the dragon was the creator of the master. It spread its wings—tiny they now seemed in comparison to its length—and soared over the men, knocking the rising Fateater back to the ground as it passed.

The gust picked up dirt and grass and horse dung and carried this debris before it like the horns of a charging bull. The wind stampeded toward the rows of painted lodges. The dragon rode this wind—not as a crow rides an updraft, but as a man rides a horse, guiding it where he wants it to go.

The wind struck.

Poles snapped. Stakes gave way. Lodge hides scattered. What became of those in the lodges, Zephyr was too far away to see.

An immense, tornado-shaped, violet-colored roar rose into the sky above the remains of the camp. In its center was a tiny worm spiraling among the dancing lodge hides. Staring into the nowhere from which the roaring wind came, Zephyr realized that the dragon had not just opened the door—the dragon *was* the door.

Whistler came riding up then, and Zephyr's perspective returned to Whitefoot's back. They were nearing the horse herd. The spirits of Shamon's gelding and Fateater's stallion were already there, grazing alongside the corporeal horses, though what ghost horses could graze on, Zephyr did not know. Perhaps they thought they were in Heaven. And perhaps they were, for the song claimed that the Flamebringers' range was "Heaven for horses".

Summerwind did not see Whistler trying to match pace with Whitefoot. Her face was buried in Whitefoot's black mane. All her effort was focused on staying mounted and cradling Zephyr's body.

His dead body. That would be difficult to become accustomed to.

Whistler leaned over and caught a rein as it swung up into his hand. With his other hand, he convinced his own mount to slow, and Whitefoot did likewise. Finally they came to a stop.

Summerwind spat out mane and turned her head to look at Whistler. "Where is the dragon?" she asked.

"It went to destroy the lodges," he said, in a voice like a mourning dove's. "Does Zephyr Stormsinger live?"

"He does not breathe," Summerwind replied.

"Zephyr Stormsinger?" a voice asked. "I thought you were Zhen Dragonslayer."

Although able to see in all directions, Zephyr had somehow missed the approach of a maiden on horseback. Her eyes were red, an uncommon color in the Flamebringer tribe. Two triangular stripes came across these eyes to meet at the bridge of her nose. Another stripe, much like Summerwind's, decorated her chin. Her cheeks were as white as snowberries.

Except for two thin streaks of white, her hair was crow black. She wore it in two braids, like a maiden, but her youthful face held a taishrefi's smile.

Her deerskin dress had a simple cut, but it was elaborately painted with black stripes. These seemed to match the stripes on her exposed arms and legs, and Zephyr wondered if they truly depicted the stripes she wore underneath. The horse had stripes, too—like a person's but coarser, because it was a larger animal. No songs had ever sung of such a beast, and Zephyr realized that, being spirits instead of bodies, the horse and rider were not required to look like beings that had ever walked the earth.

"You may call me Zephyr," he told her. "The name of Zhen Dragonslayer will no longer do me any service."

"Ah, so easily you cast aside your fame," she said.

"It is not difficult to cast aside a thing so small," he replied.

"It no longer suffices?" she asked. "It seemed great enough to please you while you stayed in Brin."

Zephyr would not ask her how she knew all these things. He already felt witless enough. Admitting it would not make the situation better.

"The fame of Brin travels far among the Yolimites," he said. "But it will not be sufficient to put my name in the songs of the Flamebringers. Unlike the name of … Masked Bethi?"

Her smile widened, telling him he had won a round in the game of I-know-something-about-you.

Masked Bethi was one of the Eighty-One—the original Lashrefites who had been created in Heaven before being placed on the prairie. Yolim had used the same names for his people, and

"Bethi" was still in common use among them. To Zephyr's tribe, the names were legendary. No Flamebringer would ever think of giving children names like "Zhen", "Dan", "Kethi", or "Bethi". It would be like naming a horse "Sweetsinger".

In the songs, Masked Bethi was always up to mischief—plucking feathers from an eagle's tail, hooting like an owl to scare the mice out of her lodge, or stealing a deer from under the nose of a sleeping bear by swapping a log for the carcass. Of course, a story could change once it got into a song. Accuracy was subordinate to the demands of meter and rhyme, and truth played merely a supporting role for drama. How much had the real Bethi been like the Bethi of the songs? And how much was this thousand-year-old soul like the real Bethi?

The spirit answered the questions that had been asked only in his thoughts: "The songs may not be about the things I truly did, but they are about the woman I truly was. And yes, you are correct, a soul changes much in a thousand years. Yours seems to have changed in even a short time. It was not long ago that your fame among the Yolimites meant more to you than the songs of the Flamebringers."

"It is not so," said Zephyr. "My tribe's songs have always been dearest to me. I left only because it was clear that I would not be the one singing them."

"Ah, in this you speak truly," said Masked Bethi. "You left because you would not be 'the one'. You had forgotten that Lashrefi's songs were meant to have more than one singer."

"But Lowsinger's Band has only one kalaibo," explained Zephyr. "And that path was closed to me by my brother Greenpool."

"The path was closed to you by your deafness."

"How so?"

"The kalaibo is not the music; the kalaibo is simply the one who decides how the music will be made. But you could not hear this. Kalaibo Stormdrummer knew you had the talent to take his place, but you did not understand the duties. You wanted everyone to hear your wonderful voice. But when a song is sung truly, it is only the song which is heard, not the singer."

"Is it possible to sing too well?" Zephyr asked.

"It is possible to sing too loudly," she replied. "It is possible to ignore the other musicians because one is too enamored of one's own voice. It is possible to forget that one's part is not more important than the music."

"I do try to blend," Zephyr said.

"And when you sang with Shamon, you succeeded … until you decided to be Zhen Dragonslayer."

"You listened to us?"

"On occasion." Masked Bethi grinned. "Sometimes you sang about me."

Zephyr grinned back. "I suppose that is why I wrote a song about myself: Even if I sang it so well that they forgot the singer, they would still be thinking of me."

"Did you think the song could make you a hero?"

"It did make me a hero," Zephyr said, "until Danwel and Summerwind came to call my bluff. But I thought that was Lashrefi's way of giving me a chance to truly become the hero of the song. Ah, that game is lost now. Still, I cannot regret playing."

"No?"

"No. 'The Death of Zhen Dragonslayer' shall make a wonderful ballad. I do hope someone composes it. It is a pity that I cannot do so myself. Perhaps Shamon will."

Zephyr thought for a moment.

"I should have bid him farewell this morning," he said.

Zephyr looked at the distant, twisting cone of violet sound drifting through the sky toward the horizon. "What will happen if no one can slay this dragon?"

"Lashrefi is uncertain. She thinks the dragons may destroy the world."

"Truly? Certainly, the dragon has an appetite, but how can it eat the entire world?"

"They do not destroy the world by eating, but rather by creating. Can you not hear the gust of Motion and Air from the Elemental Realms?"

"The wind on which the dragon travels makes a sound that I can see. Is that what you mean?"

"It is," said Masked Bethi. "The dragon can make Light, as well, but you will understand this best if we talk about wind: The Elemental Realms are like a wind constantly blowing across the prairie. The world is like a summer lodge. It was built with a vent so that there would be enough of a draft to keep the smoke rising out. A dragon is like a hole in a lodge hide. The wind puffs through this hole, but there is not enough to make the lodge colder. Yet suppose that there were many holes in the lodge hide. Then the wind would blow through them all and rip the skin in between until they were one great hole. Wind blowing through this hole could knock the lodge down or rip it apart."

Zephyr thought about this. "So this dragon must be killed so that they will not reproduce." He wondered which was the male and which the female.

"You are confused," she said. "There are not two dragons; there are fifty-seven."

"Fifty-seven?" Zephyr knew this was a large number, like eighty-one.

"And they are all different," Masked Bethi said. "They will not reproduce with each other. They reproduce alone."

"Is that even possible?"

"It is for them."

"So we must kill all fifty-seven?"

"No. Others will deal with the other dragons. You and your friends need only slay the two you know about."

"Why are you telling me this?" asked Zephyr. "Are you giving me a chance to speak to them in a dream?"

"No. I am giving you a chance to wake up."

"You mean ... ?" He gestured toward his body.

"Yes," said Masked Bethi. "You are still attached to it, and it yet holds Life."

"Aha! It is well that Summerwind rescued me, then, for I doubt my body would be holding Life if the dragon had dined upon it."

"It is as you say," agreed Masked Bethi. "But although not completely dead, your body is injured. Before it becomes a pleasant place again, you must suffer through healing."

"Very well," Zephyr said. "I will do that, then. And gladly, for the chance to write my own lament is worth some discomfort, I think."

"Then return to your body," said Masked Bethi, "and I will ask Lashrefi to help you harmonize with it again."

Zephyr floated over to his corpse. With Masked Bethi's help, merging with his body seemed as simple as dressing. He slipped his spirit-legs into the legs that had held him on his horse. He slipped his spirit-arms into the arms that had played his lute.

Just before merging, he lifted his spirit-head to ask, "Will I remember any of this?"

Masked Bethi smiled. "It does not matter," she said, "for no one will believe you."

CHAPTER 22
A Second Chance

"I DO HOPE they kill that thing today," Kethi said.

"I wonder if it needs to be killed," Chamfo said. "It has done no one harm."

"The dragon at Kwoshim has done harm," Kethi said. "And this one must be killed so that Danwel can return to kill that one."

Kethi peeled a damp cloth from Chamfo's thigh, exposing his skin to the dry breeze that whispered through the lodge. She splashed the cloth in the water.

Chamfo pushed himself up. "I can do that," he said.

"You would do it wrong," she replied, spreading the wet cloth on his knee.

Chamfo chuckled. At least she was letting him sit up.

"Why are you laughing?" she asked.

"I laugh because you think you can feel my skin better than I can," he said.

"I can," she replied.

"Yes," said Chamfo. "That is another reason I laugh."

It felt good to finally be out of the sun. Even at midday, the hide-and-pole lodge held a gentle light. Chamfo was not certain what had happened to him the day before or what Kethi had done, but he knew he was healing under her care.

Dawnracer's company had also been welcome. She had made certain that the lodge held a good supply of water and rags before leaving to join the dragon hunters that morning. The compassion women would show for a sick man was universal, regardless of creator. He should mention that to Zhen. Perhaps Zhen could write a song about it.

If Zhen came back.

"When Dan said they had a plan," Chamfo asked, "did he say

who made the plan?"

"Well, it surely wasn't Danwel," said Kethi.

"But Dan was there, yes?" Chamfo insisted. "It was not only Zhen's plan?"

"I think Zhen made the plan with the councilmen," said Kethi.

Chamfo was not certain whom she meant by this term. Among her people, villages were governed by a council consisting of one representative from each clan in the village, but Zhen's band had no such structure. The gethrav held all the decision-making authority, although the taishrefi apparently had some sort of veto power. It sounded simple, but Chamfo suspected that it was as complex as boat law. A captain had the authority to make decisions that affected the entire boat, but the captain kept that authority by making decisions that the other owners would agree with.

The council that Kethi referred to was probably an ad hoc committee. Or, as Zhen had once described it: "When he has an important decision to make, the gethrav will gather some of the hunters together and ask them what they think."

"I wish I had been there," Chamfo said.

"Well, you weren't," Kethi said. "Because you are weak. You need to rest and get strong. Worrying about what other people are doing won't help."

Chamfo did worry, though. Zhen was an optimist. This was a beautiful trait, because it allowed Zhen to see the benefits of any situation. However, it had the disadvantage of making Zhen a poor planner. In Chamfo's experience, assuming everything would work out for the best usually led to disaster. Preparing for the worst was far more practical.

Zhen had returned to his band with no plan for dealing with this dragon. Chamfo did not know whether to hope for a good plan or a bad one. If the plan was bad enough, they would not find the dragon, and Zhen would be safe. By contrast, if the plan was good enough to lead them to the dragon, then actually slaying the thing would require tactics that were even better. Chamfo doubted they had such tactical genius.

"At least Dan was there," Chamfo said. "At least they had someone who has seen the dragon."

"Aye, Danwel has seen two and run from both," said Kethi.

"But you saw the dragon, Kethi. You know we had to run or die. And you say that your dragon was even bigger."

"Aye, but— Yolim's Heaven!" she exclaimed. "I do it even when he's not here."

"Do what?"

"Nothing. I—" Kethi was flustered. "Shamon, do you think I treat Danwel badly?"

Ah. That.

"I think— How to say?" Chamfo searched for something to sweeten the bitter truth that had been demanded of him. "I think you are kind," he said. "You are not always kind to Dan, but you are a kind person."

It was the best he could do, not having time to consider the phrasing. He had said it wrong, though. Little Kethi dropped her head into her hands.

"Dawnracer said I spit out poison on him."

What could he tell her? He could say that people need criticism so they know how to improve. It was a true statement, but in this context it would be a lie.

"Sometimes we wonder why you want to marry him," he told her. "You see in him so many bad things."

"I wonder if he still wants to marry me," Kethi murmured. "Now that he knows what a scold I am."

She looked up with tears in her eyes. Her face was weary. Chamfo realized that she must have awakened several times in the night to check on him.

"I want to be better," she told him. "I want to treat my boy right. But it is so hard to change."

Chamfo thought a moment. He was being asked to judge.

"If you think it is you who must change and not Dan," he said, "then perhaps your change has already begun."

"I hope so," she said.

"You are friendly to Dawnracer now."

"Aye," said Kethi. "I thought she was flighty, but she is just young. She can be serious when it is needed."

"She told me serious things, too," Chamfo said.

"What did she tell you?"

Kethi seemed glad to have the conversation drift away from her own problems. That had been Chamfo's goal, but he had not foreseen that it would drift this way.

"She said that I did this to myself," Chamfo answered, gesturing at the pot of water in which the rags were soaking and at the hide on which he was convalescing.

"Could be you did," said Kethi.

"But I thought it was punishment from the God of Justice," Chamfo told her. "I thought I deserved to suffer for helping Zhen lie to people."

"But you told Danwel the truth," Kethi said. "He was the only one the lie could have hurt."

"Dan may be hurt anyway," said Chamfo. "He followed Zhen, and now they hunt the dragon together."

"It was his choice, Shamon. And don't worry: My boy can take care of himself."

"I am not sure Zhen can," Chamfo replied. "I should be with him. Instead, I am here. I punished myself, and this has put my friend in danger. I acted wrong. Justice has the duty to decide punishment. My duty was to help Zhen, and I failed him."

"But Danwel will look after him."

Chamfo shook his head. "Dan is brave. Perhaps even strong. But the dragon is not a normal animal. I can feel this."

Kethi nodded. "There was something about it that did not seem right. Our dragon in Kwoshim seemed to be more than an animal. Somehow, this one seems to be less."

"It feels like a wind," said Chamfo. "Or a sound."

"I wouldn't say that," said Kethi.

"No, but I would. You see, my people can feel currents— movement in the water. We make these movements, and that is how we move boats. But I am crippled. I can feel the movement, but not the water. Instead I feel movement in the air."

"Oho," Kethi murmured. "So that is how you led us out of the whirlwind's path."

"Yes," said Chamfo. "I could see where it was and where it wanted to go. The dragon, too. Before we saw it—"

"You knew it was there?"

Chamfo held up a hand. The sound was faint, distant. But he knew it was the dragon because he could hear it without using his ears.

"Kethi, it is coming now."

They were still for a moment, as still as trees. Chamfo heard the dragon's wind high in the sky. Like the currents used to propel boats, the wind was a current that began Outside and flowed into the world. Chamfo tried to listen for the dragon itself, but it was small compared with the current of air on which it rode.

He stood up. Kethi's hand on his arm reminded him to rise slowly. His legs felt strong, but his head was still weak.

Chamfo waited a moment to be certain his balance would not fail him; then he crossed the lodge and ducked out into the harsh prairie sunlight.

The dragon was visible now as a silhouette against the blue sky. Chamfo could see its triangular head, its snake-like neck, the scaly bat-like wings that stretched along its ribs to its stubby knees, and the smaller pair of wings on its tail. The dragon's wings did not need to flap, partly because they rode the air current and partly because they *were* the current. The same stream of Motion that created the high wind also flowed into the dragon's body, propelling it through the sky.

The dragon passed over the lodges, flying too high to attract attention from anyone who was not looking for it. Kethi found it in the sky then—or so Chamfo judged from the way she caught her breath. She reached out and touched his leg—a gesture of reassurance he had often seen her use when standing next to a horse. He understood that this time she was trying to reassure herself.

The dragon's flight continued, and Kethi exhaled. But then the animal's path curved. For a moment, it seemed that the dragon had changed its mind and was returning to attack the lodges, but as the curve turned into a circle, Chamfo realized what Kethi put into words:

"It's circling over the horses."

It was indeed. The band's horse herd was grazing some distance away. Chamfo's own mount was among them, although at this distance, it was difficult for Chamfo to recognize any individual horse. The dragon's circle stretched into a gentle downward spiral.

Beyond the horse herd was a patch of black dots which had to be the grazing bovines. Trailing from the bovine herd was a line of seven dots which—yes—which seemed to be moving toward the horses. The riders' black-and-white skins allowed Chamfo to discern person from beast. They covered the ground rapidly, but they could not outrun the dragon's dive.

It was the thunder that caught everyone's attention. Chores, conversations, and songs were all interrupted by a boom incongruous with the bright fluffy clouds in the blue sky.

The purple lightning showed them where the action was. Perhaps no more than Chamfo and Kethi saw the dragon make its first swoop over the panicking horse herd, but the entire band witnessed the dragon's second dive, the dive from which it did not rise.

"Why did it fall?" a small voice asked.

"Did they kill it?" asked another.

Their mothers shushed them.

"I cannot see," one complained.

Chamfo tried to make sense of the scene. It seemed that most of the loose horses were escaping. The dragon was on the ground for some reason. The riders were taking turns charging at it.

Suddenly, the dragon decided that it had seen enough charges. Chamfo could feel the explosion of momentum in the dragon's body. He could see the hole into which the Motion of dragon and horse disappeared as abruptly as a hand clap.

The band gasped.

"Whose horse was that?" someone asked.

"Quick as a snake," murmured another.

"Who's that chasing after the horses?" someone wanted to know.

The dragon made a whirlwind, then. Those in the whirlwind's path reacted at once. For this, Chamfo gave thanks to the deities. It took a moment for the wind to build to its full power, and while it was doing so, it could not drift very far. The riders evaded it easily.

Chamfo recognized one of them as diminutive Dan.

While the whirlwind was gathering power, one of the hunters decided to dive off his horse and charge the dragon on foot. Chamfo was confident that was Zhen. He was the only person in the world who would feel a need to show off at such a time.

What happened next was difficult to see. Horses obscured Chamfo's view of Zhen's charge. The hunters seemed to be regrouping. Dawnracer moved to join them, but then she stopped and, with the help of another hunter, lifted something up onto her saddle.

Now she was riding away. Did she have a limp body on her horse?

"That is the gethrav there," someone commented as two riders raised their spears.

They closed on the dragon.

And a wind appeared. It came from nowhere, just like the wind that had come for Chamfo's family on that terrible night ten years before. The wind rolled over the would-be attackers and kept rolling across the plain toward the onlookers in the camp, with the dragon riding behind as casually as a farmer driving his cart to market.

Chamfo looked down at Kethi. "Run!" he told her. "Run to the creek."

She looked at him, not comprehending.

He grabbed her hand and pulled her along. "Run!" he told the confused faces around him. "Run!"

The wind rolled toward them, thundering in his body, silent to his ears.

"Run!" he roared, drawing on the power of the approaching gale to make his voice carry above the noise that only he could hear. The band's confusion turned to shock.

Then one old woman—the taishrefi—began to run toward the creek. All followed.

Kethi's little legs pumped. The skirt of her dress whipped around her calves. Chamfo hoped he would not have to pick her up and carry her. Running made his head dizzy.

A blast of dust struck Chamfo as he descended toward the

creek. Those with small children had fallen behind. They would not reach the creek before the wall of wind.

"Down!" shouted Chamfo. There was a flood of moving air crashing toward them, and he needed to tap only a small trickle of it to give the word a bone-shaking power. Immediately, every person was on the ground.

The wind struck.

CHAPTER 23

Picking up the Pieces

KETHWIN LAY CURLED in a ball with her eyes tightly shut and her hands over her ears to keep out the dust. She could not shut out the roar of the wind, nor the crash it made as it struck the nearby tents. Pegs popped. Poles snapped. Hides ripped.

And then it was gone, with only a gentle breeze left in its wake.

She was afraid to open her eyes and look around. How could she be sure the wind would not come back? And yet, what if the dragon came back, with or without the wind, and found her lying there like a loaf of bread on the serving board?

Kethwin opened her eyes.

Following the gazes of others who had dared to raise their heads, she saw the serpent coiling its way up into the sky, accompanied by whirling tatters of tent hides. Instead of circling for another dive, it began undulating lithward, leaving the tent hides to fall back to earth like oak leaves in autumn.

Kethwin watched the silhouette shrink toward the horizon until Stripedfolk murmurs drew her attention to the campsite. Only one tent remained standing.

"The dragon spared the taishrefi's lodge!" a woman exclaimed.

"It was not the dragon's will," said another, "but Lashrefi's."

Several heads nodded at this.

"Look more closely," advised the old woman known as the taishrefi.

The tent was standing, to be sure, but its hide had been pierced by a stray pole. Had the taishrefi remained there, she would have been impaled.

"Not Lashrefi's will, then," said a woman.

"Ah, but Lashrefi's will it is," said the taishrefi. "She is reminding me not to be idle when there is work to be done."

This reminder set everyone in motion. Some scuttled back to the former site of the tent village to see if any of their possessions remained. Some strode across the prairie to retrieve the bits and pieces that had been scattered. Some tended to wounds.

One little girl had twenty splinters stuck in her arm like the quills of a porcupine. Her mother had abrasions on her cheek. The taishrefi bandaged a man's bleeding eye. On skin so black and white, Stripedfolk blood looked so very red.

Kethwin had learned how to see into a body and diagnose its injuries—the principle was the same with people as it was with animals—but diagnosis required concentration and time. Right now, everyone needed help at once, and she did not know whom she should attend to first. In the end, she decided to help mothers wash their children's wounds in the creek, as Shamon was doing.

"We felt the breath of the wind on our backs," a woman told the Riverman. "If you had not warned me to get my children down, they would have been swept away."

"Wind can be destructive," he agreed.

One of the woman's sons, a small boy about Kethwin's height, had a finger-length splinter embedded in the skin of his leg. There was not enough sticking out for Kethwin to grab hold of. She wished someone could loan her a pair of quill-pulling tongs, but she knew it would be pointless to ask. Instead, she unsheathed her knife.

"Mommeeee!" cried the boy.

"Hold still," Kethwin commanded. "We can't leave this wood in your leg. Do you want to turn into a tree?"

This idea stopped him long enough for Kethwin to slice the skin that bound the splinter. It came out easily, then. Easily enough for Kethwin, anyway. The tearful boy stumbled toward his mother, looking over his shoulder as though afraid Kethwin might be following.

His were not the only fearful glances. Most of the adults kept looking at the sky, wondering when the dragon would return.

Kethwin and Shamon were still working at the creek when somber-faced Danwel found them. She rushed into his arms. "Thank Yolim you are all right."

"Kethwin," Danwel said, "Zhen is hurt. Can you come look at him?"

Kethwin looked at Shamon. Seeing the concern in the Riverman's eyes, she said, "You should come, too."

They followed Danwel to the circle of tent pegs and jumble of hides that marked the former site of Dawnracer's mother's tent. The entire family was there now: Dawnracer, her mother, her father, her oldest brother, and Zhen, lying in the middle, the object of their worries.

Legs moved aside to give Kethwin a better view of the unconscious man. Dawnracer looked down into Kethwin's eyes. "He is breathing again now. But I do not know for how long."

Danwel was quick to supply more practical information: "The dragon knocked him backward. We think he hit his head."

Kethwin nodded. She knelt down beside Zhen and laid her hands on his chest.

His heart was strong. She could feel it in her hands even before she opened her extra senses. Next she checked his bones. His legs were fine. The flow of Life through his ribs told her that they were bruised. This was not a surprising injury. Kethwin suspected he had landed on a rock.

His head also showed bruising—inside the skull—but at least the skull was not cracked.

"His body seems to be resting, not dying," she told them. "But I can't tell you if his mind is whole. I work on cattle, not people. And oxen don't really have much of a mind."

"Neither does my brother," is what Dawnracer should have replied. The fact that she remained silent showed just how worried the girl was.

The connection between head and soul was a mystery that Kethwin's sister had never explained—perhaps because she herself did not understand it. All Kethwin knew was that when a horse was to be slaughtered, Feshwin insisted that the animal be knocked in the head first so that it would feel no pain.

Zhen seemed to feel no pain. Since he was lying on bruised ribs, Kethwin was not certain this was a good sign.

"Zephyr charged the dragon," Dawnracer told her parents. "But the dragon caught his spear in mid-flight and held it in the air."

"Aye," said Danwel. "It did the same with a stone I slung at it. That was an eerie thing."

"How did it catch?" asked Shamon. "With teeth or with talons?"

"With nothing at all," said Dawnracer. "The spear just stopped in flight."

Shamon considered this. "I believe that is possible," he decided.

"Well, I didn't believe it was possible," said Danwel, "but I saw it happen. And the dragon made my second shot curve so that it hit the gethrav in the elbow. I don't think he's too happy with Danwel Broadfield right now."

"Your aim was not at fault," said Dawnracer. "That stone curved away and up. Nothing natural could have made it do that."

Danwel looked to Kethwin. "After that, there was nothing I could do. I didn't want my stones to hit anyone else, and the dragon surely was not allowing itself to be hit."

"And then it made a whirlwind that we had to avoid," said Dawnracer.

"Aye," agreed Danwel. "And after that, it made another wind that knocked everyone over while it flew away. Kethwin, it will take more than spears and stones to kill that thing. The beast has more cunning than we thought."

Kethwin looked up into her boy's eyes. "I am sure you did your best, Danwel. Are you hurt?"

Danwel blinked. "No," he said. "Tevishi is a bit lame, but she had some galloping to do today. I think I'll rest her tomorrow. If I can."

Kethwin would have liked to look at Tevishi. She felt a bit helpless with Zhen's head injury. Still, she could not leave Zhen's side with his parents watching. Maybe she could reduce the swelling.

"What of you, Summerwind?" asked Dawnracer's oldest brother. "Are you injured?"

"No, Greenpool," Dawnracer replied. "I sprained my wrist when my horse jumped out from under me, but I will mend. How do your little children fare?"

"The Zharnovite saved us," said Greenpool. "Without his warning, we would not have started running in time."

Danwel said, "Well, I reckon it's a good thing you were too sick to come with us, Shamon."

"Good can come from misfortune," agreed Shamon, but his words sounded distant, as though he were thinking about something else.

"I could see the wind," said Greenpool. "But I did not understand it well enough to recognize its danger."

"Aye," Danwel agreed.

Kethwin thought back to their flight on horseback and Shamon's hand signal. Shamon understood the dangers of wind very well indeed.

Danwel must have been thinking the same thing, for he asked, "Shamon, how is it that you know so much about wind?"

My boy is a slow thinker, thought Kethwin, *but that does not mean he is no thinker.*

Shamon did not answer. Did he think Danwel would be frightened to learn that he understood magic?

Kethwin decided to rescue him. "Danwel, Shamon can see the flow of wind the same way I see the flow of Life."

"Oho!" said Danwel. "That explains it, then."

"In truth it does not," said Greenpool. "Many of us can see how the wind flows. I have even manipulated wind to make music. But I did not recognize the danger until the Zharnovite warned us."

Shamon finally spoke up: "Some of you can use the wind for more than music."

Greenpool looked puzzled.

"I do not speak of Flamebringers," Shamon said. "I speak of another tribe. Have the kalaibos heard of the Timber War?"

"We have songs of our war with the Kashramites," Greenpool replied. "But we do not call it by that name."

"I speak of a different war," said Shamon, "the one fought ten years ago."

"Who fought it?" asked Greenpool.

"It was between Clanfolk and Stripedfolk," said Kethwin.

"Between Yolimites and Lashrefites," said Shamon.

"But not between us," said Danwel. "Other Yolimites and other Lashrefites. In a place called Dwen-Maisil."

"Not all Lashrefites live on the plains," said Shamon. "There is a tribe in the forests."

"Ah," said Greenpool. "I know a few songs about them, but we have no songs *from* them."

"And not all Yolimites live in towns—in big villages," said Shamon. "Some wanted to live in the forest."

"With the Lashrefites?" asked Dawnracer.

"Yes," said Shamon. "Or no. They wanted the same forest, but with no Lashrefites. And the Lashrefites wanted the forest with no Yolimites."

"But there is no war now," Danwel hastened to explain. "All the boundaries got settled."

"But there was war ten years ago," said Shamon. "My people—my parents—carried supplies for the Yolimites. We had a boat. Do you know about boats?"

"Yes," said Greenpool. "I have seen your people on their boats."

"We had a boat," Shamon repeated. "I was a boy then. Not very big. It was night time. The purple moon was high above the trees on the opposite bank of the river. Our boat was moored. I was sleeping."

The Riverman closed his eyes. "Then I heard a wind. It was a wind in my mind. I woke up. I knew it was big, like a tornado. I yelled and then I— I jump into river. Dive deep."

Dawnracer put a hand on the blue man's shoulder. "What happened then, Shamon?"

"I stay down. I hear things I do not want to hear. But then I think perhaps they need help. I come back up and—and my family is dead."

"Drowned?" asked Greenpool.

"Smashed," said Shamon. "The wind blew the boat into the trees. Parents and siblings smashed. One sister's body was carried far."

The blue-skinned man shuddered.

Kethwin bit her lip. There were worse things than having a family that was too big. She surely could name no one she would be willing to part with.

"But it was not truly a tornado?" asked Dawnracer's father.

"No," said Shamon. "It was the forest people's magic."

"But we do not—" said Dawnracer. "Lashrefi would not permit—"

"It was a war," Shamon reminded her.

"I have a song of this," said Greenpool. "Not of your war, but of our war against the Kashramites many years ago. In the song, our warriors create a wind that carries their spears through the air, but they are defeated by Kashramites who can give flight to stones."

"It is always Motion," said Shamon. "Your people can move Air. Kashram's people can move Earth. My people can move Water. That is how we travel on the rivers. Except for me. I do not have the sense of Water. Instead, like you, I have the sense of Air."

"For which we are grateful," said Greenpool. "Although some of us have this sense, none of us knew what we were hearing when the wind came."

"On my boat, I was the only one," said Shamon. "My siblings were normal. They could move water. They were useful. I could have saved them."

"At least we finally know why you are so melancholy," said Zhen.

"Zephyr!" Dawnracer exclaimed.

"In the flesh," acknowledged Zhen, trying to sit up. He gave a groan and lay back down. "In the dizzy, aching flesh."

"Don't sit up," Kethwin warned him.

"Thank you, Kethwin, for these words of counsel, which are both wise and truly late."

"Unfortunately, it would seem that his tongue remains whole," commented Dawnracer.

"How much did you hear?" asked Shamon.

"All of it, friend. All of it. And I must ask you this: Did it ever occur to you that if you had stayed on that boat an instant longer, you would have shared your family's fate?"

"Yes, Zhen," the Riverman replied. "But they all deserved the same chance to survive that I had."

"In this life, we do not all get what we deserve," said Zhen. "For which I must thank Lashrefi, even though she left me with an excruciating headache."

"What if you had died with them, Shamon?" Kethwin demanded. "Who would have saved Danwel and me? What would have happened here today without you?"

"You see, friend," said Zhen, "while you may be a talented lutist, you lack the ability to comprehend the machinations of the Heavens. Can you say it is not true? You cannot. Now fetch me some cold water."

At his friend's command, Shamon hurried off toward the creek. Kethwin wished he would not hasten so. Zhen was not the only one suffering from dizziness.

"He's a good man," commented Danwel.

"He is," agreed Zhen. "And his story has explained the secret of the dragon's power."

Chapter 24
Elementary

SUMMERWIND walked toward the campfire that had been built near the creek. Zephyr had decided that receiving guests in the remains of their mother's lodge was too humbling. Against Kethi's objections, he had relocated himself to a position near the perimeter of the camp. Over that short distance, he had paused to rest three times. Zephyr was still horribly dizzy, but he was willing to aggravate his condition if it meant that he could be dizzy in a place where Mother was not in charge.

Shamon and the little Yolimites were with him. As Summerwind added herself to the circle, they turned their eyes to her, awaiting her report on the meeting that had just concluded at the center of camp.

"And what has the good gethrav decided?" asked Zephyr. He was reclining against Dan's saddle, which had been propped up with the aid of a pile of rocks, so that he could see the faces of those around the fire without sitting fully upright. Despite the head injury that necessitated this measure, his voice was as bright as the song of a cardinal and good cheer touched the corners of his half-closed eyes.

"The gethrav has decided to flee," said Summerwind. "He hopes the woods along the Kailanarl will hide the lodges and the horses from the dragon."

"I had expected this," said Zephyr, feigning wisdom. "Friends, before the gethrav announced his decision, he spoke to me. We have all been invited to travel with Lowsinger's Band for as long as we like."

Kethi frowned.

Summerwind said, "I have already told our parents that I am staying with you to help you fight the dragon."

Zephyr chuckled. "You know me too well, dear sister."

"So we will not be fleeing?" asked Kethi.

"In truth, that is the question before us," said Zephyr.

Dan shrugged. "I don't see how I can run away now. I can't go home until I know how to slay dragons."

Kethi patted his arm.

"Shamon?" Zephyr asked.

"Zhen, you know I will go wherever you go. If you choose to fight the dragon again, this time I will perhaps be helpful."

"Truly, Shamon, saving my band from destruction was helpful enough," said Zephyr. "But I am glad you will travel with us. And perhaps with your new saddle, the journey shall not be so uncomfortable this time."

He gestured toward their lutes, and Summerwind saw that each lute was resting on a saddle. Beside Zephyr's battered trail hide, Shamon's saddle looked almost new—except for the bloodstains and the crudely patched hole.

"You traded your cloak for Fateater's saddle," Summerwind said.

"Indeed," said Zephyr.

"That was truly brilliant, brother. You made Shamon ride all the way here on a horse with no saddle, and now he can ride back on a saddle with no horse."

"I thought it would even things out," Zephyr said.

"Dawnracer, your father says he will loan me a horse," Shamon said. "I am grateful."

That was a good solution; Summerwind chose not to say so in case her brother could take credit for it.

Zephyr once more assumed the attitude of a gethrav. "Now that we are resolved to slay this dragon, we must discuss how it can be done. I believe we have all the information we need. We must simply spread it out before us so that we can study it. Summerwind, would you begin?"

"I?" He was picking on her because she had teased him about the saddle.

"Yes," said Zephyr. "Tell us what you know. You were the first to see signs of this dragon."

Ah, that was also true.

"It would seem that those signs have been explained," said Summerwind. "We now know the dragon can make destructive wind. It seems likely that this was the weapon it used to topple the oak trees."

"And the glowing leaves?" asked Zephyr.

"That is still a mystery to me," she admitted.

"But we know the dragon makes light," said Dan. "Its skin glows, and it sends down cold lightning. Could be it made the light in the leaves, too."

"Yes, Danwel, well done," said Zephyr, pretending he had known the answer himself. "Now, Shamon, when we first saw the dragon, Kethwin says you watched it without seeing it. Tell us what that is like."

"I felt a storm coming," said Shamon, "but there were no storm clouds in the sky. This feeling I had only once before, when my family and our boat were destroyed. I recognized this feeling, but I did not give Dan and Kethi warning in time."

"Well, the thunder and lightning were warning enough," said Dan.

"You saved us, Shamon," Kethi reminded him. "You protected us from the winds. We would have been killed if it were not for you."

"Yes, Shamon, you are a hero," agreed Zephyr. "But let us leave this challenge to your modesty aside and concentrate on the nature of your uncanny sense."

"It is simply current sense," said Shamon. "All my people can do this. Except they sense currents in water and I sense currents in air."

"Precisely!" said Zephyr. "You sensed Air in Motion. And this drew your attention because the elements were not of this world. They were being pulled into this world from somewhere else."

"Oh," said Kethi.

"Yes?" asked Zephyr.

"I think that explains what I felt with our dragon."

Zephyr nodded eagerly. Then he winced and put a hand to his forehead. What a mouse-brain.

"And that would explain why our dragon made all those crops and weeds grow so fast," said Kethi. "It draws in extra Life the same way my sister does when she thinks an injured animal is too weak to survive on its own."

"Yes," said Zephyr. "Your dragon draws Life and Emotion from the Elemental Realms."

"What do you mean by 'Emotion'?" asked Kethi. "Do you mean 'spirit'?"

"No. I mean one of the elements of spirit."

"I'm afraid I don't understand," said Kethi.

"I don't understand any of this," said Dan.

"Do you know what the elements are?" asked Zephyr.

"No," said Dan.

"Aha," said Zephyr. "This may take some explaining." He spread his hands expansively. "You see, everything in the world is made up of nine parts. Three parts are physical: Earth, Water, and Air. Three parts are energetic: Motion, Heat, and Light. And three parts are spiritual: Life, Emotion, and Thought. Do you follow me so far?"

"No," said Dan.

Zephyr shrugged. "Perhaps Kethwin will explain it to you later, then."

"There are nine of them?" asked Kethi. "You mean one for each god?"

"In fact, each deity has three," said Zephyr. "And I believe this to be also true for the dragons. For example, the dragon we have encountered seems to command the elements of Air, Motion, and Light. The dragon to which you are attuned controls the elements of Earth, Life, and Emotion. What did you sense when the dragon blew down the lodges today?"

"Terror," said Kethi. "Everyone was so afraid of that terrible wind."

"But what did you sense from the dragon?"

"I can't sense this dragon," said Kethi. "It is not like ours at all. Our dragon has the vitality of a hundred oxen. This one hardly seems to exist."

"Is that the way you would describe it, Shamon?" asked Zephyr.

212 Jason A. Holt

"Or would you say that this dragon commands an elemental thunderstorm that far exceeds its physical size?"

Shamon chuckled. "I am not as poetic as you," he said. "But that is a good description."

"So how do we reconcile these contradictory descriptions?" asked Zephyr. "We have two people who can sense dragons. Shamon affirms that the dragon is mighty, yet Kethwin cannot perceive it at all. The solution to this mystery is that the dragon is weak in those elements to which Kethwin is attuned but mighty in the elements of Air and Motion."

Summerwind knew little about the nine elements. They were described in "The Element Song", but this was not sung very often, except among the taishrefis at the spring gathering. The melody was in nine-tone, which meant Summerwind had to bend notes to play it on her seven-toned flute. Yet despite not knowing the song well, she doubted that its lyrics contained the secret to slaying the dragon. She decided to call her brother's bluff.

"I am glad that you have deduced the source of the dragon's supernatural powers, dear brother, but I regret to point out that this does not aid our cause in any way."

"On the contrary, dear sister, it gives us complete control."

"How?" she demanded.

"Shamon and I can control sound," Zephyr said.

"It's a dragon, not music," said Kethi.

"It is a dragon made of Air and Motion," said Zephyr. "And that is what sound is: moving air. Just as we use magic to alter the sound of our music, so can we use magic to control the dragon."

Satisfaction glowed on Zephyr's face. What a coyote-pup! So this was what he had been stringing them along for.

"Could be this doesn't mean much," said Dan, "but the dragon makes light, too."

"Yes, yes," said Zephyr. "Air, Motion, and Light—the dragon controls three elements. But the Light is harmless, and it will go wherever the rest of the dragon is sent."

"Is your power strong enough to stop a tornado?" asked Shamon. "I know mine is not."

"Ah, but what if we put our power together?"

"My power is not strong enough to stop half a tornado," said Shamon.

"Will you not even try?" Zephyr asked.

"I believe the blow to your head has exacerbated your arrogance," Summerwind said.

"You can't fight the dragon with strength against strength," said Dan. "It would be like trying to win a pushing contest against an ox. You've got to find the trick to it."

Zephyr frowned. Summerwind hoped they had managed to put him in his place.

"I understand," said Shamon. "You are saying do not go against the swift current. Look for the back eddy."

"I reckon I could be saying something like that," said Dan.

Zephyr nodded thoughtfully. "Yes. Yes. That is precisely the insight that is called for. What is the dragon's weakness?"

They were silent then. None of them had seen any weakness in a beast that could kill from above, strike faster than a rattlesnake, and stop spears in mid-flight.

"Danwel," said Kethi, "you have an idea, don't you?"

"Well, what about iron?" asked Dan.

"Iron?" asked Zephyr.

"I don't know anything about elements," said Dan, "but if the dragon uses magic to make storms and control sling stones, well, doesn't iron stop magic?"

"Sometimes," Kethi agreed. "It certainly makes magic more difficult. Well done, Danwel."

"How do you propose to stop the dragon with iron?" asked Zephyr.

"I was thinking we could hit it with an iron club," said Dan. "Or make an iron slingstone."

"But you are forgetting my iron-tipped spear," Zephyr said. "The dragon stopped that in mid-air."

"Well, I thought about that," said Dan. "I reckon it's like what you said about the light going wherever the wind goes: If the dragon just stops the wood, then the iron gets stopped, too. Doesn't it?"

"That makes sense," Shamon said.

"And your spear caused the dragon difficulty," Summerwind said. "Perhaps you did not notice while you were riding by, but Dan and I saw the dragon's head snap back, as though it had been struck. Perhaps this was an effect of the iron."

Dan finished his proposal: "So if we made a club or a big knife or something that was just iron, no wood, could be we could slay the dragon with it."

Zephyr considered this. "My father is a blacksmith," he said. "But I doubt he has enough iron to make a club. He uses small bits to make spear points. Rarely, a knife."

"In truth, I believe he has a blade," said Summerwind. She held her hands apart to indicate the length of the thing she had seen among her father's supplies. "A blade this long with a curve. Yolimites made it for cutting grass, but it was wrong somehow, so they traded it to Peltswapper as scrap iron."

"A scythe?" Dan mused. "I reckon I could wield a scythe blade well enough. Do you reckon your father could give it an iron handle?"

"I will ask him," said Summerwind.

* * *

Danwel was impressed by how much Dawnracer's father could do with charcoal and a few rocks. Well, actually the rocks had been cunningly fitted together to make a compact forge pit—Buckslayer said his tribe had one at nearly every campsite—but it still looked primitive compared with Clan Ironmonger's smithy in Ashturn. Good thing iron didn't care about looks.

Buckslayer cut off the blade's end so that the remainder was mostly straight, with only a slight curve to betray that it had once been intended for a scythe. He worked on the new tip until it was as sharp as his spear points. At the other end, he shaped a handslength of the blade into a stub onto which he attached an iron handle. It was competent work, and it took him only one day.

Danwel was grateful that Buckslayer stayed to shape the blade for them while the rest of the band disappeared, horse by horse, over the rolling plain. And Danwel was glad Buckslayer had decided not to rejoin the band until the dragon was slain. But there was one complication:

"Father," said Dawnracer, "you swing that blade as though you intend to use it yourself."

"I do," said Buckslayer. "I made it for my hand."

"But it will fit as easily in mine," said Dawnracer.

"Yours?" asked Zhen, who reclined against Tevishi's saddle. "I'm the dragonslayer here."

Dawnracer looked down on him. "Your head is weak, dear brother. You cannot even mount a horse."

"I could mount," Zhen protested. "The only difficulty would be that I would fall off the other side."

"Ah, thank you for clarifying," she said. "Should we desire to see such a demonstration of horsemanship, we will be certain to fetch your steed at once."

"I am the strongest," said Buckslayer. "So I must be the one to wield the blade."

"Danwel is just as strong as you," said Kethwin. Danwel wasn't sure if she was saying he should have the blade or if she was just sticking up for him. He reckoned he probably *was* as strong as the Stripedman, but that didn't seem important.

"It does not matter who is the strongest," said Dawnracer. "For it is quickness that will win the day. As I am the quickest, I should be the one to wield the blade."

Dawnracer was quick, Danwel knew, but she was not as quick as the dragon.

"Dear sister," said Zhen, "if we but wait a day or two, I shall be fully recovered. And then—"

"And then I shall still be quicker than you."

"But the blade is heavy," said Buckslayer. "You need strong wrists."

"And mine are strong from playing the lute," said Zhen.

"But mine are strong from hammering iron."

"I tell you, it is quickness …"

As the Stripedfolk argued around, Danwel realized they were paying him no attention at all. In the village of Kwoshim, there would have been no argument: Everyone would have expected Danwel to do it. But here, on the prairie among the Stripedfolk,

Danwel didn't have to be a hero. He could let someone else try to slay the dragon. And if the trick of using an iron blade worked, he could take that lesson back to Kwoshim. If it didn't …

Well, if it didn't, one of his friends or their father would probably be dead. And it would be Danwel's fault.

Danwel looked up at Buckslayer and held out his hands. The Stripedfolk's argument trailed off. Buckslayer met his gaze.

"This is my job," Danwel said. "Give the blade to me."

Buckslayer considered a moment. "It is heavy," he said. And he let the blade fall into Danwel's hands.

Danwel caught it, careful not to wrap his fingers around the sharp edge. Buckslayer was right. The blade *was* heavy. But Danwel reckoned it needed to be heavy to cut through the dragon's magic. He shifted his grip to the handle. Both hands fit comfortably.

"But truly the task is not Dan's," Dawnracer protested. "It is our responsibility, for it is our dragon."

Buckslayer fixed his gaze on Danwel. "She speaks the truth," he said.

"I reckon it's a job for a dragonslayer," Danwel said.

"As I have been saying," said Zhen.

"No offense intended," said Danwel. "But my village needs a *real* dragonslayer."

"I have slain as many dragons as anyone," said Zhen.

Shamon chuckled. Dawnracer rolled her eyes.

Danwel looked up at Buckslayer. "You think I'm small," he said. "But back home, I'm huge. They expect me to come back and save them."

He looked at Kethwin. She bit her lip and nodded.

"I don't know if I can," Danwel admitted. "But I reckon taking on this dragon is the only way to find out."

Buckslayer's expression remained skeptical. "Show me your swing," he said.

Danwel took a step back, lifted the blade, and guided it through an overhand arc, letting the weight of the blade carry itself down.

"You look as though you are chopping wood," observed Zhen.

Danwel saw nothing wrong with that. "I reckon chopping gives it the most power."

"A stab is quickest," said Dawnracer.

"Aye," said Danwel, "but I don't think I can be quicker than the dragon."

"And you believe you can be stronger?" asked Buckslayer.

"Well, if I put my strength behind the weight of the blade—"

"That is not the way to kill with a knife," said Kethwin. "You need to slice its throat."

"This will not be a beast tied up for slaughter," said Zhen.

"No," said Dawnracer. "In truth, it is quite agile."

"What if it *could* be tied up for slaughter?"

Everyone looked at the Riverman.

"He speaks!" said Zhen. "Tell us, Shamon, have you an idea?"

"I have an idea that you all see this thing wrong," said Shamon. "You are all heroes, but a hero cannot slay this dragon. It is too quick. Too strong. Too magical. To kill it, we must all work together. Or else we shall all die."

"Ah, friend, what you lack in merriment you make up for in wisdom," said Zhen with a smile. "Shamon is correct. The blade is merely a weapon. We need a plan. Shamon, have you a plan?"

Shamon inclined his head. "Yes, Zhen. I have a plan."

CHAPTER 25
According to Plan

DANWEL SPENT THE NEXT DAY training with the blade. Kethwin had been right: Buckslayer's weapon was not an axe for chopping nor a spear for stabbing; it was a scytheblade, with power in its slice. Now that his hands knew its balance, slicing with the blade felt as natural as cutting hay.

It was Redmonth. They would be cutting hay in Kwoshim, soon. Danwel had already been gone about twenty days. Benwel and Bethinesi would be grumbling about all the extra work he had left them to do.

Danwel didn't want to rush Zhen, but he was surely glad the next morning when the Stripedman declared himself healed.

They mounted, and Zhen led them down the creek. Zhen seemed steady enough in the saddle, but Danwel reckoned he was still a bit dizzy, for he set a gentler pace than usual.

By midday they were riding in a broad canyon. The creek wound its way through a grassy floodplain between steep bluffs. Sparse cottonwood groves provided occasional shade. Cottonwood fluff floated on the wind.

Zhen led them downstream until they came to a cutbank, a place where the bluffs were so steep that they could not hold vegetation. Floods long forgotten had carved out a curve of exposed earth. The creek now flowed elsewhere, and the land within the cutbank's curve was a grassy meadow. The riders dismounted.

The Stripedman walked across the open meadow, measuring the cutbank's curving wall with his eyes. Finally, he stopped and said, "Here." A smile lit his face. "Try it, Shamon."

The Riverman moved to stand beside Zhen. He opened his mouth and sang, "Aaaah." The tone echoed back and sang itself.

"That was surely eerie," said Danwel.

"Sound bounces," Zhen explained. "Normally, it strikes the ground and bounces away. But here, the ground bounces the sound back to us." He spread his arms to indicate the curve of the cutbank.

Danwel knew about echoes. A child clapping in a courtyard would hear the sound bounce off the wall of the house. A chop into an oak tree would send reverberations throughout the forest. But Danwel had never heard anything like this. The echoes off the bare curve of the cutbank carried the life of the original sound.

Dawnracer stood beside her brother and sang, "Da, la, da, la," alternating pitch, harmonizing with her own echoes.

"Not too much of that yet, please," Zhen warned. "We do not want to summon the dragon until we are ready for it."

Dawnracer laughed. "You are always so certain of your most outlandish ideas, Zephyr. But whether it attracts the dragon or not, I shall enjoy singing at the Echo Bank."

"You may certainly sing with Shamon and me," said Zhen. "But when the dragon arrives, your duty is to distract it so that Danwel can maneuver into close quarters."

Without being eaten, Danwel added to himself.

The Stripedwoman played with her wrist. Obviously, it was still sore, but she had managed well enough with her practice throws that morning.

"My spears are ready," Dawnracer said. She indicated a row of five spears she had stuck into the ground. Nearby stood Buckslayer with another row of five.

"Kethwin?" asked Zhen. "Do you have your rocks?"

Kethwin nodded and raised her slender arms to show the stones she held in her fists. A thrown rock was unlikely to harm the dragon, but it would be one more distraction that would draw its attention from Danwel and the blade.

Shamon went over to Snowmane, the horse he was borrowing from Buckslayer, and fetched his rope. The end was weighted with an iron hammer head, also borrowed from Buckslayer. This had been his idea to keep the dragon from flying away. When Riverfolk wanted to go ashore in the wilderness, they would swing a weighted rope at a tree. The weight wound the rope around the tree, tethering the boat. Shamon hoped the same technique could be used to bind the dragon.

The Riverman tied the loose end of the rope to a slender, beaver-gnawed stump, the stoutest tether point available in the middle of the meadow. "You must be quick, Dan. The dragon may not be long held by this."

Danwel nodded. He went to Tevishi's saddle and fetched his own weapon.

The iron was cold, but it fit well in his hands. Danwel raised the blade to eye level and moved through the stroke—a sideways motion that started with his legs and used his entire body to draw the blade through the air. He could execute the slice. He just needed Shamon's rope to hold the dragon still long enough.

"It seems we are all prepared," observed Zhen. "Let us hide the horses so we can begin."

They hid their horses in a small grove of cottonwoods downstream—"trusting to Lashrefi" that the dragon would choose to attack people in the open rather than horses among the trees. On the way back, Dawnracer chatted merrily with her father, while Zhen and Shamon reviewed their plan for attracting the dragon. Danwel put his arm around Kethwin. She looked so small and pale.

She answered with an arm around his waist. "Be careful," she said.

Danwel didn't know what to say to that. He was planning to charge a monster and cut its throat with a scythe blade.

"Danwel, I'm so proud of you for standing up to them, for telling them that you should be the one with the blade, but— Well, just take care of yourself. Because I need you around to take care of me."

"Don't worry, Kethwin. I can handle this." *Yolim, please help me handle this.*

She looked up into his eyes. "Danwel, if anybody can, I know it's you."

Danwel grinned. "Aye. I'm pretty good with a scythe."

As he walked back into the meadow with his arm around his girl and the iron blade in his hand, Danwel thought, *This is why I should marry her. She gives me the courage to do what I never thought possible. I won't let her down.*

Zhen stopped in the center of the meadow. Smiling, he said, "As soon as you are all prepared, we can begin."

And so the singing began. It was the strangest song Danwel had ever heard. Zhen and Shamon each sang a note—not the same note, but two different notes that sounded good together. The echo off the cutbank sustained their song so that when either man took a breath, he was able to resume the flow of sound before the echo had died away.

At first, that was all the two men did, and it sounded magical enough, for over top of their two notes, a third one somehow emerged, as though it had been hiding in the grass. On a cue from Zhen, the sound grew larger, until it saturated the air, filling all the soundless spaces. It was loud, of course, but it did not hurt Danwel's ears. Instead, it pushed against his bones. The magic had begun.

Dawnracer took a position beside the two men and added a new voice. A moment later, Buckslayer joined in.

It was only four notes, but they had power. The singers looked as though they were in a trance. Zhen and Shamon added to the chord an eerie magical warble that danced with a life of its own. The force of the sound pulsated against Danwel's body, squeezing his chest and then releasing—an uncomfortable feeling until he realized he could breathe in rhythm.

When they had been singing a long time—longer than the longest song at a wedding dance—strain started to show in Buckslayer's face. Zhen held up a hand. Whether because he had noticed his father's discomfort or because his own body was beginning to falter, he ended the singing with a gesture.

Four heartbeats later, the echo was also gone, leaving a silence into which the prairie wind crept back.

"Perhaps that will get its attention," said Zhen. "Let us wait a while and see."

They sat down and waited. They waited until the lith rose, but still they saw no dragon in the sky.

So the four singers faced the cutbank and sang their notes

again. This time Zhen and Shamon twisted the sound so that it became an eerie, piercing call, unlike anything Danwel had ever heard from anyone's voice. It seemed to flap like a tunic in the wind. In the tail of the tunic they tied a knot, which snapped and snapped and snapped. The snapping accelerated into a buzz, which became another note in the intricate dragon-summoning chord.

Danwel and Kethwin scanned the sky. Still they could see no dragon.

Yet Shamon could see with his eyes closed. Still singing, the Riverman held up his thumb to point over his shoulder.

Danwel saw nothing there, but it was wise to believe Shamon. Buckslayer and Dawnracer pulled their notes out of the song and moved over to their lines of spears. Kethwin moved to stand beside them, a stone in each shaking hand. Danwel bent down and picked up the blade.

There were only two singers of the dragon call now—Zhen and Shamon—but the mysterious third note was still hidden inside the sound. A fourth note was added from somewhere—a throbbing bass hum. As the hum grew louder, it climbed in pitch, passing through harmony and dissonance, ripping the singers' dragon call in half. It occurred to Danwel that the magic of this fourth note might not be coming from Zhen and Shamon.

On the bluffs opposite the cutbank, a puff of light appeared. The dragon followed.

It plummeted like a diving falcon, swooped above the creek, and shot straight toward them. Danwel jumped back. The dragon flashed between him and the others in a blur of purple and blue scales.

Shamon and Zhen lay flat on the ground. The dragon must have missed them by a handsbreadth. It arced away from the cutbank and spiraled up into the sky.

"Well done!" exclaimed Zhen as Shamon moved to pick up his rope. "If past behavior is any indication, it should now dive. Be ready to catch it, my friend!"

Danwel swallowed. If past behavior was any indication, it would be diving for the kill.

Purple lightning struck among them. Thunder echoed off the

cutbank with a force that made even Zhen jump. The dragon dove.

The tiny, twisting, sky worm became a plummeting, reptilian monster. Shamon swung the weighted rope in a wide circle above his head. Kethwin ducked, though she was well distant from the flying weight. Danwel tensed his legs, ready to leap out of the dragon's path should he be the chosen target.

But the dragon did not choose Danwel. It dove toward the circle that Shamon's rope was scribing above the meadow.

With contempt, the diving dragon clamped toothy jaws on Shamon's rope, jerking Shamon to the ground. In defiance of the fact that all its weight had been hurtling downward, the dragon stopped in mid-air. Then it allowed its serpentine body to drift down and land in the meadow as gently as cottonwood fluff.

For an instant, Danwel and his friends were all still, in awe of the dragon's power, in awe of its quickness and arrogance. But the iron weight, tethered by the dragon's teeth, continued to wind round, round, and round until it struck the monster in the head.

The dragon screamed—a warbling, tortured sound that writhed like a wounded snake. Shamon, kneeling by the tether stump, put his hands over his ears. Danwel, too, lifted his hands protectively, but, of course, he was still holding the blade.

He cursed himself for a fool. He had a job to do.

With a yell of his own, Danwel charged toward the dragon.

On the opposite side, Dawnracer and Buckslayer loosed their spears. Had their aim been off, the spears could have struck Danwel, but their aim was true, and they drew the dragon's attention.

The spears stopped motionless in mid-air. Danwel wished he had started his charge sooner. He wasn't going to reach the dragon before—

The dragon whipped its head around, and the tethering rope snapped. The rope's frayed end rose lazily into the air, fibers catching golden rays of sunlight.

"Ah," said Zhen, helping Shamon to his feet, "we may need to alter the plan."

The dragon's reptilian gaze fixed on Danwel. Its glowing purple eyes held no trace of intelligence—only hunger.

Still charging, Danwel raised the blade to defend himself. He was too far away to strike, but in the pit of his stomach, he knew he was well within reach of the dragon.

Jump. He had to jump out of the way.

As Danwel planted his foot, he saw the rope descend into Zhen's outstretched hands.

The Stripedman grinned. Then the slack went taut, pulling him off his feet.

Danwel leapt sideways, drawing the blade through the air between himself and the onrushing dragon.

Zhen's extra weight barely slowed the monster's strike, but it was enough. Danwel raised the blade to meet the dragon's neck. He sliced through flesh as soft as a boiled carrot.

Light poured out of the wound and filled his eyes. As he landed from his leap, a crack of thunder shook the ground and seized his ears.

Blinded by the flash, deafened by the noise, Danwel could not be sure what his weapon had done. He turned to where he thought the dragon must be, held up the blade, and awaited his fate.

CHAPTER 26
Light and Sound

WISHING THE THUNDER WOULD STOP, Kethwin lay with her face in the grass, pressing the stones in her hands against her ears. Her only hope was that the dragon would not be hungry after eating her friends.

She had most likely killed them with her cowardice. Surely Danwel would be eaten, yet she begged Yolim to spare her from meeting the same end. She feared the dragon would snatch her up at any moment, as a fox snatches a duckling, but the thunder diminished to echoes, then silence, leaving her on the ground still breathing.

She opened her eyes and stood up.

The dragon lay in the center of the meadow in a pool of glowing purple liquid. The body looked not just dead, but empty, like a sack with all its contents poured out.

The giants stood around the corpse of the monster. Even Zhen's face showed more amazement than triumph. Dawnracer reached down to pick up her spear from where it lay in the grass. Ashamed, Kethwin dropped the stones she had been unable to throw.

Danwel stood ready, bathed in a purple glow, with his blade upraised in defiance. Her boy had done his job. They had won.

"You see?" shouted Zhen, showing them his blood-smeared palms. "Strong hands. From playing the lute."

He shouted, yet to Kethwin's ears, his voice was muffled, as though her head were bound with cloth.

Zhen turned his hands over to admire the shredded flesh and concluded, "Perhaps I shall sit down now."

Shamon and Dawnracer moved to console Zhen and inspect his wounds. Kethwin would have done the same, but her eyes were drawn to the glow of Danwel's uncertain face.

"Danwel?"

Even as she approached him, the man did not move.

"Danwel?" she asked, reaching up to touch his shoulder.

They both jumped back, and the blade sliced above her head. Danwel's face showed panic.

"Kethwin?" he yelled. He turned in place, calling her name louder and louder, as though lost in the forest and begging her to come find him.

Buckslayer stepped in and seized Danwel's arm. Her boy's body tensed, but he did not strike this time. The giant gently removed the blade from Danwel's grip.

"It is done," said Buckslayer. "It is done." His voice was like Zhen's—loud, and yet muffled.

Kethwin tentatively touched Danwel's elbow. His hand scrabbled for hers and seized it.

"Kethwin," he breathed.

She looked up into a pair of glowing purple eyes that did not look back at her.

"Danwel?" she asked. "Can you see?"

There was no reply.

"I myself am not seeing well," said Dawnracer. "That was truly a bright flash."

"What about hearing?" asked Buckslayer. "Can everyone hear?"

Dawnracer nodded.

"I am having trouble with hearing," said Shamon, sitting beside Zhen. "But I hope this trouble will pass."

Standing behind Danwel, Buckslayer gave a loud clap. Kethwin jumped. Danwel did not move.

"He seems to be deaf," said the weaponsmith.

Danwel deaf? And blind? How would he take care of her? What work could he do?

"Perhaps we should let him rest a moment," Shamon suggested.

Kethwin nodded at the Riverman and smoothed the fuzzy hair on Danwel's head. Purple light from his cheek reflected off her palm. She realized that Danwel's skin was not reflecting the light of the dragon. He was glowing himself.

"Danwel," said Kethwin into his ear. "Oh, Danwel."

His hand squeezed in response to her squeeze, but his glowing eyes saw nothing.

* * *

Danwel sat inside a ball of purple light, listening to the thunder roar. He reckoned he must be blind, but he did not feel blind. He felt like he was staring into a purple fire, even when his eyes were closed. His seat informed him that he was, in fact, riding a horse. His arms told him that Kethwin sat in front of him, holding the reins. But his eyes and ears were still caught in the instant of the dragon's lunge.

That lunge had happened two days ago. Or maybe three. Danwel could no longer tell day from night. They rode. They stopped. They ate. They rode. It never grew dark. Sometimes Danwel napped, but he never slept, for his dreams were filled with light and thunder. Or perhaps he slept all the time, for whenever Kethwin's touch asked him to stand up and come with her, he felt as though he were being awakened.

Kethwin was the only real thing left to him. Time was not real. The light and the thunder were not real. But the touch of his girl's hand, the softness of her body in the saddle in front of him, the smell of her hair—those things were real. The food he ate came from nowhere, becoming real only when Kethwin put it to his lips. The water he drank did not exist until Kethwin led him to it. Even Danwel himself was brought back into existence by the touch of Kethwin's hand.

Were any of the others still riding with them? How many had survived? He knew he had struck a blow, but what had happened after that? Was the dragon dead, or had he failed them? This did not feel like success.

But he had not lost everything. He remembered that instant of panic when Kethwin had touched his shoulder and he, expecting the dragon, had almost killed her. Yolim had spared him that sorrow, and he had no right to ask for more. If Kethwin's touch was the only thing the world had left for him, that would have to be enough.

* * *

Rosy patches of moonlight dappled the tall grass underneath the trees lining the river. Kethwin moved from patch to patch until—having climbed her third fallen log—she decided she had put enough distance between herself and the pointed tents of Dawnracer's band. She remained sitting on top of the log, listening to the dark river's ripples, which almost covered up the singing coming from camp.

As Zhen had promised, Stripedfolk knew how to celebrate. And they had reason to. Her own people would have done the same if Danwel had killed their dragon—assuming any of them were still living.

She should feel guilty about leaving them. Her journey had never been about helping her village. It had always been about getting as far away as possible until Danwel came back. And now he had proven that he could kill a dragon—but only once. Kethwin should feel guilty or angry or—or something!—because he had killed this one and not that one, but Kwoshim seemed so far away.

She did feel guilty, but not about Kwoshim. She felt guilty for leaving Danwel among the Stripedfolk and guilty for being so desperate to get away from him for one evening.

I can't do this, she thought. *Not for the rest of my life.*

That admission made her feel worse, because taking care of Danwel was not so difficult. He surely was not as much trouble as her sister's year-and-a-half-old daughter. He could feed himself when she brought him food. He could take care of private needs when she led him to privacy. Caring for Danwel did not take much of her time.

Then why did she feel she needed to watch him constantly?

Because it was her fault. If she had thrown those rocks instead of cowering, could be he wouldn't have gotten hurt. And why did he have to be the one who got hurt? If she hadn't pushed him so much, he would have let Buckslayer take the blade. In fact, if she had kept her mouth shut and just let Danwel be a plowman, he would never have left Kwoshim.

She had done this to him. She had pushed him into danger until he was blind. And now—now when he needed her—she realized she did not have enough strength for him. She wasn't strong enough to spend the rest of her life leading the remains of Danwel Broadfield by the hand. She needed a husband who would take care of her.

She had never deserved him. And now that she had ruined him for everyone else, she didn't have the courage to stay by his side. What would she tell his mother? What would she tell his sister?

She wouldn't tell Dawnracer, that was certain. She could take care of Danwel until they parted ways. The Stripedwoman need never know how heartless Kethwin was, how cold she was, how calculating.

But she wasn't heartless. She was just weak.

Kethwin had known she would cry. Tears of weakness. Great blubbering sobs of cowardice. Wasn't that why she had to get so far away from the camp?

And if a wolf came now, attracted by her pathetic misery, to gobble her up and leave behind nothing but her bones, well, she would be better off. Then Danwel would never have to know how much she had failed him.

However, it was not a wolf that found her.

"Kethi? Kethi, is that you?"

Dawnracer glided along the trail, her stripes seeming to writhe across her face as she passed through light and shadow. Behind her stomped Shamon, his blue skin almost black in the ruddy glow of the moon.

Kethwin didn't answer. Either they could see it was her or they could not. She wasn't sure which would make them go away.

Dawnracer drew quite close before she stopped.

"It is you. Kethi, are you—?"

"Perhaps we should come back later," suggested Shamon, standing in the shadows.

But instead, Dawnracer sat down on Kethwin's log. "Ah, Kethi, you have been hiding it so well."

Kethwin wiped her face with her sleeve and tried not to snuffle.

"I'm fine," she said. "You can go back to the singing."

"We were worried about you," said Dawnracer, not moving.

"Shamon said he saw you come this way. It is late to be looking for parsnips."

"Perhaps she wanted to be alone," said Shamon.

"Of course she did," said Dawnracer. "But now that she has cried it out, she needs someone to talk to."

Kethwin wasn't sure she had much to say.

Shamon stepped out of the shadows to take a seat on Kethwin's other side. "When I want to be alone, I jump in the river. Zhen never follows me there."

Dawnracer laughed. "I suspect you have employed that maneuver quite often. My brother can be a trial."

"No," said Shamon. "Zhen is important to me. He is a good friend. But sometimes I need room to be myself."

"When I want to be alone, I ride," said Dawnracer.

Kethwin said nothing.

"Zhen and I know a healer in Brin," said Shamon. "I did not want to give you false hope, but perhaps you need some hope."

"A healer won't help Danwel," said Kethwin.

"He is very good," said Shamon. "A carpenter in Brin injured his eye. He did not see, but the healer healed him, and now he sees again."

"Danwel is not injured," Kethwin told them. "I have looked at him. His eyes and ears are healthy."

"Then why can he not hear?" asked Dawnracer.

"I don't know," said Kethwin.

Shamon suggested, "But perhaps the healer—"

"I can see inside him," Kethwin said. "Nothing is wrong. And that means he can't be fixed."

That silenced them. For a bit.

"Kalaibo Stormdrummer knows a song about a deaf man who learned to hear," Dawnracer said. "Perhaps Dan will heal himself."

"Perhaps," said Kethwin.

All of them had been deafened or blinded by the dragon's death, but Danwel was the only one who had not shaken off the effects quickly. Danwel's condition had shown no improvement at all.

"I will make Zephyr learn the song," said Dawnracer, as though knowing a song could turn its fiction into truth.

"Kethi, there is always hope," said Shamon.

Dawnracer murmured, "At the ceremony tonight, when every-one took turns clasping his hands, I almost saw him smile. Or so I think. Kethi, you are so close to him: Do you think Dan is still in there?"

"Yes," said Kethwin. "Yes, he is."

They were his friends. They had a right to know.

"Danwel is still in there, but he is terribly lonely. I can feel this with my— Well, it is not my beastshaper's sight. I thought it was, but Zhen says I can see Emotion as well as Life. Anyway, I can feel what Danwel is feeling."

And it was easy—easier than resonating with the flow of Life, which had always required so much concentration. Once Zhen had explained that Emotion was an element, her talents and blind spots had made so much more sense. She really could understand ani-mals' drives and feelings better than her sister could. It was some strange cosmic consolation for being unable to color animals—which probably relied on an affinity for elemental Light.

"What is he feeling?" asked Dawnracer.

"He is afraid," said Kethwin. "Sometimes he is as afraid as I am. And sometimes he feels guilt—shame about something." *Although not as much guilt as I feel.*

"What has he to feel shame for?" asked Shamon.

"Nothing," said Dawnracer. She grasped Kethwin's hands. "Kethi, you must know that Dan did nothing inappropriate before you came. I— I wanted you to be jealous, but he never gave you cause."

Kethwin could not help but smile. "I know. Dawnracer, you are a beautiful woman, but Danwel's affections cannot be won in a night. His head is like a plow: It takes a team of oxen to turn it."

Dawnracer sighed. "Now that I know him, I see why you love him so. And watching you care for him, I see now why he loves you."

Don't say that, Kethwin thought.

"He is fortunate to have you," said Shamon.

Don't make me cry again.

"I am so sorry for what I tried to do," said Dawnracer.

And I am sorry for what I did—and for what I will do as soon as you are gone. I wish I could be strong enough for two, but there it is. I am not even strong enough for one.

Shamon offered her the end of his cloak to dry her eyes.

"He may not always be this way," Shamon said. "But if he is, he may find things he can do. He still is strong. He can walk. There must be work he can do."

Kethwin couldn't think of any, but she nodded anyway.

"Dan Broadfield is a determined man," said Shamon. "If he decides to be a farmer again, he will find a way. He just needs you to point him in the right direction."

"Aye," said Kethwin.

She wouldn't really be abandoning him. She could come visit him from time to time. She could help his folks take care of him. Point him in the right direction. That was all anyone could do with him now—just point him and hope he figured out what he was supposed to do.

"If I could even talk to him," Kethwin said. "He's in there, but there's no way to get him out."

"Kethi," said Dawnracer, "it has occurred to me that perhaps there is a way. But I am not certain you will like it."

CHAPTER 27

The Journey Back

WITH A START, DANWEL realized he had been asleep. Had he been dreaming? Had he dreamed the whole thing?

Perhaps he cried out then, for Kethwin's hand was instantly on his shoulder, soothing him.

He was sitting … on what? A hide, his fingers told him as they explored the edges. He was sitting on a furry hide, like those the Stripedfolk slept on. He really was in the Stripedfolk camp. It hadn't been a dream.

It was a memory, his first memory since the explosion of noise and light that was still crashing into his senses. It felt like his first memory ever.

He had clasped hands with the Stripedfolk. Children's hands as small as his, giant hands meaty like steaks, working hands with raspy calluses, old hands with bones barely covered by thin, soft skin—he must have clasped hands, two-by-two, with everyone in the band.

And then someone had handed him the jawbone. It was long and curved—and slightly sticky, as though the meat had only recently been removed. His index finger had found a tooth. Then another. Four rows of teeth that ran along its entire length. No animal that large needed teeth like that. Danwel had held the jawbone of the dragon. The dragon was dead, and the hands of the Stripedfolk had been thanking him for his part in killing it.

He wished he could share the memory with Kethwin. Instead he gave her a hug, hoping he could at least show her how happy he was that it had not been a dream.

When Kethwin let go of him, her hand did not slip into his. She was not taking him with her, wherever she was going. Usually, this meant she was getting him food. Danwel waited patiently, sitting on the furry hide, smelling the dry odor of smoke against the humid background of riverside trees.

He had not been waiting long when a pair of giant hands engulfed his head. Was this someone else thanking him? How far away was Kethwin?

The hands held his head gently in place and a warm forehead pressed against his. Braids brushed against his cheeks, carrying a smoky, musky smell he had not known he could recognize, but one that had left a memory from that first night of camping, so long ago, under the thatched roof of the lean-to.

What was Dawnracer doing? And where was Kethwin?

He raised an arm to push the Stripedwoman away, but a small hand grasped his. Kethwin was still there. She knew what was going on.

Danwel, for his part, was bewildered.

Perhaps Dawnracer was praying for him—but she served Lashrefi. Anyway, she was no priestess. And if Kethwin was appealing to Heaven, why not to Yolim?

Their foreheads were moist with sweat before Dawnracer finally broke contact. Then she was gone—whether two paces away or across the prairie, Danwel did not know.

What did the women expect from him? If there was something he was supposed to do, he would gladly do it—if it was something a blind man could do.

What could a blind man do? And how could a deaf man learn that he was supposed to do it?

He was useless. His girl deserved a man who could take care of her, not some walking tree. He needed her so much now, but what did he have to offer in return?

He had grown up knowing that health, land, and stock—the three legs of wealth—were his. But without health, it all crumbled. If he could no longer use the stock to bring food from the land, he had nothing.

But why would Yolim punish him? He had held up his end of the bargain. He had helped slay the dragon. Last night, the Stripedfolk had treated him as a hero. Didn't Yolim care?

Could be he didn't. Kethwin said she didn't believe Yolim

looked after her. She had to look out for herself.

But what did Danwel believe? The crops had always come up in the spring. The harvest had usually been good in the fall. He was not sure if Yolim had ever answered his prayers, but that was not the same as believing that Yolim had never given him anything.

Danwel decided that he did not know whether Yolim looked after Danwel Broadfield, but he reckoned that Danwel Broadfield had always been given the means to live a life that pleased Yolim. So what he said to Yolim was this: *If there is something a blind and deaf man can do in this world, then I will try to find it. But I can be a bit slow, so you might have to give me a hint.*

And that was all he could do.

* * *

Once again it was time for Summerwind to part with her band. Strictly speaking, she had made no bargain with Dan to help his village, but strictly speaking, bargains were for Yolimites. Lashrefi had chosen her to be a part of the song from the beginning. Summerwind would sing it through to the end.

Zephyr had no plan, of course. They would ride to Brin, look for the healer that Kethi said would be unable to help, and then do whatever flittered through Zephyr's head. But there was no reason to think one of Zephyr's flights of fancy would be worse than one of his plans. Lashrefi would guide them and put them where they needed to be.

As Summerwind adjusted Whitefoot's saddle, her father approached, carrying a bundle.

"I have decided to leave this in your care," he said.

Summerwind hefted the bundle's weight. "The blade!"

"Dan Dragonslayer can no longer wield it," her father said. "But who knows what shall happen between now and when you face your second dragon? Your brother is a good hunter, but when the time comes, he may not be the best choice. I cannot trust him to understand this. Instead, I give the blade to you, knowing that you will not be too proud to give it to the one who can best make use of it."

Was she not too proud? True, she was not as arrogant as

Zephyr, but could she truly consider passing the blade to another when the chance for glory was in her hands? Her father was asking her to be wise. No one had ever expected that from her before.

She could be wise. If her father was putting this much faith in her, she could control her pride. She promised him, "Father, I shall do my best to choose the right dragonslayer."

* * *

Danwel sat on the log with his forehead pressed to Dawnracer's. Apparently, she planned to do this every time they stopped. Was it supposed to be some form of Stripedfolk healing? Dawnracer wasn't a healer.

The Stripedwoman finally let go, and as always, disappeared from Danwel's realm of perception.

Kethwin, never far away during the forehead touchings, sat down beside Danwel and handed him a root.

Usually they ate them cooked, but this one was raw, with the top still on. Lumps of dirt clung to it.

Danwel didn't want to eat dirt. He brushed the root off, reasoning that Kethwin could not mistake this for a criticism because she had obviously made no effort to clean it herself.

She grabbed his wrist when he had the root halfway to his mouth.

Now what?

Kethwin tugged on his knife.

Oho! She wanted to cut the top off. Danwel unsheathed his knife and held it out for her.

Kethwin pressed his fingers closed against the handle.

Danwel Broadfield was not renowned for being quick-witted, but even he could figure out that Kethwin was asking him to cut his own root. Fair enough. It couldn't be that hard. He held the root against the log with his thumb near the end. He brushed the flat of the blade with his thumb tip to be sure the knife was in the right place. Then, with a firm hand, Danwel sliced the top off the root.

He could do this.

More roots tumbled into his lap—dirty things with the tops still on. Kethwin wanted him to clean them. To cut them. Kethwin wanted him to work.

Danwel beamed as a tear rolled down his cheek. It was ridiculous how happy this made him. She had found something he could do.

He was Danwel Broadfield, the parsnipslayer!

* * *

They stared at him as their boat passed by—blue-skinned men and women from the life he had led. Chamfo knew their thoughts: *What is a Child of Justice doing on a horse?*

Zhen waved as though the boat were traveling the river just to see him. Chamfo did not wave, but he would not bow his head, either. He knew what he was—a lutist with a sensitivity for wind. He knew what he was, and now he just needed to find his place. Or perhaps he could make a place.

Through the trees ahead rode Dan Broadfield Dwen-Tarthilen, the blind and deaf dragonslayer who glowed in the dark. The man had done so much, and now he suffered so much. What place was there in the world for a man like that?

It was unjust. But Chamfo's people knew that life often was. They had not been promised that the world would be fair to them. They had been given a responsibility to be fair to each other.

Would the Children of Wealth be fair to Dan? What could Chamfo do to help him?

* * *

Danwel had lost track of the days again. He had tried to count stops or meals or something that would help him remember how long it had been since leaving the Stripedfolk camp, but he had lost track.

At least he had things to do now. He had chopped all the vegetables for this meal, and Kethwin was giving him a chance to turn the roasting rabbit on its spit. He did not need to see the fire to know where it was hot. He only needed to be shown the location of the spit. He had no way to know whether he was cooking the meat evenly, but at least his nose would tell him if it started to burn. Someone else would probably have to finish the job for him, but he was grateful that his friends were letting him try.

Kethwin touched his arm long before the meat smelled cooked. His girl was insistent, however. She led him over to a log away from the fire, and Danwel knew what was coming next even before Dawnracer cupped his head in her hands.

How many times had they done this? And never any answer to the mystery. What sort of game was it supposed to be? *Fist.*

Kethwin took his hand and held it with her own slender fingers. She had such gentleness about her. *Fist.* He could see why she was so good with the animals.

Danwel relaxed and waited for the forehead pressing to end, but Dawnracer was unrelenting today—tonight?—and she kept their heads in contact until Danwel wondered why he kept thinking the word "fist" right at the top of his mind.

"Fist?" he asked, curling his fingers.

Kethwin's hands sprang away. Dawnracer gripped his forehead more tightly.

Danwel was not sure if the women had reacted to the gesture or the word. He knew he had made the gesture, but his ears had heard nothing above the rolling thunder.

While he was puzzling this out, he perceived another word: *Palm.*

Danwel opened his hand and said, "Palm."

Evidently this was good. Kethwin pressed his hands eagerly and Dawnracer kissed him on the forehead. Someone else was slapping him on the back. He hoped this was not some Stripedfolk marriage ceremony.

Dawnracer put her forehead to his once more, and soon he heard the words, *Good job.*

There was no plausible explanation for any of this, so Danwel felt obliged to consider the implausible.

"Is Dawnracer thinking thoughts in my head?" he asked. He could feel the words tickle his throat. He hoped that they left his mouth as an intelligible sentence.

Yes. Yes. Yes.

"How?" he asked.

Like this.

Fair enough. Why was he wasting questions, anyway? If Dawnracer had found some Stripedfolk magic that would let her talk to him, he needed to take advantage of it while it lasted.

"Who got hurt when we fought the dragon?" he asked.

You did.

"Who else?"

All safe.

All safe. No one else blinded. No one else deafened. Danwel was the only one.

He felt so relieved. He had done his job.

* * *

Kethwin got Dawnracer to teach Danwel a code—fist for yes, palm for no—so that any of them could answer his questions. Usually this task fell to Kethwin, for she was most likely to be the one holding his hand, but the giants took turns with him sometimes, for which Kethwin was grateful.

Only Dawnracer could ask Danwel questions, however. Once she had her breakthrough, the Stripedwoman began working with him more intensely. She reported that Danwel was getting better and better at hearing her thoughts, and soon they were able to communicate almost as though they were speaking. Forehead contact became unnecessary, and she could even talk to him from horseback.

Dawnracer had been right: Kethwin didn't like it. The bond that Dawnracer was forming with Danwel was so important to him that Kethwin kept her jealousy in check, but she could not change the fact that she was jealous.

Can people ever change who they are? Kethwin wondered. She had resolved, after her quarrel with the Stripedwoman, to speak more kindly to her boy, and she had kept to that resolution, but only with effort. She played the part of devoted, strong-willed caregiver, but she knew she was a coward who would abandon him as soon as they got home. She had told Dawnracer and Shamon that she would be only glad if Dawnracer could communicate with her boy, but of course she was jealous.

Kethwin was a weak, sharp-tongued, jealous woman, and she was powerless to change that. But she would control it. She would not let her jealousy cut Danwel off from what Dawnracer could tell him of the world.

And could be there was a way she could talk with him, too.

* * *

This wasn't going to work. Danwel understood why Kethwin kept trying to share thoughts with him, but the fact was, she lacked the talent.

Dawnracer had explained that she and Zhen had been sharing thoughts since they were small children. It was a talent she had always had, but she had never tried to use it with anyone else. Danwel didn't have the talent, but that didn't matter because as long as he made space in his mind, Dawnracer could put thoughts there and see his thoughts in his head.

With Kethwin, it didn't work. He cleared space in his mind for her, but no matter how long she held his head, she would never be able to put any thoughts there.

This session was lasting too long. He enjoyed Kethwin's touch, and he wanted to do his best for her, but he was surely getting thirsty. As gently as he could, he removed her hands from his temples and asked, in what he hoped was a kind voice, "Could we try again after I have had some water?"

Kethwin disappeared at once, but instead of fetching water for him, she came back with Dawnracer.

Kethi says, "Good job."

"I only asked for some water," Danwel said.

Kethi wanted you to be thirsty.

That made no sense.

Kethi can feel what you feel. She is trying to help you feel what she feels.

"Oh."

She wants to try again.

"All right."

As Kethwin took Danwel's hands, he tried to clear a space in his mind for her again. Then he realized that maybe this wasn't like the way he talked to Dawnracer. It was about feelings, not thoughts.

What was he feeling? He yawned.

That's it, said Dawnracer.

"What?"

The yawn. She wanted you to yawn.

Well, this wasn't good.

She wants to try another one.

"All right," he said.

Danwel tried to catch her this time, to spot what she was making him do before she made him do it.

"Are you making my leg itchy?" he asked.

Kethwin made a fist for yes.

This was just too eerie. He was pretty sure he didn't like it.

She wants to know what is wrong, Dawnracer told him.

Well, there was no good reason to hide it. Apparently, they could see it on him anyway. "I don't like it," he said.

Why not?

"I don't want to be told what to scratch."

He waited for Dawnracer to translate Kethwin's reply, but instead what came into him was a feeling of apology, blowing through him like a puff of wind that rustles the leaves of the wood.

"Did Kethwin just apologize?" he asked.

"Yes," said Kethwin's fist.

"That was all right," he said.

From then on, he and Kethwin could talk. They could not exchange ideas, but they could share how they felt. And although this was inadequate for many practical purposes, often it was exactly what they needed.

CHAPTER 28

Brin Again

FROM THE FERRY, ZHEN had a splendid view of the beautiful city of Brin. Mill wheels rolled, turning yesterday's grain into tomorrow's bread. Carts hauled goods to and from the docks. Dainty Yolimites bustled between the houses that clustered around the clan mounds. Above it all loomed the verdant High Mound, marked by stone steps rising from each of the three cardinal directions to meet at the Round House sitting regally at the summit.

Zhen's own people, who valued horses, grass, and rain, would not understand what made Brin beautiful. They never sang about mill wheels.

The Yolimites had songs about mill wheels, mill ponds, mill streams, millers, and millers' daughters. And whether Zhen sang Yolimite songs about mill wheels turning in the river or Lashrefite songs about horses running in the wind, he could find an appreciative audience in Brin.

That was what made Brin beautiful. Zhen felt he was coming to a place where he belonged, just as he had felt riding down to the band's lodges at Spring Creek. A Yolimite merchant had once told him, "I love Brin because it is home." Zhen understood what the man had meant.

The houses and mill wheels grew larger and the trees behind them shrank as the ferry drew closer to the Brinnen docks. Zhen congratulated himself on avoiding the ferry with the bigot who had tried to cause trouble for his sister.

Summerwind seemed to have forgotten that unpleasant encounter. She looked eager, rocking back and forth on her heels, grinning madly at the shore. Kethwin, by contrast, seemed apprehensive as she studied the Brinnen skyline with tight-lipped silence. Shamon was squinting at the wharf, no doubt trying to identify the boats that were docked there. Danwel was the only one who did not react to the sight of Brin. Ah, but Fen the Healer would soon mend that.

Finally, the ferry reached the docks and Zhen's little band was allowed to step ashore.

"Shamon, does it not feel good to have returned to our glorious city?" Zhen asked.

Instead of answering, Shamon said, "I see people that I need to talk to." He was gazing at a nearby dock where tiny Yolimites scurried and lanky Zharnovites lumbered about, moving crates.

"Are they your friends?" Zhen asked.

"They are the owners of a boat I lived on," Shamon replied, which—typical of Shamon—did not precisely answer Zhen's question.

"Very well, Shamon. We can stable Father's horse for you."

"Thank you," said Shamon.

Zhen's accompanist walked away toward the dock with his coin chest under his arm. Zhen could not say why this troubled him.

They helped Danwel find his rope ladder so he could climb onto Tevishi's saddle. Their plan was to keep Tevishi with them so that she could act as Danwel's eyes. The other three horses could be stabled close by, so no one else mounted. Instead, they led the horses on foot.

Kethwin had assumed control of Danwel's money, and she walked toward the stables with a swagger that clinked the pouch of coins against her hip. Zhen did not know whether this swagger was natural or intentional, but it certainly drew the stablemaster's attention. He greeted Kethwin with respect.

When the stablemaster learned that she was a Walker, respect turned to delight, for he was a member of the same clan. Then his smile faded to concern:

"You must be the cousin who was sent to find the dragon-slayer."

"And indeed she found me," Zhen replied.

Kethwin read the stablemaster's face. "What have you heard?" she asked. "Has the dragon attacked Kwoshim again?"

"Kwoshim is your village in Dwen-Tarthil?"

She nodded.

"I'm not sure which villages have been attacked and which have been spared," said the stablemaster. "We've heard some eerie stories."

"Stories of what?" Summerwind asked.

"Stories of never-bred fillies birthing twin foals. Stories of ducklings covered in scales instead of feathers." He looked at Kethwin: "And stories of a gaping hole in the ground that swallowed up a mill stream."

Kethwin swallowed. "So they still need their dragonslayer."

"Very much so."

Kethwin looked at Danwel, hooded, sitting his high saddle.

"And I shall go to them," Zhen assured the Yolimites. "But first we have some business to attend to in Brin."

"Aye," Kethwin said. "Cousin Stablemaster, do you have room for these three horses?"

He looked at Whitefoot doubtfully. "That one looks like a Broadfield filly."

"She is not!" said Summerwind. "Whitefoot belongs to my brother Frogfoot."

"Whitefoot's stocking is on the left," Kethwin said. "Clan Broadfield marks the right." She nodded at Tevishi.

"I know that," said the stablemaster. "Doesn't change the fact that she looks like a Broadfield filly. I can't take her in. We don't want the Broadfields to say we Walkers are shading them."

Kethwin said, "Well, take the horses under Danwel's name, then. He's a Broadfield."

The stablemaster looked up at the silent, hooded figure, then back at Kethwin. "Then how come he doesn't say so … cousin?"

"He's deaf," said Kethwin.

"And blind," added Summerwind.

She probably thought this would help, but it only made the Yolimite more suspicious.

"Deaf and blind and won't show his face, aye? Well, I have to run an honest stable, and this smells like trouble."

Zhen could see that Kethwin was about to drop the reins on

her temper. He took her by the shoulder and said, "Let us try our luck at the inns instead. Prices are similar if our stay is brief. And we do hope our stay shall be brief."

"Seems we don't have much choice," Kethwin grumbled.

"Now, there, Mister Dragonslayer," said the stablemaster, "your horse I can take. You have a good name here."

Zhen grinned. "Ah, but I fear that my companion is the one with the money."

"I will stable both unmarked horses on credit," said the stablemaster. "It's just the marked horse I can't accept."

"That does me little good," said Zhen. "The marked horse is my sister's. If she rides while I walk, I shall be disgraced."

Strictly true was that Summerwind would mock him, but Zhen deemed his version to be more persuasive than strict truth.

"But see here, I can't just—"

"Take all four," said Danwel.

Usually the deaf man's voice was too loud, but on this occasion, the volume was precisely what was required. Not only was it sharp enough to cut through the stablemaster's words, but it also carried enough weight to drive the point deep.

"I shall walk," said Danwel. "Help me down, Kethwin."

"I thought you said he was deaf."

"He is," explained Zhen.

"I am his ears," said Summerwind, with another foal-witted attempt to be helpful.

As soon as Danwel had his feet on the ground, he commanded, "Hand me my pouch."

Kethwin did so.

Danwel reached in, pulled out a handful of coins, and silently counted them with his purple fingertips.

"Here are ten brinnacs," he said, thrusting his fist out in front of him. "Take them from Dan Broadfield Dwen-Tarthilen, and stop harassing his friends."

"Ah, well, ten brinnacs would be enough for—" The stablemaster blinked. "What happened to your eyes?"

"A dragon blinded him," said Zhen. What Summerwind failed to understand was that incredible statements from a mouse-brained girl sounded like lies, whereas such words spoken by Zhen Dragonslayer could become legends.

"His skin is purple, too," said the stablemaster.

Danwel had been instructed to keep his hands inside his cloak, but now they were plainly visible, bright as fireflies at twilight.

"His skin has been stained by the dragon's blood," said Zhen.

The stablemaster squinted up at Zhen, as though trying to hear his thoughts. Zhen remained calm. Like the hero of "Fim's Last Game", he was "a man so bold that he could bluff with the truth".

The stablemaster said, "I thought *you* were the dragonslayer."

"My apprentice has just completed his first lesson," said Zhen.

The stablemaster looked at Danwel a moment more, then reached out and took his purple hand. Coins clinked. The stablemaster shook them twice and dropped them into his pouch. It gave the impression that he trusted Danwel so much that he did not need to count the coins. In truth, he was one of those Brinnen businessmen who could feel the difference between nine and ten as easily as Zhen could tell one from two.

"The horses will be well fed and watered, ready for whenever he needs them."

"We shall tell him," Zhen said.

They handed over the horses with no further discussion. The stablemaster seemed convinced that Danwel was a Broadfield, but he clearly had no desire to delve deeper into the matter. Kethwin leading Danwel, they took their leave.

Without Undersong, Zhen had to carry his belongings himself. Most of these fit into his pouch, but the dragon's jawbone was too large. Instead, Zhen had wrapped it in a hide that he had begged from Peltswapper. This bundle was tied to the end of his spear, which he rested on his shoulder on top of his lute strap. Zhen was afoot once more.

I knew there would be trouble, Summerwind told him as they walked up the road leading along the river bank.

No trouble, he assured her. *Just discussion.*

Summerwind had always shared thoughts with Zhen, but since discovering how to communicate with Danwel, she had been doing so more often. Zhen had been surprised at how their abilities had expanded after only a few days of practice. They were still limited to simple thoughts, but at least the conversation could go beyond an exchange of one-word insults.

The wharf was still bustling by the time they arrived, walking at Danwel's shuffling pace. Despite the crowd of Zharnovites, Zhen had no trouble finding Shamon, who had allowed himself to be recruited for the task of loading crates of linen.

"Do wait here a moment, please," Zhen told the others. He strode over to talk with his friend.

Shamon spotted him and met him on the dock.

"Are you ready to come with us to the healer?" Zhen asked.

Shamon's bald head wrinkled in an apologetic frown. "I told Jiwan I would help with these crates. We have things to say after they are loaded."

Now it was Zhen's turn to frown. What did they need to talk about? And why was it more important than healing Dan Dragonslayer?

But what he said was, "Very well, Shamon. Do come and meet us later."

The women watched Zhen return without his quarry.

"Shamon's not coming?" Kethwin asked. Her face reprised the frown motif.

"He will meet us later," Zhen assured them.

Summerwind gave him a look. "How will he find us?"

"Shamon knows Brin, and he knows me," Zhen explained. "He will find us."

So they set off to see the healer. Zhen led the way. Kethwin led Danwel.

Summerwind led people to stare at them, but this was not as problematic as it could have been. As long as everyone was looking at the giant striped woman, they would not notice the little glow worm hidden under the cloak.

The healer lived on the other side of Brin. It was a long walk for people who had spent half a month riding, but eventually they found themselves in front of a tidy whitewashed house decorated with a red floral pattern. Zhen knew the place. He had never needed the healer's services himself—for which he thanked

Lashrefi—but one morning, he and Shamon had taken turns carrying an innkeeper's daughter through the streets of Brin after an accident involving a knife and a loaf of bread. Zhen was glad that the walk with Danwel was calmer—and less bloody.

"And here we are," he told the women, pleased that he had been able to find the place again.

Summerwind smiled down at Kethwin and squeezed the little woman's shoulder.

"Well, here we go," said Kethwin.

The healer answered Kethwin's knock at once. He was much as Zhen remembered him—a man of middle years, with fuzzy brown hair on his head that did not yet show the white of age, but also with brown hair on his face, which meant he was no longer a young man. No one knew why Yolim had thought that beards would compensate for denying his males the ability to grow beautiful long hair on their heads. But to Zhen the greater mystery was why they did not cut the unsightly things off. The healer looked as though he were eating a marmot.

"Can I help you?" he asked.

"I am Kethi Walker Dwen-Tarthilen, called Kethwin of Kwoshim. I am looking for a healer."

"Fen Ironmonger, called Fen the Healer. Do come in." He looked at Zhen and Summerwind. "I believe I can find room for all of you."

There was certainly no standing room in the tiny house, unless Zhen wanted his head in the rafters. To make some space, the little man picked up one of his benches and carried it to the back room, calling over his shoulder, "The dragonslayer and his companion may sit on the floor there."

Zhen had been recognized. It was good to be back in Brin.

Only when Fen returned did he notice Danwel's eyes. Out of the bright daylight, it was difficult to hide Danwel's glow. Of course, this was no longer the time hide it.

"Are you a man?" the healer asked.

"He is," said Kethwin. "But he is blind and deaf."

The healer approached, stopping an arm's length from where Danwel and Kethwin sat on the bench.

"Pull back his hood," the healer said, clearly reluctant to do so himself.

Kethwin pulled back the hood of Danwel's cloak, revealing the purple lights of his eyes and the luminous skin of his face.

"And you are sure he is a man?" the healer asked. "Clanfolk, I mean," he added, looking at Zhen and his sister.

"Danwel is big," said Kethwin. "But he is no giant. I have known him all my life."

"Very well, Miss Walker. Am I right to think you brought him here hoping to cure his unusual skin condition?"

Kethwin looked at Danwel's face. "I can live with his skin," she said. "I need you to mend his eyes and ears."

"Hmmm," said the healer, waving a hand in front of Danwel's face. "How was he blinded?"

"He was blinded—" Kethwin glanced at Zhen, "—by a dragon."

The healer raised an eyebrow. "I have heard of this dragon," he said. "In fact—"

He turned to Zhen: "Forgive me, Mister Dragonslayer, but rumors of the dragon's arrival reached Brin shortly after your departure. There are those who said you would never return."

"Their fears were misplaced," Zhen assured him, "for we have fought the dragon and slain it."

"Well, they were not exactly 'fears'," said Fen. "You see, the dragon was rumored to be in Dwen-Tarthil, and you were last seen heading up the Kailanarl."

"Ah. I understand you now," said Zhen. *Doubting fools!* "But I assure you, I had good reason to travel that way, for my sister had informed me that a dragon threatened my people, as well."

"There were two dragons," Kethwin explained. "And Danwel agreed to slay the one on the prairie first. When he did, it blinded him."

From the way the healer's eyes shifted, Zhen could tell the little man was trying to decide whether to believe them. Luckily, Zhen had brought proof.

"This is its jaw," he said, unwrapping the bundle for the healer to see.

The little man reached out toward the dragon's sharp teeth, but then thought better of it and drew his hand back.

"I am sorry there were those who doubted you, Mister Dragonslayer."

"But he is not the dragonslayer," said Summerwind. "The true dragonslayer is Dan Broadfield."

The healer looked to Zhen with questioning eyes.

"It is as she says," Zhen acknowledged. "All of us had a hand in it, but it was Danwel who struck the fatal blow ... and who paid the dearest price."

"You must have quite a story," said Fen the Healer. "I hope you will sing it for us some time."

"I shall," Zhen assured him. In truth, he was already working on "The Ballad of Dan Dragonslayer", but he needed to find a stronger chorus.

"Well, let me see what I can do."

The healer fetched a three-legged stool for himself and sat down facing Danwel. After a deep breath, he reached out and put his hands on the patient's temples.

Kethwin closed her eyes. Zhen suspected she, too, was examining Danwel's eyes and ears, even though she had so far been unable to discover what was wrong with him. Kethwin was good with horses, but she was not the greatest healer in Brin.

Fen released Danwel's head and sat back with a sigh.

"His eyes and ears are whole," Fen said. "I do not know why he is unable to use them."

Kethwin's shoulders sagged.

"But—" said Zhen.

"I am sorry," said Fen. "I don't see what I can do."

Kethwin shrugged. "I was unable to see anything either. But I had hoped you could see what I had missed."

"But you are the greatest healer in Brin!" Zhen said.

Kethwin shook her head sadly. "I tried to tell you, Zhen: Danwel can't be cured because his eyes and ears are still healthy."

"Are you a healer's apprentice?" Fen asked.

"No," said Kethwin, blushing. "I am a beastshaper's apprentice."

"Oho!" said the healer. "Then you understand what has happened to his skin."

"No," said Kethwin. "I have no talent for coloring—which makes me a poor beastshaper."

"A beastshaper without affinity for Light? That will cut your custom in half, won't it?"

"I can't expect much custom at any rate," said Kethwin. "My sister is the beastshaper in our village. She has tried to teach me coloring … but I simply cannot see it."

Fen cocked his head to one side. "Have you considered becoming a healer instead?"

"A healer?" asked Kethwin.

"We only work with Life," Fen said. "It wouldn't matter that you can't see Light."

These last words caused a strange expression to steal across Summerwind's face.

"He means Kethwin cannot sense Light the element," Zhen explained to his mouse-brained sister. "Of course everyone can see light—except Danwel."

Summerwind gripped his arm. "But Dan does see light. He sees light constantly. That is what is wrong with him."

"Yes," said Zhen. "You have said that before."

"But, Zephyr, that is why Fen and Kethi cannot heal him: They have no talent with the element of Light. We must take Dan to someone who does—someone who can take the dragon's Light out of his eyes."

"Sister, of all the—" Zhen thought about it. He looked at Fen. "Could she be right?"

The Yolimite scratched his chin hair. "It surely is worth trying," he said. "Perhaps we should pay a visit to Sil the Illuminator."

CHAPTER 29
Illumination

THE EVENTS of the past few weeks had seemed like a series of trials, but they became an adventure story as Chamfo related them to wrinkle-faced Jiwan and pretty, green-lipped Pugoku. Jiwan, the negotiator for *The Mud Mother*, was the woman Chamfo had to impress if he wanted to return to life with his people, but he found himself telling the story to please Pugoku. It was a sign that he had been away from his people for too long: Children of Justice ought to present facts simply, without concern for who might be impressed.

The three of them sat on one of Brin's many wooden docks. Chamfo had asked for an audience with Jiwan, but Pugoku had drifted over to join them. Jiwan had not objected. Chamfo had been pleased.

"That was very brave of you to capture the dragon," said Pugoku, once Chamfo had concluded his tale. "You even acted as the bait for your own trap."

"I had not thought of it like that," said Chamfo.

The negotiator gave them a bland smile. "May I ask some questions now?"

"Of course," said Chamfo. Jiwan would be relaying Chamfo's story to the other owners so that they could judge whether he was worthy to join the crew of *The Mud Mother*. She could not do her job without asking questions.

"Why did you put the smallest person in the position with the greatest danger?" asked Jiwan.

"Dan Broadfield argued that he needed the experience more than the rest of us," said Chamfo.

"And don't forget that Chamfo was still recovering from exhaustion and dehydration," Pugoku said.

Jiwan gave her a look. As a daughter of the boat, Pugoku had certain privileges, but Jiwan usually negotiated alone.

"Can you explain why you allowed yourself to become exhausted and dehydrated?" Jiwan asked.

"Bathing during overland travel requires more planning and effort than I was accustomed to," Chamfo said. "I believed I deserved punishment, so I did not make the effort."

"But your friends were in a hurry," Pugoku said. "You couldn't have spent more time bathing without delaying them."

Ignoring Pugoku, Jiwan asked, "And why did you deserve punishment?"

"I deserved punishment for failing to correct people when they interpreted Zhen's song as truth," said Chamfo. "But that punishment should have come from the God of Justice. It was wrong for me to punish myself. That left me less able to help my friends."

"And yet you saved the Children of Luck from the dragon's winds," said Pugoku. "If you had been with your friends, those people could have died."

"I am glad I had that opportunity," said Chamfo. "But I was not put in that position by my own wisdom."

"You say you deserved punishment," said Jiwan, "but that it was wrong to punish yourself. Does that mean you still need to be punished?"

"That is for the God of Justice to decide," said Chamfo. "It was wrong to let people believe the song, but we have made the song come true. And we would not have become dragonslayers if Dan and Dawnracer had not believed the song. As Zhen says, it seems the Goddess of Luck has been guiding us. I will punish myself no more."

The wrinkles in Jiwan's forehead deepened. "And what restitution will you offer to those who were harmed by your lie?" she asked.

"No one was harmed," said Pugoku. "They believed the song because they wanted to."

"The one called Dan is now blind and deaf because he believed the song," said Jiwan.

"Chamfo told him the truth when they were still a halfday from Brin," said Pugoku. "You can't blame his injuries on Chamfo."

"Why do you think you are his advocate?" asked Jiwan.

"Why do you think you are his judge?" asked Pugoku.

"Because Chamfo has requested to rejoin *The Mud Mother*, and the others will want his answers to these questions when they consider his request."

Pugoku's green lips rounded into a silent, "Oh."

"I'm sorry," said Chamfo. "Perhaps I should have told you before I asked to speak with Jiwan."

"You really want to come back?" Pugoku asked. "To play your lute for us instead of for those who will pay you?"

Chamfo smiled. "I can do more than play the lute. I thought I was useless because I could not move the boat, but now I understand that there are other useful skills. I believe I would make a good negotiator, if Jiwan would teach me."

Jiwan nodded thoughtfully. "Yes, your time among the Children of Wealth would serve you well. But how close are you to being able to buy your own boat?"

"I have enough for a one-sixth share," Chamfo said.

Pugoku's eyes grew wide, and she took Chamfo's hand. "I know some others who are close to buying a boat. Would you like to meet with them some time?"

"Only if you are among them," Chamfo said.

"Whether we give Pugoku money for a boat will depend on many things," Jiwan reminded them. As a daughter of the boat, Pugoku was entitled to a boat chest, but only if the owners of *The Mud Mother* approved of the marriage.

"So that there is no misunderstanding," said Chamfo, "please make it clear to the others that Pugoku is the chief reason I wish to return."

Pugoku squeezed his hand.

Jiwan nodded. "We shall take that information into consideration."

"Oh, but you'll take Chamfo back," Pugoku pleaded. "When he left, we said he'll always have a place with us. Time has not changed that."

"Think carefully, daughter," said Jiwan. "He is not asking for his former status."

This was true. When he had been taken in as an orphan, he was a frogger—a member of the crew, but not related to the owners and not entitled to boat money when he came of age. Now he was asking to return as a turtlet—a legitimate suitor to a daughter of the boat. The difference was slight. The boat had no financial obligation to turtlets, but if the owners allowed him to return under these circumstances, it would mean that Pugoku was free to marry him.

"He left because he knew you would not adopt him and give him his boat money," said Pugoku. "It would be unjust to spurn him now simply because he has earned what you could not afford to give him. Please take him back."

"I will be certain to present your argument to the other owners," Jiwan said with a smile. "I suspect they will agree with you, but I must ask them first."

"Then call the meeting at once," said Pugoku, "so that Chamfo can leave with us today."

Chamfo shook his head. "Dear Pugoku, let the owners take the time they need, for I cannot leave with you now. My friend needs to be healed, and then he will need help to slay another dragon. I cannot rejoin you until that work is done."

* * *

Kethwin hated waiting. How long had Danwel been in there? And what were the illuminator and the healer doing to him?

A black curtain separated the examination room from the well-lit living room where Kethwin and Dawnracer waited. Usually when one described a room as "well-lit" one thought of rushlights or an open door, but the illuminator's house was unusual. A rock glowed in each of the room's four corners. Each stone was like a small moon, brighter than a torch, emitting a silver light that never flickered. The light was not as bright as day, but there was no part of the room that could be described as dim. Kethwin had no idea how it was done, but she hoped that a man who could work such miracles would also be able to help Danwel.

A knock at the door made Kethwin jump. Who was trying to interrupt the examination? Well, Kethwin would deal with them.

She should have known it would be Zhen.

"I found him!" said the Stripedman.

"I thought I found you," said Shamon as the two giants ducked into the room. "You were just standing there."

"Ah, but I was standing there waiting to find you," said Zhen. "And here you are."

"Oh, do sit down and be quiet," said Kethwin. "You'll disturb the examination."

"Why should we be quiet?" Zhen asked. "They are trying to heal his sight, not his hearing."

"No harm done, Miss Walker," said Fen the Healer as he pushed aside the black curtain. "We are finished."

Kethwin brushed past him and into the examination room, which was lit only by the light of Danwel's skin. The skinny young man who called himself Sil the Illuminator raised an eyebrow at her for entering without his invitation, but she ignored him. She slipped her hand into Danwel's and offered him feelings of concern.

Kethwin was beginning to understand the things she could do with Emotion. Simply giving the element its proper name had been the first step in discovering how Emotion differed from Life. Her sister had taught her to think of Life as a flow, but that flow was always contained within the body. Life flowed from one part of the body to another; Emotion, however, began in the center of the spirit and spread out into the surroundings. Emotion affected the body, but was not contained by it.

This meant that when two bodies touched, their emotional auras interacted. It wasn't magic—or perhaps it was, but it was magic that everyone practiced. A hand on the shoulder could comfort a friend or enrage a rival. A hug could ask for courage, forgiveness, or reassurance—or it could offer these things. People interacted with each others' emotions every day of their lives.

Kethwin's talent allowed her to go beyond this everyday interaction. She could control the way her spirit interacted with his. She could see feelings he would not show on his face. She could give him a hug without even touching him.

So when Kethwin wanted to know how the examiners had treated her boy, she touched her spirit to his and allowed him to feel her concern. Danwel squeezed her hand, and she felt that he wished to assure her that he was all right. That was the message he sent, but Kethwin could also tell that he was relieved that his pre-examination anxieties had been proven groundless.

She was focused on Danwel, but whenever she opened herself to these resonances, she was also aware of others nearby. She could tell that Sil the Illuminator was offended by her concern for Danwel and also that he was trying to mask these feelings with politeness when he said, "Please, after you."

Kethwin tugged Danwel's hand gently upward, asking him to stand and come with her. The gesture was automatic. In those first hopeless days after the dragon, it had seemed to be the only communication she and Danwel would be able to have. Tugging on Danwel's hand was not magical, but Kethwin's magic allowed her to see the tug's effect. Danwel had been expecting to leave the room, and the instant she tugged, Emotion flooded out to all his limbs, as though spilling from a bucket she had tipped. Elemental Emotion encompassed more than just the way a person felt. It also included the drive to act.

Kethwin led Danwel into the room where the giants waited. As she helped him find a bench to sit on, Dawnracer asked him about the examination. Kethwin knew this because she could feel Danwel's desire to assure the Stripedwoman that he was all right. Of course, with Dawnracer, Danwel could use actual words. Kethwin couldn't be sure whether Danwel meant, "They were actually very kind to me," or, "It wasn't nearly as bad as I had feared."

The skinny, straw-haired illuminator followed them out of the examination room, walking with an air of importance that far exceeded his years. Kethwin hoped he was as good as he thought he was. The illuminator waited until Kethwin and Danwel were seated. When he was certain he had everyone's attention, he announced, "It can be done."

Dawnracer grinned. Zhen nodded, as though he had known it all along.

"But it will take time," cautioned Fen the Healer. "Sil and I have never worked together, so we must proceed slowly and cautiously."

"I can sense the Light in his eyes," explained the illuminator. "But I must rely on Fen to tell me if the eyes are healthy. Our plan is to remove the Light gradually until his eyes can see other things again. Since I have never worked on a living creature before, I will need Fen to guide me."

"We believe his sight can't get any worse," said the healer. "So it can't hurt to try. And he's got two eyes, so we have two chances to get it right."

Kethwin didn't like those calculations. She expected "the best healer in Brin" to get it right the first time.

"Sounds good to me," said Danwel, once Dawnracer had translated.

"The light in his eyes makes him not see?" Shamon asked.

Sil nodded. "That is his only trouble. Fen assures me that his eyes are whole."

"Then perhaps sound in his ears makes him not hear," suggested Shamon.

"Could be," said Fen. "But unfortunately, we have no one in Brin who can do with sound what Sil is proposing to do with light."

"You propose to remove the light," Shamon said. "If you do, you can teach me how to remove the sound."

The illuminator looked at the Riverman dubiously.

"In truth, that is not a bad idea," said Zhen. "Shamon is even better than I am at manipulating sound."

"I reckon hearing is more important than seeing," said Danwel. "If Shamon thinks he can figure out a way to fix that, I'd surely like him to try."

"If you would like to attend," the healer told Shamon, "we plan to begin the first treatment tomorrow morning."

Shamon nodded. "I will be here."

"Tomorrow?" Kethwin asked.

"Yes," said the illuminator. "I wish to experiment with the technique this afternoon before I begin working on a living being."

"Practice makes perfect," Zhen agreed.

"How long will this take?" asked Danwel.

"The sessions should be rather brief," said the illuminator—to Dawnracer, since he expected her to do the translating. "To be safe, we will stretch it out across multiple treatments over five to ten days."

"Ten days?" asked Kethwin. Kwoshim needed Danwel now.

"The eye is a mysterious organ," said Fen Ironmonger. "No one knows how it functions. We're afraid that if we take out all the light at once, then the eye might not work anymore. But Sil believes that if he takes out a little bit every day, I can watch the eye and see whether his magic is hurting it."

"Exactly," said Sil. "The idea is to replace the light inside the eye with the light that comes in from outside. I don't want to remove all of it at once and just hope for outside light to pour in and fill the space. We need to take our time."

"That makes sense," said Shamon.

"You have to go without me, then," said Danwel.

Zhen waved a hand. "Ah, what is a few days of waiting in Brin, when the result of such waiting is to see a friend healthy again?"

Danwel shook his head. "My people needed you a month ago, Zhen. Please go to them. Tell them I will come as soon as I am able, but …" He shrugged.

Danwel was right, but oh so wrong. Their village didn't need Zhen; they needed a dragonslayer. And yet, Danwel had already paid the price. He shouldn't have to fight another dragon. What if he lost this time?

Shamon put his hand on Zhen's shoulder. "You told me once that the kalaibo is important not just for entertainment but for knowledge. Now you have knowledge that those people need. You must take it to them."

"Every day is another day of risk for Dan and Kethi's village," said Dawnracer. "Shamon will miss you, brother, but we must go."

"But we are so much stronger when we are five," said Zhen.

Dawnracer shook her head. "You are playing the wrong game, Zephyr. Five is more than three; that is certainly true. But three is more than zero, and that is the choice that is now before us."

Three? Why not two? Dawnracer couldn't expect Kethwin to

go with them. That would leave Danwel all alone. Kethwin couldn't do that. He needed her. Who would lead him places? Who would hand him food?

Danwel put an arm around her. She allowed herself to resonate with his Emotion, hoping that she would feel him begging her to stay.

But no. He was only telling her that he would miss her. He wanted her to know he understood why she had to go.

"Do not worry, Kethi," said Shamon. "I will take care of Dan while you are gone. If all goes well, he will not need my care long."

They couldn't make her go. Not back to that terrible beast. They couldn't make her face it again. Not without Danwel.

Zhen sighed. "Very well. We cannot ask Danwel to fight a dragon when he is like this. Shamon, help these men heal our friend so that we may one day be five again. The women and I will go to Kweshil."

"Kwoshim," Kethwin whispered.

CHAPTER 30
The Road to Kwoshim

SQUIRRELS CHATTERED as Kethwin rode Undersong through the oak wood. Sitting behind her, Zhen plinked on his lute, humming and mumbling to himself. Kethwin wondered which annoyed the squirrels more: the horses, the Stripedfolk, or Zhen's plinks.

Dawnracer kept pace beside them riding Snowmane, the horse her father had lent to Shamon. Against Dawnracer's objections, Whitefoot had been left with Tevishi in Brin. Although most people in Dwen-Tarthil would have recognized that Whitefoot's left stocking was not a Broadfield mark, occasional misunderstandings would have been inevitable.

It would have been so much simpler with Danwel. He could have explained why a Stripedwoman was riding a marked horse, and Kethwin could have ridden with him on a real saddle. Instead she alternated between Snowmane in the mornings and Undersong in the afternoons, sitting on something the Stripedfolk named a saddle even though it was really nothing more than a scrap of hide providing a way to strap spears and lutes to a horse's back. It made her thighs ache.

At least the Stripedfolk let her hold the reins. Stripedfolk reins were different. They hung down well below the ears and were attached to a chunk of iron that the horse held in its mouth. The only way to guide the horse was to tug on its mouth (which Kethwin lacked the strength to do) or to swing a rein against its neck.

At first, Undersong had balked at Kethwin's neck reining. The mare had insisted on her own way unless Zhen took the reins and tugged. But it had only taken a couple days of travel for Undersong to accept Kethwin's direction. This left Zhen's hands free for lute-playing, which he was doing now.

Seemingly oblivious to the squirrels, the Stripedman plinked idly on the strings until: "Aha! I think I see the iron shrine your cousin mentioned. We must be getting close to that village."

There was indeed a shrine at the place where the woods gave way to a green wheat field. Before long, they could see a village's whitewashed houses. Kethwin sighed and prepared herself for another entrance.

"That looks like a good crowd gathering," Zhen commented as they drew near the thatched roofs. "Sister, would you join me this time?"

They rode into the village with Zhen singing, "Rola dolamin hai lo hai!" and Dawnracer warbling similar nonsense accompanied by exotic tongue trills. Kethwin just blushed, which was actually an improvement over the dirty gray color her skin usually took when she rode with the Stripedfolk.

It was the stupidest entrance Zhen had made yet, so of course it drew the biggest applause. Zhen was the only person she knew who could offer idiocy and receive admiration in exchange. Oh well. His showmanship did make it easier to convince cousins to take in two extra guests.

When the Stripedfolk had finished their performance, a round man wearing an embroidered vest and a gilded medallion stepped out of the crowd and said, "On behalf of the council, let me welcome the dragonslayers to Shortbridge!"

Kethwin and Dawnracer exchanged looks. The dragon had been attacking villages along the Grigolin for a month and every village along the Tartholin was telling the stories, but this was the first village that had guessed why two Stripedfolk and a slender Walker girl might be traveling toward that valley. They had been overtaken by the rumors of their coming.

Kethwin slid off Undersong's back. The round councilman was so quick to embrace her that he nearly caught her before her feet touched the ground.

"Cousin Kethi, please say you and your companions will accept my hospitality tonight."

"Thank you ... Cousin Councilman," she said, noting that his gilded medallion bore the footprint symbol of Clan Walker.

He eyed her with concern. "Are you worn out from your journey, cousin? If you would like to rest before the festivities, I can have my wife show you to our home at once."

"Festivities?"

"Oh, nothing elaborate," the councilman assured her. "We have a beef roasting, and some of our cousins have put together a welcome song they are hoping to perform for you after dinner. I assure you, the celebration will be very informal."

"But— Thank you, but why all this trouble?"

"Now you confuse me," he said, and Kethwin could feel his sudden burst of panic. "Are you not the Kethi Walker who was sent to find the dragonslayer of Brin?"

"I am," she admitted.

"And that's him, isn't it?" he asked, gesturing to Zhen, who was tuning his lute in front of a crowd of admiring girls.

"I reckon so," she said.

"Good," said the councilman, with a sigh of relief. "We have heard of your adventures in the wilderness, of course, but we hope you'll have a chance to tell us the stories first hand."

Squeals of delight interrupted the conversation, as Zhen began the opening verse of "When the Miller's Daughter Smiles".

Dawnracer leaned down and murmured in Kethwin's ear, "Will every village welcome us this way from now on?"

"I don't know," said Kethwin.

"I truly hope not," said Dawnracer. "My brother will become unbearable."

* * *

"Wake. Up."

"Mmf," Zhen replied, because it was easier than saying, "Stop shaking me; I will rouse myself later."

But his sister was having none of it. "Zephyr, it is not our fault that you stayed up late again."

"You were right," said Kethwin. "He's been useless since Shortbridge."

Ah, Shortbridge—that wonderful place where his fame in Dwen-Tarthil had first been matched to his face! Zhen sighed happily. Since that delightful evening, every village had felt like Brin. Smiling faces eager to hear his stories, hearty bearded men full of praise for him and his brave band, sweet-faced Yolimite girls sighing over his love songs—he was getting the attention a hero deserved.

Zhen realized the women were correct. To sleep through the sunny morning would be a disservice to those on the road ahead who hoped today would be the day they finally heard the voice of Zhen Dragonslayer.

He leaned over the edge of the hayloft to call down to Kethwin, "How can you say I am useless when word of my arrival earns us meals and such fine accommodations?" He swept his arm to indicate the hayloft and the stalls which held their horses.

"Kethi's people were offering us food and lodging even before every village turned into your own personal spring gathering," Summerwind told him.

"Aye, all we need is a bowl of porridge and a few forks of hay," said Kethwin. "We don't need a celebration everywhere we stop, when we've done nothing to earn it."

"'Nothing' you say? Was slaying the terror of the plains nothing?"

"Danwel killed that dragon," said Kethwin. "You just helped him."

"And yet could he have done it without us?" asked Zhen. "He could not!"

"I don't know about that," said Kethwin. "But I know we can't slay any dragons without him, so I wish you would stop leading people on!"

"Ah, Kethwin, have faith. Have our adventures taught you so little? I miss Danwel and Shamon as much as you, truly I do, but we have no cause to underestimate ourselves."

"You don't even have a plan," Kethwin accused.

"But I do!" Zhen said.

The women regarded him with skepticism.

"Let us hear it," Summerwind said.

"Gladly!" Zhen proclaimed. He swung his legs out of the loft and landed on the floor in front of them.

"The plan needs no variation," he said. "We merely redistribute the roles. Kethwin, you shall create an elemental disturbance which summons the dragon. Summerwind, you shall use Shamon's rope trick to bind it. Then I shall step in, swift as a swallow, and slice its throat before it can think of doing any more harm."

"I can't call the dragon," Kethwin said.

"Ah, but you can!" Zhen said. "We have deduced that this dragon's three elements are Earth, Life, and Emotion. You have command of two of those three. Just as Shamon and I were able to manipulate Air and Motion at the Echo Bank to attract that dragon, you will be able to manipulate Life and Emotion to create an elemental disturbance that this dragon, given its elemental nature, will sense even from a great distance. When he comes to investigate: we have him!"

"We have him?" asked Summerwind.

"Truly," said Zhen.

"Truly, I think not," said Summerwind. "You seem to be forgetting the difference in size."

Kethwin nodded. "Our dragon is a lot bigger, Zhen."

"Summerwind can use a longer rope," Zhen suggested.

"Do you recall how the sky dragon broke Shamon's rope and nearly dragged you to your death when you tried to hold it?" Summerwind asked.

Zhen did recall, and the description was wholly inaccurate. In truth, he had been pulled through the air and hardly dragged at all.

"We shall use a stouter rope," he promised.

"Any rope can break," said Summerwind.

"I shall be so swift that the rope need hold for only an instant. You need not concern yourself with hanging on."

"And what if this dragon does not choose to make its appearance within range of the rope?" Summerwind asked. "Or what if, instead of appearing, it simply opens a pit under our feet and swallows us whole?"

"If the dragon should swallow me, I shall slice it open from the inside!" Zhen declared.

"Truly heroic, brother. But Father entrusted the blade to my care, and if you wish for me to hand it over to you, you must invent a better plan."

"But how can one improve upon a plan that has already succeeded?" Zhen asked.

"By adapting it to circumstances," said Summerwind. "You need a more certain way to bind it once Kethi has summoned it."

"And I can't—" Kethwin began.

"Adapting to circumstances! Sister, you inspire me. Yes, yes, what are our circumstances?"

"A bigger dragon that attacks from underground," said Summerwind.

"And wooded terrain," Zhen observed, drumming his fingers on a post.

Ah, and it was a keen observation!

"Consider this," he suggested. "If we were in a tree, the underground dragon would be forced to reveal itself before it could attack us. If the woods were thick, then the dragon could not use its size against me, for I could dodge behind trees and dart in at its vulnerable spots while its own motion would be hindered. And if we set a giant snare around the place it is most likely to appear— Kethwin, do you think you can create an elemental disturbance in the air above a particular point?"

"I can't call your dragon," Kethwin said.

"But you can," said Zhen. "You command the proper elements. We settled this already."

"I can't do it because I'll panic," Kethwin said. "Just like I did when we were supposed to be helping Danwel. You were all fighting, and …"

And what? Zhen looked at his sister.

"She collapsed and curled up into a ball," said Summerwind.

"You knew?" asked Kethwin.

"Yes," Summerwind replied.

Kethwin was horrified. "Why didn't you say anything?"

"I did not want to be unkind," said Summerwind. "Although, now that I do not need to remain silent, I would like to tell you that what happened to Dan was not your fault."

"Who said it was my fault?"

"No one," said Summerwind. "But you blame yourself because

you were hiding while the rest of us were fighting. Kethi, Dan was not injured by the dragon's attack; Dan was injured by the dragon's death. There was nothing you could have done to protect him."

"Could be you're right," murmured Kethwin. "But I should have fought, even if it was useless. Instead I was helpless, and that's worse."

"Kethwin," said Zhen. "Dear Kethwin. Has it occurred to you that perhaps this second dragon gives you a second chance?"

"Zhen, I can't face it," she said. "You don't understand, it's not just bigger. It— With your dragon, I was simply fighting against my own fear. But this dragon can do with fear what you do with sound. Its magic makes my cowardice ten times worse. Please don't make a plan that depends on me, because we'll all just end up dead."

Zhen put an arm on the little woman's shoulder.

"Kethwin, we have spent enough time together to see each other's strengths and weaknesses with acute clarity. You may lack the hunter's instinct, but you do not lack courage. You chose to face the sky dragon with us, fully aware of the danger.

"That is all I am asking of you now, and you know you can do it. You will not have to fight. Our lives will not depend on you. All I am asking is that you do what needs to be done to attract the dragon.

"Once it arrives, it will not matter whether you run or hide. All the fighting will be up to me and Summerwind. You will have done your job, and it is a job you can do."

Kethwin bit her lip.

Zhen gave her an encouraging smile.

Kethwin nodded. "All right, Zhen. When you and Dawnracer have your plan ready, I will try to call the dragon."

* * *

Kethwin knew that would not be the last time the Stripedfolk argued over the plan, but it did turn out to be the last time a late-night celebration would give Zhen an excuse to sleep in. Later that day, they entered the valley of the Grigolin, where the mood was far from festive. The thatch-roofed villages still welcomed the arrival of the "dragonslayers", but now Kethwin and her companions were met with pleas, not parties, and any smiles they received were anxious ones.

Kethwin had feared that Zhen would continue his habit of singing a jolly song to attract attention every time they entered a village, but she should have realized that Zhen would play to the audience. He rode toward the anxious crowds with his chin high, his back straight, and his face solemn—and he no longer let himself be seen riding with Kethwin holding the reins. Once introductions had been made, of course, Zhen was easily convinced to perform a song or two for his audience, but he understood that the people in this valley were not looking for a performer: They expected him to be a dragonslayer.

The dragon had been sighted frequently during the month that Kethwin had been gone, and it had not confined its rampages to Kwoshim. It had made its mark all along the valley, striking some villages and sparing others without any apparent pattern. Stories of what it had done were bad enough, but Kethwin's cousins seemed even more afraid of what it might do next. The untouched villages feared their good fortune would not hold. The damaged villages feared what could happen if the dragon returned.

No one knew the worst that could happen, but everyone knew the worst that had happened. In the town of Hickory Hill, where courtyards were few and the buildings were close together, a block of five houses had collapsed into the earth. The only survivor was an eight-year-old girl who had been buried for two days.

It was now common knowledge that sinkholes could open up anywhere. Cowherds were told to watch for depressions in the earth or cracks that might indicate unstable ground. Some stories told of villages that had not even known they had been attacked until an ox had been lost in a sinkhole. Kethwin was unable to determine if this had really happened multiple times or if all the stories were just different versions of what had happened to Danwel's family's ox.

The word "dragongrowth" had been coined to describe the parts of the forest where the dragon's passage had left impenetrable walls of lush undergrowth and grotesquely overgrown trees whose branches drooped under the weight of excess leaves and bark. Woodsmen had followed these trails deep into the forest, searching for a "lair"—a hypothetical hiding place where the dragon rested between attacks on villages. All through the valley, farmers were trying to decide what to do with hay meadows that had become overgrown in one night or with swaths of wheat that had grown shoulder high without producing seeds. The only benefit to dragon-caused growth was that some gardeners were able to harvest their root vegetables in Redmonth and plant a second crop.

"No catastrophe is without opportunity," is what the Walkers of Bwenim said, recounting the bass pond that was sucked dry overnight, necessitating a village-wide fish fry. Others were less successful in finding opportunity in the wake of the dragon's thirst. Twelve-month springs went dry, tributaries of the Grigolin were swallowed by dragonpits, and the Walker mill at Ashturn remained idle. However, Ashturn's water had found a new path to the Grigolin. The water that disappeared at Kwoshim came seeping out of the middle of an Ashturn hay meadow, forming a new tributary.

We can count on nothing anymore, Kethwin thought. *Streams and springs disappear to reappear somewhere else. Crops grow wildly. Even the ground we walk on is no longer trustworthy. Why haven't they done something? They should have found a way to kill the dragon themselves instead of depending on Danwel to solve their problems. Oh, but I wish he were here now.*

CHAPTER 31
A Spontaneous Meeting

ALTHOUGH ATTACKS had occurred throughout the valley—most recently, at a wedding dance in Praizhin—there was never any question that their destination was Kwoshim. Zhen said it was important to start at the source. Dawnracer said that if the dragon could strike anywhere, then they might as well wait for it in Kwoshim. Kethwin just wanted to get home to be sure everyone was all right. She finally understood why Zhen had been more focused on finding his band than on fighting the dragon.

It was hay-cutting time, but people left their scything when they saw Kethwin and the two Stripedfolk riding toward the village. Children went running to their cousins' meadows to spread the news and to brag that they had seen the dragonslayer first. By the time the riders reached the center of town, Walkers, Broadfields, Highmeadows, and Springwaters were flocking in along the four main streets, as though gathering for a meeting.

The four councilmen, of course, jumped right into the center of excitement.

"Will Danwel be coming?" Councilman Broadfield asked as Kethwin slid off Undersong's saddle.

"No," she said. "If he comes home, it will not be for several days."

Her answer seemed to make Councilman Broadfield grumpy rather than concerned. He relayed the news to Councilman Walker, who smiled. Because Kethwin had come back without Danwel, her clan had the honor of speaking first.

In a voice loud enough to quiet the crowd, Councilman Walker said, "Kethi Walker, on behalf of the council of Kwoshim, we welcome your return."

Everyone seemed to expect a response, so Kethwin said,

"Thank you."

She scanned the smiling, curious, and hopeful faces of the people she had known all her life. She was glad to see them, of course, but where was Feshwin? She should have stayed on the horse, where the view was better.

"Would you like to introduce your companions?" Councilman Walker asked.

"Oh. Surely. Allow me to introduce—"

"A bit louder, please," the councilman suggested.

Kethwin sighed. Why did everything have to be a show? She just wanted to see her family again. Oh, well. People had their expectations.

"Allow me to introduce Dawnracer and Zhen ... Flamebringer." That probably wasn't strictly correct, but it didn't sound right to introduce someone without a clan name. Dawnracer gave Kethwin a grin.

"Zhen is the person Danwel and I were sent to find," Kethwin added. She wouldn't tell her village that Zhen was a dragonslayer—not when it was poor Danwel who had slain Zhen's dragon.

"Zhen Flamebringer, we thank you for coming to our village in our time of need. As you may know ..."

Kethwin reckoned her part was probably done now. When it came to exchanging speeches with village councils, Zhen had surely received enough practice to be able to continue from here. "Excuse me," she mumbled. She slipped between the shoulders of those who gawked at the Stripedfolk and tried to make her way out of the crowd. She hoped someone was home at her house.

A hand grabbed her sleeve.

"Kethwin."

It was Bethinesi, Danwel's sister.

"Kethwin, where is he? What happened to him?"

"Bethinesi, he—" Well, Danwel's family needed to know the story. Kethwin could find her own family soon enough.

"There was another dragon," Kethwin explained. "Danwel said we had to fight it first because it threatened the dragonslayer's family. Only he isn't really a dragonslayer. Danwel killed the Stripedfolk dragon for them, but— Well, the dragons are magical,

Bethinesi. When Danwel killed that one, it left him blind and deaf."

Bethinesi's face was blank. Kethwin knew it would be difficult for Danwel's family to imagine him as anything but the biggest, strongest, most reliable man in the village. Actually, he still was that. The only difference was that now he would depend on others as much as they depended on him.

"We left Danwel in Brin," Kethwin continued. "Some men there think they might be able to heal him. If they do, well, then Danwel will come on his own. If they don't, then we'll go back to Brin and get him once this dragon has been dealt with." *If any of us survive*, she added to herself.

"So it's curable?" Bethinesi asked.

Kethwin shook her head. "Tell your folks not to get their hopes up. He'll probably be blind and deaf for the rest of his life. But he's still Danwel. He can still speak to us, and I'll show you ways you can answer him. It won't be easy, but I'll be there to help you."

Danwel's family would need her help more than Danwel would. That was a strange thought, but Kethwin realized it was true.

"All right, Kethwin," said Bethinesi. "Thank you. I'll tell Mom."

You poor thing, Kethwin thought as Bethinesi Broadfield walked away. *You want to cry, but to do that, you would have to let yourself believe it's true.*

Kethwin negotiated her way out of the press of bodies, exchanging polite greetings with those people who felt the need to say something to her as she passed. When she finally did escape to the edge of the crowd, she was frozen in place by the sight of her sister Feshwin talking to Zhoswin Highmeadow. Zhoswin's hair was covered by a widow's scarf.

Feshwin's face broke into a grin when she saw Kethwin a moment later. She scooped up eighteen-month-old Hafwin from the dirt and hurried over to greet Kethwin, who was too shocked to take even one step toward them.

Kethwin's niece jumped into her arms with a cry of "Kefwin!"

"Oh, Kethwin I'm so—" Feshwin stopped. Kethwin couldn't take her eyes off Zhoswin's widow's scarf.

"Oh," said Feshwin. "With all the stories going around these days, I guess you didn't hear that one."

"What happened?" Kethwin asked.

"The dragon came back about ten days ago," Feshwin said. "It opened up a hole in the middle of their sleeping room. When Tholom jumped out of bed, well, we imagine he fell in. And then the wall collapsed into the hole on top of him—not the wall holding their bed, but the other one. Zhoswin stayed in bed, so she was safe. That's where her cousins found her the next morning— sitting in bed with her back against the remaining wall, with no floor underneath her."

"Poor Zhoswin," Kethwin murmured.

Tholom and Zhoswin had been the ones who had told everyone about dragons. Now Tholom had been swallowed by one.

"Why didn't people do something?" Kethwin asked. "Why did they just sit and wait for someone to get killed?"

"Oh, Kethwin, they did do something. Didn't you hear about the woodcutters?"

Kethwin had heard a story of one group of woodcutters that had actually found the dragon. The important detail of that story had been that not all of them had come back.

"That was here?" she asked.

"Yes," said Feshwin. "When Tholom got killed, Zhoswin's brothers got mighty angry. They said they didn't need to wait for a giant dragonslayer. They said men with axes should be able to take care of themselves. So they organized a group of woodcutters—"

"Oh, no," said Kethwin. "Not Vanim?"

"Our brother is fine," Feshwin said. "Or, that is, he survived. He will be fine, if he does what he is told."

"What happened?" Kethwin asked.

Feshwin sighed. "Maybe you should just come and see him."

* * *

Summerwind knew how it was. It was only natural that Kethi would disappear into the crowd of friends and relatives whom she had not seen for so long. And it was only natural that Zephyr, when surrounded by Yolimites giving him an opportunity to act like a puffed-up robin-chest, would choose to prolong the occasion. And thus it was only natural that Summerwind would be left holding the reins for both horses.

On the prairie, she would have just turned them loose, but Yolimites were particular about which animals grazed where. Every blade of grass was claimed by somebody. And if the horses wandered into the forest, they might never be able to find the way back. So Summerwind held the reins and hoped that Kethi would remember to arrange fodder for the horses before nightfall.

Ah, but there she was! Kethi and another woman were leaving Zephyr's crowd. Summerwind could see the wisdom in that. She hurried to catch up, trusting the horses not to step on Yolimites and trusting the Yolimites not to get underfoot.

"Kethi?"

Both women stopped and turned.

Summerwind smiled. "Ah, I bid you good afternoon. I am Dawnracer."

"Glad to meet you," said the second woman, who was holding a tiny toddler. "I'm Feshi Walker, Kethi's sister."

Although it was true that all Yolimites looked similar—their faces had no distinguishing stripes—the relationship between the two would not have been difficult to guess. Feshi was a slightly older version of Kethi.

"And I am pleased to meet you, Feshi."

"We were going to check in on our brother," Feshi explained as Kethi took Undersong's reins. "Would you like to come along?"

"I was thinking that someone should stay here and keep my brother under control," said Summerwind, glancing at Zephyr, who was now telling some tale, waving the dragon's jawbone for emphasis. "But I suppose I could leave him to make a spectacle of himself, as that is truly what he enjoys."

"Aye, come with us, Dawnracer," Kethi said. "Vanim has actually seen the dragon. Let's see what he has to say."

The women led her to their mother's lodge, which was small, square, and white. Its thatched roof reminded Summerwind of the brush-lodge Dan had helped her build so long ago. Wooden fences connected the lodge to others just like it, delineating rectangular patches of bare ground that the Yolimites referred to as "courtyards". They turned the horses loose in the courtyard, and

Feshi led the way into the lodge, apologizing to Kethi, "He can't climb into the hayloft anymore, so I put him in your bed."

The bed was a sort of low platform built into the wall of the lodge. Summerwind recognized it as another way in which Yolimites tried to make themselves taller. They had ladders by their courtyard gates so they could mount their horses. They sat on wooden boards called "benches". So it was not surprising that they slept on platforms.

Van Walker was not asleep, but he did not attempt to get off the platform when introductions were made. Feshi explained that this was not laziness, but rather necessity. The man had an injured knee.

In the dim light, this was difficult to see, but as Summerwind's eyes adjusted, she observed that his left leg was naked, swollen, and twisted so that his foot pointed off to the side. His sisters were full of pity for him. The poor thing needed it: He was grotesque. No doubt Zephyr could have thought of something cheerful to say to the wretch, but Summerwind was at a loss.

"At least you are alive," said Feshi. She turned to Kethi. "Two woodcutters from Ashturn were crushed to death."

"Oh, Vanim," said Kethi. "How did you let them talk you into this?"

"Well, what else could I have done? All the woodcutters were going after the dragon. What was I supposed to tell them? 'Good luck, boys. Can I have your job if you don't come back?'"

"Oh, Vanim."

"And anyway, after it killed Tholom Highmeadow, well, I had to do something. At least try something."

"Kethwin has brought the dragonslayer," said Feshi. "Except that she says—"

"Except he's not really a dragonslayer," finished Kethi. "He helped us fight a dragon in the Stripedfolk wilderness, but he didn't kill it. Danwel did."

"Oho!" said Van. "Aye, that Danwel is a handy boy. You sure picked a good one, Kethwin. How did he kill it?"

"With a scythe blade," said Kethi.

"A scythe blade?" said Van. "How did he cut that hide with a scythe blade?"

"I don't think the two dragons are similar at all," said Feshi, to whom they had already told some of the story. "That's why Dawnracer is here. She wants to know more about our dragon."

In truth, Summerwind was there because she belonged nowhere else in the Yolimite village, but there was no need to mention this. Feshi was correct: If they were to go dragon hunting, they needed to learn more about their quarry.

"What do you want to know?" Van asked.

"Perhaps you could just tell us what happened," said Summerwind.

"All right," said Van. "A couple days after the dragon killed Tholom, we got together with some of the woodcutters from Ashturn and headed into the forest, following the line of dragongrowth it had left behind. At first I was a bit scared, but as we marched along, I thought, 'There must be nearly fifty of us here. We all have axes. No beast can be so big that it can fight off fifty men with axes.'"

He frowned. "Well, I was wrong.

"We got a ways into the forest and the trail disappeared. That's the way those dragongrowth trails are. It seems that sometimes the dragon leaves trails and sometimes it doesn't, like the way a spider can choose whether or not to leave a trail of silk.

"Anyway, we kept going in the same direction until we came to that clearing that Clan Highmeadow made two springs ago. We stopped for a rest. Some of the boys started talking about what a good place it would be for a fight. They reckoned we could completely surround the dragon without having any trees in our way.

"Some of them got to prancing about, like stallions ready to get to work, and they were telling each other all the things they would do if the dragon came." He shrugged. "And then it came."

"Right there in the clearing?" asked Kethi. "Right where you wanted it?"

"Right where we thought we wanted it," said Van. "Once it showed itself, most of the boys decided they didn't want it so bad.

"The rumbling came first. That got their attention. Shimeth

Broadfield pointed out how the rumbling was shaking the leaves of the trees. So we all looked at the branches, and as we watched, they began turning greener. New leaves were bursting out. I looked down beneath my feet, and all kinds of little plants were popping up out of the ground, like they thought they could get away from the thing if they grew fast enough.

"We all realized at the same time that none of us wanted to be standing on the spot the dragon chose to break through. Some ran then—the smart ones. The rest of us just stood there to see which spot it would pick.

"And then the ground splashed like a puddle does when you drop a rock into it, except it was more of a pond-sized splash that sent dirt raining down on all us fools who were still there.

"All I could see was falling dirt and a moving wall of orange scales. Well, I reckoned that if I was still fool enough to be standing there, then I must be fool enough to try to do what we said we would do, so I rushed at the thing and hit it as hard as I could with my axe.

"Feshwin, show them my axe."

Feshi reached under the bed. Summerwind knew why the object in question was not kept far from its owner: Every storyteller values an illustrative conversation piece. Feshi withdrew the axe and handed it to her brother so that he could display it.

The blade was not simply nicked. It had been flattened, as though it had struck a rock.

"I reckon not even Dad has ever struck a blow that hard," Van said. "But that monster has a hide of iron. The axe just bounced off it.

"Next thing I knew, my leg sank into the ground." Van grimaced. "I lost my balance then, and my knee twisted as I fell. The dragon was passing through at a good clip, so it didn't stop to finish me off. I reckon it never even knew I was there."

Van sighed. "Well, about as soon as the dragon showed up, it was gone again. That was good for me because it meant that some of the others hadn't had time to run very far. Two of the Broadfield boys picked me up and packed me away from there. I don't know what I would have done without their help. I surely cannot walk."

"Look at his leg, Kethwin, and tell me what you see." Feshi almost seemed excited.

Kethi put her hands on her brother's thigh and closed her eyes.

She frowned. "I don't know what I'm seeing," she said. "There is so much there."

"He tore his knee when the dragon passed, and the dragon's magic caused it to try to regrow itself," said Feshi.

Kethi stuck out her tongue. "That's ghastly," she said.

Summerwind had to agree.

"This happened eight days ago," said Feshi. "But it was as though his leg had been left to heal wrong for months. I reckon it will take a year to change it back to the way it should be."

"A year is a long time," said Kethi. "But it is not a lifetime."

Summerwind put her hand on Kethi's shoulder. She knew Kethi was thinking of Dan.

"I reckon Feshwin can fix me up in a month or two," said Van. "She just says it will take a year because she wants to cut on me."

"I don't want to cut on you, Vanim," Feshi said with a sigh. "But if this doesn't work, the only way to heal your leg will be to undo all the bad healing the dragon did."

"By 'undo' she means 'hack up'," Van explained to Summerwind.

Summerwind was not certain how to respond to this.

"We should tell this story to Zhen," said Kethi.

Summerwind nodded. "We should, though I doubt he will listen to us when he has so many admirers to entertain."

As it happened, Zephyr came along to Kethi's mother's lodge a short while later, looking for the horses. Kethi let him into the courtyard.

"You went away with my spear," Zephyr told Summerwind as he unstrapped the weapon from his saddle. "Some of the children wanted to see it."

Summerwind replied, "You may take the blade as well, for all the good it will do you, Dragonslayer."

"Truly?" Zephyr cocked an eye at her like a magpie. "Thank you, sister."

He unstrapped the bundle from Snowmane's saddle.

"But, Zhen, listen," said Kethi. "She's trying to tell you that the blade is useless against this dragon."

"Ah yes," agreed Zephyr. "'Bigger than a wall with a hide of stone'? I have heard the tale."

"It's no tale," said Kethi. "It's what happened."

Zephyr shrugged. "And yet I may be able to put this blade to use," he said. "There are ways to deal with walls. The councilmen have agreed to hold a meeting this evening so we can discuss my plan."

"But you have no plan," Summerwind pointed out. What a mouse-brain!

"I will have one by this evening," said Zephyr. "But I am certain it can be improved by your insights. I do hope you and Kethwin will both come."

He walked back toward the crowd of Yolimites with his spear in one hand and the bundled blade tucked under his arm.

What Zephyr did for the rest of the afternoon, they did not know. He was resourceful among Yolimites and had probably found someone who would feed him.

Kethi's family took in Summerwind. The food was mushy and tasteless, but the company was cheerful—especially Kethi's niece. The little girl happily toddled over to Summerwind and helped herself to mush from Summerwind's bowl. Of all Kethi's relatives, she was the one least afraid, probably because she was accustomed to being around people much bigger than she was.

The adults discussed somber events, but their faces were full of hope and expectation. Summerwind and her brother had arrived to put things right. For a month, the village had been expecting a hero, and nothing Kethi said could dissuade them from the idea that Zhen Dragonslayer would find a way to rescue them.

The mood among Kethi's family was matched by the rest of the Yolimites. When the time came for Zephyr's meeting, everyone was eager for it to begin. They swarmed around a huge lodge in the center of the village, buzzing with excitement.

Summerwind stood with Kethi's family, wondering why no one had lit a fire circle yet and why so many people were entering the big lodge. Not until Kethi's family led her inside did Summerwind realize that the lodge had been built for meetings. Summerwind had to duck to get through the entrance, and the passage was so narrow that she was more comfortable passing through it sideways, but the interior was large enough to hold everyone in the entire village.

They had built a square amphitheater out of wood. Those who had to sit behind could still see, because they were higher than those in front. Everyone could be a part of the circle. The only disadvantage was that the circle was a square.

The little bearded man who had welcomed them to town invited Kethi and Summerwind to sit in the front row. This pleased Summerwind, for it meant she could sit on the ground, with Kethi sitting beside her on the end of the bench.

Sitting not far from them, Zephyr was of good cheer. He flashed them a smile, and to Summerwind, he thought, *I think you will like this.*

Summerwind just smiled and shook her head. Zephyr always wanted to be the center of attention, but he also wanted to please. She could not help but feel fond of him.

The buzz of excited voices faded away, like the whispers of the instruments after the last note has been played. Four bearded men sat down on the stools in the middle of the circle. They now had everyone's attention.

One of them stood.

"Good people of Kwoshim, I am sure you all know why we have gathered here this evening. Over a month ago, Dan Broadfield—oh, and Kethi Walker—" he flashed a smile at Kethi, but did not wait to see if she would return it, "—set out to find the dragonslayer. Today, he has come."

Hundreds of little hands clapped together. Summerwind congratulated herself on not jumping. After attending so many celebrations for Zephyr, she had learned to anticipate this curious demonstration of approval.

When the applause had died away, the little man continued his speech. "I know we are all anxious to hear what he has to say. After our last encounter with the dragon, many must be wondering, 'Can a dragon be slain?' Well, I have spoken with Zhen Dragonslayer, and the answer to this question is, unequivocally, 'Yes!'"

This caused some to cheer. The cheer was immediately followed by more hand clapping.

They need Zephyr to be their hero, Summerwind realized. *More than getting rid of the dragon, they need to believe it can be done. With luck, he will appear a fool only to Kethi and me. I do hope Kethi can hold her tongue.*

When the clapping had died down enough, the speaker raised his hand and received a quiet circle once more.

"The dragonslayer has warned me that this task will not be easy," he said. These words were met by silence. "Every dragon is different, and there is much the dragonslayer will need to learn from us. But he assures us that dragons can be slain, for he has already slain one. Please welcome Zhen Dragonslayer and listen to his story."

The clapping was noise, like a waterfall or a high wind, but it was also like a song. It bound everyone together into one mood. As part of the circle, Summerwind could tell how the entire village felt.

This round of clapping was not the joyful relief that everyone had expressed the first time the speaker had said Zephyr's Yolimite name. The tiny people had heard the note of warning in the speaker's voice, and they were anxious to discover what Dragonslayer had to say.

Zephyr arose smiling. He slowly rotated, spreading his smile to all four sides of the circle. Then he walked over to the largest stool and sat down upon it.

Kethi put her head in her hands and murmured, "He doesn't know the difference between a stool and a desk."

Whatever the difference was, no one chose to mention it. The four bearded men exchanged glances and pushed their little stools away from Zephyr's big stool.

Zephyr, who must have known he had struck a wrong note, simply smiled and said, "Thank you."

A few people giggled nervously.

Zephyr said, "I would like to begin with a song, if I may. Now this is not the song you have heard so much about. That one was just a song, but this one is a ballad. It tells the true story of the true dragonslayer. You are the first to hear it. But Kethwin, Dawnracer, and I—we lived it."

His fingers began walking across his lute strings, picking out the melody that he had worked on whenever Kethi had his reins. The practice had been worthwhile. He played the tune almost as well as Shamon could have, and Zephyr's technique gave it a style that would be difficult for anyone to imitate. The notes flowed like water, and over top of them Zephyr began to sing:

There once was a monster that owned wind and thunder,
A beast that made giants feel small.
I'll sing of its flight, its speed and its hunger,
And how it brought terror to all.

The song told their story. Summerwind remembered some details differently, but the story it told was true.

Kethi looked at her. "He's singing about Danwel," she said. "I thought his song would be about himself, but it's about Danwel."

"It is about all of us," said Summerwind. "But, yes, it is especially about Dan."

The people must have been wondering what had happened to Dan Broadfield who had left on a short journey such a long time ago. And when Dragonslayer finally did arrive, they must have wondered why Dan did not arrive with him. Now Zephyr's song was telling them all.

Some people gasped when the dragon lunged for Dan, and Summerwind realized how long it had been since she had heard a song for the first time. Ballads were sung so that stories would be remembered, but first they had to be written. Zephyr had done a masterful job.

Zephyr showed them the dragon dead at their feet, with Dan standing over it, blade upraised, and the listeners' "oooh!" became part of the song. But Zephyr was not done. There was a price to pay, and as Zephyr affirmed that Dan had paid it, some wept.

Zephyr would not leave them crying. He sang:

Though deafened and blinded, Dan is a hero.
The dragon is dead by his hand.
His arm brought us hope, and his blade brought us justice,
Remember the courage of Dan.

We'll fight with the courage of Dan!

At the last note, there was silence—two full heartbeats of silence as the people listened to the note echo in their own heads. They were enthralled.

Except for Kethi. She seized Summerwind's hand and parted her pale lips to speak.

The crowd roared. They cheered for Zephyr, they cheered for his song, but most of all—and Zephyr must have known it—they cheered for Dan Broadfield, their dragonslayer.

In that roar, Kethi's voice was lost. But her lips said, "The dragon."

CHAPTER 32

The Dragon

KETHWIN had agreed to lure the monster in, but the Stripedman had done it himself. Zhen had inspired an emotion that could not be ignored. Every heart in the crowded Meeting House was celebrating Danwel's courage. Each resonated with the others, so that individuality was swept away by the enveloping emotion that everyone was part of.

In the center, Kethwin was overwhelmed by the crowd's power. This joy was a thing that an animal could not possibly understand. Some animals flee when they encounter the unknown. Others become curious. Kethwin felt the dragon's curiosity come bobbing to the surface like a fly in the milk jug.

She wished Danwel were there. He was a hero who would do the right thing without wasting time wondering what should be done.

Well, Kethwin knew what should be done, but she was failing again. She had to warn them, but she was powerless. No one could hear her even if she shouted, and all her voice could do was squeak. She could feel the crowd's elation, she could feel the dragon's curiosity, but her body was ruled by her own Emotion, and she was once again caught by her paralyzing panic.

Their cheers grew louder, and they did not know why. They could not tell that the dragon was drawing in their joy and sending it back to them stronger and stronger as it drew nearer and nearer. Only Kethwin and Dawnracer knew what was coming. The rushlights danced in the Stripedwoman's eyes as she stared at Kethwin in alarm.

Dawnracer could speak with her thoughts. She looked at her brother.

His eyes widened.

Dawnracer put her face in Kethwin's and shouted, "Where? Where is it coming from?"

Kethwin lifted a hand and pointed.

"Silence!" Zhen shouted.

No one else could have called for silence, but the Stripedman pitched the word so that it cut through the noise. The urgent tone of his voice and the anxious expression on his striped face confused everyone. This did not produce silence, but it did quiet them enough so that some became aware of the rumble. As the dragon's rumble grew louder, the cheering died away.

Zhen looked at Kethwin and the tiers of Walkers that she was pointing to. "You should run," he suggested.

A sudden hand clap will send a flock of blackbirds into flight. Zhen's words had the same effect. Kethwin's cousins rose to their feet and began scrambling down the tiers. A few jumped over the side to reach the narrow exit passages ahead of the crowd.

Kethwin knew Zhen's words had been meant for the Walkers, but all heard them, and all panicked. The other clans were attempting to flee their tiers, too, pushing on the backs of those already in the passages. When people were calm and orderly, it could take a long time to get out of the Meeting House. Now, with everyone trying to get out at once, everyone was trapped.

There was no longer a conflict between the feelings of the crowd and Kethwin's panic. It was like the time that she and Vanim had been fighting over a bucket and he had suddenly let go. Kethwin's willpower fell with a crash. She sank to her knees, and her outstretched hand fell limp at her side. As her scrambling cousins vacated the middle of the tiers, Kethwin's eyes fixed on that space, for she knew that was where her doom would appear.

The panic in the Meeting House was so strong that even the dragon became apprehensive as it approached. Its thunderous rush began to slow. The thinking part of Kethwin suspected this was important somehow, but the rest of her was immobilized by the internal panic that filled her heart and the external panic that filled the room.

Only the two Stripedfolk felt anything different.

Dawnracer was afraid, but like Danwel, she was a hero. Her fear did not keep her from thinking of others. She wrapped her striped arms around Kethwin's tiny body and heaved Kethwin onto her shoulder like a sack of flour. Kethwin went limp and allowed the woman to carry her to the opposite side of the Meeting House.

As they passed Zhen, Kethwin caught his Emotion as well. He was affected by the panic around him, but underneath was a foundation of determination. Zhen was not a hero, but he wanted to be. Could be that would be enough.

Could be that would just get him killed.

There was no way out. All four passages were jammed with panicking souls. But the seats were clear, and Dawnracer climbed the Springwater tiers, finally setting Kethwin down when they reached the top.

No. No, she couldn't sit here. This was the Springwater section. Kethwin rose shakily to her feet.

A breath of cool evening air brushed her face. Dawnracer had broken through the thatch.

"Take my hand and I will lower you down," she said.

Kethwin's mind struggled with the idea. The Meeting House had only four exits. How was it possible to go out through the roof?

It's only thatch, Kethwin told herself.

But you can't have a door in the roof, said the other part of her mind.

But we do have a door in the roof, said her practical side.

Kethwin got control of her legs. She did not climb out Dawnracer's exit. Instead, she ran to the edge of the tiers and looked down at the Springwaters and Highmeadows who were trapped between the walls of the passage below. "This way!" she shouted. "Dawnracer has made a hole in the roof!"

Those in the middle looked up at her helplessly. Caught in the crush, they could not choose where they moved. But some in the rear raced up the tiers, shouting, "Out the roof! Out the roof!"

Benwel Broadfield climbed up out of the passage at the other end of the tiers.

"Out the roof!" he shouted.

He reached down and pulled up his cousin, Pafweth. The two of them raced to the upper tier to make a second hole.

Kethwin looked across the Meeting House to see if the people struggling toward the other two passages would get the same idea. At that moment, the Walker tiers began to bulge into the room.

Wood snapped and splintered—slowly, like the fall of a great tree. The bottom tier popped, sending a beam springing out into the space where Kethwin's head had been while Zhen was singing. The second tier popped, then the third. The Walker tiers opened like the incision made on a slaughtered ox, spilling earth onto the floor like entrails.

Having tossed the meeting desk to one side, Zhen had been standing his ground in the center of the floor, but the flow of earth and wood forced him to leap back.

Kethwin could sense Dawnracer at the top of the tiers. The Stripedwoman did not allow the splintery cracking of wood on the opposite side of the Meeting House to distract her. If anything, Dawnracer intensified her focus, accelerating the pace at which she picked up people one at a time and lowered them to the ground outside.

Those brave enough to jump after Benwel and Pafweth were also escaping. Some of the panic was diminished by hope and relief. But in the two passages being crushed by the expanding mound of earth and debris, panic was turning to despair as people began suffocating.

Kethwin could feel all these emotions shift around her. And in the center was a curiosity that demanded satisfaction.

Eight claws, four on each side, emerged from the mound of earth where the Walkers had been sitting. The dragon's toes were as long as Zhen's legs. The claws glittered green in the rushlights.

Long feet followed, as the claws wrapped outward to grasp the dirt. With a push, the dragon's head emerged, filling the Meeting House with earth and the smell of snakes.

Kethwin could feel Zhen's resolve waver. The viper-like head was as broad as a house and taller than the Stripedman. Atop this orange head was a menacing green crest. Red eyes blinked in the rushlights. In that huge head, the eyes seemed tiny. How much could they see?

Did it really need to see?

Kethwin felt the Emotion of the Meeting House mirrored inside the dragon. It could sense all of them at once, and Kethwin could feel the dragon sensing them. The dragon's own capacity for Emotion was equal to all of theirs put together. And it drew on more Emotion from—from someplace outside—not outside the Meeting House, but outside the world.

Kethwin could draw on this Emotion, too. That was part of her gift. But the elemental currents could not give her courage. Panic ruled her heart, and she could only draw in more panic. It blew through her heart like a chill wind through an open door. The door could not be closed because the dragon's spirit remained in the doorway.

But Zhen did not panic. Though afraid, he raised the blade and roared in defiance: "Have you come to devour the great Zhen Dragonslayer? I dare you to try it, worm!"

The brave and pitiful fool. What could he do against a beast with a hide of stone?

Dawnracer's hand clenched Kethwin's shoulder. "I should have brought my spear," she murmured. Then she cried, "The eye, Zephyr! Aim for the eye!"

But the dragon's eye was high on its head, not easily within Zhen's reach.

Aware of Zhen's courage amid the chaos, Kethwin could feel him rock back on his right leg, anticipating a chance to spring.

Zhen cried, "If you will devour me, then open your loathsome jaw!"

Zhen was waiting for his chance. Kethwin could feel his anticipation resonating with a mirror image inside the dragon's spirit.

The mouth cracked open, revealing teeth that were boulders of craggy granite.

Kethwin felt Zhen's excitement, the tension in his legs. She realized he had decided to attack the dragon from inside.

Dawnracer must have had the same realization. Kethwin felt the anguish behind the Stripedwoman's cry: "No!"

Dawnracer descended the tiers in three strides, drew her knife, and leapt at the dragon's eye. Her brother leapt for a gap between the teeth.

The dragon flinched from Dawnracer's pain, twisting its head enough to protect the gap that Zhen had seen. The scythe blade struck a granite tooth and Zhen bounced off the dragon's jaw.

Dawnracer's body slapped against the dragon's cheek. Her knife slipped along the scales of its closed eyelid and she fell away to tumble among the councilmen's benches.

Zhen struggled to his feet. His determination to kill was like two fierce flames, one burning in his heart, one mirrored in the heart of the dragon.

Oh, but the flame inside the dragon was a tiny thing! A tiny flame in the dark forest of panic and despair. And amid that darkness, Kethwin knew she would find a burbling black pool of cowardice that was her own.

The dragon sniffed. Damp night air poured in through the rents in the ceiling and blew against the back of Kethwin's neck.

She had found the pool of cowardice and the dragon had found her. Its awareness of her grew, separating her from its impression of the terrified people still trapped inside, separating her from the despair of those suffocating in the crushed passages. It had found her because, of all the people in the village, she was the most afraid.

Her soul alone held no courage, no will to fight—nothing but fear, fear, fear, despair, and a tiny, little voice that said to her, *You can use this.*

Because she could. She could make use of her fear because it was inside the dragon.

Kethwin reached for the souls still struggling to escape and opened herself to their desperation. She invited their panic into her body. How much could she hold?

The dragon lowered its crest and drew back. Kethwin had its full attention. Zhen's puny defiance was irrelevant when compared to the panic flooding through Kethwin.

Kethwin focused on her pool of cowardice within the dragon, filling it with her awareness of the trapped villagers' terror, filling it with their desire to escape. Their desperation began to seep through the dragon's heart.

Kethwin reached for her own fear reflected within the dragon.

She opened her soul to it, allowing it to flow through her again.

Her awareness of the reflection was also reflected inside the dragon—as she had hoped. Oh, but she would not let the dragon sense her hope. No, she gave the dragon only her fear amplified by her awareness of the dragon's fear, reflected again and again and again.

With each reflection, the flood of fear grew higher, dousing any flames of ferocity, suffocating any defiance, drowning all desires except the desire to turn, to flee, to escape from this raucous world and its dreadful emotions.

"Out," Kethwin whispered. "Out the door. Out the door and never come back."

The dragon left the world the way it had come, and behind itself, it closed the door.

CHAPTER 33

Return to Brin

"KETHI SCARED IT AWAY?" Shamon asked.

Zhen shook his head. "She banished it."

They were in Brin, sitting in a private room at the Dry Mill Inn. Nesi, the innkeeper, had offered it to them free of charge so that Zhen could escape from the Yolimites who were demanding to hear how he had slain "their" dragon. It was a shrewd business tactic, for the room had only one exit. Likely, many of Zhen's admirers would remain as Nesi's customers until he chose to come out again.

Word of the triumph at Kwoshim had reached Brin long before Zhen had. He had heard several versions of the story. Many believed that Zhen had simply slain the dragon with his spear. Others said he had used "Stripedfolk magic". A few were convinced that the true dragonslayer was a Yolimite whose skin emitted an otherworldly glow, but most scoffed at such a preposterous idea.

Shamon said, "None of the stories mention Kethi."

"We have been telling Kethi's story," said Summerwind. "Perhaps it spreads more slowly because her magic is difficult for people to understand. No one could see what she did. All they could see was Zephyr with the blade in his hands."

"However, they all felt the terror," said Zhen. "Everyone was panicking and screaming. When our attack failed, all the screams went up an octave. I thought it was because they feared for our safety, but in truth, it was because Kethwin had discovered how to amplify fear the way you and I amplify sound."

Shamon nodded. "Kethi is clever."

"Kethi told me it was the weight of her cowardice that made her strong enough to defeat it," Summerwind added with a smile.

"Regardless of how she did it," said Zhen, "I am glad that it was done, for my plan was to step inside the dragon and fight from within."

"So you planned that Kethi would call the dragon and you would slay it," said Shamon. "And instead you called the dragon and she banished it."

"Precisely so," said Zhen. "I fear I am not as much of a dragonslayer as I would like to be."

"But neither are you a coward, brother," said Summerwind. "Where others would run, you stand and fight. Lashrefi did not choose you to be the one who strikes the final blow, but you have earned the right to sing her song."

Dear Summerwind! She could be so kind.

"Yes," Zhen agreed. "I shall sing a song for Kethwin. For all of them."

Zhen and Summerwind had helped excavate the ruins of the building, working all night beside the Yolimites. At first, the work had been glorious—freeing frightened, injured people and reuniting them with their loved ones. But then he had found the first of the four dead bodies. He did not want to tell Shamon about that tiny, lifeless leg poking out of the debris. Not yet. He would share the story later.

For now, best to dwell on the survivors—the heroes.

"Ah, Shamon," he said. "You should have heard my song of Danwel. In fact, you must learn it at once, for it will sound even better with you on the lute."

Shamon shook his bald head sadly.

"Zhen, I have something to tell you."

"What is it?" asked Zhen, adding to himself, *Please do not say what I know you are about to say.*

"I am leaving Brin," said Shamon. "I need to return to my people."

"When?" asked Zhen.

"Tomorrow morning," said Shamon. "The boat would have left yesterday, but I believed you were coming. They said they would wait so I could tell you farewell."

"I am glad you are returning to your people," said Zhen, quietly.

In truth, he felt miserable. "I wish I could go with you."

Shamon nodded. "But you need to go back to the prairie."

"What?" said Zhen. "Truly I do not. I was just there."

"But it is your home," Shamon told him. "It is where you belong."

"Brin is my home," said Zhen. "But perhaps I do not belong anywhere."

"I understand that feeling," said Shamon. "But I can no longer live with it. I need to belong."

"And you belong with your people now?" Summerwind asked.

"I believe I can allow myself to belong again," said Shamon. "I thank you for that."

Summerwind smiled. "All I did was build you a bath." But her voice wavered as she spoke.

"Zhen, I wish I could take you with me," said Shamon.

"I understand."

"I do not," said Summerwind. "Why can you not take him with you?"

Silence, Zhen thought at her. *He cannot take me because he does not want me.*

Lower your quills, porcupine, she thought back. *He just said he wants you. When has Shamon ever been able to bend the truth?*

"Dawnracer, no Child of Luck has ever traveled with the Children of Justice," said Shamon.

"My brother can be the first. He would like that."

Zhen knew he should stop her, but he found that he did not want to.

Shamon's blue face became perplexed. "Would you, Zhen? Would you like that?"

"Shamon, I cannot know until I have tried it," Zhen replied. "Do you think I could talk my way onto your boat?"

Shamon frowned. But it was because he was thinking, not because he disapproved.

"I had thought I must choose between life as a musician or life as a boat owner. Perhaps I was looking at this wrong."

"That is why you have friends," said Summerwind. "To help you see things differently."

"Perhaps," said Shamon, which was almost like agreement. "Zhen, if you do want to come, you should let me do the talking."

"I can let you do the talking."

Summerwind snorted.

"I can," Zhen protested.

"But you would have to leave your horse behind," Shamon said. "You cannot bring more than you can carry."

"I will take care of her, brother," Summerwind assured him. "Undersong will be happy in the band's herd, and she will be glad to see you when you finally choose to visit us again. As will I."

"That will leave you with three horses to take back," Zhen reminded her. "Mine, Father's, and Frogfoot's."

"I had not lost count, brother."

"And what about Danwel's mare?" asked Zhen. He turned to Shamon. "For that matter, what about Danwel? How is your cure coming along?"

"We succeeded."

"You did?"

Shamon nodded. "It was 'like spearfishing in muddy water' as my people say. The illuminator and I could not see. We depended on the healer. But he was a good guide. I took much of the thunder from Dan's ears. My work was not perfect, but he can hear again."

"And the illuminator healed his eyes?" asked Summerwind.

"Dan can see now," said Shamon. "But his eyes and his skin still glow. We all agreed on caution. The healer thought that if the illuminator removed too much light, it could blind Dan again. We decided to declare him cured once he could see.

"By that time, we had heard that you had defeated the dragon. Dan hoped to meet you, but he said he must go home 'the long way'. I believe he will be sorry he missed you."

Summerwind bit her lip.

Zhen took his sister's hand. "And we are sorry we missed him," Zhen said. "But we are all seeds in the wind, and we may meet again at the whim of Lashrefi."

Summerwind gave his hand a squeeze.

"Can you tell me of Kethi?" Shamon asked. "Why is she not here?"

"Ah," said Zhen. "Kethwin had other things to do."

CHAPTER 34

Tarthil

TARTHIL lay scattered across the plain like grain spilled from a sack. Mounds rose everywhere, and each was surrounded by clusters of houses, green fields, and vegetable gardens. Unlike Brin, Tarthil was a city without a plan.

From the summit of the grassy Broadfield mound, Danwel gazed on this city with grateful eyes. He was grateful that he had finally seen Tarthil and grateful that he could see at all. Colors were strangely vibrant. Clouds and whitewashed walls were tinged with purple. But Danwel could see again. It did not matter that his eyes and skin still glowed.

A bearded man, old enough to be Danwel's father, approached from the direction of the stables. He started when he met Danwel's gaze. He turned to the dark-haired, yellow-cloaked man walking beside him and murmured something Danwel had no hope of hearing over the growl of thunder that still lurked in the depths of his ears. The younger man—he was about Danwel's age—answered with an uneasy shrug.

The bearded man approached and asked, "May I take your horse, cousin?"

"Aye, thank you," said Danwel, handing him the reins.

The bearded man—Cousin Stablemaster—put a hand on Tevishi's shoulder, pretending she was the one who needed to be calmed down. "Will you be long?" he asked. "Should I feed her?"

Danwel didn't know how much time he needed to spend with the Marriage Clerk, but he reckoned it would be long enough that Tevishi would not need to hurry through her meal. "Please," he said. "But not too much grain for her. She's used to grass."

As the stablemaster led Tevishi away, the younger cousin put on the smile that people wore when they were pretending to ignore

Danwel's glowing skin. "Welcome to the Clan House," he said. "I am Pol, the door steward."

"Glad to meet you, Cousin Pol. I am Dan Broadfield, called Danwel of Kwoshim."

"Glad to meet you, Cousin Dan. If you would let me know your business here today, I would be happy to help you."

"Oh," said Danwel. "I'm here to see the Marriage Clerk."

"On what business?"

"I want to get married."

Pol smiled uneasily. "But cousin, you cannot get married without the girl."

"Well, that's fair enough," Danwel said. "But my girl is at home and I am in Tarthil. Now, I'm willing to go home, get the girl, and bring her here, but before I do, I reckon I ought to make sure the Marriage Clerk will have a mark waiting for us, aye?"

"Yes, cousin, but—" Pol was having trouble meeting Danwel's eyes. "The Marriage Clerk is short on marks right now."

"Aye. So I heard."

"Is your girl by any chance a Redfield, a Wildwood, or a Fairweather?"

"No," said Danwel.

"Then perhaps you should consider marrying out," Pol suggested. "We hold marks from only those three clans, and no Broadfield marks will be available until more people marry out."

"I heard there were three marks left," said Danwel.

"Cousin, forgive me if I have misjudged your wealth, but when there are few marks, they become very difficult to obtain. That's the Principle of Rarity."

"Well, cousin, you have not misjudged my wealth," admitted Danwel. "But I won't be leaving until I've seen the Marriage Clerk. I have a story for him that might just be rarer than his marks. Could be I can persuade him to make the exchange."

"And does this story relate to your … condition?"

Danwel chuckled. "Aye, you could say that."

The door steward shuffled his feet. "Very well," he decided. "Follow me."

Like the city of Tarthil, the Broadfield Clan House did not

appear to have been planned. Wings radiated off the round central building like petals on a daisy. Some wings even seemed to be wilting and drooping down the hillside.

The door steward led Danwel into a hall that seemed to have no purpose other than to display a mural depicting how the Broadfield Mound had looked before all the wings had been added. They passed into the central building, which housed the chamber where the Clan Council discussed and revised Broadfield clan law. Danwel had always wanted to see the Council Chamber—he'd heard the benches were upholstered with dyed leather—but instead his cousin led him along a passage that curved underneath the tiers of seating. In the candlelight, Danwel's purple glow seemed garish, even to his purple-tinged vision. He moderated his glow and changed the color to yellow, matching the candlelight. He couldn't make himself look normal, but he could at least fit in.

Cousin Pol gave him a sidelong glance.

They passed several doorways before Pol indicated that they had come to the Marriage Clerk's wing. He called it "the White Wing", but the chamber they entered had been painted green. No mural graced the walls, but the floor was covered with a woven rug depicting the plow-and-furrow of Clan Broadfield. The candles illuminating the room were supported by iron stands ornamented to resemble sheaves of ripe wheat.

The room also held a short bench, to which Pol gestured as he said, "The Marriage Clerk is seeing someone right now. Please wait here. I will inform Cousin Clerk at an appropriate time."

Danwel sat down and adjusted his color to match the green walls of the room. It actually felt good to rest his legs, but he wondered why he was being kept waiting. If there were no marks left, then how could the Marriage Clerk be busy? He could hear voices floating in from the next room, but the curtain muffled them just enough that they blended into the noise in his ears.

Danwel reckoned that Pol could hear the voices quite clearly. The door steward stood by the curtained doorway, apparently so he could listen in and find "an appropriate time" to interrupt. Danwel wondered what it was like to have a job where you were expected to stand in doorways and listen to other people's conversations.

The voices grew louder. Pol frowned and looked sideways at the curtain. Then came an outburst that even Danwel could hear:

"He's not an invalid!"

Kethwin?

Danwel jumped off his bench and crossed to the doorway. Cousin Pol made no move to stop him. On the contrary, the door steward had one hand on the curtain and was on the verge of actually going through.

"He's just blind and deaf," Kethwin was saying. "He can still work. His body is whole. His back is strong. He's a real person."

"Yes, Miss Walker. Yes. I'm sure the boy is very capable," said the elderly voice of the Marriage Clerk. "But Broadfield clan law is quite clear—"

"Then change the law."

"Beg pardon?"

"Change the law. Because any law that says my boy can't be a good husband is a bad law."

Danwel passed through the doorway and entered the room. Kethwin sat on a bench that was designed for two. The white-bearded official sat behind a tidy writing desk. Two shelves of ledgers recorded all the Broadfields who had entered or left the Clan by marriage during the five-hundred-year history of Dwen-Tarthil. The wall behind the Marriage Clerk was studded with rows of pegs. Three marriage marks hung there. Ninety-seven pegs were empty.

Kethwin and Cousin Clerk both looked up at Danwel.

"I'm all right," he told them.

Kethwin jumped up and hugged him tight about the ribs.

Cousin Clerk looked from one to the other. "I take it that this is your boy?" he asked.

"He is." Kethwin stepped back to look up at him. "Oh, Danwel. You came."

Danwel grinned. "Well, that was your plan, wasn't it? I was supposed to slay a dragon and then convince Cousin Clerk to give us a mark. What are you doing here?"

"The same, I reckon."

"Thank you, Pol," said the Marriage Clerk. "You were right to let him in."

"Ah … yes," said Cousin Pol, standing in the doorway. "Yes. Of course. Do you need anything? Or should I return to my post?"

"That will be fine, Pol," said the Marriage Clerk.

Kethwin helped Danwel sit down on the bench beside her.

Danwel patted her hand. "You don't need to do that anymore. I can see now."

"Oh, I'm sorry."

"It's all right. I'm still getting used to it myself."

"I for one am quite glad to hear of your recovery," said the Marriage Clerk. "It makes my decision a good deal simpler."

Danwel nodded at the wall of pegs. "Does that mean you'll give us a mark?"

"I believe that Clan Broadfield should seize the opportunity to corner the market on dragonslayers," the Marriage Clerk said with a smile.

Danwel frowned. What did he mean by that?

"Didn't you know that Miss Walker defeated the dragon of Kwoshim?"

Danwel looked at Kethwin. "No. I heard that was Zhen."

"Rumors," scoffed the Marriage Clerk. "It was Miss Walker's doing, and she has a letter from your village councilman that proves it."

"Zhen and I worked together," Kethwin explained. "And if it hadn't been for Dawnracer, the dragon would have eaten me before I came to my senses. But I can tell you the story later."

"All right," said Danwel.

She took his hand. "You came," she said. "You really do want to marry me."

"I do," he said. "But you— You came, too. And you thought I was still blind and deaf, didn't you?"

"I just decided that it didn't matter."

"Oh," said Danwel.

He thought on this a bit.

"I still glow," he pointed out.

She patted his hand. "That's all right, Danwel. Right now, I feel like I am glowing, too."

Epilogue

ALL OVER THE WORLD, people were winning battles against the elementals, and the deities were helping. Yolim said he had an obligation to aid his people. Zharnov said he intervened to defend Nature's law. Lashrefi said nothing, but she smiled to herself. She liked the odds.

Many battles remained to be fought, but it would always be so. The world had been at risk from the moment it had been created. It was threatened by the evil that lurked below, by the chaos that surrounded it, perhaps even by the good that dwelt above. Yet without these threats, it would no longer have a reason for being. Risk and existence were intertwined.

Only resourceful and courageous people could stand in the winds of chaos and risk their lives against the unknown. Not even Lashrefi could predict where such resource and courage would be found.

Ah, but she did know where to place her bets.

Lashrefi found a man sitting on a boat and listened to him sing of dragonslayers.

Acknowledgments

I'D LIKE TO THANK MY WIFE, SIERRA, for reading multiple drafts, lavishing me with encouragement, and making everything possible.

Justin Barba and CthulhuBob Lovely organized the MisCon programming and writing workshops where I learned so much. From the MisCon workshops, I'd like to thank Patty Briggs, Mary Jane Engh, and Jim Glass for advice I used to improve multiple scenes. From ChiCon 7, I'd like to thank Oz Drummond for putting the writing workshop together and Lorraine Heisler, Martha Wells, Gregory Wilson, and John Wiswell for helpful comments on the first chapter of this novel.

Andrea Howe of Blue Falcon Editing was my editor for the final draft. (But I did my own copy editing and typesetting, so if you see any mistakes, blame me.)

Rose Stoneberg, D.V.M., advised me on veterinary science and helped me explore ways that very short people might ride comfortably on a tall horse. (But don't try ear reins on your own horses, please. They won't like them.)

I'd also like to thank my parents, my wife's parents, and my children for support and encouragement all along the way.

About the Author

JASON A. HOLT has a Ph.D. in mathematics. He is fluent in Czech, and he lives on a remote Montana cattle ranch. In other words, he is well qualified to write fantasy novels.

To learn more about Jason, visit JasonAHolt.com.

To learn more about the world of Edgewhen®, visit edgewhen.com. Or look for *The Artificer of Dupho*, the next Edgewhen® adventure.

www.ingramcontent.com/pod-product-compliance
Lightning Source LLC
Chambersburg PA
CBHW021503240626
47154CB00002B/483